DAWN OF RA

BLOOD OF RA PREQUEL BOOK ONE

M. SASINOWSKI

KINGSMILL PRESS

ISBN 978-1-7324467-8-6

ISBN 978-1-7324467-7-9 (ebook)

This is a work of fiction. Names, characters, and incidents are the product of the author's imagination, except in the case of historical figures and events, which are used fictitiously.

BLOOD OF RA SERIES

Book One: Heir of Ra

Book Two: Daughter of Ra

Book Three: Legacy of Ra

Book Four: Dawn of Ra

To Sarah,
I love you bigger than space.

Even though Dawn of Ra is technically the fourth book in the Blood of Ra series, it was written to stand on its own, so if you have not read Heir of Ra and the sequels, and just want to dive into Horus's story, enjoy the read! If you did read the first three books, I hope you will have fun reconnecting with the characters you met in Alyssa's flashbacks. Considering it may have been a while since you read the original trilogy, I provided a brief summary in the next section. If you do plan on reading Alyssa's adventure at any point, I urge you to skip that section as it is filled with massive spoilers for Heir of Ra, Daughter of Ra, and Legacy of Ra.

Giza Plateau—1913. Lord GEORGE RENLEY, ruthless collector of antiquities, stands at the entrance to the mythical Hall of Records beneath the Sphinx. Lord Renley savors his triumph…then the screams begin.

Present time—High in the Peruvian Andes. ALYSSA MORGAN receives a phone call from her father, KADE MORGAN. He has unearthed the hidden entrance to the fabled Hall of Records beneath the Sphinx. Minutes later, Alyssa's camp is attacked. While trying to make a daring escape, she crashes a plane and is knocked unconscious.

American geneticist, GEOFF BAXTER, is abducted by the enigmatic TASHA MENDEVA, a ward of British aristocrat, GEORGE RENLEY, who is the great-grandson of the original discoverer of the Hall of Records. Lord Renley is also a member of THE SOCIETY, a ruthless group of ultra-rich individuals obsessed with seizing the genetic power of an advanced civilization whose ruler is said to be buried in the Hall of Records.

Kade Morgan and his partner, ED WALLACE, unearth the entrance to the Hall in the Giza Plateau. Disaster strikes when their protective biosuits fail, and a lethal virus is unleashed, killing Ed Wallace and sending Kade and his team fighting for their lives.

Alyssa awakens in a hospital in Cusco, Peru. Upon hearing news about her father's expedition, she races to the World Health Organization in London. There, she receives unexpected help from intern, PAUL MATTHEWS, and computer geek extraordinaire, CLAY OBONO. They discover a mysterious object that her father found in the Hall of Records, a fist-sized crystal pyramid, and uncover the nature of the artifact: it is a storage medium that safeguards ancient memories. Clay constructs an ingenious virtual reality device that unlocks the memories and immerses Alyssa into the world of Egyptian mythology. The first flashback into the world of the artifact reveals a strange ceremony joining a young boy with a falcon. Alyssa has trespassed into the mind of the Egyptian falcon-headed god, Horus!

An attack by The Society sends the trio fleeing for their lives. As they continue to elude their pursuers, Alyssa relives other memories from the past: a conflict between two ancient races, the PUREANS and Horus's people, the HYBRIDS. Horus's grandfather, THOTH, created the virus as a weapon and reveals that Hybrid blood offers protection from it. Thoth also reveals his life's work to Horus: a device to safeguard memories, the artifact now in Alyssa's possession.

Based on information Alyssa gleamed from the artifact, she

and Paul travel to Egypt in hopes of obtaining additional insights from her father and uncovering the cure. On the plane, Alyssa is attacked by an assassin of The Society, but she is saved by George Renley, who has been following them. Lord Renley offers Alyssa and Paul protection from The Society in exchange for the artifact, but Alyssa refuses.

In Egypt, Kade Morgan's friend and scientist, KAMAL KHANNA, recognizes that the virus has broken containment in the hospital and is threatening to become an epidemic. Alyssa realizes that the cure for her father's illness lies in Horus's blood, but the knowledge comes at a price. She is shot and wounded by Tasha. Desperate to save Alyssa's life, Paul contacts George Renley, who betrays them, leading to their capture by the leader of the Society, WILLIAM DRAKE. Alyssa learns that her father's friend and partner, Ed Wallace, staged his own death and masterminded the disaster at the unearthing of the Hall of Records. Ed Wallace is William Drake, the leader of the Society!

In captivity, Alyssa is forced into a final immersion: Horus attacks his home island, the mythical Atlantis, where he uncovers a terrifying truth and strikes Atlantis from history.

Alyssa is coerced to open the Hall of Records, filled with the deadly virus. When Horus's sarcophagus is opened at the top of a vast subterranean pyramid, they find it empty. Wallace's dream of immortality and Alyssa's hope for a cure have vanished. Furious, Wallace injures Paul and attacks Alyssa, damaging her biosafety suit and exposing her to the virus, spilling her blood into the sarcophagus. Kamal Khanna, who has been alerted by Paul, follows the group into the Hall. He arrives during the altercation and shoots Tasha. An instant before an enraged Ed Wallace has a chance to kill Alyssa, her blood reaches the bottom of the sarcophagus. Alyssa enters a trance-like state. Filled with Horus's power and fury, she kills Wallace. Alyssa is recognized to be of the Rathadi bloodline and proclaimed as the Daughter of Ra. By virtue of ancestry, the cure for the illness is in her blood.

Alyssa's father is cured of the virus, and the pandemic is averted. Alyssa takes off in pursuit of clues and additional information about Horus and The Society—and a mysterious, golden-eyed woman who may hold answers to Horus's mystery and the disappearance of Alyssa's mother.

DAUGHTER OF RA

After several months of following leads about The Society, Alyssa winds up at the National Library in Prague in search of information that may bring her closer to the Hybrids. Unaware that The Society is also hunting her because of the ancient genes in her blood, Alyssa is ambushed, and only narrowly escapes being captured.

After Professor Baxter's death, his assistant, DR. YURI KORZO, has taken over the scientific effort to re-synthesize the ancient blood. As Korzo's research reaches a dead end, a mysterious golden-eyed woman provides him with a sample that matches Alyssa's Hybrid genes. A splinter group of The Society, who is obsessed with the power of the ancient race, allow themselves to be injected with the Hybrid blood, but they are betrayed by Korzo and the golden-eyed woman.

In Europe, Alyssa hears ominous news. There was an attack on the National Museum in Cairo, and the artifact was stolen.

Alyssa rushes to Cairo where she learns that her father kept the artifact safe and lied publicly to throw off The Society. He gives Alyssa the artifact for safekeeping. They are surprised by a call from Kamal Khanna, who informs them of a gravely ill woman who shares the Hybrid genes with Alyssa; the woman is one of the members of The Society who were injected with the ancient blood. Eager to find out more about the woman, Alyssa breaks into the hospital room and sees a single-word message on the woman's mobile phone: *Valediction*. Alyssa is exposed but is able to escape; however, her father is arrested.

On the run, Alyssa calls Paul, who suggests that George Renley could help her. Alyssa reluctantly contacts Renley, who sends a private plane to smuggle her out of Egypt. At his manor in England, she is reunited with Paul and Clay, and Renley informs her that the *Valediction* is the name of The Society's mega-yacht, used as their headquarters and safe haven. To try to obtain more information, the group hatches a plan to break into the *Valediction's* supercomputer that stores The Society's information database.

With Lord Renley's help, Alyssa and Paul infiltrate the ship, posing as stewards. On board, Alyssa overhears a conversation about a HYBRID FEMALE who may be working with Yuri Korzo against The Society. Alyssa and Paul successfully break into the server and create an uplink that allows Clay to download data, but as they make their escape, Alyssa is recognized by DR. CLAUDIA TIBALDI, whom she encountered during her first meeting with The Society. To save Alyssa and allow her to get away, Paul creates an explosion that damages the ship, sacrificing himself in the process.

Back at Renley's manor, Alyssa is despondent about Paul's

apparent death. Clay comes across a scrambled photo of the Hybrid woman in The Society's data. The photo is geotagged to a mountain location in Nepal. When Alyssa makes it clear that she will not abandon her pursuit, Lord Renley discloses to her that Tasha has survived and convinces Alyssa to allow Tasha to accompany her to Nepal.

In Nepal, Alyssa and Tasha locate a mysterious mountain temple at the geotagged location. They devise a plan to get inside, but the plan fails, and they are captured. Their captors are led by the golden-eyed woman, NEPHTHYS, who tells Alyssa that she can help her uncover information about her missing mother and unlock her full potential as a Hybrid. When Alyssa refuses, the woman destroys the ancient artifact. Alyssa and Tasha manage to escape the temple and are rescued from the mountain by a handful of mysterious soldiers in an advanced jet. Their rescuers are revealed to be a group of surviving Hybrids, called the RATHADI, who are led by DHARR. This group of Rathadi also saved Paul from the explosion on the *Valediction,* and Alyssa is united with her friend.

The Rathadi fly Alyssa, Paul, and Tasha to Hong Kong, where she is astounded to learn that several hundred Hybrids hide in plain sight in a downtown skyscraper that serves as their home. Her exhilaration at reuniting with Paul and finding the Rathadi is cut short when she blacks out. The Rathadi realize that her body is reacting adversely to her experience in the Hall of Records, and that she is in danger. Her only chance of surviving is to undergo the Rathadi joining ceremony. The ceremony goes horribly wrong, severely injuring Alyssa. As she lies dying, the leader of the Rathadi appears and saves her. He is HORUS.

Alyssa recovers and learns that this "Horus" is a descendent of the original Horus whose memories were stored in the artifact. For millennia, Horus's memories have been passed down from father to son, preserving his legacy and leadership over the Rathadi. Horus confides in Alyssa that he and her mother had been lovers, and he is Alyssa's father, and that Nephthys, who is Horus's half-sister, killed Alyssa's mother.

As Alyssa struggles to come to terms with the revelations, the Rathadi are ambushed by Nephthys and her soldiers, the descendants of the PUREANS. Nephthys allowed Alyssa and Tasha to escape, and Yuri Korzo secretly infected Tasha with an altered virus that is harmful to the Rathadi. Battle ensues. Nephthys manipulates Alyssa's mind and forces Alyssa to shoot Horus, mortally wounding him. Most of the Rathadi and Alyssa manage to escape, but Nephthys captures Paul and Tasha. Before Horus dies, he transfers his consciousness and memories to Alyssa, to great dismay of his son, HERU-PA, who was in line as the rightful heir to his father, and to become the next Horus.

LEGACY OF RA

A guilt-ridden Alyssa, together with her Rathadi friend, Dharr, and Horus's son, Heru-pa, join the surviving Rathadi in a secret shelter in a remote cave system in Indonesia. Even though neither Heru-pa nor any of the other Rathadi realize that it was Alyssa who shot Horus, Heru-pa is furious with her and blames her for the attack on his people. The Rathadi are divided in their allegiance and whom to recognize as the true legacy to Horus: Heru-pa, his son, who has been groomed since birth to become their next leader, or Alyssa, his daughter, who has just been revealed to them, but who now holds Horus's memories. To complicate matters further, even though Horus passed down his consciousness to Alyssa, his memories remain hidden to her.

Alyssa pleads with the Rathadi elders to rescue Paul and Tasha, but the Rathadi refuse, claiming they lack the strength to mount an assault against Nephthys and the Pureans. Alyssa strikes a deal with Dharr; she will allow him to teach her how to open herself to Horus's memories in exchange for his help in launching a small rescue mission to save Paul and Tasha.

Alyssa and a handful of her Rathadi friends, led by Dharr, travel to an abandoned arctic base where Paul and Tasha had been located with the help of Lord Renley and Clay. When Alyssa finds them, she is horrified to discover that Paul lost his right hand and is at the brink of death. In the fight to rescue the prisoners, the Rathadi jet is damaged, and Tasha stays behind so that Alyssa, Paul, and the Rathadi can escape.

Upon their return to the base in Indonesia, Dharr and Alyssa's Rathadi friends are reprimanded for the unauthorized rescue mission and for allowing Alyssa to endanger her life. As punishment, they are stripped of their rank, and Alyssa is confined. Despite Alyssa's and Dharr's best efforts to unlock Horus's memories from her mind, they have made little progress. Desperate to find any information that may give them an edge over Nephthys and help them save Tasha, Alyssa and her friends steal the jet. Their escape is disrupted by Heru-pa, but Dharr and the other Rathadi subdue Heru-pa as he follows them inside the plane.

The group travels to Nigeria, where XANDER HART, an inventor and friend of Lord Renley's, offers help by using deep brain stimulation and a machine he invented to recover memories. However, Xander reveals that the process is extremely time consuming because of the computational power required. Running out of time, Alyssa suggests that they join forces with The Society and use their supercomputer against their shared enemy, Nephthys.

Alyssa contacts The Society's senior scientist, Claudia Tibaldi. After the initial shock, Dr. Tibaldi assents to Alyssa and the others coming onboard the newly repaired *Valediction* to use their server in exchange for information that will help The Society find and defeat Nephthys. As Alyssa's memories are recovered, her friends and Heru-pa discover that Alyssa was the one who shot Horus.

Unwilling to concede that Alyssa acted under Nephthys's control, Heru-pa challenges Alyssa to a duel for killing his father. With the help of Horus's memories and instincts, Alyssa defeats Heru-pa. Disgraced, Heru-pa attempts to assassinate Alyssa then steals the jet and flees. Heru-pa travels to Nephthys and offers her a deal: he will deliver Alyssa to Nephthys, and Nephthys will help him eliminate her, so Heru-pa can become the leader of the Rathadi. In a moment of Nephthys's complacency, Heru-pa attacks her, infecting her with lethal poison that he had smuggled into the Purean's base inside his own blood. As Heru-pa dies, Alyssa finds Horus's golden amulet that Heru-pa left for her onboard the *Valediction*, and realizes that Heru-pa has been planning his sacrifice all along, so he could kill Nephthys.

Desperate to survive, the mortally wounded Nephthys injects Hybrid blood into Tasha, so she can serve as a vessel for Nephthys's consciousness. However, the transformation must be finalized in the sacred site beneath the Sphinx, so Nepthys, Tasha, and the Pureans race to Egypt.

Alyssa's clues also lead her and her friends to the Hall of Records. When they arrive in Cairo, they are ambushed, and they discover a military perimeter around the Sphinx. Alyssa suspects that Kamal Khanna, who was the only person who knew about their plan, may be working with Nephthys. She contacts the MINISTER OF ANTIQUITIES for help. The Minister, upon seeing a Rathadi, believes Alyssa's story and agrees to help her. Together with the military, they defeat a group of Pureans who were left to guard the entrance to the Hall of Records after Nephthys and Tasha entered it. Just as Alyssa and her friends gain access to the Hall, more Pureans arrive and overwhelm the military.

When Alyssa and her friends reach Nephthys, Alyssa realizes that she has arrived too late. Nephthys has already transferred her consciousness into Tasha's body! Alyssa and her friends are attacked by the Pureans who followed them, but Rathadi reinforcements arrive and buy Alyssa and Paul enough time to slip inside the sacred pyramid. Inside it, the couple find the true "Hall of Records:" a vast collection of Rathadi statues, each holding a triangular crystal containing the memories of that Rathadi, including the memories of Ra himself, inscribed in a red crystal. Nephthys, in Tasha's body, follows them inside, gravely wounds Alyssa, and overwhelms Paul. As Nephthys hauls them back outside the pyramid, they find the Rathadi have been defeated by the Pureans.

When the Rathadi cause a distraction, Paul slides the red crystal into Horus's amulet around Alyssa's neck. Filled with the power of the Rathadi's first ancestor, Alyssa defeats Nephthys and forces the Pureans to surrender.

However, the victory comes at a terrible cost. Alyssa has lost her eyesight, and she knows that she is dying. To preserve her life, Alyssa decides to be placed in hibernation inside of Horus's sarcophagus atop the sacred monument in a ceremony witnessed by her father, friends, and the remaining Rathadi.

Xander's machine is used to wipe Nephthys's memories from Tasha, which seemingly erases her mind completely...

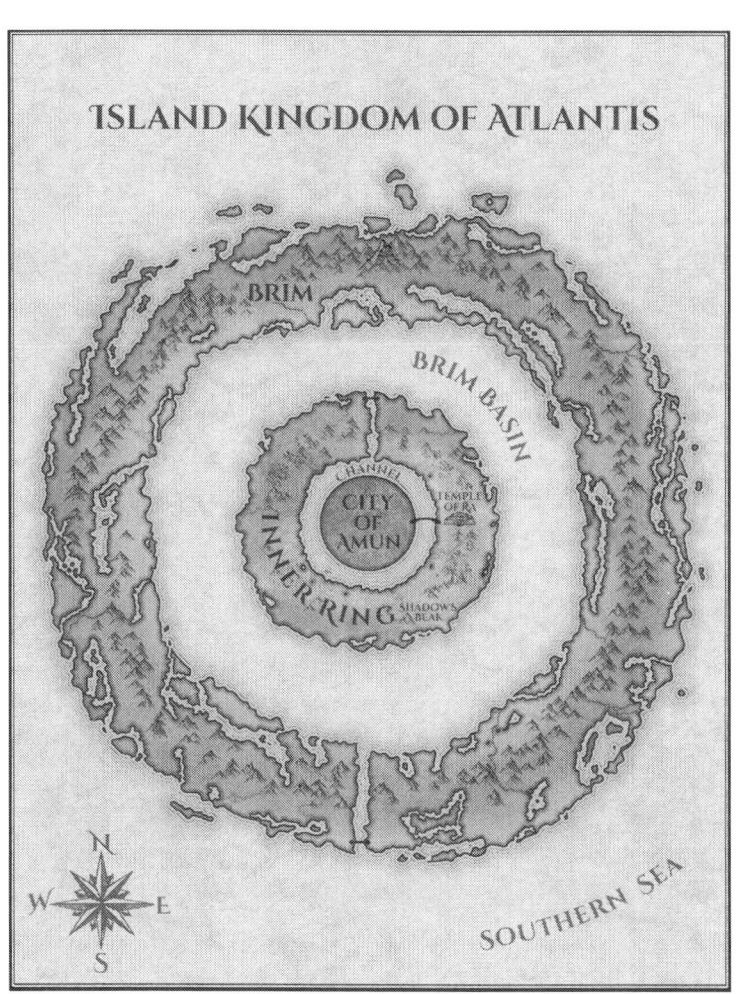

ISLAND KINGDOM OF ATLANTIS

BRIM

BRIM BASIN

CHANNEL

CITY OF AMUN

TEMPLE OF RA

INNER RING

SHADOW'S BEAK

N
W E
S

SOUTHERN SEA

THE PUREAN TRUTH-SEER gazed over the flames lapping at the edges of the divination bowl. The burning oils swathed the chamber in scents of metopion, and the fire cast soft shadows against the walls and the solitary bed that occupied the space.

A scream cut through the silence. The Rathadi female writhed against the damp sheets, her skin stretched firmly over her bulging stomach.

The birthing woman seated between the Rathadi's thighs cried out, "He is crowning! Push now, hard."

The young woman's panting quickened.

An old Rathadi at her side grasped her palm. "You're almost there. Push, Daughter!"

His face twisted into a grimace when she crushed his hand with the next contraction.

"Clam up! All of you!" the woman grunted between labored breaths. Her large feline eyes glazed over, then her voice crescendoed into a piercing cry that melted into the wail of a newborn. Moments later, the young woman's sobs joined the nascent squeal of her child.

The old Rathadi turned to the guard stationed at the door. "Tell King Osiris that his wife and son are both healthy," he said, unable to keep the quiver from his voice.

"Yes, Archsage," the woman replied, and rushed out.

The birthing woman passed the newborn into his mother's waiting arms. As the boy suckled, the truth-seer approached. The young mother watched warily as the Purean pricked the heel of her son with a silver needle, allowing the red liquid to coat the metal. She moved back to the divination bowl and loosened a pouch from her belt then poured the contents inside. The flame took on a bluish cast. The truth-seer raised her arms and muttered an incantation before throwing the needle into the fire.

The flames grew, spreading out like a pair of golden wings. The truth-seer gasped.

"The blood of Ra," she whispered. She closed her eyes, calling for the vision to descend upon her.

A face, strong and chiseled.

She allowed the trance to pull her in deeper.

Darkness. Countless pinpoints of lights. A strange-clad girl. She raises her arm, palm clenched around a dark object. A crack, loud as thunder. The single eye in the face widens. Another crack. And another. The face twists with pain as he slumps to the ground.

Without warning, the vision pulled the truth-seer inside like a whirlpool, drowning her. Images flooded her mind like cruel, shattering waves, more vivid than ever before.

The island burns in ruined waste. Carnage and horror

surround her as screams ring out from a thousand ravaged souls.

The truth-seer groaned. She resisted, trying to pull away.

The face contorts into a snarl, dragging her back into the nightmare. The single eye burns into her, razing everything in its path, wiping out all it meets into emptiness, leaving death and destruction in its wake.

The truth-seer cried out and staggered. The old Rathadi rushed forward and guided her to a chair. Slowly, the vision receded, and the smell of ash and blood ebbed. She focused on the deep lines of his face, the bristly canine jowls and gray eyes, then moved her gaze from the archsage to his daughter.

The young woman stared at her, the joy melted away, replaced by dismay. "What did you see?" she demanded.

The truth-seer trembled. She opened her mouth, but her voice failed.

The old Rathadi grasped her shoulders. Fear and worry etched the lines of his face even deeper. "Speak, Harwa! What have you foreseen for my grandson?"

The old woman fixed on him, unseeing. The air in the chamber was sucked away, and sweat sprouted on her forehead. Darkness closed the world to a tight, agonized knot, then the truth-seer slumped against the back of the chair.

PART 1

DAWN

CHAPTER 1

THE BOY STALKED through the tall grass, noiseless as a shadow, eyes glued to his mark. The afternoon sun caught the smooth scales in the brush ahead, sprinkling the vines with dancing sparks. The two-foot-long reptile seemed oblivious to the boy's presence as it raked leaves from the sinewy branches of the brittlebush with its powerful jaws.

He braved another step, rolling his foot in the soft soil from heel to ball. The lizard lifted its head and flicked its forked tongue in and out of its mouth, tasting the moist summer air. The crest around its neck flared then fluttered nervously, displaying a brilliant green.

The boy froze mid-step and held his breath. This was as close as he had ever stood to a Malachite Lizard. It was an immature male, the neck crest half-grown and still almost translucent, but the boy knew that what this razor-toothed menace lacked in size it made up for in speed—and wicked temper.

For several heartbeats neither moved. Then the boy pounced.

The reptile twisted and scurried for the undergrowth. For a moment it looked like it might escape, but the boy leaped in the air and stretched—

He landed on the lizard with a grunt and snatched it around the midsection with both hands, pinning it to the ground.

The beast hissed, its neck crest on full display. The boy pressed down, mindful of the reptile's claws and the twin rows of sharp teeth that lined its jaw. He slid up and pinned the animal's neck to the ground while he used his free hand to reach behind him and pull the large canvas sack from his belt.

He shook the sack open with his left while he slid his right palm along the body of the reptile until he reached its thrashing tail, then grasped it firmly. With a grunt, he lifted it off the ground, keeping the snapping jaws as far away from his body as he could manage. A triumphant smile spread across his face as he moved the bag under the squirming beast.

Abruptly, the lizard dropped to the ground and scurried away. The boy blinked, staring at his right fist, still clenched around the writhing tail. His mind struggled to catch up with what just happened.

The snickering behind him snapped him back.

"Behold, Heru-pa, mighty conqueror of lizard tails!" the young voice called out.

Heru-pa whirled. Set's ice-blue eyes crinkled with barely concealed amusement. He scrutinized the tail in Heru-pa's hand with exaggerated curiosity, revealing the gleam of white teeth against the dark of his face. "What a magnificent specimen you've ensnared. Mia is going to be so impressed."

Heru-pa flung the wiggling appendage at his friend. "I forgot they did that."

Set dodged the flying tail with annoying nimbleness, still grinning shamelessly.

"You could have helped, you know," Heru-pa grumbled, his shoulders sagging. He pointed to the dagger at Set's hip. "Could have put your heirloom to good use."

"And miss all the fun? Not for Ra's wings!" Set replied, struggling to keep his composure. He slipped the dagger from its scabbard and lifted it theatrically. "This noble blade was not forged to slay fledgling lizards. It was made to drink of the blood of ancient draccans."

Heru-pa glanced at the onyx blade enviously. He leveled his friend with a withering stare, but could not contain the laughter bubbling up in his throat. "Go kiss a joltfish. Next time, you can play the lizard wrangler, and I'll be looking out for his mom."

"I wouldn't dare!" Set cackled. "It seems like you need all the time you can get to sharpen those trapping skills. You'll be putting them to use soon enough."

Heru-pa's face darkened. "I won't be trapping lizards." He glanced south, beyond the highlands. It seemed like only yesterday that the hybrid nature of the Rathadi was unveiled to him during the Ceremony of Revelation. At that time, his sojourn to find his own sentinel had seemed a lifetime away.

"I know," Set said, the mirth fading from his voice. He slipped the blade back into the scabbard and clasped Heru-pa's shoulder. "You will find a mighty sentinel that is worthy of you. And you of him."

Heru-pa gave his friend a grateful smile.

"Still," Set said, an impish grin spreading across his face

again. "It's a good thing there's plenty of time left before your Rite of Valediction."

Heru-pa smacked Set's hand off his shoulder and punched him in the arm.

Set yelped and rubbed his sore limb. "You may be stronger, but I'll always be faster. Not even joining with your sentinel will change that."

"Only in your visions," Heru-pa shot back.

"Well, then it's as good as true," Set replied smugly.

Heru-pa sighed and picked a shoot of honey grass before plopping onto the meadow that extended over the valley below them. He nibbled on the stem, letting the sweet juice coat his mouth as he peered northward across the grass, past the coastline of the Inner Ring, and to the Center Island beyond the water. The sprawling terrain of the Inner Ring, the home of the Rathadi, stretched out to the east and west, before curving north and connecting again on the far side of the island. The contours of the Ring rose and dipped in concentric layers, from low-lying prairies at its edges to the soaring highlands at its interior, as the landmass completely encircled the island metropolis that rose from the water: the city of Amun.

The Purean capital was completely enclosed by an immense defensive wall that towered one hundred feet above the shimmering, turquoise water of the channel that separated it from the Inner Ring. Every hundred paces, bastion towers rose another one hundred feet into the sky. Yet even the bastions were dwarfed by the single alabaster spire that jutted out into the blue sky from the palace grounds in the center of the island.

"We should head back soon," Set said, drawing Heru-pa back, "before they catch on we snuck out again."

Heru-pa extended his arm toward the western horizon and used his palm to measure out the distance between the sun and the highlands below. It stood two hand spans above the horizon. "Let's stay another half span," he said absent-mindedly.

Set gave him a playful shove. "You daydreaming about Mia again?"

Heru-pa spit out the honey grass, his somber expression reflecting his spirit.

Set noticed the shift in his friend's mood. He eyed Heru-pa quizzically. "Why the glum face?"

"My Rite of Valediction," Heru-pa started, then stopped, unsure of how to continue.

Set sighed. "You know I was just having fun with you. If anybody is worthy of Ra's sentinel, it is you. He will seek you out, and you will—"

"It's not that," Heru-pa cut in.

Set raised his eyebrows. "It's not?"

"Will you…" Heru-pa swallowed. "Will you join my mother and father during the ceremony, and complete the Triad?"

Set opened and closed his mouth, but no sound came out. Finally, he managed to stammer, "M-me? The Third Pillar? But… but I'm not Rathadi. And besides, shouldn't your grandfather—"

"I talked to Grandfather," Heru-pa said. "And to my parents."

"And they agreed?"

"You know how they feel about you. Besides, they think that it would be good for our people."

"A Pure One? As a Pillar?" Set shook his head. "Have they talked to my parents?"

Heru-pa hesitated. "Not yet, I… I wanted to talk to you first."

Set rose and stood as proud and tall as his five-foot frame allowed. "Heru-pa, son of Isis and Osiris, it shall be my honor."

Heru-pa allowed a smile to spread over his lips. He got up and extended his arm to his friend. "Brothers forever."

Set clasped his forearm. "Brothers forever," he replied. "So, have you thought about your adult name?"

Heru-pa nodded.

"And?" Set asked.

"You know I can't tell you."

"Not fair!" Set groaned. "Not even now that I'm going to be—"

A cacophony of bells froze the next word on his lips. Heru-pa's thoughts spun at hearing the sound.

"Th-the alarm?" Set's face mirrored Heru-pa's own disbelief.

Heru-pa returned his friend's bewildered gaze. "We have not been attacked since…"

"Maybe it's a military exercise?"

Heru-pa shook his head.

Blood drained from Set's face as realization struck. "I need to get back to the capital!"

Heru-pa glanced to the temple on the east side of the Ring. It would take them the better part of a span running at breakneck pace to get there. They would then have to cross the long bridge over the channel to the Center Island. He turned and looked south to the highlands.

"No," Heru-pa said.

"No?" Set croaked.

"It will take too long to get to the temple, let alone across the bridge to the capital. And what if we don't make it in time? We could be trapped on the bridge during an attack."

"We could take the sky carriage when we get to the temple." Set pointed to the tethered gondolas shuttling between the Rathadi temple and the Purean palace.

"And risk being fried by the Eye while we're dangling in the air?" Heru-pa shot back. "We'll be safe in the highlands. If we head for Shadow's Beak, we'll get a better view of the Outer Ring and what is happening."

"You want to get closer to the Brim?" Set's voice shrieked into a falsetto. "Are you crazy?"

"Don't you want to see what's going on?"

"Our parents are going to kill us when they find out!"

"We'll just tell them we thought we'd be safer hiding in the highlands, rather than risk racing across the bridge," Heru-pa replied, a mischievous look on his face.

Set stared at him, as if unable to believe what he was about to say. "I am so going to regret this."

Heru-pa whooped and took off, racing for the high ground.

"Wait, slow down!" Set yelled before rushing after him.

"We're not going to miss it!" Heru-pa yelled back, trying to carry his voice over the ringing of the alarm bells. He continued racing at full speed, weaving his way between branches as they made their way up the small mountain.

A quarter span later, they arrived at a steep cliff, panting hard.

"Why'd you stop?" Set asked. He pointed right. "Serpent's Pass is that way."

"The path will take too long," Heru-pa replied. "Besides, we want to get up as high as we can, not just cut across the highlands."

Set gaped at the cliff before them. He gave Heru-pa a pleading look. "Please tell me you're not thinking what I think you're thinking."

"It's less than fifty feet. And it's an easy climb, just like going up a ladder."

"Maybe for you," Set said. "My mom told me—"

"Don't be a craven. Mia could do this climb in her sleep."

Set's jaw tightened at the mention of the girl's name.

"I'll lead the way. Just do what I do." Heru-pa studied the cliff face. A route seemed to appear in his head as if sketched by an invisible hand. He stepped to the wall and reached for the first handhold then grinned over his shoulder. "See you on top."

The surest handholds seemed to seek out his fingers all by themselves as Heru-pa scaled the wall, and before long, he was halfway up the cliff. He glanced down. Set was a dozen feet below him, clinging to the rock with white-knuckled fingers.

"You're doing great. Just keep doing what you're doing," Heru-pa called down.

Set grunted a reply that sounded like a reference to a foot and Heru-pa's backside, but he pressed on.

A short while later, Heru-pa crested the ridge. He reached down and helped Set over the edge.

"Told you that you could—*Ow!*" he yelped when Set smacked him in the head.

"I can't believe I let you talk me into this!" Set called out between ragged breaths. "This has got to be the most stupid thing that you've ever—" He looked to the sea, and his jaw dropped.

Heru-pa followed Set's gaze south. Beyond the Inner Ring, separated by another, wider, circular basin of water, stood the vast Outer Ring, known as the Brim, which completely encircled the Inner Ring and served as the first defense of their island home. Past the Brim, in the open waters of the South Sea, six massive black warships held station, their red, rectangular sails billowing in the wind.

"It *is* an attack!" Set called out, the words frosted with fear.

Heru-pa took in their surroundings. They were on the edge of a cliff, a sheer drop of at least two hundred feet on the side facing the Brim. He recalled his grandfather's lessons about the formidable natural defenses of the island. The ringed outer and inner landmasses and the two circular bodies of water formed a defensive perimeter that had repelled assaults on the island for millennia. Thousands of treacherous rocks hidden from view just beneath the water that surrounded the Brim made a night attack impossible, forcing any fleet to attack by day and exposing them to the terrifying power of the sun weapon.

"Calm down," Heru-pa said, trying to keep his voice steady. "We're safe here."

"What are they waiting for?"

Heru-pa reached into the bag he had strapped around his back and pulled out a metal cylinder. Set's eyes widened.

"A farseeker? Where did you—"

"I borrowed it from *Amah's* observatory," Heru-pa said, expanding the device and lifting it to his eye.

"You what?"

Heru-pa ignored him and aimed the farseeker north, back to the Center Island and the massive bowl-shaped mirror that crowned the tall spire in the heart of the capital. The Eye of Amun was designed by his grandfather and used the power of the sun to keep the island safe. A dozen Purean and Rathadi soldiers, the Guard of the Eye, stood in position on the platform, their own farseekers trained on the ships.

"Why aren't they using the Eye?" Set asked.

Heru-pa swung the glass out to the sea again. "The ships are still too far. At that range it won't be strong enough."

"They're going for the gate!" Set cried out. Heru-pa watched with morbid fascination as five of the six ships broke off and steered for the massive water gate that protected the single entrance from the open sea to the Brim Basin, the circular body of water between the Brim and the Inner Ring. The ships formed a wedge, picking up speed as they drew closer. Huge battering rams at the bows of the ships skimmed just over the surface of the water.

The warships collided with the gate. A blinding light then a huge explosion swept over the island. The shockwave traveled across Heru-pa's skin and through his body, stealing his breath. He gasped, almost losing hold of the farseeker.

"Amun's grace," Set muttered.

Heru-pa blinked through the flickering spots that assaulted his vision. His heart plummeted as the smoke cleared, revealing a gaping hole in the outer gate.

The air stilled, and perfect silence hung in the air, then the ringing of the alarm bells intensified and changed pitch.

"The breach alert!" Set gasped.

The sixth ship changed course and targeted the remnants of the massive gate hanging from its vast hinges.

Heru-pa focused the farseeker at the Eye of Amun. The Guard moved in a coordinated bustle, and the huge mirror tilted down and toward the ship, preparing to unleash the energy of the sun upon it.

"They are doomed," Heru-pa whispered.

The air grew still and heavy, and the chatter of birds hushed. A chill rolled in, as if bearing the threat of a storm, swallowing the sultry day. The landscape dimmed, but not into the dull gray of a cloud-covered sky. Instead, a faint yellow engulfed the island, like the glow cast by a fading torch.

Set raised his head and pointed at the sun. "Look!"

Heru-pa squinted, shielding his eyes with his hand. A dark disk moved in front of the sun.

"A black sun!" Set exclaimed.

An eclipse? A cold shock rippled through Heru-pa. *The Eye...* He honed in on the spire. The soldiers on the platform stood frozen, their gazes raised to the skies.

The warmth ebbed, and the sky darkened while the black disk swallowed the sun. Fireflies winked on as a chorus of crickets began their twilight song. A star materialized, then another. A few final ripples of light rushed over the ground before darkness descended on them.

Heru-pa forced his gaze back to the sea, just in time to see the black ship break through the battered gate and enter the narrow channel that led into the Brim Basin.

"It... it got through..." Set moaned. An instant later the batteries of catapults on both sides of the narrow channel sprang to life.

The first volley of the boulders missed its mark, and the ship continued its course untouched.

"Come on!" Set pleaded.

A second volley took to the air. Most of the projectiles splashed harmlessly into the water again, but one of the giant rocks scored a hit, turning the ship's center mast into a rain of splinters. Heru-pa stared mesmerized as the huge beam pitched and collapsed onto the deck, crushing everything in its path.

"Take that!" Set hollered.

A glimmer of light appeared in the sky, then the sun brightened, returning daylight to the island.

A moment later the ship erupted in flames. The screams from dozens of throats reached Heru-pa's ears. He blinked to dim the flashes of light inside his eyes then pointed the farseeker at the ship again. The sailors scurried around the deck to keep the ship on course, even as the searing heat from the Eye continued to burn and consume them. Heru-pa zeroed in on the men's faces. Their skin was covered by strange, swirling markings.

"Why aren't they jumping off?" Heru-pa cried out. "Why aren't they saving themselves?" A figure caught his gaze. He focused the farseeker. A woman stood on the bridge of the ship, seemingly unaffected by the blaze. Even though the sky was bright, and the ship was alight with flames, shadow pooled around her like smoke. Fire lapped at the wood surrounding her, but no flicker of its light reached the woman's form. She lifted a wooden staff in her right hand.

No, not wood.

Heru-pa blinked. The staff coiled around her hand like a serpent. She moved her arms and her mouth, barely visible beneath the dark hood, as if in a chant or incantation. Before her, sinuous shapes that looked like thick ropes coiled together began moving, their jet-black scales shimmering in the flames. Heru-pa's chest tightened, and dread pooled in his stomach.

Serpents?

"Set—!" he called out when another salvo of stone projectiles took to the air. This time three of them scored direct hits, gouging huge chunks of wood from the deck and port side of the vessel. The hooded figure stood still as a statue, surrounded by the smoke, yet seemingly unscathed by the flames. She turned her head and fixed Heru-pa with a piercing gaze, her eyes burning into him with spellbinding intensity.

Heru-pa gasped and reeled back. He yanked the farseeker from his eyes as if it were on fire.

"What happened?" Set asked. "What did you see?"

"I… I…"

A hand grasped Heru-pa's shoulder. He screamed and whirled—and stared into a pair of reptilian eyes peering down at him.

"Q-Qar?" Heru-pa stammered.

CHAPTER 2

HERU-PA AND SET stood shoulder to shoulder, heads bowed. Qar's even breathing echoed behind them as the fading sunlight streamed into the vaulted interior of the elegantly appointed chamber, shining across the gilded columns and the silk tapestries suspended between them.

A tall, regal woman rested in an exquisite chair against the far wall that was covered by a blanketing mural painted by the Pure One's master artisans. The woman wore a deep-blue robe that left one shoulder bare. Her slender jawline and prominent cheekbones looked carved out of dark marble, and her almond-shaped eyes glinted like polished sapphires, matching the stones in the slim crown that adorned her head. A dozen Purean guards and twice as many court attendants lingered against the other three walls of the hall.

Heru-pa rocked from one foot to the other, doing all he could to prevent himself from fidgeting with his tunic. After what seemed like an eternity, the woman turned to Set. "Are you hurt?" she asked.

Set shook his head without looking up.

"Have you any idea what you put me through?"

"Mother—" Set began.

"Don't you 'mother' me!" she interrupted. "Instead, explain to me why the crown prince of the Pure Ones is roaming around the Ring during an attack, instead of being safely behind city walls?" She leaned forward, her palms digging into the armrests. "And why, of all the souls in Amun's realm, it is the Rathadi weapons master who finds him and brings him home?"

Heru-pa and Set flinched at her tone. The woman stood and approached.

"Where were they?" she asked Qar.

"Shadow's Beak, Your Majesty," the weapons master replied. "Fortunately, one of our lookouts spotted them, and I was able to reach them quickly."

"Shadow's Beak?" the queen's voice went up an octave. "How did you get up there?"

Set shuffled his feet. "We… we climbed."

"You what?"

"I…" Set started but stopped under her glare.

"You are the crown prince to the Pure Ones," the queen said. "You must learn to act like one."

"Yes, Mother," Set said meekly.

Heru-pa stirred. "Your Majesty, it was all my fault. I—"

"Hold your tongue, boy!" the Purean queen snapped at him. "I shall get to you in good time. You may be a Rathadi princeling, but never forget that Set is the crown prince of the Kingdom Island of Atlantis, the heir to the ruling family. You are not his equal. Have you any idea of the risk to which you exposed him?"

Heru-pa flinched again. He felt heat rising behind his eyelids.

The queen waved one of the attendants over.

"Take the prince to his chambers. He is not to leave until I have spoken with him again."

"Yes, Your Majesty," the attendant said, and scurried to Set. She grasped his arm and nudged him along. Set shot Heru-pa a dejected look over his shoulder as he followed the woman out.

"Now to you, Rathling," the queen said to Heru-pa. "You have endangered the prince's wellbeing and his life, and once again brought discontent to me. We shall make certain that this is the last time. One night in the castle cells should make you think twice before you decide to endanger the crown prince's life again."

"The castle cells?" Heru-pa whimpered, unsure he heard right. Behind him, Qar's steady breathing hitched for the first time since they had entered the queen's chamber.

She nodded to one of her royal guards. "Captain Nebet, take this miscreant below."

Heru-pa tensed as the captain approached him. His lower lip began to tremble.

Qar stepped in front of Heru-pa. "Your Majesty…" he began. The guard stopped and hesitated.

The queen's eyes narrowed. "You dare to defy my order, Weapons Master? In my own palace? You have my gratitude for bringing my son to me unharmed, but you forget yourself." She addressed the guard again. "Take him, Captain."

Nebet reached for Heru-pa.

The huge door to the throne room opened loudly, and a

quiet voice filled the chamber. "If you lay your hand on my boy, Captain, it will be the last thing it will ever touch."

The guard froze.

Heru-pa whirled. "Grandfather!" he sobbed.

"Silence, boy," Thoth directed a burning glance at him.

Queen Nuit glared at the old Rathadi. "You dare to come into my hall and threaten my captain?"

"I will take care of the boy, Your Highness," Thoth said, and approached Heru-pa.

"Your *Majesty!*" Queen Nuit bristled. "You will address me properly in my own palace, and you will learn your place, Archsage!"

"Enough!" another voice called out from behind Heru-pa's grandfather. All the soldiers in the room snapped to attention and sank to one knee.

Geb, the High King of Atlantis, entered the hall. His bronzed face was all angles and hard corners, sharpened further by a carefully trimmed beard that was streaked with fingers of silver. He crossed the chamber, his white and gold cloak rippling around him.

Qar took a knee and pulled Heru-pa down to the cold stone.

"Thoth, take your grandson to his parents," King Geb said. "And tell King Osiris I have need of his council. Return with him soon as you can."

Thoth bowed. "As you wish, Your Majesty." He glanced to Heru-pa. "Let's go, boy."

The queen opened her mouth, but the king cut her off with a raised hand. "My Queen, I understand your displeasure, but we have more important things to worry about than two runaway princelings."

Heru-pa tried to keep a stoic face as he hurried after his grandfather. Qar bowed low to the king and queen and followed them out.

They left the throne room and stepped through a vaulted gateway into a corridor. A thick red carpet lined the marble floor beneath their feet, muting their footsteps as they aimed for the stairs to the sky carriage terminus that would take them across the channel to the Temple of Ra. Arched supports held up walkways that encircled the high walls overhead.

"Your mother is displeased," Thoth said. "What in Amun-Ra's name were you thinking?"

"We just wanted to explore the Ring, Grandfather. Soon I will have to go out and—"

"Soon, but not yet," Thoth interrupted gently.

"When the alarm rang, we thought it would be safer to stay where we were, rather than to head back." Heru-pa pulled at his collar. "And... and we thought maybe we could see Amun's gaze," he added, with a trace of guilt. "We didn't mean to upset anybody."

Thoth stopped at the bottom of the wide stairs that led to the terminus. He faced Heru-pa and took a knee. His gray lupine pupils shone with an intensity that stirred the fine hairs on the back of Heru-pa's neck.

"Do not rush to know destruction and death," Thoth said. "Both will seek you out of their own volition, and before you know it, you will wish they had never found you." He paused. "I understand your youthful fascination, but the relationship between the Rathadi and Pure Ones is strained, at best. We can ill afford your childish games complicating matters further. You and Set are old enough and wise enough to know better. You are both princes. Learn to act like them."

Heru-pa winced at his grandfather's words.

"Do you understand the importance of what I am telling you?"

Heru-pa nodded.

"Good," the old Rathadi said, and stood. "No doubt your mother and father will attempt to convey the same message. Perhaps not quite as calmly."

Qar chuckled softly, and Heru-pa shot him a glare.

They climbed the stairs in silence and reached an expansive terrace on the east side of the palace that served as the entry point onto the sky carriage. Two Purean guards greeted them. Manned by Pureans on this end and Rathadi on the side of the temple, the thick tethers that held the moving gondolas spanned the channel and connected the Purean palace and the Temple of Ra. Constructed to provide a quick way for the Rathadi and Purean royals to interact, it was yet another marvel of engineering that had been conceived and developed by his grandfather.

They entered one of the gondolas, and Qar latched the door behind them. Heru-pa felt the slight lurch as the cables engaged, and the carriage began its journey to the temple. Soon they had left the grounds of the Center Island and were traveling over water. The trio sat in silence as Heru-pa watched the channel beneath them. The view of the dark water stirred memories of the burning ship.

"Who attacked us, Grandfather?" he asked.

Thoth regarded him silently before replying. "We do not know."

"They knew about the eclipse, didn't they?"

Thoth nodded. "Even we have not been able to master the overlapping cycles of the moon and the sun, despite years of trials and observations."

"*Amah* told me she was close to understanding it." Heru-pa gave his grandfather a timid smile. "I'm sure the two of you will figure it out soon."

Thoth's lips curved up whimsically. "Your words in Ra's ears, my boy."

They continued in silence as they approached the vast rooftop of the temple. Surrounded by four spires that rose up from its roof, the Temple of Ra was capped by the most revered symbol of the Rathadi, their sacred monument: an enormous pyramid.

The gondola stopped on the high terrace, the Rathadi terminus of the sky carriage. As they exited, they were greeted by a pair of guards. Heru-pa smiled, savoring the feeling of being back home. Even though only the narrow channel separated the Purean city and the temple, they could not have been more different. Unlike the Pureans and their monolithic and urban architecture, the Rathadi preferred spacious designs and open ranges. The temple and the sacred monument were the only substantial structures in the Inner Ring and were home to the royal family and the few who worked in the temple. Most of the Rathadi lived in smaller settlements surrounding it and in the eastern part of the Inner Ring.

They descended the stairs into the high gardens. Heru-pa found his mouth going dry, unable to forget the images burned into his mind through the farseeker. He swallowed to gain his voice. "Grandfather?"

"Yes, my boy?"

"When I watched the ship through the farseeker, I saw the men's faces… They were covered by strange ink."

"Like the Purean truth-seer?"

"Yes—" Heru-pa considered—"and no. They were different patterns."

"What kind of patterns?" Thoth asked.

Heru-pa chewed on his bottom lip, pondering how to best describe the swirling lines that covered the men's faces.

Thoth stopped and picked up a fallen branch. "Could you draw it for me?" He broke it in half and handed a piece to Heru-pa.

"I… I think so," Heru-pa said, and took the stick.

He stepped off the walkway and cleared a patch in the dirt, forcing himself to recall the details of the serpentine lines that covered the faces of the men on the ship. One particular shape came to mind. Two concentric circles, bisected with another swirling line. He squatted and drew the design as best he could.

His grandfather bent down and studied the drawing, stroking the gray fur of his jaw. "Are you certain?" he asked.

Heru-pa nodded. "What—?"

"Did you see anything else?"

"When I watched the ships, I thought I saw…" He stopped, unsure of how—or whether—to continue.

"Go on, boy," the old Rathadi urged.

"A woman," Heru-pa said.

"On the ship that broke through?"

Heru-pa nodded again.

"Was there anything you noticed about the woman?"

"She wore a dark robe. And seemed unaffected by the

flames. And… she had a staff." Heru-pa hesitated. "It may have been a trick of the light, but it looked like the staff was moving… coiling… like a serpent. I know that sounds—"

"Coiling like a serpent?" Thoth interrupted, his voice hardening. "Are you certain?"

"Y-yes," Heru-pa stuttered, flustered by his grandfather's shift in demeanor. "I… I think so."

Thoth stood and faced Qar. "Take the boy home. And tell King Osiris that the Purean king requires his presence." He used his foot to erase the drawing. "You must not speak of this to anybody," he said to Heru-pa. "Neither of you," he added, then turned and rushed back across the gardens before either of them could muster a reply.

"Wait," Heru-pa called after him when he found his voice. "Where are you going?"

"I must consult the royal archives," Thoth replied without slowing down.

Heru-pa flicked a questioning glance at Qar. The weapons master met his gaze halfway and shrugged.

"Who do you think they were?" Heru-pa asked.

"I do not know," Qar said. "I do not have your grandfather's wisdom, but few goals are worthy of sacrificing a small flotilla." The weapons master placed a palm on Heru-pa's shoulder and nudged him on. "Let's get you home."

They continued on wordlessly. Heru-pa's trepidation grew with every step.

"Is *Amah* really mad?" he asked.

"She is not too pleased."

"I really messed up this time, didn't I?"

"It is not for me to judge the actions of a prince," Qar said.

"But I would advocate a downcast gaze and multiple instances of the use of the words 'I'm sorry.'"

Heru-pa's shoulders sagged. "That bad?"

They turned the corner into the corridor for the royal living quarters, and the two guards that stood at the end of the corridor nodded when they spotted them. Qar raised his arm in greeting as they approached.

"The majesties are expecting you, Prince Heru-pa," one of the guards said.

Heru-pa sighed woefully as Qar knocked on the tall double doors.

"Enter," came a voice from within.

Qar opened the door. "Good luck," he said, and patted him on the back as they entered the chamber.

Fading sunlight poured into the spacious, vaulted interior through a west-facing wall that consisted of nothing more than a row of arched windows and a tall doorway that opened onto a sprawling terrace. Long, flowing curtains danced in the warm evening breeze as Heru-pa's parents stood on the sunbathed platform overlooking the channel and the Purean capital.

His father turned. "The adventurer returns," he said, his voice carrying the subtle confidence of one shaped from birth to lead. King Osiris wore his customary black trousers, but his chest and feet were bare. As one of the few Rathadi ever to live with the gift of the scorpion, he preferred the feel of the sun on his onyx skin. He appraised Heru-pa with vertical pupils, their deep black splitting an amber, rich as the sun rising over the Eastern Sea. "I heard you gave the Purean queen a sour stomach today."

Before Heru-pa could think of a reply, his mother

approached. At first glance Queen Isis could not have appeared more different from her husband. Flowing hair framed an elegant, bronzed face. A long, white robe covered a body that was petite and slender enough to almost seem delicate. At a second glance, a subtle edge of threat shined through her features, and watching her move was like witnessing a panther stalking prey in a tree. She embraced him tightly, then held him at arms-length. Her deep, feline eyes seemed to look through him as she studied him with an equal measure of relief and scorn. "Are you alright?"

He simply nodded.

"What were you thinking?" she asked.

"I'm sorry, *Amah.*"

"You have to be more responsible. I heard the queen was very upset," she said.

Osiris gave a chuckle. "I do wish I could have seen the look on her face."

Heru-pa turned to his father, mouth agape. Instead of the anger he expected, his father's scaly lips curved into a hint of a smile. The fading sunlight behind his tall form caught his skin at just the right angle, and the scales on his broad shoulders shimmered a trace of blue and green.

Isis frowned. "Truly? You are not helping."

"The boy was curious. That is a worthy quality in a future leader."

"His *quality* was going to land him in a Purean cell for the night!"

"I doubt the queen had any intentions of following through. She was vexed and wanted to give him a scare," Osiris said, and chuckled again. He quickly raised his hands when he saw his wife's glare, worthy of the Eye of Amun. "But I am certainly not saying he did not deserve it," he added.

"I'm just glad they were spotted, and Qar got to them when he did, before anything else happened during this assault."

"A handful of ships, My Love," Osiris replied. "That hardly qualifies as an assault."

"One of the ships breached the outer gate," Isis countered.

Qar, who had been standing by the door quietly, cleared his throat. "Majesties," he chimed in hesitantly with a bow. "My apologies for intruding, but King Geb kindly requested King Osiris's presence."

"He is calling the King's Council?" Osiris asked.

The weapons master nodded.

Osiris sighed. "The fearless ruler of the Pure Ones beckons." He reached for his black cloak that hung draped over a tall sofa then ruffled Heru-pa's hair. "Take care of your mother while I'm gone."

"Yes, *Tato*," Heru-pa said.

The king gave Isis a tender embrace. "Don't be too hard on the boy," he said before stepping through the door.

Qar bowed to the queen and followed him out. When the door closed behind them, Heru-pa's mother eyed him seriously. "Your valediction ceremony will take place in less than two months' time. You must make certain that you are worthy of your adult name."

"Yes, *Amah*," he said.

"I was worried about you."

"I know, *Amah*. I'm sorry." He stood in silence for several moments before he began trembling. He blinked to keep the tears from his eyes.

"It is alright," his mother said. "I am sure the queen was not that upset with you."

Heru-pa shook his head. "It's not that."

"What is it?" she asked gently.

"When I saw the men. On the ship. They… they just stood there as they… burned. As they burned alive."

Isis pulled him close. Heru-pa closed his eyes and took in the familiar scent of jasmine in her hair and the metopion oil on her skin. The images of the men burning and screaming on the ship slowly dissolved, draining the tension from him.

"Try not to think about that. Let us find something more enjoyable to discuss, shall we?" his mother offered.

Heru-pa swallowed and nodded.

"Did you ask Set about your valediction ceremony?"

A small smile flickered across Heru-pa's lips. "Yes."

"And?"

"He agreed!"

"Did you really expect anything else?"

"No," Heru-pa replied. His face grew somber. "It's just… with what happened today, I don't think that the king and queen will give their consent."

"Give them a few days. Unity Day is coming up. And your grandfather can be very persuasive," Isis said. "Sometimes a little too much for his own good," she added. "You know the king values his council, and I'm sure he can help sway both of them to allow Set to participate."

"If you think so," Heru-pa said, not quite convinced.

"I do." Isis pulled him in again, crinkled her nose, and shoved him away playfully. "You definitely need a bath before sleeping."

"But, *Amah*..."

"No arguments," she said. "I will have a bath drawn for you. Wash up and put your night clothes on. I will see you afterward."

Heru-pa nodded meekly and lumbered to the bath chamber.

Half a span later, he laid in his bed. Isis came in and eased down on the side.

Heru-pa reached for her hand. "I'm sorry, *Amah*, I didn't mean to worry you, or make the queen angry."

"I know," Isis replied.

He scooted over. "Will you stay with me? For a little while?"

Isis nodded and laid down beside him, holding him in her arms. Heru-pa closed his eyes and listened to his mother's breathing until he fell into an uneasy sleep.

In his sleep, the boy did not see his mother as she rose and blew out the candle, casting the room into complete darkness to all but those blessed by the gift of the sacred cat. Isis kissed him gently on his forehead then placed her palms on his head, her thumbs and forefingers shaped into the triangle that represented the rays of the sun bathing the earth.

In his sleep, the boy did not hear his mother when she leaned in and softly whispered, "You are Horus, son of Isis and Osiris. You shall know no fear."

CHAPTER 3

OSIRIS TOOK a sip of his seaweed tea before leaning back into the padded chair opposite the Purean monarch. Flickering flames from the wall sconces cast ghostly shadows on Geb's expressionless face as he studied the five individuals at the circular table of the royal council chambers.

After several moments of silence, King Geb pushed aside the short staff of black ash and ivory that served as one of the few symbols of his position and placed his palms on the cool marble. "Who were they?" he asked, unable to fully strip the trepidation from his voice.

The tall woman on the king's left stirred. He nodded, granting her permission to speak, and Admiral Kiya stood. She wore the deep blue tunic of a naval officer, and the pair of oval sapphires that adorned each of her lionfish skin lapels marked her as the supreme commander of the Purean fleet. Her left temple was shaved, and she brushed back the single braid over her right shoulder.

"We do not know," she said, her voice calm and measured.

"We are combing through the wreckage and are looking for survivors, but it appears that the entire crew perished with each vessel."

"Even the ship that made it through?" Osiris asked.

The admiral nodded.

The Purean king shook his head in disbelief. "They chose to be burned alive, rather than to abandon the vessel?"

"It appears so, Your Majesty."

"Who does such a thing?" the king asked.

"Those who fear the consequence of disobedience more than they do being burned alive," the man next to the admiral replied. General Mehet was a wiry man with a high domed forehead and scarred cheeks.

The king eyed him in silent contemplation for several heartbeats. "Are there any signs as to their origin?"

"From the preliminary analysis of the salvaged pieces, it appears that the attackers went through a great deal of effort to ensure their identities, and origins, would remain unrevealed," the admiral replied.

"We have not been challenged by sea in decades," Geb said, stroking the streaks of silver in his square cut beard. "Why now?"

"A vanguard? To test our defenses, perhaps?" A raspy voice to the left of Osiris rang out. The Rathadi high priest's leathery face matched the roughness of his words. So'bek shifted his gaze from the Purean king to Osiris and regarded him from behind yellow, reptilian eyes.

Osiris pondered the priest's words. "A costly price to pay," he said, then shook his head. "We must be missing something crucial."

The admiral took her seat again, and for several moments no one spoke as they considered the circumstances. Finally, Geb turned to the woman on his right who had been following the discussion silently, her face covered by a low hood.

"Do you have anything to add, truth-seer?" he asked.

The woman lifted her head and pulled back the hood. Her ageless skin was smooth and completely hairless and was covered in swirling ink that glowed faintly in the dim light of the wall sconces.

"The visions have been silent, Majesty," Harwa replied.

Osiris stirred uneasily at the woman's voice. Truth-seers had been in the services of Purean monarchs for millennia, and they commanded universal trust because a single willful lie that passed their lips came at the sacrifice of losing their power. Despite it, Osiris had never grown comfortable around the old woman.

"Perhaps we are thinking about it too much?" she offered. "Perhaps they were simply barbarians looking to pillage us for resources?"

"Barbarians who happened to mount an attack during a total eclipse, rendering useless our most powerful weapon?" Osiris challenged.

"A coincidence?" Harwa suggested.

Admiral Kiya shook her head, her thick braid swinging with the motion. "They waited until the exact moment. They were able to predict the black sun to the instant. These were no mere barbarians."

Osiris nodded his support at her words.

"Still we are not a step closer—" Geb stopped when the

door opened and Thoth rushed in. "Archsage, how kind of you to join us."

"Forgive my delay, Majesty," Thoth replied, breathing heavily as he slumped into his seat across from Harwa. Osiris furrowed his brow at the tightness in his father-in-law's voice and his demeanor.

"Despite your tardiness, it appears you have not missed anything of essence," the king groused. "All we seem to concur on is that the entire crew chose to burn alive rather than abandon their vessels."

Thoth's face sank even further.

"Have you anything to add?" Geb asked.

"I may have found a clue regarding the identity of the invaders," Thoth said.

The room fell silent.

"I had to consult the archives to confirm my suspicion," Thoth continued. "I found references to an enemy from a time long past. An enemy we have not—"

"Archsage," Geb cut in. "If you have something to say, do so. I am already burdened with interpreting the jumbled visions of one truth-seer." He pointedly ignored the glance Harwa flicked at him.

"The Ba'ulati," Thoth said.

"The Ba'ulati?" Geb asked.

"Impossible," Admiral Kiya said. "The Ba'ulati perished centuries ago."

"At great cost to the Rathadi," Osiris added.

The admiral scoffed and opened her mouth, but Thoth jumped in before she could reply. "We are aware of the history of our island, Admiral, and of the price that victory demanded.

However, I have reasons to believe they were responsible for today's attack."

"The Ba'ulati have not been seen in centuries," General Mehet said. "Since—"

"Since they were annihilated when they challenged the island the last time," the admiral cut in. "To claim that they were responsible—"

Geb silenced her with a raised hand and turned to Thoth. "How do you come by this information?"

"My grandson, he—"

"*The* grandson?" the king interjected with a glance to Osiris.

"He may be young, but he is more mature than most boys twice his age," Osiris replied, holding the Purean king's gaze. "If my son says he saw something, his words should be considered."

"And it appears that, through his youthful folly, he was positioned closer to the ship than most of our soldiers," Thoth added.

Geb considered for several moments. "Continue," he said.

"It appears that young Heru-pa had his farseeker trained at just the right place and time," Thoth said. "He described men that bore inscriptions on their skin consistent with the Ba'ulati tribal markings on the ship that broke through our defenses."

"Our *first line* of defenses," the admiral corrected.

"Why the Ba'ulati?" General Mehet asked. "And why now? They must have known this attack would be futile."

"The Ba'ulati are not famed for their knowledge of the heavens," Geb added. "How did they know about the eclipse?"

"As the admiral recounted, the last time our people met in

battle was centuries ago," Thoth said. "Many things may have changed."

"There could be dozens of other explanations," General Mehet offered. "Not the first one of which is that the boy was simply mistaken in what he saw."

"I agree with the general's skepticism," Admiral Kiya said. "We had dozens of farseekers aimed at that ship. None of my sentries reported seeing Ba'ulati markings."

"We all know that none of your soldiers can match my son's sight," Osiris said. "Despite his young age," he added, turning to King Geb.

"His descriptions are too detailed to be a coincidence," Thoth said. "This is more than just a Rathling's imagination."

"Be that as it may," Geb said. "Are we to rely on a child's story?" He regarded their faces. "Is that the best my council can offer?"

High Priest So'bek stirred. "And yet, if Heru-pa and the archsage are correct, this is a warning we dare not ignore."

A heavy silence fell over the room. Finally, the Purean king spoke up. "Did the boy see anything else?"

The old Rathadi seemed to hesitate for a heartbeat. It appeared as if he was going to reply, but he shook his head. Osiris raised his eyebrow, but remained silent.

The truth-seer sneered. "You bring us a theory, based on the account of a Rathling. We require more than just the ideations of an old man and his grandson."

"Guard your tongue, witch," Osiris scolded. "This old man has done more for the Kingdom than your sorcery ever could."

Thoth laid a calming hand on Osiris's shoulder. "This has been a trying day, and tempers are strained. We must remember that the island is impenetrable, as long as we stand united."

"Then what is to be our course of action?" So'bek asked.

"If the Ba'ulati attacked us, we must retaliate," the general replied.

"I advise against that, Your Majesty," Thoth said.

"I agree with General Mehet," the admiral said. "If it was truly the Ba'ulati who assailed us again and tested our defenses, we must move against them before they are able to mount a full campaign."

"You are suggesting we mobilize our fleet and sail west to confront them on their ground?" King Geb asked.

"They will only grow bolder if we allow their attack to go unchallenged," the general replied.

"I do not believe this to be the wisest course," Thoth said.

"What in the Three Seas would you have us do?" the admiral fired back. "Cower and wait for them to return in full force?"

"It is not the coward who steers clear from conflict, but the wiser man," Thoth said. "Our defenses are sound. The island is safe."

The admiral stood up. "I would rather send out our fleet—"

"That is not—" Thoth cut in.

"Enough!" the king snapped. "The Day of Unity is upon us. I shall not have my trusted advisors bicker like children."

Thoth bowed. "Forgive us, Majesty. I merely advocate restraint over rashness."

The king pressed thumb and forefinger against his eyes and cursed softly. "Until we have additional information, I must agree with the archsage," he grumbled.

The faces of the general and admiral tightened, but both nodded wordlessly. "We shall inform His Majesty of any new development," the admiral said.

"And I shall consult the visions once again," Harwa said.

King Geb nodded and stood. The others rose with him.

"One other item," Geb said. "Have there been any new developments regarding the death of the merchant?"

The general shook his head. "I have placed Captain Nebet in charge of the investigation, but there have not been any leads as of yet."

Geb sighed. "Amun curse the timing. As if we did not have enough to agonize over. Let us hope nothing else befalls us between now and the Day of Unity celebration."

CHAPTER 4

HERU-PA HELD his breath and thrust the pitchfork into the muck. He lifted the foul blend of horse excrement and hay then backed out of the stall. Once a safe distance away, he rested the prongs on the ground and inhaled deeply, wiping his brow. He muttered a soft curse that would have earned him an extra day of this torment if his mother or the Purean queen had heard it.

"Stable duties suit you, Prince Heru-pa," a girl's voice rang from the gate. Heru-pa whipped about. Mia was perched on the wooden fence that enclosed the royal stables, not even giving him the courtesy of feigning sympathy for his plight. Her bright grin stood out against her olive skin, and her long blonde hair was skillfully braided into a lace in the latest fashion of Purean noble-borns.

Heru-pa felt the heat rising in his cheeks, but he forced himself not to dignify his friend's quip with a reply. He piled the muck onto a wheelbarrow then threw the pitchfork down and kneaded his sore palms, wincing at the budding blisters on his skin.

"It's your own fault," Mia continued, seemingly unperturbed. "What in Amun's name were you thinking? And dragging Set with you?"

"It's not like I kidnapped him!" Heru-pa snapped back. "Besides, he's the crown prince of the Pureans, so shouldn't he be the responsible one? Why am I the only one getting punished?"

"Because *he* is the crown prince of the Pureans," Mia snickered.

Heru-pa sighed then picked up the wheelbarrow and wrestled it toward the gate. "I wanted to do something special, to ask him to participate in my Rite of Valediction," he said, grunting. "How could I have guessed this would be the day we are going to be attacked?"

The gate opened as he approached, revealing Set enrobed in a crisp new vest and leggings.

"Amun's blessings, Heru-pa!" his friend greeted him.

Heru-pa dropped the wheelbarrow and pushed up the sleeves of his filthy tunic. "Oh, his royal highness himself," he grumbled. "You are looking splendid today. Just waking from your midday nap?"

"Not fair," Set said. "You should have heard the sermon I endured from my mother last night. *And* I've been with Harwa since sunrise, scouring her pots and helping organize her herb collection."

Mia laughed. "Now you know what I have to deal with every day."

"You chose to be her acolyte," Set said. "You've got nobody to blame but yourself. Besides, I still don't understand why a healer like you would want to spend her time studying under a truth-seer."

"I have to know my herbs to be a healer," Mia replied. "And nobody knows herbs better than old Harwa."

"Nobody smells stronger like herbs than old Harwa," Set mumbled. "Ugh... it's still in my snoot…" He wiped at his nose theatrically.

Mia giggled, bright and cheerfully.

"Are you seriously going to complain about herb smell while I'm shoveling horse dung?" Heru-pa grumbled.

"When I'm king, I shall ensure that—" Set started.

"Well, until then, Your Highness," Heru-pa cut in, "why don't you make yourself useful and pick up another pitchfork?"

Set shot him a surprised glance.

"Come on, Set, the Day of Unity is almost upon us," Mia chuckled. "What better way to honor unity between the Pure Ones and the Rathadi than having our princes lead by example and work together?"

"Very funny," Set said, but couldn't help flinging her a grin. "Fine, let's get this done with, so we can go do something fun." He took off his vest and hung it on the corner of a stall. "Just don't tell my mother. I'm not even supposed to be here. I just snuck out to see you before weapons training."

Set reached for a halter and entered the next enclosure. He spoke softly as he approached the horse then stroked its neck. The animal nickered and pressed its snout against Set's palm. Heru-pa couldn't hide his smile as Set skillfully haltered the horse then led it out and tied it to a hitching post.

"You know, if you keep this up, you'll be training the Rathadi animal handlers soon," Heru-pa said.

"It's always been easier for me to talk to beasts than people," Set said, then picked up a pitchfork.

Heru-pa emptied the wheelbarrow and pushed it near the stall Set was mucking out. Mia jumped down from the fence as Set dumped a pile of the dirty hay. She drew closer, a conspiratorial expression framing her face. "Did you hear about the merchant they found yesterday?"

"What merchant?" Heru-pa asked. Set glanced up, equally puzzled.

"They found him just inside the city gates." She lowered her voice. "Dead."

"Was he murdered?" Set asked, dismayed.

"Not just murdered. Mauled," Mia replied. "They say it looked like he was attacked by a wild beast."

"A wild beast? Inside the city walls? That's crazy," Heru-pa said. "Who said that?"

Mia blushed. "I overheard my father talking with the captain of the guard."

"You were eavesdropping on the general?" Set asked.

"The captain seemed ruffled when he got to our home early in the morning. I figured it had to be important."

Heru-pa leaned against the wheelbarrow, trying to process the information. "Why would somebody kill a merchant?"

"I don't know, but the captain said he wasn't even robbed. They're trying to keep things quiet because of the Day of Unity celebration."

"People are bound to find out," Set said. "You did."

"What a day," Heru-pa said. "First the murder, then the attack on the island…"

A heavy silence fell between them. Finally, Mia spoke. "Did you really see it? What happened to the ships?"

"Heru-pa had the farseeker," Set said.

"What was it like?" Mia asked.

Heru-pa's jaw tightened. "Grandfather told me not to say anything…"

"Come on. We can keep a secret. Did you see Amun's glare?"

"It was horrid," Heru-pa said, struggling to keep his voice from breaking. "I never want to see it again. The Eye of Amun… it was everything Grandfather described in his stories. The men on the ship… they… they did not stand a chance."

"I'm sorry," Mia said. "You don't have to talk about it."

Heru-pa swallowed. "There is more. But you have to promise not to tell anybody."

Set and Mia nodded.

"I mean it, no soul may know about it," he said.

"Amun's promise," Mia said. Set propped up his pitchfork and echoed her words.

"There was a woman on the ship."

"A woman?" Mia asked.

Heru-pa nodded. "I saw her as clearly through the farseeker as I see you, but her face…" He trailed off, recalling the shadows pooling around the woman like a cloak. "She held on to this… strange staff."

"A staff?" Mia asked.

"Yes, it was curved and coiling, like… like a serpent." Set opened his mouth, but Heru-pa held up his hand and continued. "And the strangest thing, she wasn't even affected by Amun's glare. She just stood there while all the others…" He shuddered as the images of the burning men swept through him. Heru-pa closed his eyes, trying to push the images from his mind. He blinked his eyes and wiped a tear.

"Amun's grace," Mia whispered.

"Did you tell your grandfather about the woman?" Set asked.

Heru-pa nodded. "Well… not everything," he said.

"Not everything?" Set and Mia stared at him with bated breath.

"I… I think there were serpents."

"Serpents?" Mia asked.

"On the ship. Then the woman signaled to them, and they slithered into the water."

Mia gasped. Beside her, Set's mouth hung agape.

"And you didn't tell your grandfather about the serpents?" Set asked.

"When I told him about the woman, he just took off. I didn't even get a chance to say another word."

"But what if it's something important?" Mia asked.

"It seemed I caused him enough grief for one day," Heru-pa replied. "Anyway, I probably just imagined the serpents."

"And what if you didn't?" Set asked.

Heru-pa considered then nodded. "Very well, I will tell him." He picked up the pitchfork. "But you have to promise not to tell anybody, especially not your mother. I don't need any more of her wrath after yesterday, or she'll never agree to let you be in my valediction ceremony."

"You should ask her on Unity Day," Mia suggested. "It'll be hard for her to refuse you then."

Set nodded. "That's not a half-bad idea, Mia."

"Gee, thank you for your kind words, My Prince," Mia said mockingly. "Perhaps you should just stick with talking to animals, after all."

"I thought it was brilliant," Heru-pa said without thinking.

Mia shot him a look, and he felt heat rising in his cheeks.

Heru-pa faced Set. "But Mia does have a point," he said, eager to move on. "If we both ask your mother on—" His words died on his lips when Set's eyes rolled back into his head. "Set!" He rushed to his friend.

Mia froze.

"A truth-vision!" Heru-pa called out. He lowered Set to the ground and cradled his friend's head. Set's breathing slowed, and his skin began to radiate a strange warmth. A calming seclusion spread through Heru-pa's limbs.

"Is he going to be alright?" Mia asked.

"Yes," Heru-pa replied, uncertain of where he found the confidence. Set closed his eyes. His body quivered gently, and his eyelids fluttered.

Heru-pa's skin tingled an instant before Set clutched his arm, squeezing it tightly.

Images flashed before him.

A corridor. A huge claw strikes down in a vicious slash. Darkness.

The darkness dissipates. Slowly. Too slowly…

A body. He floats above it. A grisly wound spills from the man's head. Four long slashes, as if mauled by a great beast.

An icy numbness spread through Heru-pa. Gradually, the dark walls of the corridor dissolved, and the familiar surroundings of the royal stables emerged, then Mia's face, a panicky daze tainting her features.

"Set! Heru-pa!" she cried out. "What is happening to you?"

"I… I'm fine," Heru-pa managed. "Set?"

"Fine," Set replied weakly. "I… I had a truth-vision."

"I know," Heru-pa said. "I saw it."

"Y-you saw my vision?"

Heru-pa nodded.

"You shared your truth-vision with Heru-pa?" Mia asked, mystified. "I didn't know you could do that!"

"Neither did I," Set said. "What was that?"

"I don't know," Heru-pa replied, "but I think we'd better find my grandfather. Now."

CHAPTER 5

THOTH STOPPED before the tall door at the end of the corridor and knocked.

"Enter," Isis's voice came from within.

Thoth stepped inside. The Rathadi queen's work chamber was a treasure trove of models and trinkets that they had constructed together over the decades. His lips curved into a smile at the sight of his daughter scrutinizing their favorite construct.

Isis glanced up.

"Ra's blessings, Father," she said, and embraced him.

"Ra's blessings," he replied, returning the warm hug.

She studied his face. "You look troubled. The King's Council?"

"And when have you become a Purean mind reader?" he asked.

"Do not try to change the topic."

Thoth's smile faded.

"Shared troubles are halved troubles," she pressed, quoting

him.

"I know you have a great deal of things on your mind. I do not wish to bother you—"

"You may be the greatest intellect among the Rathadi," she said, "but I am your daughter, and you have taught me well."

Thoth chuckled. "Sometimes I wonder if not perhaps too well."

He turned to the astronomical model and scrutinized the complex mechanisms and gears that allowed it to mimic the diurnal movement of the sun and moon around the earth, and the motions of the five celestial wanderers that roamed through the night sky against the vast canvas of the stars. He and Isis had painstakingly catalogued the motions of those objects over years, and he had designed this mechanical marvel based on their shared observations.

"Father?" his daughter's voice cut into his thoughts, drawing him back.

Thoth focused on the golden disk that represented the sun and the silver one that was the moon. He plucked the moon disk from its slot and studied it in his hand. "The eclipse took us by surprise," Thoth replied. "We are relying on the Eye of Amun to keep us safe, but if we are unable to predict when the island is most vulnerable…"

Isis remained silent, as if lost in her own thoughts.

"I shall have to build a stronger farseeker," Thoth continued, "one that will allow me to peer farther into the vastness. Perhaps we are not measuring the motions precisely enough, or perhaps—"

"What if a stronger farseeker is not the answer?" Isis interrupted.

He looked at her quizzically.

"I have been thinking about something." She approached the model but then hesitated.

"Speak, daughter," the old Rathadi coaxed her. "I have not known you to be meek in declaring your opinion."

She plucked the golden disk from the model and held out her hand for the moon disk. Thoth handed it over, and she put the disks on top of each other. They aligned perfectly, just as he had designed them.

"What if we have been going about this the wrong way? What if the sun and the moon are not the same size?" She paced to her desk and picked up a leather-bound notebook. "I have followed and noted the whereabouts of the five wanderers for months; how they switch positions against the rotating background of the stars. What if… what if the sun and moon do not both go up and down around us? What if, instead, we traveled around the sun?"

Thoth stared at her, dumbstruck, struggling to process the concept. He studied the model, trying to visualize the patterns. "That… that is not possible," he breathed.

"But if you only open your mind to the possibility," she pleaded. She rearranged the disks. "If the sun was at the center —here—and we, and the other wanderers, moved around it—"

"No," Thoth interrupted. "If we revolved around the sun, then the view of the sun disk would change. It would shrink in size when viewed from the side. It—"

"Unless the sun was not a disk." Isis moved to the corner of the table and picked up a golden glass ball then placed it in the center of the model. "What if the sun was a sphere?"

Thoth opened his mouth, but she continued before he could

jump in. "Recall the four daughters that circle Iovis, the Great Wanderer? On some nights we could glimpse only one of his daughters, but on others all four would reveal themselves to us." She moved the earth and the moon disks close together. "What if the moon was our own daughter and revolved around us like the four daughters journey around Iovis, and we—" she moved both the earth and moon disks farther away from the golden glass ball—"traveled around the sun?"

Thoth gaped at her open-mouthed. When he spoke, his words were slow and measured. "If the distance between the earth and the moon is as close as the distance between Iovis and his daughters, and the distance to the sun is so much greater…" He paused, considering the implications. "For the moon to cover the sun completely during an eclipse, the difference in size between the sun and the moon would have to be—"

"Vast," Isis finished his sentence. "By my calculations, at least two hundred times."

"Are you saying the sun is two hundred times farther from the earth than the moon?" Thoth whispered.

Isis nodded.

Thoth stared at the astronomical model as if seeing it for the first time. His heart pulsed at the sight of the golden ball resting at the center of the arrangement and at the consequences of what Isis had revealed. "This could change everything…"

"So you agree?" Isis asked.

"I must review the notes you collected and your calculations, but—"

The door burst open, and Heru-pa surged in, followed by Set and Mia. All three were panting. The guards glanced at Isis, embarrassed.

"My apologies, Majesty," one of them started. "Your son insisted—"

"Heru-pa!" she scolded. "What is the meaning—?"

"Grandfather!" Heru-pa called out as Set and Mia stopped and bowed to Isis. "We've been looking all over for you! You wouldn't believe what happened. We were just talking, and Set had a truth-vision, and he grabbed me, and suddenly these images—"

"Slow down, grandson." Thoth raised a calming hand. "Take a deep breath."

Heru-pa quivered with excitement, but he forced himself to suck in a deep breath and let it out. Isis dismissed the guards with a wave.

"Now, from the beginning," Thoth said.

"We were talking in the royal stables," Heru-pa began, struggling to maintain his composure. "When I turned to Set, he was in a truth-vision daze. He grasped my hand, and then there were images in my head." Heru-pa shuddered. "A corridor and a dead Purean."

"You two shared a truth-vision?" Thoth asked.

Both boys nodded.

Thoth turned to Set. "You channeled your truth-vision into Heru-pa?"

"I-I didn't mean to do it, Honored One," Set stuttered.

"It is quite alright, Young Prince," Thoth said. "I know you would never do anything to harm your friend."

He waved the boys closer. "Did either of you recognize the body?"

Heru-pa and Set shook their heads.

"Is there anything else you remember?"

"There was a great claw that came down on him," Heru-pa said.

"A great claw?" Thoth asked. "Like that of an animal?"

"I… I think so," Heru-pa replied.

Thoth looked to Set.

The boy shook his head. "I'm sorry," he said. "It happened so quickly."

"It is quite alright," the old Rathadi replied. "Did you get any idea about the time of the event? Or the place?"

"Not the time, Honored One," Set answered. "But I think it was somewhere in the palace." Heru-pa nodded his agreement.

Thoth regarded them seriously. "The subject of your vision is disturbing, but your location makes it even more so."

"What are you going to do?" Heru-pa asked.

Thoth remained silent for several moments. "Thank you all," he said when he finally spoke. "You have done the right thing to tell me and the queen about it."

Heru-pa stirred. "We need to—"

"*You* need to trust us to do what is necessary," Isis cut in, her voice quiet but firm. "And I give you my word that we shall come back to you if we believe you can help us further." She eyed them all seriously. "Is that clear?"

"Yes, *Amah*," Heru-pa grumbled.

"Yes, Your Majesty," Mia and Set said, and bowed.

The queen eyed the two princes. "I believe you two have lines to practice for the Day of Unity celebration, do you not?"

Heru-pa and Set nodded.

"Then you shall spend the remainder of the day on it, and again tomorrow," she said.

Heru-pa's face twisted. "Can we still go to weapons practice tomorrow morning?"

"If you know your lines," the queen replied. "You may now take your leave."

Isis waited until the children had left the room then faced Thoth. His glum face mirrored her own concerns.

"Another slaying?" she asked.

Thoth nodded absentmindedly. "So it would appear."

"Do you think this vision might be linked to the body that was found yesterday?"

"I do not know," Thoth replied.

"We have to tell Geb and Nuit."

"And what would you expect them to do with this knowledge? We do not even know when this event from the vision may occur. It could be tomorrow, years from now, or never. At best, we would stir up tempers that are close to boiling over. At worst, we would create a panic." Thoth stood silently for several moments, contemplating. "The visions, the deaths, the attack…"

Isis gazed at him curiously.

"Never mind," he said. "Will you inform Osiris? I have some duties to which I must tend."

"Preparing for the festivities?" Isis asked.

"I wish it were so." An uncomfortable expression crossed his face. "It is work of a different nature." Thoth forced a smile. "Amun-Ra protect you, Daughter."

Isis's eyebrows raised for an instant, but she did not press him. "His wind guide you, Father," she replied, before Thoth turned and left the room.

CHAPTER 6

QAR'S TRAINING flashed through Heru-pa's mind as the blade slashed at him.

Hold...

Now!

He raised the hilt of his sword and pivoted just in time to deflect the oncoming weapon. Set's sword slid down the edge of Heru-pa's wooden blade, and the momentum of the charge carried the Purean prince forward. Heru-pa spun and thumped his friend across the back.

"Ow!" Set yelped, and raised a hand to pause the sparring match. He lifted the visor of his helmet and took a gasping breath while contorting to reach the sore spot on his back. "Did you have to hit so hard?" he asked, rubbing it.

"It's a practice sword," Heru-pa said, "and you're wearing more padding than a hillock duck during cold season." He lifted his own visor and grinned smugly at Qar who stood at the edge of the small arena observing them. "That's seven strikes to five."

"The contest goes to Heru-pa. Take a thirty-tick break, then one more bout," the weapons master said. "Then you're done for the day. And keep the strikes below the neck during the last match. Neither of the queens would be too pleased if her prince showed up with a bloodied face for the Unity Day celebration tomorrow."

Set sighed as Heru-pa nodded. Heru-pa removed his helmet and scanned the training pavilion set inside the courtyard of the temple. The staccato beats of wood and metal rang out as several dozen Purean and Rathadi children darted about, engaged in their own sparring matches. Most wore the cloth padding and wielded the same type of short wooden swords as Heru-pa and Set, but three pairs of the taller children were clad in silver-colored armor and fought with real steel. The tradition of training the Rathadi and Purean children together had stood as long as the two races coexisted. Heru-pa's father had told him that it served to strengthen the bond between them; the same bond that would be celebrated tomorrow during the Day of Unity.

Heru-pa honed in on the pair in the center ring. He marveled at the speed of the older Purean boy and Rathadi girl as they continued their skirmish, the clashing of their steel ringing out against the high walls of the courtyard. The girl was a hand-breadth shorter than the boy, and narrower in the shoulders, but her quickness more than made up for the lack of physical size. She parried each of the boy's blows skillfully, dancing away at what seemed like the very last moment. He overextended his next uppercut, and she went in with a quick strike to his lower body. She let out a whoop when the dulled steel connected with his thigh.

The boy ripped off his helmet. His face was narrow and sharp, and his long black hair clung to his forehead. Sweat poured from his brow into his striking blue eyes. "Lucky hit, Bast," he grunted.

The girl removed her helmet with a flair. A fine coating of dark fur covered her skin and a broad grin split her face. "I guess that makes it three lucky hits in a row. Six strikes to six. Next one takes the glory, Takhat."

Heru-pa moved to replace his helmet, but he spotted the other combatants stopping their matches and edging closer to Bast and Takhat. He shot Qar an imploring glance, and the weapons master gave him a slight nod.

He beamed and turned once again to the center ring. The boy and girl donned their helmets and squared off again. With the duel on the line, Takhat approached more cautiously, ensuring he didn't leave himself open for a quick counterstrike again.

Heru-pa sensed Mia squeezing in between him and Set. "His mother won't like it if he loses the champion's badge," she said.

"The admiral will get over it," Set said. "And some humility will serve Takhat well."

Mia snickered as Heru-pa stared wordlessly at the pair of combatants, analyzing each other's strikes and parries. Takhat had stood undefeated for the last two seasons, but during the last few weeks, Bast's increasing quickness has been chipping away at his dominance.

"She has never before been able to challenge him for the last point," Set said.

Takhat's quick flurries pushed Bast closer to the edge of the ring, but just when he seemed to be gaining an advantage, she rolled under one of his swings and slid back into the center of the ring.

A chorus of impressed oohs and aahs rang out.

"Her animal sentinel is coming into being," Mia said. "She is learning to use the gift of the feline."

"It's just not fair," Set grumbled, giving Heru-pa a bump with his elbow. "How am I supposed to keep up with you once you join with your sentinel and transcend?"

A scaly hand settled on Set's shoulder from behind. Heru-pa tore his gaze from the match for a tick and looked up. Qar kept his eyes on the duel before him, his yellow, slitted irises focused on the combatants' every single move as he spoke. "The gifts of our animal sentinels are mighty, Prince Set, but those of the Pure Ones who are fortunate to be blessed with powers, and disciplined enough to hone them, can become formidable warriors, as well."

Takhat leaped forward, blade at the ready, slashing out. Bast whirled, like a dagger on its point, and ducked close into Takhat's reach, then followed up with two quick counterstrikes that drove Takhat back.

"Truly? And how is my power of truth-telling supposed to help me defend against that?" Set asked.

Before Qar had a chance to answer, Bast came in with a third strike that Takhat just managed to deflect. On the way down, his blade connected a glancing blow to Bast's flank.

"Yes!" the boy whooped, ripping off his helmet.

"Come on, that wasn't a real hit!" Bast cried out. She removed her helmet. "Tell him, Weapons Master!"

"Bast speaks true, Takhat," Qar said. "Incidental contact. The strike is invalid."

"What?" the boy challenged. Heru-pa noticed the Purean children frowning.

"Stop whining, already," Bast said. "Come on!"

Takhat grumbled, but he replaced his helmet and assumed a fighting stance. Bast mirrored his pose, and they restarted the contest. For almost a minute, they weaved and bobbed, matched evenly. With time, Takhat's strikes became clumsy, but the girl seemed to be getting faster and more precise as the fight progressed, as if growing more accustomed to her body.

"See?" Set said. "What are truth-visions or healing skills compared to the agility of a feline?"

"Takhat is a fierce competitor," Qar replied evenly, but Heru-pa sensed a hint of unease creeping into the weapons master's usually confident tone. He glanced up at Qar's face. His scaly lips were pinched, matching the tightness of his voice.

She is just toying with him now. And Qar sees it, too.

Bast surged forward, forcing Takhat to dodge a flurry of particularly vicious strikes. His balance was off, but rather than retreat to regain his footing, he charged forward, countering with a reckless upward slice. His power and speed almost allowed him to break through Bast's defenses, but the girl parried the strike and side-stepped, then kicked him in the back of his knee, driving him down.

Takhat's frustrated grunt rang out as he fell face first to the ground.

Bast yelled triumphantly and charged. Takhat turned just in time to see the Rathadi girl's sword barrel down at him.

A shout of power filled the courtyard, stirring the air and

reverberating from the tall walls. Bast's high-pitched shriek followed, and she sank to the ground, clutching her head.

Before Heru-pa realized what had happened, Qar roared and rushed into the ring.

"Fool!" he yelled, and kicked the sword out of Takhat's grasp. He dropped to the ground beside Bast and gently removed her helmet. Heru-pa gasped when her face was revealed. The girl's eyes were clouded over, and her face was knotted with pain.

"Fetch a healer, now!" Qar called out.

Two of the older boys took off for the temple.

"I… I'm sorry…" Takhat stood dead still behind Qar. "I didn't mean to…"

Mia raced across the courtyard and sank to her knees at Bast's side.

"Let me," she said, and took Bast's head between her palms as the Rathadi girl whimpered.

"Shhhh…" Mia spoke. Heru-pa watched her recite an incantation. The air seemed to shimmer between the two girls, and slowly Bast grew calmer, and her sobbing ebbed. By the time the Purean healer arrived, Bast lay quietly with her head on Mia's lap.

The woman bent down. "I have her now, young one," she said gently to Mia. The healer examined Bast before reaching into her bag and pulling out a vial. She dripped several drops of a clear fluid into the girl's eyes then covered them with her left palm and pressed the other to the girl's chest. The air crackled again with swirls of power, stronger now, and a few moments later Bast breathed more evenly. When the healer removed her left palm, Bast's eyes had regained their sheen, but their whites were stained with crimson threads.

Takhat approached uncertainly, his head cast down, as the woman slowly helped the girl to her feet. "Will... will she be well?" he asked.

"She will recover in time," the healer said. "What happened?" she asked Qar.

The weapons master flicked a piercing glance at Takhat. "Why don't you ask the boy?"

Takhat's shoulders slumped even lower. "I... I didn't mean to..."

"And yet you allowed it to happen," Qar said.

The healer's face shifted as understanding dawned. She glared at Takhat. "You used your powers in a sparring match?"

"I... I don't know what happened. When I saw the blade come down, I just..."

"Thank Amun the girl did not get seriously hurt!" the healer cried out. "If Mia had not acted as quickly as she did, the girl could have suffered permanent damage!"

Takhat's face caved as he held back a sniffle. He approached the girl. "Bast, I'm so sorry."

The girl drew back. Takhat moved after her, but Qar grasped his arm, holding him in place. "You've done enough," he said. "Give her time. You hurt her—and you scared Ra's light out of her."

The weapons master lifted Takhat's sword from the ground and addressed the boys and girls who were watching the scene, frozen in place like statues.

"Do not forget what you witnessed here today," he said. "And let this be a valuable lesson and a warning. Fighting is about control. If you lose control while you spar, you will hurt your friend. If you lose control during a battle, you will forfeit your life." He paused for a moment to let his words sink in. "Do you understand?"

"Yes, Master Qar," a chorus of timid replies rang out.

"Tomorrow we celebrate the Day of Unity," Qar continued. "Amun-Ra has smiled upon us and averted serious harm. For that we are grateful." He handed the sword to Takhat. "Lesson is over for today. Go home."

He regarded Bast as the children collected their belongings. "Can you walk?"

The girl replied with a cautious nod.

Qar faced Mia. "You did well today," he said. "Will you accompany Bast home? It seems I have matters to attend that involve the admiral and her son."

"I'm at your service, Weapons Master," Mia replied.

"May I walk Prince Set across the bridge?" Heru-pa asked as the two girls left the training pavilion.

Qar considered. "Very well, but afterward you will head straight home, understood?"

"Yes, Weapons Master."

Heru-pa followed his friend out of the pavilion and through the temple gates. They trudged along in silence, each in their own thoughts. They turned onto the cobblestone road leading to the Bridge of Amun-Ra that connected the Inner Ring and the capital. The small number of Pureans who periodically visited the Ring had swelled in anticipation and preparations for the Day of Unity festivities. Dozens of merchants, both Rathadi and Purean, had been crowding the road for days, trading their goods and wares that were to be sold during the upcoming celebration. Several Purean guards strolled along the path, patrolling and offering help to the merchants.

As the boys approached the bridge, a pair of Rathadi guards stationed at the entrance gave them a wave. One of them, a gray-skinned guard who lived with the sentinel of the mighty rhinoceros, gave Heru-pa a wink. "All prepared for tomorrow?" she asked, her voice deep and booming.

"We sure are!" Heru-pa answered brightly. When they passed the guards, he turned to Set. "By Ra's wings, if anybody else asks me that question one more time…"

Set clapped him on the shoulder. "Act your part. And—more importantly—do not blow it tomorrow."

The preparations continued on the bridge with dozens of Rathadi and Pureans dressing up the parapets and capstones with vibrant flowers and bows. The boys took in the sights and sounds, letting the excitement spread through them as they approached the Purean guards that flanked the gate to the capital.

"Welcome back, Prince Set," one of the guards called out. "And welcome, Prince Heru-pa. Ready for the ceremony?"

"We sure are!" Set answered with entirely too much enthusiasm.

When they got out of earshot, Heru-pa shook his head. "You're really enjoying this, aren't you?"

Set flicked him a self-contended grin, and they entered the city, continuing along the wide boulevard that led to the palace grounds. The tall trees and buildings that lined its sides had been decorated with a kaleidoscope of flags, and bright streamers were strung across its entire width. Hundreds of Pureans and Rathadi bustled side by side, erecting scaffolding and setting up vendor stands. The crowd parted as they recognized the two boys. Some greeted them with small bows and blessings, some simply smiled. Heru-pa glanced up at a pair of simian Rathadi who nimbly traversed the tall façade of the grand bathhouse, stringing colorful banners between them. Heru-pa smiled wistfully, lost in thought and envious of the workers' task and the feel of wind in their hair.

A poke in his side snapped him back. "Hey!"

"Wh-what?"

Set sighed in mock exasperation. "The serpents," he repeated. "Have you told your grandfather about the serpents yet?"

Heru-pa shook his head. "He's been cooped up in his work chambers."

"My father and mother have been acting strange, too," Set said, kicking a small stone and watching it bounce into the drain. "But they pretend like nothing is wrong! How are we supposed to learn and be effective rulers if they keep things from us?"

Heru-pa nodded in agreement at his friend's frustration. Set's lips pinched.

"What is it?" Heru-pa asked.

"You really should tell your grandfather about the serpents."

"I will."

"I just have this feeling, like it's really important."

"I said I would do it."

"When?" Set asked.

Heru-pa bit back a snide remark when he met his friend's gaze. He simply nodded. "I will find him now."

"Good. And after that make sure to go through your lines

again." Set's face brightened once again. "I don't want you to make me look bad during the celebration tomorrow."

"The only time I make you look bad is when I whoop you in sword fighting," Heru-pa shot back, and ran off before his friend could muster a reply.

Heru-pa raced back through the boulevard and across the bridge, then trotted into the courtyard of the temple. He bounded up the wide stairwell, making for the east wing that housed his grandfather's work chambers. Even though his grandfather served as archsage to both kings in the diarchy, he kept his main workplace in the temple.

Heru-pa reached the upper level and was just about to turn into his grandfather's hallway when he spotted the silver armor and blue capes of the Purean royal guard in front of the archsage's chambers. He skidded to a halt and scrunched his brow.

King Geb's personal guard?

He recalled his conversation with Set. People *had* been acting strange, and now the Purean king was paying his grandfather an unannounced visit? An idea stirred in his head. He studied the arcade at the end of the corridor, picturing the narrow overhang that snaked to the terrace attached to his grandfather's office.

This is not a good idea.

But as the Rathadi prince, wasn't it his responsibility to find out as much as he could? Also, if he listened in, he would know if his grandfather was too busy to be bothered about the serpents.

Before he had time to debate the wisdom of his resolution, he dashed to the arcade, and stepped out onto the narrow ledge. The eastern side of the temple faced the plains of the Inner Ring and the highlands beyond. He paused a moment to savor the view. He never understood either Rathadi or Pureans who became queasy at heights. For him there was only exhilaration. The higher, the better.

Heru-pa turned to the wall and scooted along, creeping for the terrace of his grandfather's work chambers. He climbed over the stone balustrade and tiptoed to the door.

"… it cannot be done, Geb," the voice of his grandfather reached his ears through the open window. "Even if I agreed with the principle of your request, the technical challenges are beyond even my skills. To provide the stability required to keep a mobile mirror trained on the sun would prove an infeasible task."

Heru-pa started at the familiarity his grandfather took with the king. *He calls him by his first name when they are by themselves?*

If the king took issue with his grandfather's tone, his reply did not seem to betray it. "Admiral Kiya and General Mehet insist we must be more ardent in the defense of our island."

"More ardent in its defense?" His grandfather laughed. "To construct a version of the Eye to be carried by ship is not being more ardent in our defense. It is a weapon of unmitigated aggression. The Eye was created to be used for a single purpose: to protect our island from invaders. To place that kind of a power on a ship that could sail anywhere, destroy anything in its path…" Thoth trailed off. "I am sorry."

"What if they mount another assault? What if they plan their next offensive during another eclipse? Perhaps one that lasts much longer and will allow them to make landfall in the Inner Ring? Or even the capital? What if the recent attack served merely to test our defenses and explore how long it would take their ships to traverse the Brim Basin?" Geb pressed. "Shall we be defenseless?"

"We are not, nor shall we ever be, defenseless," Thoth replied. "No invaders will pass the Inner Ring."

"How can you be certain? There are but a thousand of you."

"Believe me, Majesty," Thoth said, adopting a formal tone. "We are not defenseless, and our warriors will prove sufficient to hold back a far greater force."

At that, the king seemed to pause. "What have you up that long sleeve of yours, Archsage?"

"I beg for your indulgence, Your Majesty, and your trust."

"I allow you too much leeway," King Geb grumbled.

"And I am grateful for it."

The king seemed to concede. "You will tell me if there is anything else I must know?"

"At once, Your Majesty."

"Very well. Amun protect you, Archsage."

"His wind guide you, Majesty," Thoth replied.

Heru-pa wrinkled his brow as the door opened and closed. He replayed their words in his mind, trying to make sense of them.

He waited for a few moments longer, then crept forward and peeked inside. The spacious chamber was paneled in black walnut and smelled of pipe tobacco. His grandfather sat at his wide desk, elbows resting on top of the piles of papers that completely obscured the surface, and his head was cradled in his hands, as if in deep contemplation. Rows of rare books stretched along the walls and reached to the tall ceiling, requiring rolling ladders to get to the highest shelves. The familiar surroundings of his grandfather's space almost gave Heru-pa the courage to step out and reveal himself when the old Rathadi stood and crossed the room to the door. He locked it, then paced to one of the bookcases, climbed two rungs of the ladder and tilted back a book. Heru-pa stifled a gasp when a section of the bookcase swung open, revealing a hidden passage behind it. His grandfather slipped inside, and the bookcase swung shut behind him.

Heru-pa waited several moments then tiptoed into the chamber. He chewed his bottom lip as he considered following his grandfather. He hesitated, but something about his grandfather's secretive demeanor after the king's visit pushed him forward.

He climbed up on the ladder and pulled the book his grandfather touched. He heard a soft click, and the bookcase swung open again.

Heru-pa crept to the opening. A gust of cool, musty air wafted over him as he entered a stairway lined with low-glowing sconces that cast an eerie orange light. He followed the stairway, counting twenty steps before reaching its bottom. The passage led straight for another fifty feet. An rancid smell reached Heru-pa's nose before the corridor opened up into a cramped circular room. The small hairs on his neck bristled when he peered inside. The room was vaguely reminiscent of a laboratory, though he didn't recognize any of the equipment. Several glass cages with animals lined the curved wall to the right. His grandfather stood on the opposite side, hunched over a long table that held all manner of flasks, bowls and other paraphernalia filled with various fluids.

Heru-pa hid in the shadow, his heart thudding against his ribs, as Thoth paced to the wall with the glass cages. He selected one that held a small rabbit and brought it back to the table.

Heru-pa moved closer to get a better look. His grandfather dipped a glass rod into one of the flasks, lifting a drop of liquid, then dribbled it into the glass container. The fluid hit the bottom with a barely perceptible hiss, and a veil of purple mist rose up and engulfed the rabbit. The animal scampered for several heartbeats, then thrashed wildly before collapsing lifelessly.

Heru-pa reeled back, gorge rising up in his throat. He bumped into a crate on the floor.

Thoth whipped around at the noise. His face flushed.

"Heru-pa? You should not be here, boy!"

"I'm sorry!" Heru-pa called out before he whirled and rushed forward—crashing straight into a narrow metal table. His impact toppled the table, knocking him down on a large shape covered with a white cloth. Heru-pa pushed to regain his feet, and his hands touched something soft and sticky. He glanced down, and stared in horror at the blood-covered Purean beneath him.

The Purean from his vision.

Heru-pa's breath hitched. Then he screamed. His limbs flailed, trying to get away from the bloody corpse. He managed to scurry to his feet and took off into the passageway.

"Heru-pa, wait!" Thoth yelled after him, but Heru-pa was already racing full-speed up the stairs. He shouldered open the door and tore across the work chamber and out onto the terrace. His body shook as he scrambled over the railing and across the ledge. He reached the corridor and raced down the stairs, rushing out of the temple and through the gates of the courtyard, weaving his way between the Rathadi and Pureans who cast him bewildered stares.

"Heru-pa!" his grandfather's voice rang behind him.

He glanced back—and barreled into a wall of flesh. He bounced off with a grunt, landing flat on his behind on the cobblestones.

Heru-pa shook his head to clear it then looked up, meeting the vexed gaze of the captain of the Purean royal guard.

CHAPTER 7

THOTH WINCED as his grandson barreled into Captain Nebet and bounced off him like a Nikka ball off a stone hoop.

"Mind yourself, boy!" the Purean scoffed. He glanced down, and recognition flooded his face. "My apologies, Prince Heru-pa," he said hastily, extending his arm.

Thoth arrived as the captain helped Heru-pa to his feet. He reached for his grandson, but the boy shrank away from him. The captain's eyebrows raised for an instant before he pressed his palm to his heart and inclined his head at Thoth. "Amun's blessings, Archsage."

"Greetings, Captain Nebet," Thoth replied curtly before turning back to Heru-pa. "All is right, my boy," he said. "Come with me."

Heru-pa stared at him wordlessly, his body rooted to the ground.

"Prince Heru-pa? Is everything in order?" The Purean captain asked.

"It is quite alright, Captain," Thoth asserted. "My grandson and I were playing, and I'm afraid I gave him a bit of a scare."

"He does look like he has seen a ghost," the captain said.

Thoth became aware of the ring of onlookers that had started to form around them. Two more Purean guards appeared and held the people at a distance. He spotted one of the Rathadi court attendants taking in the scene, then scurrying away into the temple.

"Captain, the poor boy is frightened out of his mind," he said. "I wish to take him home."

"Of course, Honored One," Nebet replied with a bow. "May Amun's—" he stopped as his gaze fell on Heru-pa's hands. His eyes narrowed. "Is that blood?"

Thoth glanced down and bit back a curse. "Amun!" he said. "He may have scraped himself up when he fell in my chambers."

Before he had a chance to react, Captain Nebet took Heru-pa's palms in his own.

"This is not the prince's blood," he said, a hint of suspicion frosting his voice. He stepped closer to Thoth and whispered, "I beg your indulgence, Archsage, but there has been another disappearance, and we are still looking for the body. May I ask the prince some questions?"

Thoth fought down a surge of frustration. "Another disappearance?" he asked, trying to keep his voice level. "Of course, Captain. We are at your disposal."

The captain faced the boy. Thoth moved behind Heru-pa and placed his palms on his grandson's shoulders. Heru-pa flinched but did not move away.

"Do not fear," the captain said. "You and your grandfather will be free to take your leave in a few moments."

Heru-pa nodded shyly.

"Did you see something that scared you?"

Heru-pa nodded again. He took a shaking breath. "I… I…" he choked out, his lips quivering. "I think I saw—"

Thoth gave Heru-pa's shoulders a firm squeeze. Heru-pa closed his mouth.

"You saw what?" the captain asked. After a moment of silence, the Purean captain looked to Thoth.

Thoth met his gaze. "I'm afraid the boy is too scared to talk. Perhaps he can answer your questions after he has recovered?"

"Archsage, with all due respect," Nebet countered. "The boy is clearly upset and we must investigate—" He stopped at the sounds of commotion behind the onlookers.

"Make way!" a strong voice rang out a moment before the Purean guards parted and bowed respectfully.

Isis approached, accompanied by the court attendant Thoth spotted and four Rathadi soldiers, dressed in the green and gold of the royal guard.

"What is the meaning of this?" she asked the Purean captain.

"Queen Isis," Nebet bowed. "It is an honor—"

"Are you holding my son?"

The captain looked aghast. "I assure you, Highness, we are not holding anybody, least of all the prince." He lowered his voice. "He looked quite distraught and… there appears to be blood on his hands."

Isis blinked. "What?" She bent down to Heru-pa.

Nebet continued to whisper. "We are on full alert given the latest events and the second disappearance, and I wanted to—"

"Be that as it may," Thoth interrupted. "As you see, the boy is in no condition to talk at this time. I believe it is time for him to return home. You may continue your investigation at a later time." He shot Isis a glance.

She returned his gaze for a long moment, tilting her head. She turned to the captain. "Thank you for your assistance, Captain. You are dismissed."

Captain Nebet composed his face stoically. "As you wish, Your Highness," he said with a curt bow. He beckoned to the Purean guards, and they withdrew.

Heru-pa scurried to his mother, and the queen embraced him tightly. "Let's get you home," she said. "Father, will you walk with me?"

Thoth nodded and fell in beside them as the Rathadi guards cleared a way through the crowd. They walked in silence for several moments until they left the busy street and entered the temple courtyard. Isis sent Heru-pa ahead of them.

"Second disappearance? What did you not want Nebet to know?" she asked quietly.

Despite the situation Thoth bit back a smile at his daughter's astuteness. "Our guards found the second dead Purean last night," he replied quietly. "They brought the body to me."

Isis inhaled sharply. "The Purean from the boys' vision?"

"We cannot be sure, but that is the presumption."

"Why was I not informed?"

"I wanted to investigate the cause of his death before I brought it before you and Osiris."

"You kept this from both of us?"

"The Purean king cannot blame you or Osiris for withholding information you did not have."

"Do you truly believe it is wise to keep this from the Pureans?"

"The relationship between Osiris and Geb is already strained. Tempers are frayed. We are on the eve of the Day of Unity." He sighed. "We shall inform the Pureans when I have more information on the cause of death. Besides, the body was found on sovereign Rathadi territory, so the investigation is technically our responsibility."

"Technically?" Isis asked with a tired smile. "I am uncertain the Purean king will share your point of view."

Thoth sighed again.

"What do you know so far?" she asked.

"The man was found under the bridge, near the water. Another Purean merchant, from the looks of it. He seems to have been attacked by a wild animal… likely an Ursus."

"An Ursus?" Isis stared at him, alarmed.

Thoth nodded gravely.

"An Ursus attacking Pureans, one inside the city walls, the other this close to the Temple? That's—" she stopped when she saw Thoth's expression. Isis paled at the implication. "You cannot possibly think…" she whispered.

"I am considering all possibilities," Thoth said.

"A shifter?" Isis blurted out. She gave a small curse when Heru-pa faced about with wide eyes. She sucked in air to calm herself before continuing in a softer voice. "Here? To even suggest that a Rathadi shifter is killing Pureans—"

Thoth stopped. "Yet I fear that would be the first conclusion the Pureans would draw. Now you understand my reluctance to share the second slaying with Geb before I could gather additional information. One death may be interpreted as a random accident. Terrible, but an accident nonetheless. Two attacks within two days will not be so easily ignored. The Pureans will demand answers."

Isis looked like she was about to argue, but her lips tightened, and she simply nodded.

"I will get to the bottom of it, Queen Daughter. You have my word."

They continued in silence, stopping before the royal chambers.

"Will you come in?" Isis asked.

Thoth smiled. "As tempting as your company and sweet treats are, I have work I must finish before tomorrow." He beckoned to Heru-pa. The boy approached him wearily, but allowed his grandfather to embrace him.

"Grandfather," Heru-pa whispered. "What happened in your work chambers. I…"

"Shush, my boy," Thoth silenced him. "There has been enough excitement for the day. We shall talk about this at a later time." He pushed him back gently and held him at arm's length. "Get a good night's rest—and prepare yourself for the best fireworks in the history of the island."

Heru-pa's face brightened, and his mouth quirked into a hesitant smile. "Ra's promise?"

"Ra's promise," Thoth replied, then turned and strode away.

CHAPTER 8

ISIS LIFTED the porcelain carafe and regarded her son as he rested on the plush sofa in her chambers. With his shoulders hunched and drawn in, his body looked even smaller against the oversized furniture, and she was suddenly reminded of his young age. She poured a cup of ginger tea and placed a lemon biscuit on a plate. He accepted both quietly, and she eased down next to him.

"It was the Purean from the vision," he said. "The one Set and I shared."

Isis nodded silently, her suspicions confirmed.

They sat quietly as Heru-pa nibbled on the biscuit. "Are shifters real?" he asked.

"Your ears are too perceptive for your own good, my son," Isis replied. "And I should be more mindful of what I say."

"Set says shifters aren't even real."

"Shifters are very rare," Isis said, "but they are real."

Heru-pa took a moment to digest this. "What causes one to become a shifter?"

"Nobody knows for certain. Some think that certain Rathadi are born that way. Others believe it is caused when a Rathadi's *Ka* and that of their sentinel fall out of balance during their joining."

"Have you known a shifter?"

The shadow of a smile ghosted Isis's face. "Several."

"Is it forbidden to shift?"

"No, but those who can shift, avoid it."

"Why?"

"The pull is strong to enter the form of your sentinel. It is exhilarating. But every time a Rathadi shifts, they grow closer to their sentinel. Even in their animal form, they are restless, aggressive. They become more and more the wild beast, until the pull to shift is so strong that they cannot resist it."

"Is that when they become…" Heru-pa hesitated, as if unwilling to speak the word.

"A forsaken," Isis said. "Yes."

Heru-pa swallowed. "And no forsaken can come back to the Rathadi form?"

Isis shook her head somberly.

"Do you think a forsaken could have—"

Isis placed her palm gently against Heru-pa's cheek. "I think that's enough for today, my son."

"But Grandfather thinks that the slayings may be linked to the attack on the island."

"He told you that? Grandfather should not be discussing these matters with you. I shall have words with him."

"No…" Heru-pa started. "He…" He trailed off and remained silent, but she saw the struggle in his face. His lower lip began to tremble. "I… I didn't mean to listen in on them. It just happened."

"Listen in on who?"

"Grandfather… and King Geb."

"The King? You eavesdropped on a conversation between Grandfather and the Purean king?"

Heru-pa nodded timidly.

She leaned forward. "And just how did you accomplish that feat?"

She listened as Heru-pa recounted how he sneaked onto the terrace and overheard the conversation between his grandfather and the king. She forced a level expression when he described the hidden laboratory and the deadly vapor.

His eyes teared up. "That's when I got scared, and I just ran and… and I didn't see where I was going and…"

Isis's mind reeled as she processed the information and weighed how to respond. She wrapped her arms around her son. "All will be right," she said.

"What is happening?" Heru-pa asked. "Why did Grandfather kill that animal? And why are those Pureans getting killed?"

"I do not know, my son," Isis said. "But it is very important that you do not tell anybody about this. Do you understand?"

Heru-pa nodded.

"Not even Set or Mia."

Heru-pa nodded again.

She gave him another hug. "Very well," she said. "We shall discuss it again, but for now, you must try to put it out of your mind and get some rest. We all have a big day ahead of us tomorrow." She gave him a kiss before leaving the room, then stepped through another chamber into Osiris's private office.

Her husband stood at his desk, immersed in a document. His bare back was turned to her, but she recognized by the subtle shift in his stance that he knew she was behind him. She drew near and wrapped her arms around his stomach, pressing her body against his back. He put down the paper and placed his palms over her hands. The muscles beneath his scaly skin rippled against her fingers as he exhaled deeply.

"Still working, My Sun?" she asked.

"The representatives from the high council have formally requested seats in the royal pavilion for tomorrow," he grumbled. "We are reeling from an attack on the island, yet the most important issue for those court puffers is to sit close enough to their majesties so they can stick their noses right up the royal—"

Isis slapped his shoulder.

He turned and shot her a grin. "Feisty!"

She smiled back, but it was distracted. She took his hands into hers. "We have to talk," she said.

His grin faded at her tone.

"There has been another slaying," she continued. "A Purean merchant."

"What? When?"

"They found the body this morning. My father has been examining it."

"Your father has been examining the body? Why am I just now learning of this?"

"Please hear me out," she said. She relayed to him the conversation she had with her father.

When she finished, Osiris stared at her, speechless.

"Father says a shifter could have been responsible for the deaths."

Osiris shook his head. "I know every single shifter among our people." She did not miss the look in his eyes. "I do not believe a Rathadi, shifter or not, is responsible for the slayings."

"He believes that the wounds may have been inflicted by an Ursus."

"An Ursus?" Osiris mulled over her words. "There is one, but I have known that shifter since I have been a Rathling. He lives beyond the Northern Highlands with his family on a farm they have tended for generations. To suggest he is somehow involved in this is preposterous."

"Then what do you believe it is? Random maulings?"

Osiris furrowed his brow. "I do not know…"

Isis stood in sullen silence, unease coiling inside her stomach.

"What is it?"

"There is something else. Concerning my father. Heru-pa saw him working on something."

She told him about the lethal vapor and the animal. When she finished, Osiris remained strangely still.

Realization rose inside her chest. She pulled back, lips pinched. "You knew about this!"

Osiris took a step toward her, but she drew back.

"Both you and my father kept this from me? Why?"

Osiris seemed to have no immediate answer to that, opening and closing his mouth as though biting back half-formed thoughts. "It's… complicated."

"Tell me," she said in a tone that brooked no argument.

Osiris nodded, then led her to a sofa and eased her down. He took a seat beside her and reached for her hand, placing it between his palms. His fingers were tight and cool against her skin.

"It goes back to the war against the Ba'ulati."

Isis blinked at her husband's words. The victory against the Ba'ulati had come at a terrible cost to the Rathadi and had brought the island to the brink of a civil war. "If your grandfather and the Purean monarch had not called for a Kings' Conclave, they may not have succeeded in salvaging peace between our people," she said.

"My father was a young prince, barely a Rathling, when he witnessed the slaughter," Osiris continued. "He vowed that he would never allow that to happen again when he reigned." His gaze grew distant. "He never forgave the Pureans for sealing the gates while so many Rathadi still remained outside the safety of the wall."

Isis squeezed his hand. The relationship between the Rathadi and Pureans had been strained during Osiris's father's reign, with her husband still struggling to undo much of the damage wrought during that time.

"When my father ascended to the throne, he tasked a promising young scholar to develop a weapon capable of keeping our people safe even if hostile forces managed to invade the Inner Ring again."

Slowly, comprehension dawned. "The young scholar was my father," Isis said.

Osiris nodded. "Thoth was tasked with creating a means to protect the Rathadi—at any cost."

"At any cost? Meaning this weapon he developed, this vapor… it is lethal to the Pureans?"

"Your father was young, and he followed a mandate from his king. He spent years studying the features of our blood before creating what he called the Breath of Ra, a vapor that can be released on the outer perimeter of the Ring, lethal to any invaders, yet completely harmless to the Rathadi."

"But what of the Pureans?"

"Your father knew that the highlands would block the vapor from moving inland, and that the wind would disperse it well before it could reach the capital and cause harm to them. For decades the weapon stood ready to be released at a moment's notice. By the grace of Ra, it never had to be deployed."

"What happened to it?"

"As your father matured, he realized the potential physical and political peril the weapon posed. He dedicated decades of his life to develop another device powerful enough to convince my father to abandon the Breath of Ra."

"The Eye of Amun," Isis said.

"Once my father witnessed the power of the Eye, he allowed himself to be convinced that the Breath of Ra was no longer necessary to keep the island safe."

"How do you know this?"

"Before my father passed, he disclosed the existence of the lethal vapor to me. When I ascended to the throne, I had contended with Thoth to reinstate it, but your father was as persistent as he was persuasive. Because of my respect for him, I relented and agreed that the Eye of Amun was sufficient to keep our people safe, without endangering the Pureans."

"But after the latest attack…"

"When the vulnerability of the Eye of Amun was exploited in the latest attack, I tasked him with reviving the Breath of Ra. He agreed, under two conditions. The first was that I allow him to continue working on ensuring the Pureans are afforded the same protection as the Rathadi—work he had already begun decades ago."

"And the second?"

"That we share its existence with the Pureans, but only after the weapon has been made completely safe to them."

"He was worried that revealing it in its current form would raise questions, or could even be perceived as a threat," Isis said.

"Precisely. Your father and I wished to ensure that if the Pureans discovered it prematurely, you could not be held accountable for keeping the information from them. Also, your innocence in this matter would allow you to act as a mediator in whatever fallout may ensue between our people."

There was a long silence as Isis processed the information, reluctantly agreeing with the reasoning. "What is the status of the weapon now?"

"Your father is continuing his work on something he calls an 'inoculation' to train the Pureans' blood and prevent them from falling ill should they become exposed."

"Does he know when it will be ready to be shared with Geb?"

"He thinks soon." Osiris lifted her hands to his lips and kissed them. "We have a very busy day ahead of us," he said. "Let us focus on that. Let us forget about these things for now and celebrate tomorrow."

Isis considered. "Very well. You will get a brief reprieve,

but after tomorrow I want you and my father to come completely clean with me."

Osiris smiled. "As you wish, My Queen. We will tell you anything you wish to know." He pulled her closer and raised his palm to her cheek, his fingertips skimming the outline of her face, then moved his lips to hers.

Isis kissed him back, cherishing the familiar feel of his smooth scales beneath her lips. "Ra's promise?"

"Ra's promise," Osiris replied.

CHAPTER 9

HERU-PA'S MIND buzzed restlessly as he took in the wilderness of bodies that lined the bridge leading to the capital. Vibrant costumes and elaborate face paints shifted and shimmered in the midday sun as the colorful mob danced and swayed to cheerful beats of drums. He strutted proudly between his parents, a large grin pasted on his face that would not be curtailed even by the chafing of his dress shoes or the weight of the velvet cape. The king and queen, draped in their ceremonial robes, waved to the crowd as they led the column of hundreds of Rathadi through the tall gates. When they entered the capital, the Pureans fell in behind them, growing the procession as they made their way up the winding promenade that led to the palace.

Heru-pa's stomach growled at the smell of spiced breads and roasted meats that filled the vendor stands, mixing with a mélange of incense and flowers that showered down on them. On either side, florid tassels swung gracefully with the move- ments of the dancers' bodies, like reeds of switchgrass in the foothills of the highlands. When they neared the palace gates, an honor guard of two dozen Purean soldiers, dressed in shining silver cuirasses, snapped to attention. They split their formation and lined the tall gates, then saluted briskly with their fists against their hearts, holding their stance until the procession passed onto the palace grounds.

The parade snaked through the royal gardens when Heru-pa caught sight of the Purean monarchs and Set, seated atop a stone terrace. The king wore a sleeveless tunic that reached to his knees, and a wide cape draped loosely over his shoulders. The queen's long white dress was girdled at the waist by a wide, golden belt. An azure blue cloak rested on her shoulders, held below the neck by an oval clasp adorned with diamonds and sapphires. Matching crowns of black marble and gold rested on their royal heads.

When the procession entered the inner court, the king and queen rose. Osiris and Isis stopped, bringing the mass of bodies behind them to a halt. The drum beats and merry noises ceased, and every pair of eyes turned to the royal balcony.

King Geb lifted his arms. The long cape slid back, revealing his sun-bronzed skin beneath it.

"Amun's blessings, Osiris, King of the Rathadi, and Isis, Queen of the Rathadi," he called out, his voice deep and powerful. "On this day, the Day of Unity, we bid welcome to you and all of our Rathadi brothers and sisters as we celebrate the roots of our creation and all that binds us."

The crowd below him and in the procession broke into a cacophony of cheers and applause. When the noise subsided, Osiris stepped forward. "Ra's blessings on you, Geb and Nuit, King and Queen of the Pure Ones, Sovereigns of the Island

Kingdom of Atlantis. You have the gratitude of the Rathadi. We accept your hospitality in the spirit in which it is given."

The royal guards who stood at the bottom of the stairs to the balcony parted, and Heru-pa followed his parents as they ascended the stone stairs, accompanied by more cheering and hollering. When they reached the balcony, Osiris bowed to Geb, who returned the gesture. He then moved aside and allowed Isis to stand next to Nuit, as he took his place beside Osiris.

Heru-pa moved next to Set and shot him a quick grin before King Geb addressed the crowd again.

"On this day, we celebrate the unity between the Pure Ones and the Rathadi. Let us cast aside our differences and welcome each other into our hearts and homes as brothers and sisters."

Below him, the crowd stirred and mingled into mixed pairs of Rathadi and Pureans.

"I call on Set, Prince of the Pure Ones," Geb proclaimed.

Set stood and moved beside his father at the edge of the terrace.

"Who have you selected as your Rathadi brother today?"

"Heru-pa, Prince of the Rathadi," Set called out.

"Do you grant leave, Isis and Osiris of the Rathadi?"

"With honor and joy," Heru-pa's parents responded in unison.

Heru-pa stood and took his place beside Set. The crowd below him cheered again, their movements and vibrant colors reminding him of flocks of birds dancing around a watering hole.

"Prince Set and Prince Heru-pa," Geb continued, "will you recite the words of our creation to begin the celebration of unity?"

Heru-pa and Set bowed to him, and the Purean king took his seat between Isis and Osiris.

A hush fell over the crowd as Set cleared his throat. He began, lifting his thin voice above the audience. "At a time before any future destinies have been foretold, there was only the primordial infinite sea, the Waters of Chaos, known as the Waters Nu."

Below him, the throngs of Pureans and Rathadi opened small flasks of water and poured it onto the ground. "Blessing to the waters," they called out.

"The One God, Amun," Set continued, "he who is both within and without, moving and unmoving, far and near; he rose out of the waters and breathed."

The crowd lifted their arms to the sky. "Blessed be The One," they said in a single voice.

"Amun spoke a word, and a mound emerged from the Waters of Chaos. That mound grew higher and taller and became our home, the Island of Atlantis."

The people dipped their hands into bags of sand and scattered it onto the ground.

Set stepped back, and Heru-pa moved forward. "The island was green and lush, and Amun saw it and judged it fit as a home for those he made in his image. And so he created the One People to inhabit the island and watched over them as his children."

"We are children of Amun," the crowd responded, "The One People."

"The children lived in peace for generations, thriving on the fertile land and bountiful sea that surrounded them, but they grew lonely and restless," Heru-pa continued. "'The land is so

rich,' the children said. 'We long to share it with other creatures.' Amun listened to their pleas, for he was kind and wished
for his children to rejoice, so he created animals that roamed the
land beside them. At first, all the children delighted in their new
companions, but soon some grew discontented."

Heru-pa backed up, and Set moved up again. "'Amun likes
his new creatures better,' they said, and before long many of the
One People became jealous and displeased," Set said. "Many
wanted the beasts gone."

"But some wanted them to stay," Heru-pa said.

"In the course of time, the loud voices of the One People
begged him to separate them from these new creatures," Set
said. "Amun listened to his children and created a ring of land
around the island and carried the animals there."

Heru-pa continued. "Amun told the animals, 'This shall be
your new home. Here you can live free and in peace.' But some
of the One People were despondent and missed their animal
companions. To console them, Amun spoke to the Sun, who
took the shape of the falcon and emerged from the waters at
night and visited upon the island. The falcon came upon a
young woman who sat at the shore, gazing forlornly across
the water.

"'Why are you crying, child?' the falcon asked. 'I miss the
beasts,' the woman replied. The falcon peered into her soul and
saw that she spoke true. 'You shall never again be without an
animal,' he said. 'For I am the Amun-Ra, the Sun, and I give
life to all you see. An animal shall be your sentinel, and you
shall carry her inside you for all time.' Ra took on human form
and blessed the woman, giving life to the first Rathadi. Before
he left, he turned to the woman and spoke. 'I leave you now,

those who live with the gift of your sentinel and those who live without it. Together you shall rule over the island, undefeated. Divided you shall fall.'"

Heru-pa finished, and a silence fell over the crowd. Their parents stood and took place behind Set and Heru-pa.

"On this day, let us remember that our ancestors were wrong in casting out the animal companions," Geb said. "For it is through them that we learn about our world and live to enrich it. We are all children of The One."

Set and Heru-pa raised their hands and spoke in unison. "Together we shall rule over the island, undefeated. Divided we shall fall."

"Together we shall rule over the island, undefeated," the crowd repeated. "Divided—"

Without warning something crashed into Heru-pa, and he tumbled to the stone. The ground shook again. For an instant it seemed as if everything around him stood still, then the screaming started.

"Earthquake!" Osiris yelled out. He reached for Heru-pa when the balcony collapsed beneath them.

They smashed to the ground. Heru-pa's head rang with the impact, and he rolled off the stone balcony onto the ground. The tremors continued to rage all around them.

"Look out!" Osiris cried out as a fissure opened up near Heru-pa. He stared in horror as a Purean noble teetered on the precipice before the ground swallowed him. Heru-pa's face twisted at the man's scream.

"To me!" Osiris shouted, rushing for Heru-pa.

The ground shifted again. Before Heru-pa realized what had happened, another chasm opened up, the crack in the earth racing for him. Osiris reached him and snatched him off the ground, diving to safety.

"Set!" Nuit's bloodcurdling scream and Geb's bellow rang over the rumble. The Purean king raced to the fissure and dropped to his knees. He peered into the void and tried to squeeze inside, but the crack was too narrow for a grown man to do more than get a limb in.

Heru-pa wiggled himself from his father's grasp and raced to Geb, straining to stay on his feet amid the tremors. He dropped down next to the king. His breath hitched when he spotted Set's motionless body wedged in the rock ten feet below him. Before he realized what he was doing, he slipped between the rocks and into the darkness below.

His mother's terrified scream barely reached his ears. He descended, clinging to the rock as the shaking continued all around him. He tried not to think about what would happen if a boulder dislodged from above, or if the earth shifted, and the fissure closed. He inched his way down. When he finally reached Set, he wedged his feet on either side of the crevasse and shook the Purean prince.

"Set! Set—wake up!" he pleaded. He shook his friend's shoulders again.

Set opened his eyes groggily, his head rolling listlessly.

"We have to get out of here!"

Set's eyes glazed over again.

"Set!" he screamed.

"Heru-pa!" A shout came from above. He glanced up just in time to see Qar pitch a rope to him.

"Tie it about him, quickly!" the weapons master called down.

Heru-pa snatched the rope and wrapped it around Set, securing it under his friend's arms. He rushed to tie the knot, willing his quivering hands and the swaying walls surrounding him to be still. The rope slipped through his fingers, and he had to try again, then doubled up just to be sure.

"Ready!" he yelled.

A moment later Set lifted up. Heru-pa climbed along him, guiding his ascent past the jagged rocks as the walls continued to shudder around them. As they reached the edge, Set was pulled out of the crevasse. A tick later a pair of strong hands locked around Heru-pa's wrists and lifted him out.

Heru-pa's legs cleared the fissure when a large slice of the side wall broke loose and plunged into the depth below bringing with it the sound of stone grinding on stone. He collapsed on top of his father who clutched him tightly against his chest.

"Foolish boy!" his father called out, but Heru-pa could discern another note in his voice.

A few moments later the shaking stopped, and Osiris and Heru-pa slowly rose to their feet. Isis rushed to them and pulled both into her arms. "What were you thinking?" she cried into Heru-pa's ear, her body trembling.

Heru-pa squirmed in her embrace. "Set? Is he alright?" He twisted and looked behind him. A Purean healer knelt beside Set as the queen and King Geb watched their son, pale-faced. A group of Purean and Rathadi guards formed a ring around them.

A moment later, the healer raised his head, and Set stirred before slowly sitting up.

Nuit cried out and sank to the ground, wrapping her arms

around her son. Heru-pa rose and approached them uncertainly when the queen's gaze caught his eyes.

The tears streamed freely down her face, but her expression was one of relief and gratitude. "Thank you," she said. "Thank you for saving my son."

CHAPTER 10

HERU-PA STOOD on the high terrace of the temple, overlooking the city of Amun. The rooftops sparkled with brilliant light as the rising sun at his back illuminated the capital. He fidgeted absentmindedly with the bandages that covered his scraped palms, trying to process the events from the prior day.

He recognized his mother's footsteps as she drew near. She stopped behind him and wrapped her arms about his shoulders.

"How many?" he asked.

Her arms clenched tighter. "Seven Pure Ones, three Ratha-di," she replied, her voice heavy.

Heru-pa's breath hitched in his throat.

"It could have been so much worse," Isis said. "If you had not saved Set…" She trailed off, and her palms slid down to his hands. She glanced at the dressing. "May I take a look?"

Heru-pa nodded absentmindedly.

She unwrapped the bandages and examined the scrapes that covered his palms. "They are healing well," she said.

"Old Harwa saw to them yesterday, before we returned to the temple."

They stood wordlessly for several moments, each lost in their own thoughts. Their silence was interrupted by soft footsteps. They both turned.

"Amun-Ra, *Tato,*" Heru-pa said in greeting.

"Amun-Ra, son," Osiris replied. "How are your hands?"

"*Amah* says they're healing well."

"*Amah* knows best," Osiris said, and smiled, but Heru-pa recognized the grief beneath it.

"How are people doing?" Heru-pa asked.

"We shall recover."

Heru-pa nodded somberly.

Osiris put one arm around Heru-pa and the other around Isis. "Your mother and I have matters to discuss with you," he said.

Heru-pa glanced up at him, a fluttering feeling settling into the pit of his belly.

"What you did yesterday was reckless and impulsive," Osiris said.

"But I thought that saving Set—"

His mother stopped him with a gentle squeeze on his shoulder. Heru-pa lowered his head.

"I'm sorry, *Tato*," he said, shoulders slumping.

"It was reckless and impulsive," Osiris repeated, "and unbecoming of a Rathling."

"*Tato*—" Heru-pa started.

"Unbecoming of a *Rathling*," Osiris stressed.

A suspicion crept into his mind. His father faced him, and

their gazes locked. Heru-pa's throat closed up at the sheen coating his father's amber eyes.

"What you did yesterday was one of the bravest things I have ever witnessed," Osiris said.

"Our hearts swell with pride at your deeds," his mother added. "You made your people proud to be Rathadi."

Heru-pa stood perfectly still, willing himself not to react, fearing to spoil the moment.

"You may not yet realize the magnitude of your actions," Osiris continued, "the magnitude of the catastrophe you have averted." His expression darkened. "The death of the Rathadi and Pure Ones who perished yesterday is a terrible tragedy, but in time and with Amun-Ra's grace we shall overcome this tragedy and heal. But if the Pure Ones had lost their crown prince on the Day of Unity…"

"What your father is saying," Isis said, "is that the relationship between the Rathadi and Pure Ones has been difficult, and we do not know what may have happened if Set had perished."

"At the very least," Osiris said, "you have prevented what could have been a terrible stain in the Unity Day celebration."

Heru-pa finally allowed himself a breath. "Wh-what does this all mean?"

Isis drew herself up and assumed the regal demeanor he knew so well. "We have declared that through your deeds on the Day of Unity you have proven your worthiness to face the Rite of Valediction." Her voice rang with pride, but she could not hide the wistful flicker that crossed her features.

A cold wash swept through Heru-pa, raising goose bumps on his arms. "B-but I have not yet reached the age of sanction."

"You are braver and wiser than most Rathadi many years your senior," Osiris said.

Isis cleared her throat quietly.

"On most occasions," Osiris added with a small smile.

Heru-pa's heart quaked inside his chest. He opened his mouth, then closed it and considered. A concern crept into his mind. "What I did yesterday… that's not the only reason to move up my ceremony, is it?"

Osiris shot Isis a bemused look. "The boy has too much of you in his blood." He gave a small chuckle before addressing Heru-pa again. "You are correct."

"It has to do with the trouble between the Rathadi and Pure-ans." Heru-pa said.

"Among other things," Osiris replied.

"So how does moving my ceremony help?"

"Queen Nuit gave her permission for Set to be the Third Pillar," Isis said.

"She what?" Heru-pa's mouth gaped open.

"It is a valuable gesture," Osiris said. "And one that could not have been more timely. To have the Purean prince partici-pate in your valediction ceremony will serve to heal many wounds."

"And you want to make sure the ceremony occurs before something else happens, or the queen changes her mind."

"Is this not what you wanted?" his mother asked.

"More than anything, but this feels… contrived."

His father leaned toward him. "As prince of the Rathadi, you must do what is best for your people."

"What will the others say? What about the Council of Elders? Will they not scoff at my age?"

"They understand the circumstances better than most, and will agree that it will benefit the Rathadi," Osiris said.

Heru-pa pondered their words before nodding. "I will do what you think it best for our people."

His parents smiled.

"Can I see Set and Mia and tell them?" Heru-pa asked.

"Not yet," Isis said. "But soon," she added when his face fell. "Set is still recovering."

Heru-pa frowned, but kept his mouth closed.

"We shall make the announcement and make preparations," Osiris said. "People will welcome some good news."

CHAPTER 11

HERU-PA GRIPPED the package tightly under his arm as he and Mia paced along the wide corridor to the Purean prince's chambers. Five days had passed since the earthquake, and he had been cooped up in the temple preparing for his valediction ceremony—and champing at the bit to see his friend. Finally, after much begging and bargaining, his mother had relented and allowed him to pay Set a brief visit, and to deliver his present to the Purean prince himself.

"So how does it feel to be the youngest Rathadi ever to face the Rite of Valediction?" Mia asked, drawing him back.

Heru-pa fidgeted with the package and shifted it to his other arm. "I don't know," he shrugged. "Like there are lots of expectations."

"You know, if anybody can do it, you can," she said.

Heru-pa gave a grateful smile at her words as they turned into the corridor leading to the royal living quarters. Two soldiers flanked the entrance to the prince's chambers. Heru-pa swallowed, recalling his last two encounters with the Purean guards.

"I hope they'll let us in to see him," Mia said, as if sensing his trepidation.

Despite their apprehension, or perhaps because of it, they quickened their pace and stepped briskly for the tall double doors. To Heru-pa's surprise, the guards snapped to attention and saluted them.

"Prince Heru-pa," one of the guards said in greeting. "Their Majesties have been expecting your visit."

"Th-the king and queen are here?" Heru-pa mumbled.

"Indeed. They are within."

Heru-pa tried to ignore the surge of butterflies rising in his stomach as the guard opened the door. Set's sleeping chamber was easily three times the size of Heru-pa's quarters in the temple and was appointed in leathers and exotic woods. The Purean king and queen stood beside a tall canopy bed, observing a healer who was bent over Set's body. He shined a light into Set's eyes, then made the prince follow his finger as he traced shapes in front of the boy's face. Mia and Heru-pa stood still, afraid to break the silence.

The healer finally straightened and faced the king and queen. "The Prince is recovering well," he said.

"I told you I feel just fine," Set said, sitting up.

The queen sighed audibly, and the king squeezed Set's shoulder then turned to the door. When he spotted Heru-pa and Mia, his face broadened into a smile.

"Ah, Prince Heru-pa," he said. He waved them closer. "Your quick thinking and selfless act saved the prince from grave injury, perhaps even death. You have our unceasing gratitude."

The queen pulled him into an embrace. Heru-pa stood awkwardly. After several moments, she released him. "Set apprised us of your desire to have him serve as the Third Pillar in your Rite of Valediction."

Heru-pa shifted uncomfortably, his gaze bouncing between the two royals. "Yes, Your Majesties."

"It shall be our honor to allow him to be your attendant," the queen said.

Despite his mother telling him the news a few days ago, a wave of excitement rushed over him at hearing the words from the queen's own mouth. "Thank you, Your Majesties," he said, and bowed low.

The queen turned to Mia. "And you, young Lady Mia. Word has reached us of your deeds at the sparring pavilion. It appears that your talents as a healer are blossoming. Harwa has taken on a most promising pupil."

Mia blushed. "You are too kind, Your Majesty," she said.

The queen smiled graciously. "We shall leave you to yourselves. Enjoy the day and each other's company, but be mindful of the prince's recovery."

"Yes, Your Majesties," Heru-pa and Mia said, and bowed again as the royals and the healer left the room.

"Well, that's certainly a different type of reception than I'm used to," Heru-pa mused after the guard closed the door.

"It appears saving the prince's life has its perks," Mia teased. She turned to Set whose face split into a broad grin.

"I suppose you won't let me forget this one for a while, huh?" Set asked.

Heru-pa grinned back and gave Set a firm hug, patting him on the back. "Not a chance. How are you feeling?"

"Ready to go on a hunt—as long as it doesn't involve any climbing."

"From the looks of it, it may be a while before they let you do anything half as exciting."

Set groaned. "I've been dying of boredom, pent up here by myself for nearly a week."

"My mother and father thought it best to give you time to recover."

"But when they found out Heru-pa's begging could be heard all the way to the palace, they decided to cave in and let him see you," Mia quipped.

"Thank Amun for that," Set snickered.

"Laugh it up, both of you." Heru-pa shot them a glance. "When you're done jestering, I've got something for you." He held out the package.

Set accepted the bundle and unwrapped it. He regarded the finely spun white fabric. "A Rathadi robe?"

"If you are going to partake in a Rathadi liturgy, you should look the part," Heru-pa said.

Set turned the robe over in his hands. "It's exquisite," he said, his voice heavy. "Thank you."

Heru-pa nodded awkwardly.

"So, you ready for your big day?" Mia jumped in.

Before Heru-pa had a chance to reply, there was a knock at the door, and three royal attendants entered bearing plates that brimmed with sweet treats and pitchers filled with colorful nectars. One of them, a young woman with short auburn hair, approached and gave a shy curtsy.

"Prince Heru-pa and Lady Mia, it would please Her Majesty if you would join the prince for dessert," she said. "May I inform her that you accept?"

Heru-pa glanced at Mia who was sizing up the delicacies. He swallowed before speaking—it would not do to drool on himself. "Please give Her Majesty our sincere gratitude," he said. "It would be an honor, if it pleases the prince, of course."

"Are you kidding?" Set called out. "I've been dying for some company!"

"I shall be glad to inform Her Majesty of your acceptance," the young woman said, and motioned them to the large table on the terrace.

They took their seats and waited until the servers set the table and stepped away.

Set reached for his glass of dragon fruit nectar and raised it. "Amun's light!"

"Amun's light," Heru-pa and Mia echoed, lifting their own glasses.

They clinked and took a sip. Heru-pa let the sweet taste burst in his mouth.

"Well, what are you waiting for?" Set pointed at the spread before them. "Dive in!"

Heru-pa didn't wait for a second invitation. He stabbed his fork into an artfully carved piece of muskmelon while Mia picked up a lychee and nibbled on it. They inhaled the first three servings, delighting in the treats and relishing in each other's company before Mia finally broke the silence.

"So what's going to be your valediction gift to Heru-pa?" she asked Set between bites of her mangosteen tart.

"Mia!" Heru-pa mumbled with his mouth fuller than his mother would have approved. "You know he can't tell me."

"And you can't tell me that you're not the least bit curious," Mia retorted. "Besides, just because he can't tell *you*, doesn't mean he can't tell me, so why don't you just hold your ears shut and—"

"Nice try, Mia," Set said. "I won't be telling anybody. I guess you'll just have to wait until tomorrow and find out yourself."

"If they even let me in," Mia said.

"I'll make certain there's a spot saved for you," Heru-pa said. "I want my friends close."

"Deal," Mia said, carrying another morsel of pastry into her mouth with a silver fork. "And you begin your valediction sojourn right after the ceremony? To find your sentinel?"

"We find each other," Heru-pa said. "That is why the next sacred liturgy is called convergence."

Mia nodded thoughtfully, chewing on her treat. "How long will it take for you to find each other?"

"Only Ra knows," Heru-pa replied. "Some Rathadi's valediction sojourns have lasted a day, some stretched for weeks before they were divined with convergence. But my father said that his sentinel found him on the beach, as soon as he set foot on the Brim."

"That was lucky! How did he know it found him?"

"The scorpion stung him," Heru-pa said.

"What?" Mia almost spit out her pastry. "You are joking!"

"I am not. It stung him, but the sting did not cause him pain or illness. Rather, he felt stronger and keener than ever before.

As if the scorpion's poison unlocked something in him that had always been there."

Mia stared at him, open-mouthed, forgetting about the half-eaten pastry on her plate.

"Amazing," Set said. "Rathadi are so wicked."

"The powers of the Pure Ones are nothing to scoff at, either," Heru-pa countered.

"If you're a mind controller like my father, perhaps," Set replied. He gazed out wistfully for a moment, before sitting up and stuffing the last bit of fruit tart into his mouth. "You know," he said, licking his fingers clean, "Mia and I have been taking bets on what your adult name will be."

"Oh, yeah?"

"Yes. Mia thinks it will be Hechepsut, but I'm going with Wakshakwi."

Heru-pa chuckled. "I wish I had considered those."

"Alright, seriously," Mia laughed. "I think it will be Herit."

"It sounds like a strong name," Set said. They both stared at Heru-pa, unblinking.

"Is that the best you can do?" Heru-pa laughed. "I'm not telling you. Patience is a noble virtue. You'll have to wait until tomorrow."

"Not even a little hint?" Mia asked.

Heru-pa made a motion as if to seal his lips shut.

Mia groaned in mock frustration. "Fine… be that way."

Set gave a smile, but Heru-pa noticed it grew distant.

"What is it?" Heru-pa asked.

"Nothing," Set said.

"Come on, spill it," Heru-pa pressed.

Set shrugged. "It will be strange to call you by another name."

"You'll get used to it quicker than you think."

"Still. I… I just can't help but think that things will be different." Set reached for his drink.

"That's assuming that I will find a sentinel that deems me worthy," Heru-pa said.

"Are you kidding me?" Mia jumped in. "They're probably lining up on the shore of the Brim, just waiting for you to arrive and have your pick. There's probably an ox just waiting to kick you the moment you step on the beach. Like father like son."

Set snorted and nearly spit out his juice.

Heru-pa shook his head. "Seriously? I've been begging my mother for five days to spend time with you two, and this is what I get?"

"You know you're going to miss us when you're on the Brim all by yourself," Mia said. "How many times have you been there?"

"Only once," Heru-pa said, "with my father."

"What was it like?"

He thought back to the visit. "Empty," he said. "Peaceful." He had been as excited as he had been terrified. Even though the Brim lay only past the Basin, when they had pulled their boat onto the shore, it had seemed like they were a world away.

"Is it true that shifters live there?" Mia asked. "And the forsaken?"

Heru-pa's expression darkened. "I… I don't know."

"Aren't you worried?" she asked.

Heru-pa gazed at her wordlessly. An awkward silence stretched.

Set stood. "I think that's enough talk about the Brim and shifters. I don't know about you two, but after all the food, I could definitely go for a game of Nikka."

A smile spread across Mia's face. "You're on! If your healer allows it."

"We can always sneak out," Heru-pa said.

Set stared at him and opened his mouth. Then he saw the look in Heru-pa's eyes. "Nice…" he laughed. "I thought you'd never learn your lesson!"

"My mother said that there was nothing that you won't achieve once you set your Rathadi mind to it," Mia said.

"She said that?" Heru-pa asked. "About me?"

"Among other things," Mia said, pitching her voice low.

"Really?" Heru-pa leaned forward. "What else did she say?"

She gave him a teasing look, but kept silent.

"Tell me."

"Patience is a noble virtue, Heru-pa, you'll just have to wait for her to tell you herself," she replied, her laughter brightening the room.

Heru-pa threw a grape at her. "What is this? Tease Heru-pa day?"

"What else do you expect on your last day as a Rathling?" Set asked, joining in Mia's laughter. He lifted his glass. "To your last day as a Rathling," he said.

Mia lifted her drink. Heru-pa raised his own and smiled at his friends, but he could not ignore the sinking feeling in the pit of his stomach.

CHAPTER 12

THE NARROW PASSAGEWAY was dark and smelled of mildew. The woman squeezed past the tiny boat that sat at the end of the shaft and pressed her shoulder against the heavy stone door. It gave way slowly with a grating sound, and fresh air streamed inside, bringing relief to her lungs after what seemed like an eternity in the cramped dankness. Barely wide enough for a grown man to pass through comfortably, these catacombs had been used mostly for clandestine operations in the name of the Purean king and served as a last resort to escape the capital. Few knew about their existence. Fewer yet knew how to gain entry into their twisted web.

The woman tightened the hooded cloak around her and gazed out into the dark water of the channel that lay between her and the Inner Ring. Dimly illuminated by a quarter moon, the smooth surface was like a polished mirror, reflecting the pinpricks of light above. She would have preferred a moonless night, but she could not wait any longer.

They had run out of time.

She slipped off her pack and threw it inside the boat. She doubled back a few steps, squeezing past the boat once again, then began pushing it to the water. Slowly, the boat inched toward the exit. Holding back a grunt, she gave the boat one final shove, and it slid into the water with a soft splash. The woman slipped inside, picked up the paddle and began rowing south. Even though she was eager to get to the other side and complete her task, her movements were slow and steady, mindful of the sound carrying far over the still water, and the sentries standing guard along the wall.

As she approached the shore of the Inner Ring, she set the paddle down and jumped into the shallow water, then dragged the boat as far onto the sand as she could manage.

She pulled the bag from the boat and slung it over her shoulder before setting out into the lush forest toward the Southern Highlands and Serpent's Pass. Keeping a brisk pace, she cut straight through the ring island; she had to move fast to make it to the Brim with enough time to return to the capital before dawn. She could ill-afford to be discovered missing in the morning.

The plan had to work.

The air was colder, and the moon was high in the sky when she crested over the highlands along the Serpent's Pass. She gazed down into the valley. At any other time, the view before her would have been mesmerizing, even in the dim moonlight. The contours of the Inner Ring circled back gently in both directions, ringed by water that separated it from the landmass beyond, the Brim.

She picked her footsteps carefully as she descended and continued down into the woods until she reached the outer shore. A scattering of Rathadi fishing boats had been pulled onto the beach for the night and secured to pilons driven into the ground. She checked her surroundings again, making certain that no sleepless Rathadi was about, then she untied one of the boats and pushed it into the water. She slipped the oars into the water and set off across the Basin.

The slow-building ache in her back and shoulders had transformed into a constant burn by the time the bottom of the boat scraped against the inner shore of the Brim. She had aimed for a spot a safe distance from the gated water channel that connected the Brim Basin with the Southern Sea. Even though the work on rebuilding the massive gate that protected the Basin had stopped for the night, and the keen eyes of the Rathadi lookouts were trained out to the sea rather than into the Basin, she could not take any chances.

She had to succeed.

He had to be stopped.

The sacrifice had been immense. She could only hope the wyrmlings had survived and made it ashore. In time, they would have grown to adult size, and things could have been different, but time was a commodity they did not have.

She pulled the boat onto the beach and set out into the forest, clutching her pack tightly against her body. Cutting through the woods, she trekked parallel to the waterline for a full span. This was as close to the southern gate as she dared approach without worrying about the Rathadi lookouts spotting her—or one of the wyrmlings smelling her before she had time to finish her task.

Breathing hard, she slipped off her pack and reached inside. She pulled out the ampulla and the blood-stained cloth. She struggled to keep her hands from trembling as she poured the fluid in a circle and placed the blood-stained cloth inside it. Tiamat had assured her that the wyrmlings would be attracted to the smell of the tincture and then be fixed on the blood on the cloth, but she was not going to test her word. She threw the empty ampulla into her bag and doubled back, leaving as much distance as she could between her and the cloth.

Perhaps it was only in her imagination, or perhaps the slow, harsh slithering sounds converging on the cloth behind her were real. She cared not to discover which it was as she rushed back to the boat.

He had to be stopped.
No matter the cost.

CHAPTER 13

Heru-pa tugged at the collar of his golden tunic and stifled a yawn as his mother wrapped the ceremonial linen shawl around his shoulders and his freshly shaved head. Isis shot him a glance.

"It would not do to fall asleep at your own Rite of Valediction," she said.

The heat in his cheeks surged. The sun had set by the time he had returned from the Purean palace yesterday. Even after he had finally turned in, he spent hours tossing about, not able to fall asleep until well past midnight. Despite that, he woke up before sunrise, anxious about the day ahead of him.

"What if I won't find my sentinel?"

His mother let go of the shawl and clasped her palms around his shoulders. "Every single Rathadi who went through valediction shared the same trepidation. I promise you, your sentinel will find you. Your sojourn will end in convergence."

"Were you worried?"

"Being the daughter of Thoth, the greatest mind of the

Rathadi? What do you think?" A bubble of laughter caught in her throat. "I was terrified of disappointing him and being an embarrassment to my family."

Heru-pa processed his mother's words, studying her face: the graceful lines of the cheekbones and strong contour of her jaw, the slumbering fervor behind the kind, feline eyes. As his mother and the queen of the Rathadi, she had always seemed to him as fierce and courageous as she was beautiful. Always regal. To imagine her as a Rathling, terrified of disappointing her family, was a notion he struggled to accept.

"How will I know it's the right one?"

"You will know. And more importantly, so will your sentinel."

She finished wrapping the shawl, then attached a golden clasp in the shape of a triangle to the front, pinning it tight. She tugged at the sides, making sure the fabric lay straight then ran her palm along his cheek.

"You look so grown up," she said, a hint of sadness creeping into her voice.

He stepped forward and pulled her into a hug. "Thank you, *Amah*," he said. "For everything."

The smell of the metopion oil on her skin was soothing. A cord of tension released in his chest as they stood, a mother and her son, savoring the moment and each other's presence.

He summoned his strength and pushed back gently. There was a hint of resistance before she allowed him to break the embrace.

She blinked the dampness from her eyes. "Ready?"

He nodded, then turned and crossed the room. He opened the door and stepped through, mindful of the guards flanking the door. His father and Set stood to his left, waiting. Their faces were solemn, but he drew strength from the kindness in their eyes.

Heru-pa kept his gaze ahead of him and turned right. Ignoring the wobbliness in his legs, he set off, his chin high, as his parents and Set fell in behind him. His mind rushed with a thousand different thoughts and none at all as he descended the stairs into the heart of the temple. He crossed the bridge over the sacred underground lake that represented the eternal waters, and aimed for the sanctuary. As he neared the entrance, two guards blocked his way.

"Who seeks entry to the inner sanctum?" one of them asked the ritual question.

"Heru-pa, son of Isis and Osiris," he answered.

"What is your purpose, Heru-pa, son of Isis and Osiris?"

"The Rite of Valediction," he replied.

"Who are the pillars that shall stand with you?"

"Osiris, King of the Rathadi," his father replied proudly.

"Isis, Queen of the Rathadi," his mother said.

"Set, Prince of the Pure Ones," Set completed.

The guards stood aside and opened the door. He entered the dimly lit chamber. Two parallel rows of stone pillars lined his path to an elevated shrine at the far end. High Priest So'bek stood behind the shrine, his leathery face fixed on Heru-pa from beneath his hood. He was dressed in a golden mantle that draped loosely over his body. In his right hand rested a golden staff, the ceremonial *was*.

Dozens of Rathadi clad in white robes stood alongside the pillars, their faces solemn. Heru-pa made out Mia's face in the front row. When their gazes met, her lips turned upward into a hint of a smile that made his heart quicken, but he kept his expression somber as he approached the golden triangle on the floor before the shrine. The congregation closed the gap behind him, forming a circle. When he reached the center of the triangle, Heru-pa knelt and bowed his head. He could sense, more than hear, the quiet footsteps of his parents and Set taking their positions at the three vertices.

So'bek struck the *was* against the marble floor. The single sound faded into the recesses of the hall, and Heru-pa lifted his head but remained kneeling.

"The Rite of Valediction marks the passing of a Rathadi child into adulthood," So'bek began. "It marks the time when a Rathling is sent forth on a spiritual sojourn. By the grace of Amun-Ra, the separate paths of seeker and sentinel converge. If the sentinel judges the young Rathadi worthy, they shall return together to be joined in the Ceremony of Transcendence." He swept his gaze over the assembly. "On this day, we bid farewell to the Rathling known to us as Heru-pa, son of Isis and Osiris, as he sets forth on his sojourn of valediction. May his animal sentinel find him and guide him back to us safely."

So'bek struck the ceremonial *was* on the floor again, twice. Heru-pa closed his eyes, and the high priest began an incantation, his voice sonorous and surprisingly mellow. The other Rathadi joined in, and soon Heru-pa was enveloped by a hauntingly beautiful harmony from dozens of throats reverberating through the chamber.

Heru-pa lost track of time, swaying to the chorus, unable and unwilling to resist the pull of the chanting when So'bek struck the *was* three times against the marble floor, and the chamber fell into silence. Heru-pa opened his eyes and met the high priest's reptilian gaze once again. So'bek nodded.

Heru-pa rose and turned right, facing his mother.

"Isis, Daughter of Ra," So'bek's voice rang through the chamber, "what parting gift will you bestow upon this child as he embarks to face the Trials?"

Isis stepped forward, her eyes calm and filled with confidence. Her hands held a golden amulet. Heru-pa bowed his head, ready to accept her gift and blessing as she hung the talisman around his neck.

"Your animal sentinel will find you," she said, the warmth of her voice matching the love in her eyes, "and you will return home safely." She placed her hands on his forehead in the traditional blessing of the Rathadi, her forefingers and thumbs forming the sacred triangle.

Heru-pa waited until she lifted her palms then turned to his right again and faced his father.

"Osiris, Son of Ra," So'bek's voice rang out again, "what shall be your parting gift to this child?"

His father regarded him for several heartbeats. Heru-pa held his gaze, unblinking, the fierceness in his father's amber eyes giving him strength. An acolyte approached with a tablet of black ink and a golden reed. His father lifted the reed and dipped it into the ink, then moved it to Heru-pa's head.

The ink felt cool at first as his father inscribed his adult name on his skin, encircled by a powerful sigil of protection. Heru-pa gasped at the warmth spreading through his body as the power of the symbol melded with the amulet around his neck.

When Osiris finished, he spoke, his voice deep and filled

with pride. "You are Horus. Son of Isis and Osiris. You shall know no fear."

Heru-pa's knees trembled, and a wave of emotion swept through him at the sound of his adult name uttered publicly for the first time. His adult name, inscribed in his skin, ringed by the circle of protection. The name that he would bear from now until the day he died, and that he would share with his animal sentinel, if they both proved to be worthy of each other.

Horus.

Son of Isis and Osiris.

Heru-pa bowed his head, and his father repeated the blessing of the Rathadi.

He turned to the right a third time and faced the front of the triangle once again. He found the icy-blue eyes of his trusted friend.

"Set, Prince of the Pure Ones," So'bek called out, "what shall be your parting gift to the seeker?"

Set approached Heru-pa and held out an onyx dagger. Heru-pa just managed not to let his jaw drop as he grasped the hilt with his right hand and the scabbard with his left.

"May this dagger drink of the blood of those who shall attempt to harm you or your kin," Set said, the solemn words at odds with his young voice.

The boys' gazes caught, and one corner of Set's mouth tugged into a sheepish smile.

"Brothers forever," he whispered, and he repeated the triangle blessing of the Rathadi.

"Brothers forever," Heru-pa replied quietly. He slid the blade into the scabbard and fixed it to his belt.

So'bek lifted the *was*. "The parting gifts of protection,

courage, and strength have been bestowed upon you by those you love. May they guide your journey as you enter the Trials of Valediction. May they help you and your sentinel find each other and bring you safely back home."

So'bek struck the marble three times, and the circle around Heru-pa parted as the sounds rang out.

"It is time, son of Isis and Osiris," the high priest said. "Go now and leave the remnants of your childhood behind. Leave as Heru-pa, the Rathling, and return to us as Horus, the Rathadi, worthy of your animal sentinel that will know your true name and come back with you. May Amun-Ra guide your steps on your path to Convergence."

The chanting started once again. Heru-pa turned and strode out of the triangle, passing between his mother and father. He tried to ignore the pained tinge on his mother's face, yet the lump that choked his throat would not melt. He fought the crushing urge to rush to her and tell her that he would be fine, that he would return into her arms safely. Tears threatened his eyes, but he refused to let them come. Instead, he lifted his chin high, forcing himself to look straight as he paced through the corridor of bodies, and exited the sanctuary.

CHAPTER 14

HERU-PA PASSED through the gates of the temple. His heart rattled in his rib cage as if trying to escape. He breathed deeply and faced west, across the channel. The smell of cypress rinsed by a fresh sea breeze hung in the air, and the sun stood two hand spans above the tall wall that surrounded the capital. If he stepped briskly, he could use the remainder of the light to cut across the Ring, cross the highlands, and reach the inner shore of the Brim Basin before nightfall. There, he would set up camp for the night before traversing the Basin into the Brim on the following day. He wrapped his palm around the handle of the onyx dagger and took a final glance at the temple, then turned east.

He followed the trail for the Eastern Highlands, accompanied by the sounds of birds frolicking among the lush treetops, until he reached an intersection. The trail split north and south to the small settlements near the temple. He stepped off the path and continued east, across the meadow and into the valley.

A span had passed by the time he reached the wooded

foothills of the highlands. Despite his fast pace and the uphill slope, his breathing was slow and regular, but he had taken off his shawl and tunic, and wrapped both around his hips. The night would be cool, and he did not want his clothes to be damp with sweat. He continued along the pass that would take him over the mountain range and to the other side.

The sun had begun to set when he stopped to pick a handful of berries in a valley on the far side of the highlands. The heads of clover bobbed in the wind as a few straggling bumblebees darted between them before returning to their nests for the night. By the time he found a small spring-fed pool nestled among some birch trees, he could see the sky purpling into dusk through the canopy. He knelt and dipped his hands in the spring and wiped his brow and neck, then took several sips of the cool water. He rose and glanced wistfully at the refreshing water, wishing for a canteen he could fill up, but he had only been allowed his clothes and the items given to him during the ceremony.

He pressed through the scrub of the floodplain and into the woods that would eventually lead him to the outer shore of the Inner Ring. A small shiver went through him. Now that the sun had dipped below the highlands at his back, the temperature dropped quickly. He slipped the tunic back on and wrapped the shawl around his shoulders. As the skies darkened further, his mood seemed to follow. He listened and scanned the trees, straining his senses for any signs of danger, but the air was still around him. Soon the gentle sound of water lapping against the rocky shore reached his ears. He stepped out of the trees and onto the beach.

He peered at the vast landmass across the Brim Basin. He

shivered again, this time not from the cold, but from the growing sense of dread that he had strived to ignore. The outline of the Brim was dark and foreboding. Back in the safety of the temple or the Purean palace, stories of shifters and forsaken that dwelled in the shadows of the Brim were captivating and enthralling. Alone, in the falling darkness, they took on a different life. Heru-pa swallowed and allowed himself a moment of panic before forcing it down. He had a task to accomplish.

Since it was too late to hunt or fish, he looked around for some more berries, but came up empty. His stomach grumbled, and he promised himself to look for food as soon as he got up the next morning. He spent the rest of the twilight gathering dry leaves for kindling and some small branches then picked up two of the flint stones that covered the beach and started a fire.

The flames bathed the beach in an orange hue, flickering bright and holding back the night. The warmth from the fire went a long way to improve his mood, despite his growling belly. Heru-pa spread out the shawl on the sandy part of the beach and lay down.

A brilliant ceiling of stars stretched overhead, and the waxing crescent moon was back in the sky. They were in the twenty-ninth day of The Great Twins; two more days before the month of the Crayfish. He recalled the lessons from his mother and grandfather as he searched for their constellations. The exhilaration of the day slowly ebbed from him, to be replaced by a heaviness that began to settle into his limbs. Heru-pa continued gazing at the pinpricks of light in the vastness above until fatigue claimed him, and he drifted off into sleep.

————

IN THE BLACKNESS, the beast had waited. Spawned for a singular purpose, its brain had no concept of boredom, and time was irrelevant. Born into a cruel and vicious world, it had lain dormant, lingering, growing, only allowing itself to wander when hunger compelled it to venture out.

Then it had been roused, the scent stirring an impression, an echo deep inside its core, driving it into restlessness. Seeking. Pursuing.

The beast slithered through the undergrowth. Evolved for hunting at night, the faint light of the moon was soft and unreflecting on its smooth skin, but for the faint, glistening scar from a meal that had fought back. Though not yet a fully-grown adult and unknown to the creatures nearby, it was shunned by all, recognized for the lethal predator it had already become.

The beast rose and tilted its large skull, unblinking, tasting the air with its forked tongue, its abyss-like eyes embedded in an otherwise unbroken sheath of scales, scanning for the scent that had been seared into its memory.

————

HERU-PA WOKE UP WITH A START. He wiped at the sand pasted to his cheek, mystified, before recalling where he was. He sat up and gazed out into the Basin. The water shifted in dozens of shades of blue and green, and the waves lapped calmly against the black-pebbled shore. A gentle wind rose as the sun warmed the earth. He stood and took off his sandals, then tramped to the shore and dipped his feet in the cool water. A movement near his foot caught his eye. A fat crayfish scurried across the bottom. Heru-pa smiled.

Breakfast.

Before the sun rose another span, he had caught three crayfish, cooked them, and was sucking out the fresh meat from the shell of the last one. He gazed to the distant shore, his belly no longer empty, and his mood greatly improved. In the warm daylight, the Brim did not look nearly as foreboding as it had seemed to him at night.

Energized, he set forth to his next task: crossing the Basin. He recalled the lesson from his father about constructing a small raft from bamboo shoots. The morning dew had burned off, and the grass rasped about his shins as he crossed the narrow sward between the beach and the trees. He entered the forest, and in less than half a span he found a growth of bamboos. They grew by a stream that he used to quench his thirst and wash up. He selected several of the shoots that were about the width of his forearm and slipped his dagger from the scabbard.

Before long, four sizable shoots lay on the ground. He dragged them to the beach where he cut them to equal size, each about the length of his body, then tied them together with reeds. He stepped back and scrutinized his work. Not much longer and wider than his body, the small raft was just large enough to keep him afloat and allowed him to paddle with his arms and kick with his feet. It would not get him far in the Three Seas, but in the still waters of the Basin, it was more than enough to get him safely across to the Brim.

He secured his amulet and dagger about him, then pulled the small raft into the water and strode past the gentle waves.

When the water reached his hips, he hopped onto his raft and began paddling.

The sun had passed its zenith by the time he reached the shore of the Brim. He slipped off the raft and teetered onto the beach, collapsing onto his back. The sand scratched against his skin, but he reveled in its coarseness as he closed his eyes and let the warmth of the sun spread over his face and exhausted limbs.

After he regained his strength, he pushed to his feet and took in his surroundings. To both sides, the beach continued in a great arc, circling back around the Inner Ring. Ahead, dense trees with moss-lined bark melded with swaying saplings and colorful underbrush. The greenery stretched before him, rising into the vast Brim Highlands that towered in the distance, reaching for the sky.

He stripped off his clothes and sandals, rinsing them clear of the sand, and stood in the knee-deep water as the cool wind stroked his back. A strange sensation passed through him a heartbeat before a faint cry rose from above. It pitched upward until it reached its highest note, piercing the still air, then it died away.

Heru-pa looked up to the source of the sound, and his skin prickled. A falcon soared in the midday currents, circling high above the black beach. It circled in wide, graceful arcs hundreds of feet above him. It called out once again, a long high-pitched *scree*, before turning inland toward the Brim Highlands. Heru-pa followed the falcon's flight until its wings disappeared from sight, melting into the blue sky. He stood, transfixed, for a long time, his heart quaking in his chest, before he was able to move again.

His stomach growled, drawing him back. Building the raft and crossing the Basin had burned off the breakfast quickly. He needed to find food and water soon. There were plenty of roots and berries in the forest and small creeks to quench his thirst, but he did not want to head into the woods wearing wet clothes and shoes.

He hung up his clothes on nearby branches and strolled along the shore to pass time when he spotted the colorful pink of sea grapes. He twisted off a bunch and nibbled on them. Two more weeks on the vine would have ripened the taste, but their tartness refreshed him as he waited another span for the sun to dry his clothes, then dressed and set off into the woods.

Before long, the bushes and short trees had disappeared to make room for thick trunks and wide branches that formed a vaulted green roof high above his head. Soon after, the sky vanished almost completely, and only a few fragments of blue remained. The trees were tightly-knit, just one strand in a massive web of life. The air grew impossibly rich with the fragrance of leaves as the forest hummed with life all around him. Heru-pa trudged on, keeping his eyes peeled for anything edible.

Ahead, the sun broke through the cracks in the canopy, lighting up the undergrowth filled with outgrown roots, plants and fallen leaves that crunched beneath his feet. He stopped, drawing nearer to one of the plants, recognizing the green, oval-shaped leaves of a broadleaf turpin. Heru-pa pulled out his dagger and knelt beside it.

As he dug up a pair of fist-sized tubers, the trickling sound of water reached his ears. He followed it until he arrived at a small stream, flowing in a steep-sided ditch, splashing on the rocks. He climbed down and cupped a few mouthfuls, savoring the wetness on his parched throat then squatted on the bank, rinsed the dirt from the tubers and cut them into bitesize pieces. He knew they would taste better cooked, but the hunger pangs in his belly won out over his discerning palate, so he chewed them raw, washing the food down with crisp spring water.

He spotted some nuts and berries on the other side and waded across. He slipped the nuts in his pocket for later, but sucked on the sweet juice from the berries to get rid of the bitter taste of the turpin, then decided to follow the water upstream. After another span of trekking, the forest grew thinner, opening up into a glade. An enormous boulder rose up in the center of a grassy meadow. Heru-pa stepped out and froze. Perched atop the boulder was the falcon.

It—*she*, for Heru-pa was sure it was a female—moved her head to face him, her golden eyes so brilliant they looked like a source of light rather than a reflection of the sun's rays. She held her body straight, her black head raised high and proud in the manner of a peregrine. Her tawny breast was speckled with black spots, and a vertical white stripe ran between her eyes, just above the yellow part of the bill.

Heru-pa approached the falcon slowly. On his third step, she bristled her feathers, and Heru-pa froze mid-stride. She cocked her head and eyed him guardedly. Heru-pa stood completely still for several heartbeats, holding his breath, before he spoke, his voice low and steady.

"Ra's blessings, noble one. I am Heru-pa, son of Isis and Osiris." He knew the falcon didn't understand him, but he hoped the measured sound of his voice would keep her from flying away. "Did you call to me on the beach?"

The falcon spread her wings and took off. Heru-pa's gaze followed her as she rose into the sky. "I suppose I should be grateful you didn't bite me," he said, trying to keep the disappointment from his voice.

He frowned at the gray clouds advancing over the Brim Highlands and selected a spot at the edge of the clearing beside a mossy rock to build a shelter. He collected some fallen limbs and leaned them against the rock then chopped off a dozen dense branches from a nearby boxwood bush and wove them through the limbs. When he finished building the canopy, he gathered two piles of velvetleaves for a mattress.

It's not pretty, but should keep me mostly dry, he mused, trying not to think of his soft, empty bed in the temple.

His shelter for the night complete, he ventured back to the stream. He set out for the deeper pool shrouded in the shade of overhanging bushes that he passed earlier in the day. Ra willing, he might be able to catch some fish in the calmer waters. Lacking a line or hook, he kept his eyes open for something that could be turned into a fishing spear. Before long, he spotted a narrow tree limb that was about the length of his arm and forked out into three prongs near the top. He cut it from the tree and trimmed the smaller branches and leaves, then sharpened the three twigs into fine points. Armed with his new spear, he continued on.

When he reached the pool, he studied it from the bank, surveying for a site that would be popular with fish, but that also provided some cover for him. He spotted a fallen tree that was partially submerged and decided to try his luck near it, so he slipped into the creek and stalked along the fallen trunk.

When the water reached his thighs, he lifted his spear and stood, motionless, scanning the surface.

Heru-pa waited, still like a statue for a quarter span, reflecting on the lectures about patience drilled into him by Qar during their outings. After another quarter span, he lowered the spear, tired and frustrated, and rested his hand on the fallen tree. The bark crumbled beneath his palm. He glanced down, spotting several grubs chewing on the exposed rotten wood. An idea struck.

He reached for the fattest grub, then stuck it on a pointed end of a branch and wedged the other end into the trunk, making sure the grub was just below the water line.

Let's see if that gets anybody's attention.

A few moments later, a Bluegill approached, circling.

Heru-pa stayed perfectly still, recalling Qar's advice on how to account for the bending of the light in the water. The fish drew near, and he aimed the spear a hand's width below it. When the Bluegill reached for the grub, he thrust.

A splash later, Heru-pa gave a quiet curse, watching the Bluegill dart away. He reached for another grub, then glanced up, peering through the dense canopy. The light was fading quickly. He reckoned he had another half span of daylight; after that he'd have just as much luck spearfishing blindfolded.

After some time, another Bluegill appeared. Heru-pa held his breath as the fish approached the bait. He said a quick prayer to Ra and thrust again.

When he retracted the spear, the fish flopped impaled on two of the three prongs. Heru-pa gave a woot. He rushed out of the water and allowed himself to revel briefly in his success, before slipping out his dagger and killing the catch quickly.

He glanced to the sky again. He had hoped to catch at least two, one for himself and one to try to win the falcon's trust tomorrow, but traveling through the forest after the sun had set did not strike him as a good idea. It looked like he would have to share his spoils.

Half a fish is better than no fish at all.

His mouth watered when he thought of the smell of the Bluegill over a fire when a distant rumble drew him back. The blue skies had been replaced by dark gray clouds. He picked up the Bluegill and his spear and made for his camp.

A few steps later, the skies opened up.

He arrived at the clearing as wet as if he had swum back in the creek. He cursed himself for not putting some firewood beneath his shelter before setting out for his fishing trip. Despite bringing the flintstones he had found on the beach, he knew there was no hope of building a fire with wood drenched by the rain. He glanced at his catch dejectedly. For a brief moment he considered eating it raw, then decided against it. He wrapped it in leaves and buried it for the night.

I hope she'll appreciate the effort.

Heru-pa pulled a handful of nuts from his pocket and threw them into his mouth then lay back on his makeshift mattress. He pulled his wet tunic around him, trying to ignore the dripping of the water and his hungry belly as he curled up and closed his eyes.

A crack in the woods broke the stillness. Heru-pa's eyes snapped open, and his hand shot to the dagger at his hip.

The noise repeated, drawing nearer. The sound of rustling and snapping twigs followed. He sat up and listened keenly into the darkness.

Something large shuffled through the bushes near the clearing. Heru-pa drew his dagger and pressed his back against the rock.

The bushes rustled again and swayed. Heru-pa raised the dagger, his heart thudding in his chest. He held his breath—then the slim head peaked through the leaves.

Heru-pa exhaled as the Highland Ibex and her calf emerged from the thicket. The doe pulled down the branches and held them low while her young plucked the wet leaves off the limbs. Heru-pa allowed himself a smile and sheathed the dagger. He watched the pair graze at the edge of the clearing until his chin drooped against his chest.

———

HERU-PA AWAKENED HUNGRY, damp, and with the drone of insects in his ears. Gradually, layers of other sounds arose, building into nature's chorus of the forest coming alive, heralding the morning—and the end of one miserable night.

A spiderweb stretched across the entrance of his shelter, stringed with drops of morning dew, glistening in the first shards of sunlight. He slid out, ducking beneath the web, not wanting to disturb the delicate creation, then stepped into the clearing and watched the red sun rising over the treetops. Its warmth slowly evaporated the memories of the cold and mostly sleepless night. He gave a shiver beneath his damp clothes then decided to strip them off and hang them in the branches facing the sun. Despite all, he snickered to himself, realizing that his second day on the Brim was starting just like the first, naked as a newborn Rathling. He scanned the sky and the tall rock, but the falcon was nowhere to be seen.

She'll be here.

A coconut tree on the other side of the clearing caught his gaze. He crossed to it excitedly, then clamped his teeth around the dagger and climbed up. He cut down a pair of coconuts and was working on the third when a buzzing sound distracted him. A flying insect the size of his thumb emerged from the wood.

A bolt of panic shot through him.

Stingwings!

Three more appeared and charged straight at him. The first sting felt like a hot needle.

He dropped the dagger and slid down the trunk, landing hard on the ground. Before he had a chance to gain his feet, another one scored a hit. Heru-pa yelped and swatted at it, then bounced up and tore through the clearing to the stream, waving his arms about him as a dozen of the wrathful insects buzzed after him. He dove into the stream from the bank, taking shelter from the winged menace beneath the water. Stingwings minded their own business if left alone, but when disturbed, their tempers were as foul as their stings painful. He stayed submerged for as long as he could hold his breath, then slowly lifted his head above the surface and peeked around. Fortunately, as easy as they were to anger, stingwings were just as quick to forget.

He took a deep breath and chuckled at his harrowing escape and the sight he must have cut, streaking through the woods.

This part of my valediction story shall remain on the Brim.

When he took a step, he winced at the sharp pain in his right foot. He hobbled to the bank, plopped down and lifted his leg to examine the damage. A nasty gash ran the width of his right sole. He must have sliced it on the sharp rocks near the stream and not even noticed when he was bolting from the insects. Despite all the blood, it didn't seem very deep, but walking would not be fun, especially barefoot.

Heru-pa limped back to the clearing and slipped on his sandals before cautiously approaching the palm tree, keeping an eye and ear out for any signs of the stingwings. Thankfully they seemed to have retreated back into their nest, so he retrieved his dagger and the two coconuts and hobbled to the shelter as quickly as his injured foot allowed.

He eased to the ground and used his dagger to drill a hole in one of the coconuts, then drank most of the milk before using the rest to wash out his wound. The milk was soothing and the pain slowly ebbed. He split the coconut and carved out some of the meat, chewed it, then spread the paste over the gash. He covered it with a broadleaf before slipping his foot back into the sandal. Leaning back against his shelter, he feasted on the coconut meat, feeling the energy slowly returning to him.

Refreshed, he considered trying to make a fire and grilling the fish, but the wood was still too damp from last night's torrent. He laid out some dead branches in the sunniest spots of the clearing to dry. Maybe by tonight he'd be able to start one. He lay down in the grass and peered into the sky, looking for the falcon.

Heru-pa woke up not realizing he had fallen asleep. It was at least two spans past midday. He glanced to the rock, and his breath hitched. The falcon sat perched atop, regarding him alertly.

He gathered up his clothes and got dressed, then dug up the

fish and unwrapped it from the leaves before approaching the bird cautiously.

"Ra's blessings," Heru-pa said. "Remember me? Are you hungry?" He lifted his hand with the fish and tossed it to the base of the rock.

The bird stirred and spread her wings, and for a moment it appeared as if she might take flight, but she stayed put. She eyed Heru-pa, her golden eyes bright and intelligent, before swooping down to the fish. She snatched it up and returned to her perch on the rock.

Heru-pa smiled and eased onto the grass. He reached for the second half of the coconut, and scooped out a chunk of the nutty meat. He chewed in silence, watching the bird tear strips of the fish and gobble it up.

"Bennu," Heru-pa said, breaking the stillness.

The falcon turned its head to Heru-pa and cocked it.

"Bennu," he repeated. "That shall be your name. Do you like it?"

The falcon returned her attention to the fish, ripping off another piece with its powerful beak.

"I take that as a resounding yes," Heru-pa said. The falcon finished her meal and stayed perched on the rock for a few moments longer then took to the air.

Heru-pa collected the firewood he had laid out to dry and hauled it beneath his shelter. It did not look like it was going to start raining anytime soon, but it wasn't worth taking a chance. He needed something warm in his stomach tonight. He cleaned out his wound again and covered it with the coconut paste then picked up his spear and set out for the stream.

Two spans later he returned with three fish. He gutted two

of them, started a fire and hooked them over it. Soon, the smell of fire-grilled Bluegill permeated the clearing.

He smiled at the flapping of wings. "Welcome back, Bennu," he said, looking up at the falcon. "Couldn't resist the smell?"

He threw the raw fish to her. She swooped down and snatched it up, then perched on the rock once again.

Heru-pa took his fish off the fire. They were hot enough to burn his mouth, but the warm food was a blessing on his stomach. He devoured both of them, sipping on the milk from the second coconut.

After he finished, he rose and took a tentative step toward the rock. The falcon kept her eyes on him, but stayed in place as Heru-pa reached the base and climbed up. When he reached the top, Bennu eyed him guardedly, but did not bristle or move. He eased down next to the bird, sitting quietly beside it until the sky began to darken, and the falcon took flight.

"I will see you tomorrow, Bennu," he called out after her before climbing down and crawling into the shelter.

That evening, Heru-pa fell asleep with a smile on his face.

———

THE BEAST FLICKED its tongue over the sand. The faint scent it had picked up was imperceptible to even the most sensitive creatures, but the trace had led it to the edge of the creek, where the smell grew infinitesimally stronger. The beast's brain had no concept of anticipation, yet it sensed the energy that tingled through its long, writhing body, like sparks on their way to the ground.

It slid into the water.

As it glided in the dim moonlight, noiseless as a shadow, an awareness began to take shape. The beast may have lacked the words or the understanding for what stole into its mind, but it knew it had only one aim, only one target: the source of this scent.

The creature followed the trail, its senses rousing as the trace swelled with every serpentine movement. It glided to a spot on the rock and flicked its forked tongue over it. When it tasted the essence, it was as if the world had become sharper, the shapes of the trees and rocks around it more defined. It reared up its head and hissed.

The prey was within its reach.

————

HERU-PA WOKE TO A RACKET, the roof of his shelter being torn to pieces. Startled, he rushed out from beneath it. His brain took a moment to make sense of the moonlit scene. Bennu was perched atop his refuge, ripping at the branches. When the falcon spotted him, she screeched and took to the air before settling on top of the rock, beating her wings fiercely.

"Bennu," Heru-pa mumbled, wiping the sleep from his eyes. "What is wrong?"

The falcon screeched again and took flight, rising higher and higher into the air.

A warmth spread from the top of Heru-pa's head into his body and limbs. It took a heartbeat for him to realize that the strange sensation arose from the cartouche his father had inscribed. An instant later, he whirled at the noise behind him.

He froze.

A serpent, more than twice the length of a grown Rathadi and as thick as Qar's thigh slithered from the woods and into the clearing.

Heru-pa's blood iced over as recognition dawned.

A sea serpent from the ship.

The serpent lifted its body off the ground. The front third stood completely upright, its flat eyes level with Heru-pa's. Painfully slowly, he moved his hand down, wrapping his palm around the hilt of the dagger. He clenched it so tightly that the script engraved across it felt like a brand in his flesh.

The serpent hissed and lunged. Heru-pa dove aside. He pulled the dagger from the scabbard and slashed out, but it had already pulled back, coiled for another strike.

Heru-pa's mind whirled. His eyes darted to the rock. Could he make it there before the beast could reach him?

Before he had another chance to consider, the serpent lanced out again. Heru-pa twisted aside and thrust. It was blind strike, waged on instinct alone, but he felt the blade connect with the scaled skin. The serpent hissed and retreated.

Reddish-green blood tainted the edge of the dagger. Despite his dread, a thrill spread through Heru-pa. He fell into stance, his jaw set, and raised his weapon high.

"I shall not make this easy on you, beast," he said.

The serpent slithered closer and reared up again. Impossibly, it seemed to rise even higher than before. Heru-pa stared at the cold pair of eyes glaring down at him. The beast hissed again and opened its huge mouth, revealing two parallel rows of dagger-like teeth.

Heru-pa braced for the next strike.

The serpent spit.

The pain in Heru-pa's eyes was instantaneous and blinding. He screamed as the world spun around him. He staggered back, tripping over his feet.

He felt a hot knife sink into his chest and heard the clang of needle-like teeth striking metal. Panic surged through him, but the serpent hissed and drew back, as if in confusion. Heru-pa cried out and slashed wildly with his dagger. The serpent coiled, ready to strike again as he lay on the ground.

The *scree* of the falcon tore through the air. Heru-pa forced his eyes open through the burning pain to see a shadow swooping down onto the serpent's head. The serpent reared up, but the falcon held tight with her talons embedded in its scales. Before the beast had a chance to buck again, the falcon's beak plunged into its eye. The serpent coiled wildly, but Bennu held firm, her claws lodged deep in the beast's flesh. The falcon's beak pierced the other eye. The serpent reared, rising as high in the air as a grown man, then toppled to the ground, crushing the falcon beneath him.

Heru-pa cried out. He surged forward, desperately trying to protect the bird from the crushing weight of the serpent. The beast twisted and writhed, coiling around Heru-pa's body. Its grisly mouth reared open, larger than Heru-pa's head. The stench of rotten meat flooded Heru-pa's nostrils as the beast's teeth loomed over him like rows of daggers, its tips bent inward, making them appear even more grotesque.

The serpent lunged down. Heru-pa wrapped both hands around the hilt of the dagger and drove it upward through the serpent's jaw. He screamed and pushed, unleashing all his fear and rage into the single thrust, ramming the tip of the blade into the beast's brain.

The serpent thrashed wildly for a heartbeat, then two, before it collapsed on Heru-pa.

The silence was complete, as if the world was holding its breath.

Heru-pa's heart pounded in his ears as he lay pinned beneath the serpent, panting. After he gathered his breath, he twisted out of the coils and lifted up his tunic. One of the serpent's fangs was lodged in his amulet. Staving off panic, he examined the wound. A single red line trickled across his chest and stomach; it appeared that the amulet saved him and prevented a full bite. Still, there was no time to lose. He had to get back to the temple, and soon. He pushed off the ground to gain his feet when fear gripped him.

The falcon!

His eyes still raw, he crawled on his knees, desperately searching for the bird. He froze when he saw her lying motionlessly on the ground, her beak covered in the dark blood of the serpent. His hands trembled when he reached out.

The moment his skin touched the falcon, the hairs on the back of his neck stood up and stirred, as if trying to lift off.

My sentinel.

He felt the bird's quick and shallow breaths beneath his fingers. Heru-pa forced himself to rise, then pulled his dagger from the jaw of the serpent, a grim resolve on his face.

———

SET STOOD at his post outside the temple, facing the road to the

East Highlands. By tradition, it was the third pillar's duty to keep watch for the returning sojourner.

He stirred when he spotted a form in the distance. He lifted the farseeker to his eye. His heart lurched when he recognized Heru-pa, but the smile died on his lips when he noticed his friend staggering and falling to the ground. He turned to the guards.

"Fetch King Osiris and Queen Isis! Now!" he yelled, then took off.

He tore down the road as fast as his legs could carry him. He had almost made it to Heru-pa when the sound of powerful steps drew near. A breath later, the Rathadi king and queen sped past him as if he had been standing still.

Queen Isis reached her son first and sank to the ground beside him. Heru-pa's fist opened, releasing a bundle wrapped in his shawl. Set gaped at the bloody head of a giant serpent that rolled free of the cloth and came to rest at his feet.

"Amun's curse," Osiris whispered.

A moment later Thoth arrived, breathing hard. He glanced at the serpent's head, then rushed to Heru-pa.

"Did it bite you?" the old Rathadi asked, fear tainting his voice. Heru-pa's eyes rolled back into his head. Thoth shook his shoulders. "Did it bite you, boy?"

Heru-pa managed a weak nod. Isis let out a sob.

The boy's hand fumbled to his tunic, and he opened it. Set gasped at the sight of the motionless bird his friend clutched to his bare chest.

"The falcon," Heru-pa whispered. "Is it… is she alive?"

"Shush, my boy," Isis said between tears.

"Save the falcon… You must…" He swallowed, his face knotting in pain.

Isis grasped Thoth's arms. "Father! Do something!"

Thoth reached for the serpent's head and raised it to his nose. He took a cautious whiff and grimaced.

Set knelt at Heru-pa's side and reached for his friend's palm. Heru-pa's eyes fluttered open. He squeezed Set's hand. His breathing turned to slow, rattling gasps.

"I am Horus," he whispered. "Son of Isis and Osiris." He drew in a slow breath, as if to gather all his remaining energy. "I shall know no fear." His eyes rolled back, and his breathing stopped.

PART 2

TEMPEST

THE TRUTH-SEER HURRIED through the dark corridor, the light from the hanging sconces catching the flutter of her robes, casting fleeting shadows on the walls. She barely acknowledged the handful of men and women who still milled about the outer sections of the palace as they scurried out of her way and bowed their heads in a show of respect. Some among the Pure Ones revered Harwa for her gift—believing it had been bestowed by Amun himself. Some loathed her. But they all avoided her.

She ripped open the door to her chambers and rushed inside, then latched it. She pressed her back against the wood and allowed herself a moment of solace to face the turmoil of emotions that welled up.

Had she done enough to avert the vision?

There had been an age, lifetimes ago it seemed, when Harwa had been unencumbered by truth-visions. But that time had faded almost into oblivion once the visions began to make themselves known, haunting her. The first ones had arrived as she slept, sowing seeds of confusion. Later they had descended unbidden at any time, day or night, asleep or awake. Eventually, she had learned to control them—or at least to live with them.

As the Rathadi queen fell pregnant, the visions began to assail Harwa nightly: the boy's birth, then the terror, chaos and blood, screams and horror. Every night they ravaged her mind, consuming her more and more, culminating in the torment—the prophecy—that befell her when she saw him born. The one vision she could not share with his mother, or anybody.

The images that flooded the truth-seer's mind grasped at her again, almost driving her into madness as they did for the last decade, since she had glimpsed them at his birth. She pressed her hands against her temples, willing the apparitions away, but the screams of tens of thousands of throats carved at her soul.

Please... she begged silently. She collapsed onto the stone floor, whimpering. Slowly, too slowly, the images ebbed, leaving her shuddering at their shadows.

She sucked in air, trying to slow her hammering heart. She had to be strong. She had to see through the task that was placed upon her by Amun himself, for it was he who guided all visions.

Harwa forced herself up and trudged to the wardrobe in the corner of the chamber. With great effort to keep her trembling hand still, she unlocked the door, then pushed aside the thick robes on the bottom shelf. She spoke a spell and pressed a small panel on the side. The latching mechanism on the bottom of the wardrobe released with a click, and she lifted the board, widening the gap just enough to reach inside the hidden compartment.

She lifted a vial and a small box. The items appeared like any of the dozens of others that she had been using for rituals and incantations. Still, if the king or queen discovered the true nature of these items, or how she came about them, even a lifetime of service to the Pure Ones would not be able to save her. But though they may never understand her sacrifice—she had to save them.

He had to be stopped.

Harwa carefully closed the hidden compartment, ensuring it was fully concealed, then picked up a bowl and knelt down. She opened the vial and poured a drop of the dark liquid into the vessel before opening the box and reverently removing the lock of black hair from it. She took a single strand and placed it into the liquid, then suspended the bowl over a lit candle.

At first the strand clung to the surface. Finally, it dissolved and sank, hanging like a thin layer of broken silk along the smooth bottom of the bowl.

As she chanted the incantation, the mixture bubbled and hissed, and wisps of smoke rose into the air, swirling like ribbons of dye in still water. She leaned over the smoke and inhaled deeply. The ancient spellcraft coursed through her body, the familiar sensation of numbness spreading into her limbs. She recalled the first time she had succeeded in communing by dream state, after years of inquest into the deepest corners of the arts. Despite being the most powerful truth-seer in generations, her journey had been plagued by one misstep after another. Then, just over a year ago, her efforts had finally borne fruit. She relaxed her muscles and closed her eyes, allowing the drug-induced sleep to claim her.

———

WHEN HARWA OPENED HER EYES, the familiar surroundings of the chamber had been replaced by a fluid darkness. She sensed the other woman's presence before she came into view.

"It is done?" the woman spoke with a soft, almost hypnotic, voice. Only the lucid green of a pair of deep-set eyes flickered from beneath the dark hood that concealed her features.

"The boy has returned," Harwa replied.

The woman drew near, the flowing movements of the long robe ethereal against the shapeless background. "And the wyrms?"

"One has tracked him down."

The woman's posture relaxed. "Then everything is proceeding as I had planned," she said. "The poison in the boy's body will continue to spread. He will recover, in time, but not before the poison takes its toll. When the boy has been shunned, you will bring him to me."

The truth-seer stirred awkwardly.

"What is it?" the woman asked.

Harwa hesitated, staring down at her folded hands.

"Speak, truth-seer," the woman pressed, a hint of irritation creeping into the smooth voice.

"The boy has already recovered."

"So soon?"

"He killed one of the wyrms—and returned with its head. His grandfather, the archsage, recognized the poison. He devised a potion—"

The tall woman's eyes flared. Like a wraith, she shot

forward. The truth-seer winced. Even though she knew the woman could not harm her in the dream state, she drew back.

"If they succeeded in healing the boy before the poison had sufficient time…" The tall woman trailed off. "The wyrms were too young. You had assured me there would be more time."

"There was nothing more I could do to delay it further," Harwa said. "His parents were determined to move forward."

"Is there anything else I should know?"

Harwa hesitated. "The boy found his sentinel."

"He must not be allowed to join!"

"There is still a chance the poison worked," Harwa said. "Perhaps it had enough time to affect his blood and—"

The tall woman silenced her with a glare.

Harwa's throat went dry as if it had never known moisture. "Is everything lost, then?" she asked.

The woman turned, staring off into the darkness. She was silent for so long that Harwa thought she would not answer the question. Finally, she replied. "No."

Harwa leaned in and listened intently as the woman spoke.

———

THE TRUTH-SEER WOKE, her body trembling.

First the merchants, and now… him?

Harwa's mind reeled from the implication. She leaned a hand against the wall to steady herself, glad to be on the cold floor as a wave of emotions swept through. She did not fight it. It welled up out of her chest and choked her throat.

Will I be strong enough?

Harwa grasped the amulet that hung around her neck and prayed to The One for the strength to carry through the woman's bidding.

She had to be strong enough.

The destroyer must be stopped.

CHAPTER 16

THE BOY GROANED. A weight pressed against his chest. His right hand drifted toward it, the muscles responding slowly, sluggishly. The cool touch of the round metal against his fingers brought some comfort against the numbness.

"Horus?" a voice broke through the fog.

A cool palm brushed his forehead. "Horus?" the voice repeated; deep, soothing, ever in control.

The boy's mind dazed. The name rang familiar, but it was not his own.

He forced his eyes open and turned to the voice.

"Welcome back, grandson." The face that came into focus stirred with a cautious smile, but the concern that was etched in its features was not yet ready to leave.

Another hand grasped his left palm, the skin soft, the touch familiar and soothing. The boy tilted his head to the other side. His mother and father stood beside the bed, their expressions mirroring the concern in his grandfather's eyes.

"Horus, my son." His mother eased down beside him. "How are you feeling?"

Horus, the name rang through his head again.

Horus. My Rathadi name.

He gripped the metal harder as the memories slowly took shape. His mind leaped.

The serpent…

The falcon!

He lifted his head. A wave of nausea flashed through him. He clamped his jaw tight, willing himself not to get sick. A few moments later, the queasiness eased.

"The falcon?" Horus asked, surprised at the raspiness in his voice.

His grandfather placed a hand under his neck and brought a glass to his lips. "Drink," he said.

Horus lifted his hand, trying to push the glass away, but his muscles did not obey.

"Drink," Thoth repeated.

Horus took a small sip. The fluid was like sand against his parched throat. He coughed and sputtered. His mother and grandfather helped him sit up. He took another sip, then a third, before grabbing his grandfather's hand and swallowing the bitter fluid greedily until he drained the glass.

He felt the strength flowing into his body, spreading to his limbs, and pushed the glass away. "Where is the falcon? Is she…?"

His mother gave him a small smile. "Where she has been for the last three days. She has not left your side since you have returned." She pointed behind her.

Horus followed her hand. The falcon sat perched on a ledge

in the far corner of the room. The bird cocked its head when their eyes met. Horus gave a small sigh of relief.

"How is she?" he asked.

"The falcon is well," his grandfather replied, "but she would not be if you had not brought her here." He paused. "Neither of you would have survived if you had not been strong enough to return."

Isis inhaled sharply at Thoth's words and squeezed her son's hand harder.

"The falcon," Horus said. "She saved me. The serpent, it… it spit in my eyes, blinded me. The falcon attacked it when I was in its grasp."

He glanced around, fear creeping into his mind. He exhaled when he saw the onyx dagger resting on the table beside the bed.

His grandfather leaned forward. "Horus, was the falcon bitten?"

"I… I don't think so."

His grandfather leaned closer. "Are you certain, grandson? This is of utmost importance."

Horus concentrated, trying to remember. "No," he answered, after several moments. "The falcon attacked the serpent…" Horus shuddered at the memories, the twin rows of dagger-like teeth, and at the falcon's beak, stained with the serpent's dark blood. "We fought it. We defeated it—together."

"Did the falcon taste of its blood, or flesh?" Thoth pressed.

Horus nodded.

Thoth shared a look with Isis and Osiris.

"What does that mean?" Horus asked, concern rising. "What kind of serpent was that?"

"Not a serpent," his grandfather said. "A Ba'ulati wyrm. It was young, barely older than a wyrmling, but its blood had been replaced by poison."

Isis gasped at his words.

Thoth sighed. "I prayed I was wrong, but Horus confirmed what I had feared."

Isis squeezed Horus's hand even harder as his father held Thoth's gaze, his face expressionless as a slab of black marble.

Isis opened her mouth as if to say something, but closed it.

Guilt clouded his father's face. "I should have never allowed you to go. I should have been there to protect you."

Isis placed her hand on her husband's arm. "We both share the blame. I agreed to it."

"You counseled against it. You wanted to delay the valediction because of the slayings. If I hadn't convinced you..." Osiris trailed off and dropped his head.

Horus stirred. He had never seen his father look so... vulnerable. "No, *Tato*, what happened was my fault," he said.

"Don't say that, son," his mother said. "You share none of the blame."

Horus pulled back. "No, you don't understand! The day the ships attacked. I... I saw the wyrms. I wasn't sure I did, I thought maybe I was imagining it, but... but now..."

"What?" Osiris lifted his head.

"I... I wanted to tell you, *Tato*, and tell *Amah*, and grandfather too, but I thought maybe it was just a trick of the light." He turned to Thoth. "And when I told you about the woman, you were so upset..." He trailed off, fighting the heat behind his eyes.

"What woman?" Osiris asked, but Thoth gave him a look and shook his head.

The old Rathadi leaned down and cupped Horus's cheeks gently. "Do not trouble yourself with these things now, my boy. First you must rest and get stronger. There will be time to talk later."

Horus stared at his father whose scaly lips were taut with anger. "I'm sorry, *Tato*," Horus said. "I should have told you."

His father grasped his shoulder and squeezed hard. "My anger is not toward you, but those responsible for harming you," he said, fighting to restrain his voice. He gave his shoulder another squeeze and strode off.

His mother leaned down and kissed him on his forehead. "Get some sleep," she said. "You will feel much better when you wake."

Despite everything, Horus felt his eyelids growing heavy. He nodded. His mother helped him lay back down and pulled the cover over him. "Amun-Ra protect you," she said.

"I love you, *Amah*," Horus said.

"I love you, Horus," his mother replied, and the adults left the room.

CHAPTER 17

OSIRIS all but slammed the heavy door behind him. The pair of guards flanking it snapped to attention at his appearance, and flinched at the expression in his face.

Thoth motioned him and Isis to the chamber across the hall. They entered, and the old Rathadi closed the door behind them.

Thoth stood silently, stroking his beard, his gray eyes and mind distant.

"By Ra's wings, say something!" Osiris exclaimed, unable to contain himself any longer. "Who is this woman of which he spoke?"

Thoth took a deep breath as if steeling himself for what he was about to say.

"On the day of the attack, the boy told me that he saw a woman. He said that she was unaffected by the flames, and that she was holding a staff." Thoth paused. "A staff of serpents."

Isis inhaled sharply while Osiris gazed at him in sullen silence.

"There are few powerful enough to transform the blood of a

wyrm," Thoth continued. "And even fewer who hate the Rathadi sufficiently to undertake such a task." Thoth reached inside his robe and pulled out a piece of paper. He unfolded it and placed it on the table, smoothing it flat with his palm. Osiris and Isis drew closer to get a better view of the drawing.

"I have copied this image exactly from one of the ancient texts." Thoth tapped at the staff in the woman's hand. "The boy described this exact staff."

Osiris stared at the drawing. "Tiamat?"

"The Witch Queen?" Isis moaned.

Osiris barked a laughter. "To claim that the Ba'ulati came out of hiding after a century to attack us is one matter. But to suggest that somehow the Witch Queen—"

"How could she even be alive after all this time?" Isis cut in.

"She is but a myth," Osiris added.

"A myth?" Thoth's voice hardened. "As Ra is a myth?" When neither of them spoke, he continued. "Your son saw Tiamat on the ship that day. I was praying either he or I were mistaken. But Ra did not grant me that favor." He paused. "The Witch Queen has returned."

Osiris shook his head, then paced to the tall window overlooking the gardens, his hand rubbing his temples, trying to wrap his mind around the old Rathadi's words. He paced back. "Perhaps he simply imagined it."

"He described the Ba'ulati markings perfectly, as if he was standing on that cursed ship," Thoth said. "I do not believe the boy imagined anything."

Osiris opened his mouth again, but the finality in Thoth's voice froze him. He studied Thoth from beneath narrowed eyes.

The old Rathadi met his gaze. "What if the ship attack was only a diversion?"

"A diversion?" Osiris asked.

"To deposit the wyrms on our shore," Thoth said.

"To what end?" Isis asked.

Thoth remained silent for several moments before he spoke. "There are ancient stories of the Ba'ulati wyrms being used in assassinations."

Isis paled at the implication. "Are you saying the attack on Horus was planned?"

"I did not want to say it in front of the boy," Thoth replied.

"Why would anyone do that?" Isis cried out. "Why would anybody wish to harm a child?"

Thoth sensed the weight of her gaze on him. It was true that there had been stories of Ba'ulati wyrms hunting down their marks for days. But this wyrm had been different. And the poison in its blood... when he analyzed it to develop the antidote...

"I do not believe the poison was meant to kill Horus," Thoth said.

"Not meant to kill him?" Osiris scoffed. "He was on the brink of death when he returned."

"As much as it pains me to even consider these matters," Thoth said, "if somebody had wanted to assassinate the boy, they could have accomplished that task far easier." He tried to ignore the tormented expression on his daughter's face.

"That is preposterous," Osiris said. "Would there not be easier ways to poison him, too?"

"Are we truly debating—" Isis started.

Thoth lifted a calming hand. "You both must understand. I

have given this my utmost attention and considerable thought since your son's return. This poison was not meant to kill him. It was meant to work in his body over a long time. For that to happen, the boy had to be poisoned when he was on his own. If he had suffered a full bite, or if he had not been strong enough to return in time… Even if he had come back, but had not brought the wyrm's head, I would not have been able to ascertain what had happened to him, and would not have been able to prevent the poison from doing what it was designed to do in the boy and his falcon."

Isis and Osiris stared at him speechlessly, processing his words.

Osiris was the first to regain his voice. "If what you say is true, why use a wyrmling, not a mature wyrm?"

"The Ba'ulati wyrms lose their natural ability to swim as they mature. The only way to get them to the Brim during the attack was to use wyrmlings. It would be impossible to get fully grown wyrms onto the shores without anybody noticing. It was only because Horus's valediction occurred ahead of schedule that the wyrm was not fully grown when the boy encountered it."

Isis wringed her hands. "If this attack wasn't meant to… kill him…" She choked at her own words. "What was its purpose?"

"There is only one conclusion I have been able to reach," Thoth replied. "To prevent him and the falcon from joining."

"Why in Ra's name would the Witch Queen want to prevent Horus's joining?" Isis snapped, anger flaring.

"You both have known since the moment your son was born that he was far from ordinary. He comes from a union of the two oldest and most powerful Rathadi bloodlines. He is stronger and more mature than any Rathadi at his age I have ever known. His sentinel was the last step in confirming that he truly was a son of Ra. And while I do not claim to understand what the Witch Queen's plans for him might be, they should be a matter of grave concern."

"Do you…" Isis started, her voice frosted with dread. "Do you think the poison had enough time to work?"

"I cannot be certain. But I do not believe he was exposed to enough poison nor that enough time had passed."

Isis sighed in relief. "Still, perhaps we should postpone the joining ceremony?"

"The boy and the falcon have reached convergence," Osiris said. "The ceremony of joining must proceed."

"I do not believe that waiting will help," Thoth said.

Osiris swiveled his amber eyes on Thoth. "All of this to prevent Horus's joining?"

"All of this—and perhaps more," the old Rathadi replied. "Perhaps even the deaths of the Pureans."

"The deaths of the Pureans?" Osiris asked. "You said your-self the wounds were caused by a shifter. Are you implying a shifter has aligned with the Witch Queen?"

Thoth shook his head. "At first glance they seemed to have been caused by an Ursus. The types of marks, the separation between the claws, even the pattern of the swipe. But when I examined them closer—"

"You don't believe them to be caused by an Ursus now?" Osiris cut in impatiently.

"The wounds are too shallow. An Ursus would have struck with greater force."

"Someone tried to make it look like the Pureans were slain by a Rathadi shifter?" Isis asked.

Thoth nodded.

"Who?"

"Perhaps an accomplice of the Witch Queen."

"On the island?" Osiris asked. "Impossible."

"I thought so myself at first, until the boy was attacked by the wyrm," Thoth countered.

Osiris and Isis stared at him, waiting for him to continue.

The old Rathadi stirred uncomfortably. "This may be even more disturbing than everything we have discussed thus far," he said. "The victims' own blood is used to imprint the wyrms on them."

Isis's mouth gaped open, her body growing rigid. "Tiamat had access to Horus's blood?"

"She or the accomplice," Thoth replied.

"And you think this accomplice also killed the Pureans?" Isis asked.

"Why would the Witch Queen care about killing Pureans?" Osiris cut in before Thoth had a chance to reply.

Thoth pressed his thumb and forefinger against the bridge of his nose. "I could think of two reasons," he said.

Isis inhaled sharply, as sudden realization rose. "To dissuade us from assenting to Heru-pa's valediction ceremony. Giving the wyrms enough time to mature."

Thoth nodded.

"And the second reason?" Osiris asked.

"To sow discord between us and the Pure Ones," Thoth replied. "If she is indeed mounting an attack, she must weaken our alliance. She knows she cannot win if the Rathadi stand united with the Pureans."

"If there is an impending attack, we have to be prepared," Isis said. "We have to tell Geb."

"Tell him what? Our conjectures and ideations?" Osiris challenged. "About the Witch Queen and her accomplice on the island who murders Pureans, and tries to make it look like a shifter?"

"We must be prepared if she attacks again," Isis pressed. "We need Geb for that." She paused. "Unless…" She turned to Thoth. "The weapon you have been developing, is it ready?"

"No," Thoth replied.

"When Horus told me—"

"It is still not safe for the Pureans."

"But if the Witch Queen or the Ba'ulati were to mount a full offensive…"

"It will be effective against the Ba'ulati," Thoth replied.

Isis nodded, her posture relaxing. "Then we have some time. We must find the accomplice. That will provide the proof Geb requires."

"And how do you propose we go about collecting this proof?" Osiris asked.

"Perhaps we should consult a truth-seer?" Isis suggested.

"You want to involve a Purean in this?" Osiris asked.

"It is not an unreasonable suggestion," Thoth offered. "Truth-seers may be Purean, but they are bound by their blood oath to speak true."

"Harwa is the strongest of them," Isis said. "If anybody can help us, she will."

Osiris frowned. "I do not trust her."

"We do not have to trust her as long as we know that if she speaks a lie, she will lose her power of truth-telling," Thoth said.

"Be that as it may, the old hag makes me itchier than a hundred stingwings," Osiris said. He lifted his palm before either of the pair could say anything. "But if you think it may help shed light on this, I am willing to concede. As long as I am not the one who has to call on her."

CHAPTER 18

HARWA LEANED over the table and scrutinized the collection of herbs that her acolyte had gathered in the morning. Studying plants had remained one of the few indulgences the truth-seer allowed herself these days. She lifted the foxglove and plucked one of the berries from the stem. She crushed it between thumb and forefinger and lifted it to her nose. *Too bitter.* She pinched her face. *Harvested a week too soon.* After studying with her for six months, the girl should know better. She moved to the next herb and picked up a stalk of the lungwort. The red, egg-shaped leaves were subtle against her fingertips. She took a sniff and nodded approvingly. The fickle herb had been particularly difficult to find during—

The knock at the door snapped her from her thoughts. She shook off the distraction and leaned over the lungwort again, barely aware of her acolyte's light footsteps skimming across the chamber to the door.

"Mistress?" Mia called out.

"Yes?" she answered, not trying to hide the irritation in her voice. She had specifically instructed the girl she did not want to be disturbed. She lifted her head toward the door.

The air seemed to drain from her lungs, and she barely managed to stifle a gasp at the sight of the Rathadi queen, flanked by a pair of her guards.

How did they find out? And so soon?

Harwa braced herself for the guards to rush in and pin her down, shackling her into irons, but to her surprise they remained standing, and the Rathadi queen gave her a small smile.

Harwa stood and bowed low, certain that the shock in her face betrayed her. "Queen Isis," she said, unable to keep the tremor from her voice as she approached the door. "To what do I owe this honor?" Harwa eyed the guards, still standing like statues beside the queen.

"Truth-seer," the queen said in greeting. "Is there a place we may talk privately?"

"Yes, of course," Harwa said. "Please forgive my manners." She stepped aside and invited the queen in with another bow. Isis motioned for her two guards to stay outside and entered Harwa's chambers.

The truth-seer turned to Mia. "Leave us," she said. The girl nodded, bowed to the queen and scurried out, closing the door behind her.

Harwa pulled out a wooden chair and beckoned Isis to sit. "Please forgive the accommodations, Your Highness."

The queen dismissed the comment with a gracious wave and eased into the chair.

"May I offer you tea?" Harwa asked, and Isis nodded.

Harwa fetched the pot of tea from her work bench and

placed two glasses on the table. She strained to keep her hand from trembling as she poured the tea before taking her own seat.

The queen lifted the steaming liquid to her lips and took a small sip. She gave a contented sigh. "It's blissful."

Harwa gave a bow and produced a thin smile. "Your Highness is too kind. I suppose it is one of the advantages of knowing herbs."

The queen returned her smile and took another sip.

"How is the prince faring?" Harwa asked.

"He is recovering well, thank you," Isis replied.

"Thank Amun," Harwa said.

The queen only nodded. Harwa waited for Isis to continue, but the Rathadi queen remained silent, sipping her tea, as if lost in her own thoughts. Finally, Harwa interrupted the silence. "How might I be of service to Your Highness?"

The Rathadi queen raised her head, drawing back. She placed the glass on the table. "I am here in matters concerning my son."

Harwa tensed, but she took solace from the lack of anything accusatory in the other woman's tone or expression.

"Of course," she replied. "I am at your disposal. Is there anything I can do to assist with his recovery?"

"No," Isis said. "It is of a different matter. One surrounding the circumstances of what had befallen him during his sojourn."

Harwa tensed again. What game was the queen playing? Was it some kind of trick to bait her into revealing something to implicate herself?

Before she had a chance to respond, Isis spoke again. "We have reasons to believe that the attack on the island and the attack on my son are related. We wish to conscript your assistance in resolving this matter."

How—? This time Harwa was unable to hide her gasp. Fortunately, the queen seemed to misinterpret it.

"I understand how startling this revelation may be," Isis said.

Harwa swallowed to gain her voice. "D-do you have any evidence to point toward that conclusion?"

"Nothing beyond conjectures, at this time," Isis replied, and again Harwa strained to find any hint of suspicion, but came up lacking.

"Please tell me what you suspect," the truth-seer said.

Isis nodded slowly, her expression distant. Finally, she asked, "Can I trust you?"

"My entire life has been devoted to the well-being of our home," Harwa replied. "And as a truth-seer, I am bound to speak true, on pain of losing my gift of visions." She lifted the glass to her mouth and blew on the tea to cool it.

Isis nodded again, then paused, as if to prepare herself for what she was about to say. "What do you know about Tiamat?"

Harwa's hand twitched, and the hot liquid burned her fingers. She stifled a pained hiss and just barely managed not to drop her drink.

"Th-the Witch Queen?" she sputtered.

The queen nodded.

Harwa set the tea down and put on an expression of deep thought, straining to compose her face as her stomach churned and flipped. "My knowledge stems from what has been passed down in the ancient texts," she said. "The forbidden tomes," she added, lowering her voice.

The queen peered out of the window into the dark sky. "Do you know why these tomes were forbidden to all but a handful of us?"

"Because they do not agree with what we are taught, with our myth and our history."

"No." The queen shook her head. "They are forbidden because that knowledge is not meant to burden our people. That responsibility is to reside with those who rule, to show us the consequences of our actions if we allow ourselves to lead our people against each other." She pushed her glass away and rested her elbows on the table, steepling her fingers. "The Witch Queen may be attempting to finish what she was not able to accomplish millennia ago."

"How could she even be alive after all this time?" Harwa asked.

"My father seems quite certain in his opinion."

Harwa shifted uncomfortably. "Forgive me, Your Highness, it is just... so much to take in at once. Are we truly discussing the possibility that the Witch Queen is responsible for the attack on the island?"

"That and more," Isis said. "We fear that she may have an accomplice among us."

A bolt of panic went through Harwa. She forced herself not to react despite the gorge rising up in the back of her throat. "An accomplice?"

The queen nodded, once again misinterpreting the shock in her voice.

"W-why do you think so?" Harwa asked.

Isis hesitated.

"Your Highness," Harwa pressed. "You asked for my help,

but I am afraid my help will be of limited use if I do not know—"

"A second Pure One has been slain," Isis said.

Harwa inhaled sharply. "When?"

"Several days ago, before the Day of Unity."

"Does King Geb know?"

Isis shook her head. Harwa stared at her, surprised. "But why keep the information from him?"

"We did not wish to spoil the celebration. And my father needed time to investigate the slaying before we brought evidence to King Geb."

"Was it the same killer?" Harwa asked. "The... shifter?"

"According to my father, it was not the work of a shifter. But he does believe the accomplice is responsible for both slayings."

Harwa took a moment to collect her thoughts. She remained motionless while everything inside her shrieked. "With all due respect, Your Highness, these are bold statements. Have you any proof to back up those claims?"

"My father is working on it," she said.

Harwa held her breath.

"We shall share all available information with the king and queen, in time."

"You will continue withholding this information from His Majesty?"

"Our final piece of information is missing."

"The identity of the accomplice," Harwa offered.

Isis leaned forward. "We need your help, Truth-seer. We need you to help us find the accomplice. Then we will inform King Geb."

"Y-you want me to help you find the Witch Queen's accomplice?"

The Rathadi queen nodded. "Will you help us?"

"I… I shall consult the sacred waters and the visions, Your Highness," Harwa stammered.

"Thank you," Isis said.

"It is my honor and privilege, Your Highness."

Isis rose from the chair. "I am thankful for your time and hospitality, Truth-seer."

Harwa stood and bowed low. "And I for your visit and trust, Your Highness." She accompanied the queen to the door and opened it.

"Your Highness?" Harwa said, as the queen stepped out.

Isis stopped.

"You must understand that if His Majesty, or anybody, asks me about the second slaying, I shall have no choice but to answer truthfully."

"I know the oath that binds your truth-seeing to your truth-speaking. And I am aware of the risk I took by asking for your assistance." A glint of darkness broke through the queen's tranquil eyes. "It is a risk I am willing to accept in exchange for information that may bring me to those responsible for harming my son."

Harwa lowered her head, unable to hold the queen's gaze. She deftly turned it into another bow that she held until the queen left her chambers.

She closed the door behind her and took a shuddering breath. Her hands trembled when she bolted her door shut and collapsed against it. A long time later, after she had gathered herself, she rose, then shuffled to the wardrobe and unlocked the secret compartment.

She collected the items and prepared the spell. When the vapors filled the chamber, she took a deep breath and faded into the dream state.

The mist cleared, and the tall woman materialized.

"The Rathadi queen visited me!" Harwa said before the other woman's form was complete. "They must suspect something! She—"

"Quiet, you shrew," the woman silenced her. "Cease your blabbering and tell me what happened."

Harwa flinched like a young acolyte reprimanded by her mistress. She took a calming breath and relayed the visit of the Rathadi queen.

After she finished, Tiamat's lips curved into a dark smile. "If the Rathadi queen had suspected you of playing a role in poisoning her son, you would already be dead."

"She does not know?"

"No," the Witch Queen replied. "And, what is more important, and infinitely useful, she asked for your help." She paused. "We shall use it to our advantage."

Harwa nodded, but could not hide the trepidation from her face.

The Witch Queen edged closer. Harwa knew that scents did not pass through the dream state, yet an acrid smell seemed to shroud her when the other woman drew near. "When you first succeeded in summoning me," Tiamat said, her voice smooth, "you professed your loyalty in exchange for salvation of your island from the destroyer. The culmination of your efforts is almost upon us. You must continue trusting me."

"What if they ask me?" Harwa said. "What if they ask, and I will have to answer truthfully?"

"Your cunningness has served you well for decades. Use it. The plan must proceed as I have instructed."

"Yes, My Queen," Harwa said.

"We must discredit the old Rathadi before he has an opportunity to confer with the Purean king. You must tell Geb about the second body the Rathadi found. The king will want to question Thoth. The archsage will have no other recourse but to reveal that he kept information from Geb. It will strain his credibility, and their relationship."

"As you wish, My Queen."

Tiamat considered. "Now to the more important matter," she said, and drew even closer.

Harwa listened attentively, doing all she could to remain composed, as the Witch Queen outlined her instructions.

———

MIA APPROACHED the door to her mistress's chambers. She lifted her hand to knock when she heard the truth-seer's voice and froze mid-motion. She had been certain she saw the Rathadi queen and her escort depart and had assumed her mistress was alone. She stood for a moment, unsure of what to do, then pressed her ear against the door.

"Yes, My Queen," she heard Harwa say.

My Queen? Mia wondered. Harwa would not address Queen Isis that way... Had Queen Nuit paid the truth-seer a visit, as well? If that was the case, where were the royal guards?

She continued listening, but there was only silence. Finally, as she was about to lift her ear from the door, she heard Harwa's voice again.

"It shall be as you command."

Mia jumped back. She turned to leave, but Harwa had not dismissed her for the day. She stood, conflicted, for several heartbeats, before she summoned up courage and knocked.

A moment later, the door swung open. Perhaps Mia only imagined it, but the old truth-seer's face appeared even more pale than usual.

"Ah, Mia," she said.

"May I get you anything before I leave for the day, Mistress?" Mia asked.

"No, thank you, girl," Harwa replied.

"Or your visitor?" Mia added.

Harwa's eyes narrowed imperceptibly. "There is nobody else here but me. Queen Isis has already left."

"Of course, Mistress." Mia peeked into the room and caught the open wardrobe. "Would you like me to tidy up your chambers before I go home?"

"That would be appreciated," the truth-seer replied. She stepped aside to let Mia in, then closed the door.

"I shall be in my study," Harwa said, and wandered off to the other room.

Mia cleared the table and washed the dishes. She picked up the truth-seer's coat from a chair and hung it in the wardrobe when she spotted a small crack between the bottom shelf and the floorboard. She threw a quick glance over her shoulder. Harwa was still in her study. Mia lifted the board and gasped when a hidden compartment was revealed. An assortment of vials and small boxes filled the space. A larger rectangular box was wedged against the back wall. Mia glanced behind her again. Her heart pounded when she lifted the lid.

She narrowed her eyes at the sight of a metal gauntlet with four large claws in place of the fingers. A noise from the other room stirred her. She quickly closed the box and lowered the shelf.

She closed the door of the wardrobe, flinching when Harwa appeared beside her. Mia stood frozen, but the truth-seer gave her a smile. "Thank you for your help, Mia," she said.

"O-of course, Mistress," Mia stammered. "Will there be anything else you will require of me tonight?"

"Not tonight, but tomorrow, first thing in the morning, I would like you to inform the King's Magister that I am seeking an audience with His Majesty."

"Y-yes, Mistress. As you wish."

"After that, make your way here. We have much work cataloguing the herbs you collected."

"Yes, Mistress," Mia said with a bow. "Amun protect you."

"And you, child," Harwa replied.

Mia forced herself to step slowly to the door. As soon as she was through and closed it behind her, she took off running and did not stop until she reached her home.

CHAPTER 19

"No, the other way," Thoth admonished his apprentice. "Turn the dial the other way."

"I beg your forgiveness, Honored One," the young Rathadi stammered.

Thoth sighed. As the archsage to the diarchy, he had both Purean and Rathadi hopeful lining up for an opportunity to study under him. Almost without fail, he turned them all away. He preferred working alone, and—given the nature of some of his projects—it was decidedly better that way. He caved in at the request of his daughter to take on this young Rathadi. She said he was the brightest student she had seen. So far, she had been right. As usual.

It had been two days since his conversation with Isis and Osiris, yet he was still unable to put it out of his mind. By Amun-Ra's grace, Heru-pa—*Horus*—was recovering well. He smiled at the thought of his grandson, pride stirring in his chest. Not only had the boy successfully converged with the most noble of all sentinels, he had managed to defeat a Ba'ulati wyrmling in the process.

His smile wilted.

But what if the cost had been too great? Had he done enough to counteract the poison? The preparations for Horus's joining ceremony were well underway, but he could not shake the sense of dread when he thought about it. Since his grandson's birth, it had been clear that the boy was not ordinary. His valediction sojourn had silenced the last remaining skeptics. Now, on the verge of the boy's most important rite, Thoth could only pray that his own actions were sufficient to protect his grandson and Horus's sentinel.

"Honored One?" The voice of his apprentice drew him back.

"Yes, yes," Thoth said, and moved closer to the assemblage of connected glass and metal containers arranged on the table.

He had long observed the lightning discharge and surmised that the small spark that flies between his finger and an object on the ground after he had been walking on a rug were manifestations of the same phenomenon, just on a vastly smaller scale. He had seen the force of a lightning strike only once from up close, and it was an experience he would never forget, nor cared to repeat. Yet, if he could learn to harness this force at even a fraction of its scale, he speculated it would generate more power than all the thermal energy from the hot springs in the entire Kingdom.

He brought the lodestone closer to the circular coil wrapped with wires of copper that he and his apprentice had constructed.

The door opened, and he turned, annoyed, ready to admonish whomever presumed to enter his work chambers unannounced and unbidden. He opened his mouth when he spotted the frowning countenance of the Purean king.

"Your Majesty," Thoth said. "I wasn't expecting you. I—"

Geb strode into the work chamber wordlessly. Two of his guards entered behind the king and took stations on either side of the door, their faces expressionless and cold like the steel that hung at their sides.

"Leave us," the king told Thoth's apprentice. The boy cringed and managed a deep bow to the king and Thoth, then scurried out of the room.

Geb waited until the guards closed the door behind the boy then said, "It seems that my statement became prophetic."

"I beg your forgiveness, Majesty?" Thoth uttered.

"I told you that I allowed you too much freedom," Geb replied. "It appears that has indeed been the case, and you have abused my trust."

"Your Majesty—" Thoth began.

"Has another Pure One been slain?" Geb interrupted.

Thoth's open mouth closed with a snap.

"Answer my question, Archsage."

The old Rathadi's chest tightened. He forced a placid tone into his voice. "Yes, Your Majesty."

"Why have I not been informed of it?"

"I wanted to ensure that we had sufficient evidence to report. You must believe—"

"I must do nothing!"

Thoth bowed. "A poor choice of words. I beg your forgiveness. What I simply meant is that there was a good reason to wait."

"Did King Osiris know about the second slaying?"

Thoth hesitated before nodding. Geb's face grew a shade darker.

"The body was found on the eve of the Day of Unity celebration," Thoth said. "We thought it was prudent not to detract from the celebration with—"

"Was it another shifter attack?" Geb cut in.

"I... I do not believe either of the attacks was caused by a shifter."

"Then why withhold that you found the second body?"

"I needed more time before presenting the conjecture to you."

"First you speak of evidence. Now it is conjecture. Which one shall it be, Archsage?" the king asked, growing more irritated.

Thoth's mind raced, trying to salvage the situation. The face of the Purean king indicated he would not condone anything but candor.

"We believe the slayings and the attack on the island are linked," Thoth said.

The king raised both eyebrows.

"I believe that these slayings were performed to drive a wedge between the Pure Ones and the Rathadi," Thoth continued.

"To what end?"

"Together we shall rule over the island, undefeated. Divided we shall fall," Thoth replied, quoting the prophecy of unity.

"You believe somebody is trying to divide us?"

Thoth nodded.

Geb studied him intently. "And you believe the island is in danger?"

Thoth nodded again.

"Did you know it when you refused to build the weapon I tasked you with?"

"I had my suspicions."

"Yet you would leave the island vulnerable to attack, knowing we may be facing a threat?"

"We are not vulnerable, Majesty. There is a… means to keep us safe."

"Truly?"

"Yes, Majesty."

"Show me," Geb demanded.

"I am afraid that is not possible at this time. It is not yet ready."

Geb's jaw twitched. "You are not making sense, Archsage, and I grow tired of your double talk. Is it ready to keep us safe, or is it not? I demand to see it. Now."

"I assure you, Majesty, it would not be wise to—"

"Are you refusing me, Archsage?"

"No, Majesty," Thoth exclaimed. "But this weapon is different from all others I have designed."

"What is it?" Geb asked, a hint of curiosity seeping through the grumbling tone.

"It is a vapor, designed to kill."

"A vapor? Is it safe for the Pure Ones and the Rathadi?" the king asked.

Thoth remained silent.

"Speak, Archsage."

"It does not harm the Rathadi."

"Does it harm the Pure Ones?"

"It is meant to be released in the Inner Ring, in case our

defenses are breached again, so I had to ensure the Rathadi would not be harmed. I am working on providing the same protection for the Pure Ones."

"So, this lethal vapor you have brought into existence is harmless to the Rathadi—but not the Pure Ones?"

"As I said, it is not yet complete, Majesty."

"But at this point, it could be used by the Rathadi against my people?" Geb's voice grew dangerously quiet.

Thoth remained silent.

"You will answer my question, Archsage!"

"Yes, Majesty," Thoth said. "At this time it could, but please, I beg of you, allow me to—"

"You quote our prophecy of unity while you develop a weapon behind my back that could harm the Pure Ones?" Geb's voice was cold, but the hollow in his eyes was worse.

"Majesty—" Thoth began.

Geb raised a hand to cut him off. "I have heard enough for today." He pointed to his guards. "Arrest the archsage. On the charge of treason against the Kingdom."

The guards' faces twitched, but they obeyed without hesitation. They approached Thoth and positioned themselves on either side of him.

"Your Majesty," Thoth pleaded. "You are making a terrible mistake."

"Quiet, Archsage," Geb said. "I will not be swayed by your silver tongue. We shall continue our discussion in the palace dungeon."

Thoth's shoulders dropped. One of the guards grasped his arm, but he shook it off.

"I know the way," he said.

They paced through the corridor to the stairs. Thoth ignored the vexed glances of the Rathadi at the strange procession.

When they arrived at the sky carriage terminus, they found their way blocked by a formation of six Rathadi soldiers. The soldiers parted and Osiris stepped forward.

"King Geb," he said.

"King Osiris," Geb replied coolly.

"Explain this."

"The archsage and I have business together."

"Is that so?" Osiris asked. "What business?"

"That is not your concern."

"You are in my temple on my island."

Geb's face hardened. "He is being arrested on charges of treason against the Pure Ones."

"Treason against the Pure Ones?" Osiris called out. "Have you forgotten that this Rathadi has done more for the Island, including the Pure Ones, than a dozen of your own finest scholars?"

"Do not presume to lecture me, Young King," Geb said, his voice a dangerous hiss. "You knew about the weapon he was constructing, yet you chose to keep the information from me, as well."

"Because we knew you would react this way! The archsage is working on making it safe for everybody, so it can be used to protect us all."

"Yet he first designed it in such a way that it harms the Pure Ones. In a way that can be turned against us by the Rathadi."

"Why would we want to use a weapon against you?" Osiris cried out, exasperated.

"And why would you keep information about a slain Purean from me?"

Osiris's lips twisted into a grim line.

"Did you really expect my truth-teller to keep that sort of information from me?"

"King Geb," Osiris said. "You must see reason. This is not the solution you seek."

Geb inhaled. "I am willing to consider your father-in-law's service to the Pure Ones and your son's selfless deed that saved my own son's life," he said coldly. "I do not wish to tarnish Horus's upcoming joining ceremony, but this matter is not closed."

"Your Majesty," Thoth said. "I will share everything I have found out about the slayings."

"That time has passed, Archsage. We shall conduct our own investigation into the slayings, and we shall uncover the truth behind them, whether they involve a Rathadi shifter or not." He turned to his guards and said, "Release him," then strode past Osiris. The Rathadi guards parted before him, and his detail followed without a word.

After the Pureans entered the sky carriage, Thoth spoke up. "I am grateful for your intervention, yet I fear that it served to worsen Geb's mood—and his paranoia about current events." He regarded the gondola as it set off for the palace. "How did you even know?"

"Your apprentice rushed to see me," Osiris replied. "He said the Purean king seemed ill-tempered, and he feared something might be wrong. It appears his intuition was correct." He gave a wry chuckle. "I thought the poor boy was going to faint before he finished delivering the message. You should consider training him in physical vigor in addition to all the reading you force onto him."

"I shall consider it," Thoth said dryly, but he made sure to commend the apprentice for his quick thinking. "Now, I hear it is a big day for your son tomorrow, and undoubtedly there are much more important matters that require your attention. May I suggest we revisit this topic at a later time?"

Osiris studied Thoth for several moments before nodding. "Very well," he replied. "We shall continue after Horus's ceremony."

CHAPTER 20

HORUS STIRRED RESTLESSLY in the chair. His head still felt wobbly, but thankfully the bouts of nausea that had plagued him each time he sat up had dwindled. Set and Mia hovered by his side.

"I liked it better from where I was standing," Horus said.

"Enjoy the pampering," Set replied. "It won't last."

"I'm glad your parents allowed you to visit," Horus said. "With everything that's going on."

"It turns out they still have a soft spot for you," Set said.

"I can't believe your father really planned to imprison my grandfather yesterday," Horus said. "What in Ra's name is going on?"

"Everybody's been acting so strange," Mia said.

"Especially after Heru-pa's—" Set stopped himself with a soft curse. "You know, it will take us a while to get used to your adult name."

"I like it," Mia said. "It suits you. And it will suit you and the falcon."

Horus gave a small smile and rose from the chair. The room spun. Set caught him before he fell.

"Are you alright?" Mia called out in alarm.

"I'm fine," Horus replied. "Just give me a moment."

"Maybe you haven't fully recovered from the bite?" Set asked.

"We should tell your mother," Mia said. "Perhaps a healer should—?"

"No," Horus cut in. "I don't want to give them a single reason to even think about postponing the joining." He sized her up. "Besides, aren't you a healer?"

"I'm an apprentice," Mia replied.

"A mighty good one from what I've seen," Set offered.

"Just do what you do," Horus said.

Mia shot him a fretful glance.

"Come on," Horus pressed.

Mia sighed. "This isn't right," she said, but she approached Horus and placed her palms on his head.

"Thank you," Horus said. A tingling and warmth emanated from Mia's palms. A few moments later the dizziness ebbed.

"Better?" Set asked.

Horus nodded.

"Sit still," Mia said. "We're not done yet."

"Do you know what's going on?" Set asked. "Why my father wanted to arrest your grandfather?"

Horus hesitated. "I shouldn't tell you, but… there has been another slaying. The one we saw in the vision."

Mia drew her hands back and gave Horus a bewildered stare.

"And you're just telling us now?" Set asked accusingly.

"I promised my mother," Horus said.

Mia placed her palms on his head again, and the comfortable warmth continued. "How do you know?" she asked.

"I saw the dead body. Before my sojourn… In my grandfather's work chambers. He was examining it. I wasn't supposed to tell you, but with everything happening… I don't know what's right anymore."

"Did the shifter kill this one, too?" Set asked.

"I… I don't think so," Horus said. "My grandfather doesn't seem to think the shifter killed either one of those Pureans. I think he wanted to keep it from King Geb until he was certain. When the king found out about the second slain Purean and that my grandfather kept it from him, he grew angry."

"If not the shifter, then who?" Mia asked.

"I don't know," Horus said. "But my grandfather thinks that perhaps somebody is trying to make it look like it was an Ursus."

A wave of heat blazed from Mia's hands.

"Ow!" Horus yelped, jerking away. He turned to Mia. "What in Ra's name was—?" He stopped when he saw Mia's pale face.

"Wh-what did you say?" she choked out.

"I said that my grandfather thinks somebody is trying to make it look like a Rathadi shifter slayed these Pureans."

"No," Mia said. "Not just a shifter. You said an Ursus."

"That's right."

Mia stared at him, aghast.

"What's going on, Mia?" Set asked.

"Wh-when I was at Harwa's…" Mia stammered. "I saw a

hidden compartment in her wardrobe… I really didn't mean to be nosy, but…"

"Wait, start from the beginning," Set said.

"Well, it started when Queen Isis visited Harwa and—"

"My mother visited the truth-seer?" Horus asked.

"Yes, but that's not the strange part. I left so they could converse in private. When I returned, I thought everybody was gone; then I heard Harwa talking, but when she opened the door, nobody was there beside her."

"So the old hag was talking to herself," Horus laughed. "Do you really think this is so strange? She probably does it all the time."

"No," Mia said. "It wasn't like that. I've heard her mumbling to herself before. This was different."

"What did she say?" Set asked.

"I don't remember exactly. 'Yes, My Queen' and 'it shall be as you command' or something like that."

"Well, it's official," Set quipped, "the old truth-seer finally lost it."

"Maybe she was having a truth-vision?" Horus offered.

Mia shook her head. "I've been with her for half a year now, I know what that sounds like. And she has been acting stranger and stranger."

"So what does that have to do with the wardrobe?" Set asked.

"I'm getting to it. I was straightening out and hanging up her robe when I noticed a hidden compartment inside the wardrobe. I didn't really mean to pry, but when I looked inside, I saw this…" She trailed off, her face paling again.

"What did you see, Mia?" Set asked.

She took a deep breath. "A… a metal gauntlet with Ursus claws."

An icy shiver ran down Horus's back.

Set's jaw hung agape. He shook his head. "No, no, no…" He shook his head again, more emphatically. "Do you have any idea what you're suggesting? She is a truth-seer. She is bound by her oath to only speak the truth. If she lies even once, she would lose her powers."

"Perhaps she didn't have to lie about it," Horus offered.

"We have to tell the kings!" Set said.

"No!" Mia said. "We can't. We have no evidence. Besides, they would never believe me over the truth-seer."

Horus nodded. "Mia is right. Even if the claw gauntlet was there, by the time they'd get to it after hearing the accusation, she would have long gotten rid of it."

Set considered. "Then we just have to get it first," he said. "Mia's word is one thing, but if the Pure One's prince backs it up, it will carry different weight."

"What do you suggest?" Mia asked.

"We need to get inside and find that claw."

"You are serious," Mia said.

Set nodded.

"But we won't know when she will be home," Horus said.

A stretch of silence fell upon the room until Mia stirred. "The joining ceremony," she said. "Harwa will be there."

"Uh… so will I… and the both of you," Horus said.

Mia nodded, dejectedly.

Horus considered. "Unless…" An impish smile broadened his face. "You're a genius, Mia!"

"I am?"

"Well, I can't leave the ceremony, obviously, but you and Set could sneak out and slip into Harwa's chambers while she is out."

"And miss your Rite of Transcendence?" Set asked.

Horus clasped his friend's shoulder. "Knowing you want to be there means a great deal to me, but this is more important. If Harwa is truly involved in these slayings…"

Set pondered Horus's words, then nodded gloomily. "I suppose that's the only time we can be sure she will not be in her chambers."

"So how do we get inside?" Horus asked.

Mia gave him a sly smile. "Leave that to me."

CHAPTER 21

THE PUREAN KING paced along the dark corridor, flanked by two of his royal guards. He had been nursing a sour stomach since his encounter with the archsage two days ago. He could have forgiven Thoth his transgression of keeping the information about the second slaying from him, especially if the archsage had wanted to gather additional evidence, but the weapon he had been developing was an entirely different matter. Osiris and Isis were naive to blindly trust the old Rathadi. Regardless, he would have the answers to the slayings soon enough; Rathadi shifter or not.

He descended a set of winding stairs and approached a door at the end of the hall. The captain and two of his royal guards snapped to attention when they spotted him.

"Who is he?" Geb asked.

Captain Nebet stepped forward. "A farmer, Majesty. A Taurus. We picked him up beyond the Northern Highlands."

"Did anybody see you?"

"No, Majesty."

Geb glanced to the cell. "He is restrained?"

"Yes, Majesty."

Geb nodded. "Open it."

One of the other soldiers unlocked the door and held it ajar.

Geb stepped inside. Nebet followed him, but Geb raised his arm. "Stay outside and lock it," he said.

If the captain was surprised, he did not show it. He turned on his heel and closed the door behind Geb.

The tiny cell was bare and windowless. A hooded figure was shackled by his wrists and ankles to the wall with thick iron chains. The precautions were not excessive. Geb had witnessed the bull-like strength of a Taurus on multiple occasions. It would not bode well to take chances.

Geb moved in front of the figure.

"Wh-who is there?" a deep voice rang out from beneath the hood. "I have done nothing wrong!"

Geb waited several heartbeats, then pulled the hood off the prisoner. Fine brown hair covered the cheeks and chin of the Rathadi's long face, and his eyes were two huge orbs set deep inside his face. Geb scowled as he followed the bovine contours of the Taurus's countenance. He had almost grown accustomed to the looks of the Rathadi royals and even the insufferable Thoth. Still, every time he confronted a more bestial Rathadi, he could not repress a sense of revulsion.

"Your High-, uh, Majesty?" the Rathadi's black eyes widened in surprise.

"Those who live with the sentinel of the Taurus are hard workers, strong," Geb said. "But their intellect leaves one wanting, does it not?"

The Rathadi stared at him, confused. "I... I do not understand."

"Do you know why you are here?" Geb asked.

The Rathadi shook his head. "I have done nothing wrong," he repeated.

"I am told you keep company with a certain Rathadi who is of interest to me," Geb said. "An Ursus."

"An Ursus?"

"Yes. Specifically, a shifter."

The Rathadi blinked.

Geb moved forward and reached up to the Taurus's head. The Rathadi tried to pull back as Geb grasped his temples firmly between his palms. The Taurus struggled, but Geb held fast.

"Wh-what are you doing?" the Taurus asked, fear creeping into his voice. "I have nothing to hide. I will tell you what you need to know."

"That is very likely true," Geb said, his cold voice matching the icy expression in his eyes. "Yet I cannot take the chance that you would try to deceive me." He reached out with his mind, entering the Rathadi's head.

The Taurus moaned and cried out. He tried to resist Geb's intrusion, but his attempts were like straw huts in a cyclone. Geb barely heeded them attention as he tore through them and entered the Rathadi's memories. He focused on the image of the Ursus, honing in on the location of the information, ignoring the imploring shrieks as he pulled apart the Taurus's thoughts.

———

A HALF SPAN LATER, Geb stepped out of the cell, wiping the sweat from his brow. Despite his exhaustion, he could not hide the flush of excitement coursing through him, like that after a fresh kill on a hunt. Few activities left him as thrilled as reaping another's mind.

He approached Nebet. The captain held his gaze amid the trepidation he failed to hide.

"I have some insights for you, Captain," Geb said. He relayed to him the information he learned from the Taurus. "Find the shifter and surveil him. I want to know his every move."

"Yes, Majesty," Nebet said. "What would you like us to do with this one?"

"Bring him back to the Ring and drop him close to his home. He will not remember anything," Geb replied.

CHAPTER 22

HORUS STOOD at the terminus of the sky carriage. He squinted into the setting sun, gazing out over the Purean city as the gondola approached. His falcon circled high above the water before it soared to the temple and settled onto a high ledge.

Tomorrow we shall be one.

The thought woke shivers under his skin. The pressure in the pit of his stomach was as abrupt as it was intense. He took in deep breaths, working to slow his hammering heart.

The gondola drew closer, and he spotted Set's face. He broke into a grin that his friend returned. When the carriage stopped, the Rathadi guards opened the door.

"Welcome, Prince Set," one of the guards said.

"Thank you," Set replied, and stepped to Horus.

"It's about time," Horus said.

"It took some convincing to get my mother to let me come here again," Set said. "I told her you were nervous about your ceremony tomorrow, so she finally gave in. She made me promise we would not leave the temple grounds."

"I guess our parents are still cross with each other," Horus said dejectedly.

"They will get over it."

"Things seem different this time."

"They will," Set repeated. "They always do."

Horus couldn't help but smile at his friend's ever-positive attitude. "Well, in any case, I'm glad you're here."

"So, where are we going?" Set asked.

"You'll see." Horus lifted his arm, and the falcon swooped down and settled on the leather bracer that covered his forearm.

Set reeled back. "Whoa! That is amazing," he said after he found his voice. He approached warily and studied the falcon who returned his gaze with burning, yellow eyes. "May I touch her?"

Horus lifted the falcon to Set.

The Purean prince reached out cautiously. The falcon stirred, but allowed him to gently stroke the feathers along her back.

"She likes you," Horus said. "You're almost as good with animals as a Rathadi. My grandfather says that animals can sense one's *Ka*."

Set continued stroking the bird silently. After a while, he drew his hand back.

"Thank you—both of you," he said, his voice distant. "Have you named her?"

"Bennu," Horus replied.

"It suits her."

They descended the stairs from the platform and passed the sky gardens, then followed the colonnaded path into the open expanse of the high terrace on the roof of the temple. Horus led them before the vast triangular structure that stood in the center of the terrace.

"The sacred monument?" Set asked.

"You are my best friend," Horus said. "You will not be here tomorrow because you and Mia will be doing something that you believe is bigger than both of us." He shot him a grin. "You ready for a climb?"

"Are you sure we're allowed?"

"I am the Rathadi prince," Horus said. "And I'll be climbing the sacred monument tomorrow. Shouldn't I make sure I know the steps, so I don't slip and embarrass our royal family before all those watching?"

"Good point," Set replied. "But what about me?"

"You're here just in case I do slip. And that's our story."

He lifted his arm above his head, and the falcon took off into the air. Its powerful wings lifted the bird effortlessly until it was no more than a shadow against the night sky. It circled above the pyramid.

"It's almost as if she knows," Set said.

"She does," Horus replied, then began climbing. They ascended the monument in silence. Three hundred and forty-three steps led to the top. Three powers of the sacred number seven. Once for each vertex in a triangle, the shape that guided the Rathadi lives, representing the rays of the sun as they fell to the earth, giving life to all.

When they reached the summit, Set turned slowly, taking in the view around him. The Purean capital stood to the east beyond the channel, thousands of points of lights forming an outline against the far side of the Inner Ring as it encircled the Center Island. "It's breathtaking," he said.

Horus eased down onto the stone then stretched out on his back. Set took place beside him. They lay in silence for a long time, gazing up at the night sky, unwilling to break the spell of the sacred site.

"I'm scared," Horus said.

Set sat up. "You? Scared?"

"What if Bennu won't accept me?"

Set glanced at the bird soaring above them. "She has bound herself to you already. Why would you think she won't accept you?"

"I… I don't know. Just this feeling."

"No Rathadi has been denied the joining in decades. It won't happen to you."

"With everything that's been going on…"

"You and this great bird are meant to be one. I am not Rathadi, but even I can see that you are meant to grow old together. You have the blood of kings and queens in you, Horus. You will not be denied the joining."

Horus gave a weak smile. "When we are kings, we shall never fight."

"Ra's promise," Set said.

Horus sat up. "Amun's promise," he replied.

Set gazed to the capital. "When I was growing up, I wanted to have my father's powers."

Horus raised both eyebrows. "You wanted to be a mind queller?"

"He prefers you not call it that."

"We were always taught that being a truth-seer is the purest form of the Pure Ones' gifts," Horus said. "The powers that are rooted in the mystical domain."

"It may be pure, but is it really a gift worthy of a leader? As measured against the power of the voice, or a forger, or a *mind queller?*"

"You may not have the ability to forge elements or control a mind, but with your truth-visions you can avoid conflicts before they require the use of the other powers. You can shape the future based on the events that reveal themselves to you."

Set pondered Horus's words. "I have not thought of it that way."

"And having your people know that you always speak true is the greatest gift you can bestow on them."

"What if there comes a time when telling the truth is not an option?"

Horus studied his friend. "Has there ever been a truth-seer who lost their powers because they lied?"

Set nodded. "I was taught about the consequences of breaking the oath at a very early age."

"What happened to them?"

"After it was revealed that they had lost their powers because they spoke an untruth, they were cast out, never to return."

Set's words rang in Horus's mind as he approached the altar. He ran his palm along the rough edge, tracing the marks carved into the stone by the passage of time. Beneath the vastness of the night sky and surrounded by millennia of Rathadi history, he felt small and insignificant.

How many others have transcended here before me?

"You know, after this, things will be different," Set said, drawing him back. "Before long, I'll look like an old man compared to you."

"Ra's tail," Horus said. "We'll have decades together before that happens."

"Why is it, anyway, that the Rathadi age slower after joining with their sentinel?"

"It is the spirit of Ra," Heru-pa said. "The *Ka*. It is said that his immortal spirit touches us when we join with our sentinel and transcend. We cannot reach Ra's immortality, but he graces those that are worthy of a sentinel with long lives."

A breath of silence descended between them as Horus followed his falcon's graceful arcs across the dark sky. He grew somber. "Are you and Mia set for tomorrow?"

"Yes."

"And you're still willing to go through with it?"

"If what Mia said was true, we have no choice. If Harwa is somehow involved…"

"You're sure you'll be able to sneak out of the ceremony unseen?"

Set grinned. "Don't worry. We've got it all figured out. We'll take the bridge into the city. Mia will leave a window open in Harwa's chambers, so we can sneak in."

"And Harwa won't suspect anything?"

"I trust Mia to do things right."

"You're sure you're not doing it just to impress her, right?" Horus asked.

Set shot him a glance. "Look who's talking."

Horus felt the heat surge in his cheeks.

Set smiled and pushed him playfully. "She likes you better, anyway. If you weren't Rathadi…" He trailed off.

They sat in silence for another half span, soaking up the view and each other's company, both understanding the change tomorrow would bring, but neither willing to admit it. Finally, Set broke the silence. "I should probably head back."

Horus nodded.

Set extended his hand. "Next time we talk, you will have joined with your sentinel."

Horus grasped his forearm, and the boys pulled each other in for a long embrace.

"Brothers forever," Set whispered.

"Brothers forever," Horus replied.

CHAPTER 23

HARWA PORED over the page in her hand for the tenth time. The voice of her acolyte rang distant through the haze in her mind.

"Mistress?" Mia repeated from the adjoining chamber. "Is everything in order?"

"What?" Harwa drew back. "Yes… yes, of course," she replied reflexively.

"Forgive me for interrupting," Mia said, entering the truth-seer's study, "but the ceremony will be starting shortly."

Harwa put down the scroll and studied the young girl. Mia's long blonde hair was groomed into a tight bun, exposing the delicate lines of her pale face. Her slender body was covered by a long white robe, the traditional cloth worn to a Rathadi ceremony of joining. A twinge of regret passed through the truth-seer, but she cast it aside as quickly as it arose.

It has been foreseen. There is no other way.

Mia met her gaze. Unsure of what to make of the attention, she lowered her eyes.

"Of course," Harwa replied, straining to curve her lips into a smile. "It would not do to keep the Rathadi prince waiting on his Day of Transcendence, would it?"

The girl's cheeks flushed a bright red. "I shall fetch your cloak," she said, and scurried into the other room.

The smile Harwa had pasted onto her face wilted.

So many sacrifices.

Mia returned and helped Harwa slip into the cloak then opened the door. When they stepped into the corridor, the girl turned back, flustered.

"My deepest apologies, Mistress," she said. "I left my carryall in the other room." Before the truth-seer had an opportunity to reply, Mia dashed through the door and into the other room. A moment later she reappeared, holding her satchel. "Here it is."

"Very well," Harwa said. "Are we all set now?"

"Yes, Mistress."

The girl closed the door behind them, and Harwa locked it. The truth-seer's chambers were housed in the outer section of the royal palace, alongside the Purean nobility, senior palace employees, and officers. It was a short walk to the terminus for the sky carriage, and they cut through the royal gardens, aiming for the wide staircase.

"Are your parents going to be at the ceremony?" Harwa asked as they stepped through the meticulously manicured grounds.

"No, Mistress. Since the attack, my father has been quite taken with his work."

Harwa nodded in understanding. "No doubt the general has had his hands full."

When they reached the bottom of the stairway, Mia offered

her arm, and Harwa accepted it. They slowly ascended the long stairs until they reached the terminus.

The guards greeted them and helped them inside the cabin. A moment later the gondola moved out. They rode in silence, watching the temple in the Inner Ring growing larger as they drifted high above the channel.

"Have I told you of the first vision that ever visited me?" Harwa asked.

The girl turned to her, surprised. "N-no, Mistress."

"I was not much older than you," Harwa said. "It came upon me in my sleep. After the first time, I thought it had only been a strange dream, but the following night, the same dream repeated. After it recurred again the following night, I shared it with my parents."

"What was the dream?" Mia asked.

"A deer, trapped in a vine. It was in the woods, not far from the island. I recognized the spot right away."

"Did you find it and save it?" Mia asked.

"When I told my father, he went out and brought it back. It fed our family for a week."

Mia gaped at her, openmouthed. The truth-seer cackled. "I am only teasing you, girl. Yes, my mother and I went out and freed it."

Mia exhaled. They continued gliding over the water in silence.

As they drew nearer to the temple, the multitude of Rathadi and Pureans crowding the high terrace beneath the sacred monument became visible. The last joining ceremony of a Rathadi prince occurred decades ago, and for many Pureans this would be the only opportunity in their lifetime to witness such an event. The Royal pavilion that had been erected to host the Purean king and queen along with their entourage was the only other structure that rose above the assembled masses. The Rathadi prince's family would stand with the boy at the foot of the pyramid.

When they arrived at the terminus, Harwa stifled a frown as the sonorous chanting of the Rathadi choir reached her ears. The sounds were haunting, the melody complex, unlike the clean and refined notes of the Purean music masters.

The Rathadi guard opened the door of the gondola. "Amun-Ra's blessings, Truth-seer," he said. Harwa gave a small nod in reply, and they aimed for the staircase that brought them to the high terrace atop the Rathadi temple.

When they entered the terrace, Mia gasped, and even Harwa could not deny the imposing presence of the vast structure that rose like an island above the sea of bodies. She squinted toward the peak of the pyramid and spotted the Rathadi high priest standing motionlessly, his leathered body and face covered by a long, black robe. So'bek's right fist was wrapped around the ceremonial *was* staff, and he was flanked by two priests clad in similar robes, but lacking the single white stripe that denoted his status.

They had just joined the rear ranks of the assembly when a murmur rippled through the crowd. Harwa glanced to the wide stairway leading up to the terrace and spotted the throngs of Rathadi and Pureans part before the Rathadi prince, flanked by his mother and father. As the trio made their way through the assembly, both Rathadi and Pure Ones alike greeted them with a deep bow. When the procession neared the royal pavilion, they stopped. Horus bowed low to Geb and Nuit, and Osiris and Isis raised their hands in the Rathadi greeting. Geb and Nuit stood and returned the greeting while their entourage bowed.

As the procession continued to the sacred monument, most of the children fell in behind them to take their place at the base of the pyramid.

Mia turned to Harwa. "Mistress, may I join the procession?"

"Of course," Harwa said. "I shall remain right here in the back. Crowds make me uneasy. Find me after the ceremony."

"Thank you, Mistress, I shall." Mia gave a small curtsy and disappeared into the throng.

Harwa followed the girl with a smile that did not reach her eyes before she turned and headed in the opposite direction.

———

MIA DID all she could not to take off running after the procession. She blew out a frustrated breath. The old truth-seer just had to wait until the very last moment before coming here, didn't she? She needed to find Set and get out before the ceremony began, while everybody was still getting settled in and mingling about. Once the rite started, they'd risk somebody spotting them.

She kept her eyes peeled for Set as she squeezed through the crowd.

Where is he?

She finally spotted the white hood embroidered with gold threads and made a beeline for the Purean prince. He was surrounded by a flock of Purean and Rathadi youth, and appeared to be hobnobbing about merrily with his friends, but when she reached him, the tension in his eyes mirrored her own.

"Ah, Lady Mia!" he said in greeting.

"Amun's blessings, Prince Set," she replied, pointedly ignoring the possessive glances from the girls fawning about him. "Your queen mother wishes a word with you."

"Now?" Set replied with an exaggerated raise of his eyebrows.

"I'm afraid Her Majesty insisted," Mia said.

"Well, then I'd better not keep the queen waiting." Before the group even had a chance to voice their disappointment, he turned and joined Mia as she squeezed back through the assembly.

After a few steps, Mia pulled a plain white hood from the satchel and handed it to Set. "My apologies for tearing you away from your admirers, My Prince," she quipped, but could not hide the tension in her voice.

Set flicked her a half-hearted glare, then pulled the white hood over his head, covering the gold embroidery. "Let's get out of here before things quiet down," he replied.

They moved parallel to the pyramid, aiming for the outer edge of the crowd. Set kept his head low, letting Mia lead. Several of the onlookers aired their displeasure, but most simply moved out of the way, allowing them to pass.

The chanting stopped just as they reached the perimeter. Mia glanced back. The procession had arrived at the pyramid, and So'bek lifted his arms and began an incantation.

"Come on!" Set whispered, and they rushed for the wide stairs leading down from the high terrace into the courtyard. Set slipped off his royal robe and handed it to Mia who stuffed it into her satchel. They kept their hoods low over their faces as they quickly slipped by the Rathadi guards who flanked the courtyard gate.

They paced down the cobblestone road that led to the bridge. Ahead of them, a pack of young Pureans headed for the capital. Mia and Set picked up the pace to close the gap before they reached the city gates. Mia held her breath as they drew near the Purean guards, but the soldiers only gave their group a cursory glance before letting them pass.

They continued on the sloping boulevard to the palace. "So far, so good," Set whispered.

Mia shot him a sidelong glance. "Don't count your chickens…"

"Just appreciating small victories along the way," Set said before drawing the hood tighter over his head as they approached the palace grounds. The entrance to the common sectors of the palace was not heavily guarded, but there was no reason to take chances. Fortunately, the two soldiers stationed at the entrance appeared to be engaged in some heated debate, and two children dressed in the garb of lower nobility hardly seemed worth their attention.

Once inside the palace grounds, they made for the feature-less stone building near the southern wall that housed the truth-seer's chambers. They circled around the back and glanced to the partly open window on the second floor.

"Are you sure you can do this?" Set asked.

"Piece of cake," Mia replied. "I will climb through the window and open the door for you."

"Maybe I should be the one—"

"I know Harwa's chambers better than you. *And* you're the crown prince. Meet me at the door."

Set looked like he was about to argue, but his lips tightened, and he nodded. He moved against the wall and gave Mia a push-up as she reached for a ledge and wedged her feet against the wall.

"Be careful," he called out softly before dashing away and disappearing around the building.

Mia pulled herself all the way onto the ledge and stood up. She carefully shimmied under the cracked window to Harwa's study. She stretched up and gently pushed the window open another hand's breadth then stopped and listened, holding her breath. *Nothing.* She pressed it open wide enough to squeeze through, then drew herself up and slipped inside.

She hopped down and made her way across the dark chamber to the living space when the room lit up. Mia froze, blinking at the sudden brightness. When her vision cleared, she stared into the eyes of the truth-seer.

"Amun's blessings, Acolyte," Harwa said. A sickly smile flickered across her inked face.

An icy terror blossomed in Mia's chest, expanding like a tumor. She gasped for breath. "M-mistress," she stammered. "I... I thought... Wh-why are you...?"

"Why am I in my own chambers?" the truth-seer asked. "I should ask you the same thing, girl."

"I..." Mia started, but found herself unable to form words.

The truth-seer approached and lifted her right hand. "Are you looking for this?"

Mia froze at the sight of the gauntlet. Her throat dried up.

She tried to scream, make some noise, but the terror over-whelmed her.

"Did you truly believe I would be so careless to leave the compartment open by mistake?" the old woman asked, her voice colder than the sea in winter. "And that I would allow you to unlatch the window, so you can sneak in?" She barked an ugly laugh. "You are only here because I allowed you to be. And now, Acolyte, it is time to play your final role."

"Wh-what are you saying?" Mia asked, the stone of fear settling inside her gut, paralyzing her.

The truth-seer lifted her left hand, opened it, and blew. The powder that she had concealed inside her fist enveloped Mia. Before the girl had a chance to react, the truth-seer spoke a word, and a flash of light blinded her, sparing her the sight of the heavy iron gauntlet barreling down on her head.

———

THE TRUTH-SEER STARED at the motionless body on the ground. Panic rose in her chest, sharp and hot, and her hands began to tremble. She had lost her soul when she had killed the first Purean merchant, but slaying the girl...

So many sacrifices.

Her mind was slipping. She dug the fingernails of her left hand into her thigh hard enough to draw blood. She hissed with pain, but the fog lifted, and her thoughts became clearer. She was not yet done. The truth-seer granted herself another moment of terror before going coldly logical again. It had been the only way to keep her sanity.

She stepped to the front door as if in a trance. Slowly, she unlocked it and allowed it to fall open, revealing the girl's body inside. She hid behind the door as it swung into the chamber.

She heard the gasp from the corridor, then Set's terrified scream cut through the air. He rushed inside and crumpled at the girl's side.

"Mia!" he cried. He bent over the blood-stained body, pulling it into his arms, quivering.

Harwa quietly closed the door and approached him, lifting the claw over her head. Time seemed to come to a standstill as she watched Set's small form beneath her, bent over Mia's lifeless body.

She brought the gauntlet down on him in a vicious strike, the four great claws ripping through the side of his neck. He did not have time to cry out. He turned and stared at her, his gaze unseeing, his mouth opening and closing soundlessly. Pain and confusion scattered from his eyes. He opened his mouth again, and blood mixed with spittle sputtered out.

Harwa dropped the claw and collapsed next to him, cradling his head.

"Be calm, My Prince," she whispered, unable to control the tears streaming down her face. "Be calm." She pulled his trembling body against her and held him close as the boy shuddered one last time before slacking in her arms.

The nausea swelled and descended upon her in a violent rush. She turned aside and retched, heaved a shuddering breath, then retched again until the taste of acid invaded her nostrils, and she was dripping with sweat and tears. Harwa forced herself to ignore the shrieking inside her and focused on her breathing, trying to erase all other thoughts from her mind. She had to act quickly. Everything depended on it. She wiped her mouth and staggered to the secret compartment, hiding the Ursus claw. She rushed to the door and peeked into the hallway. It was empty. She picked up Set and carried him out of her chambers and down the corridor. She brought him outside and into the courtyard then sank to the floor and wailed, allowing true grief to spill from her.

"The Prince!" she cried out. "Guards! To me!"

A few breaths later she was surrounded by three guards. Their faces paled when they saw their prince in Harwa's arms.

"The Prince has been slain!" Harwa wailed. "I must bring the son to the majesties!" She pointed at one of the guards. "Follow me! Bring the prince!"

The guards stood, petrified, gaping at her in stupor.

"Obey!" she screamed.

The guards flinched, and one of them picked up the prince. She ran to the sky carriage as fast as her legs would carry her. She ignored the stupefied stares of the soldiers as she rushed into the gondola followed by the guard carrying the prince.

"Get me across. Now!" she cried out. "I must get to the majesties!" She faced the guard who held the prince. "Put him down and get out," she ordered, putting as much command into her voice as she could muster. The man obeyed, and the door closed.

The gondola sped for the temple as Harwa watched the Purean city pass beneath her. The city for which all of these sacrifices had been made. She wished she would never have to leave the sky carriage, for she knew what awaited on the other side. Her true sacrifice. Her punishment. She had lost her soul murdering innocents, but the next act would seal her fate by demanding the greatest sacrifice she could offer.

The gondola docked with a jolt, and she lifted Set's body and stepped out. The Rathadi guards' faces blanched.

"Get me to the sacred monument," she commanded.

The Rathadi moved instantly. They guided her down the stairs, supporting her as she carried the body of the Purean prince.

She entered the high terrace and cut through the crowd. The Rathadi prince had just risen from the altar atop the sacred monument, and the chanting had reached its peak. She could feel the powerful aura surrounding the young Rathadi as the falcon and the boy had joined into one.

The destroyer.

A hush arose as the crowd recognized Harwa and the body she bore. It spread like a wildfire with her at its center. Before long, the Rathadi prince's eyes found hers. A heartbeat later the singing died down, and complete silence fell over the crowd.

The truth-seer held on to her powers for one last breath, savoring for one final moment the gift that had guided her life. Only then did she allow her grief to spill, channeling all of her strength and despair into the howl that rose from within. It was as if all the lies she had held back throughout her entire lifetime spewed forth at once and crescendoed to a single anguished note.

"Prince Set is dead!" she screamed. "Our prince has been slain by a Rathadi shifter!"

The destroyer's face caved into nothing at the same instant her powers bled into the stone beneath, fading forever. She screamed in agony and collapsed to the ground as chaos erupted all around her.

CHAPTER 24

THE RIPPLE of energy was alive beneath Horus's skin. It coursed through him, the power of the falcon touching every muscle, every nerve, sharpening his senses even as the truth-seer's words rang in his ears, yet his mind refused to accept their meaning. He stared at the scene that unfolded below him from the peak of the sacred monument.

His mind caught up with the words his ears perceived, and his knees buckled.

"Set!" he screamed, and rushed forward.

Strong hands pulled him back. "No, boy!" So'bek called out.

"Let me go!" Horus strained against him, but the old priest's palms were like a pair of iron vises wrapped around his arms. He watched helplessly as a squad of Purean soldiers rushed to Harwa and formed a circle around her and Set's body, while the royal guards led their king and queen down from their pavilion.

Queen Nuit drew forward, as if in a trance. When she reached the pair, she stopped, unwilling to accept the image before her. She slowly approached the lifeless body of her son and extended a hand to touch his bloody cheek.

A piercing scream rang through the night, the anguish sending an icy wash through Horus and freezing everybody in place. The Purean queen sank to her knees. All other sounds disappeared as she wailed, her long fingers trembling, hovering over the bloody gashes in her son's neck. King Geb stood behind her, motionless, his eyes hollow like those of a man long dead.

Horus's parents pushed through the crowd and approached the Purean royals. The guards opened their circle, and Osiris moved to King Geb, but the Purean king held up his hand. Osiris froze.

The king bent down and reverently lifted his son's body from Harwa's arms. Queen Nuit reached for Set, but the old truth-seer gently held the queen's hands back and put her arms around her. The crowd parted before Geb as he carried his son to the stairs leading from the high terrace, followed by his queen and the Purean soldiers. One after another, the Pureans in attendance joined the silent procession.

For what seemed like a long time, none of the Rathadi moved. Then Osiris rushed up the stairs of the pyramid followed by Qar and three guards.

"High Priest, what just happened?" Horus cried out. "Tell me what just happened?"

So'bek's reptilian eyes were a mirror of great sadness as he gazed down at Horus. "Something that will change everything," he whispered.

Osiris reached the top of the sacred monument. "Children of Amun," he called over the crowd. "Pure Ones! Hear me!"

Below him, the Pureans who were filing out from the high terrace stopped and glanced up.

"We must not rush to judgment!" Osiris continued, his voice pleading. "The Rathadi are not your enemy."

"A Rathadi killed our prince!" one of the Pureans shouted.

"We cannot know that!" Osiris replied.

"A shifter!" another exclaimed. "Your shifter slayed him! The truth-seer said so."

"We must work together to find the one responsible for this heinous act," Thoth called out from below. "We must—"

"Lies!" a voice broke in. The Purean king's face was twisted with grief and rage. "Always lies!" he screamed, spittle spraying like venom through his teeth. "You have poisoned my mind for long enough, *Archsage*. I listened to you, and now my son lies dead!" He lifted his head to Osiris. "Enough talk, Rathadi. We have all heard enough from your kind." He turned and descended the wide stairs, followed by the other Pureans.

Osiris addressed Qar who stood three steps below him. "Escort the Pure Ones back. Ensure there are no incidents, then triple the guards at the bridge and the entrance to the temple. Be prepared to seal the temple gates."

"Yes, Your Majesty," Qar said. "Are you expecting—"

"I do not know what to expect," Osiris cut him off. "But we must be prepared for anything."

Osiris faced Horus. The pain in his face shifted into great sadness. "This was to be your day of celebration…"

"Set…" Horus said. "Is he…?"

"We must get inside the temple, now," his father said.

"Is Set dead?"

Osiris remained silent.

"I want to see him!" Horus cried out. "I want to see him now!"

"No, son. That is not—"

Horus screamed, and his father pulled him into his strong arms. They stood at the top of the sacred monument, great sobs racking through his body.

CHAPTER 25

THE PUREAN QUEEN knelt at the side of the bed, her palm wrapped around her son's limp hand. Two healers hunched over the body, but she knew their efforts were futile. She barely noticed her husband standing across the room, staring at his son's bloodied form, and the truth-seer hovering in the corner.

The door to the room opened, and the captain of the Purean guard entered and sank to one knee before the king.

Geb stood still for several more breaths before he swiveled his head ever so slightly in the captain's direction.

"This… shifter. This *Ursus*," Geb spat the word like a curse. "You know how to find him." It was a statement more than a question.

"Yes, Majesty," Captain Nebet replied without looking up.

"I want his head at my feet." Geb's voice was a strained whisper.

"Yes, Majesty," Nebet repeated. He rose and rushed out.

Geb gazed at Set one more time, his face a mask of grief,

then turned on his heel and left the room, trailed by the royal guards.

The two healers continued their work. The queen grasped the woman's arm. The healer's face was pale, and she would not meet the queen's gaze.

"Is he gone?" Nuit asked.

The other healer stopped and raised his head. "We tried everything, Majesty," he said. "The wound… it was too grave."

"Get out," the queen said.

The healers stared at her, unmoving.

"Get out!" she screamed, and the pair scrambled and scurried out.

Nuit skimmed the contours of Set's face with her fingertips. She turned to Harwa, her face maddened with grief. "You have powers, Truth-seer."

The old woman approached the queen. "Majesty, I am but a truth-seer."

"I know you have more powers than you dare to admit," Nuit pressed. Her voice was filled with the anguished hope of desperation.

"Majesty—" Harwa started.

"Do something!" the queen cried out. "Anything!"

"I am powerless to do anything, Your Majesty."

The queen wailed and pressed her head against Set's chest.

"But," Harwa continued, "somebody with greater powers may be able to intercede."

Nuit raised her head. "What did you say?"

"There may be hope," Harwa said.

Nuit stared at her with wide eyes. "What are you saying, Truth-seer?"

The old woman leaned close. "It is for your ears alone, My Queen."

Nuit waved to the guards. "Leave us. I am not to be disturbed."

The guards bowed and left the room. The truth-seer waited until they closed the door behind them before she continued.

"There is somebody who may be able to bring back your son."

"Bring him back?" Nuit's voice trembled.

Harwa nodded.

"Who? Who could do such a thing?"

"Somebody much stronger than I," Harwa said. "Somebody skilled in the dark arts."

"Dark arts?"

"The strongest one who ever lived."

Nuit's eyes widened as realization struck. "She is a myth…"

"She is much more than that, Your Majesty."

"You… you know how to find her?"

"I have communed with her, on occasion."

Nuit gasped, then she shook her head, her face hardening. "But the Witch Queen, she—"

"What matters is the life of your son," Harwa cut in. "And the longer we wait, the less likely that even she can help."

The queen grimaced at the turmoil inside her. "Who would know?"

"Just you and I… and she," Harwa said.

The queen turned to her son's lifeless body. Her shoulders sagged. "Do it…" she whispered. "Save my son."

"As you wish," Harwa said. She reached into her bag and

took out a pouch and a silver bowl. She emptied the pouch into the bowl.

"What are you doing?" Nuit placed a hand on Harwa's arm.

"Now is not the time for questions. You must trust me," the truth-seer replied.

Nuit did not move her hand.

"She is the only chance you have to bring back your son," Harwa said. "We do not have much time."

Nuit sighed and removed her hand.

Harwa ignited a candle and placed it under the bowl, then took out a locket and opened it, pulling out a single black hair.

The Purean queen watched the old truth-seer, fear clinging to her ribs, as the mixture in the bowl heated, and the vapor enveloped her.

———

NUIT AWOKE WITH A START. In place of the familiar surroundings of the chamber, she was swathed in darkness. She lifted her hand, but could not see it. The living world had disappeared, and the dark was absolute, a visual silence. Panic swelled inside her.

She flinched at the touch of a palm on her arm. The old truth-seer's features emerged.

"Wh-where are we?" Nuit asked. "Am I dreaming?"

"Yes, and no," Harwa replied. "We are in the dream realm."

"The dream realm?"

"It allows us to commune with the Witch Queen."

"But how—?"

"It would take a long time to explain it to you, and even

longer for you to understand," Harwa replied. She tensed and whispered, "Prepare yourself. Tiamat approaches."

Nuit squinted into the void. A form stepped, no *glided*, toward them. As it drew nearer, Nuit could make out the woman's features beneath a dark cloak.

The Witch Queen ignored Nuit and addressed Harwa. "You brought her," she said, her voice low and toneless.

Nuit stepped forward. Movement was tenuous, like drifting beneath the surface of the sea. "Can you bring back my son?"

The Witch Queen regarded her with a curious expression. "The love and devotion of a mother."

"Stop your games, Witch!" Nuit snapped. "I am risking everything just to be here. Can you bring him back?"

"Yes," Tiamat replied.

Nuit's breath caught in her throat.

"The question is, are you willing to pay the price?" Tiamat asked.

"No price is too high to bring back my son," Nuit replied.

"Are you certain of that?"

Nuit fell to her knees at the Witch Queen's feet. "I will give you anything and everything I have. Bring back my son."

"Anything?" The Witch Queen asked.

"Yes, anything!"

"Very well," Tiamat said, her lips curving into a smile as she approached Harwa. The truth-seer knelt and bowed her head.

Tiamat placed her palms on Harwa's head. The old woman flinched as a surge of energy seemed to pass through her. She screamed, back arching, before collapsing to the ground.

Nuit gasped. "What did you do?"

"A seed of my power now resides in the truth-seer," Tiamat said.

"Does that mean she can save my son?" Nuit asked, her voice trembling.

"All in good time, Your Majesty." The Witch Queen smiled, freezing the blood beneath Nuit's skin. "First let us discuss the matter of my payment."

NUIT OPENED her eyes to the familiar surroundings of the royal chambers. Gorge rose in the back of her throat as she recalled the Witch Queen's demands.

How could she be expected to—

"We must hurry, Your Majesty," Harwa urged, snapping Nuit out of her thoughts. "There is no time left to spare."

She looked to her son, motionless on the bed. Anguish spread through her. She had to save him, no matter the cost. No matter how painful the sacrifice.

Nuit grasped Harwa's arm. "The King must never know the truth."

The truth-seer glanced at her and nodded.

Nuit took a deep breath. "What do I do?"

"Disrobe him," Harwa ordered.

Nuit's hands quivered as she slipped Set's tunic over his head, then removed his pants and underclothes. When he lay naked before them, Harwa approached. She moved aside her cloak and drew a dagger and a vial.

Nuit gasped at the sight and smell of the sticky fluid. "Is it—?"

"The blood of the Witch Queen," Harwa said. "Freely given, a most potent artifact."

She dipped the dagger in the blood and drew sinuous shapes on Set's body. After covering his skin with the patterns, she poured three drops of the blood into the gashes in the boy's neck.

"Lift his head and open his mouth," Harwa said.

Nuit stood frozen, unable to move, realizing the implication.

"Do it!" Harwa cried. "We are almost out of time!"

With an agonizing wail, Nuit did as the old woman bid. Her stomach churned as Harwa poured the remainder of the Witch Queen's blood into her son's mouth.

"Put him down," Harwa said, "and step back."

With Set stretched out on the bed, the truth-seer lifted her arms and began chanting. The language was coarse and guttural. Nausea spread through Nuit as the dark incantation reverberated through her mind.

The symbols on her son's body shimmered with an eerie glow, then moved and coiled, like serpents roiling over his flesh. She bit back a cry when the symbols disappeared, sinking into his body, but their outlines persisted, coiling and twisting beneath his skin.

"By Amun," she whispered. "What have I done? What kind of abomination—?"

The movement stopped, and Harwa fell to her knees, then collapsed to the floor.

The room was bathed in silence. Nuit stared at Harwa. "Did it work?" she whispered.

Harwa did not respond. She lay motionless on the floor, her breathing ragged.

"Did it work?" Nuit repeated, her voice frantic. "Is my son—?"

Set took a gasping breath.

Nuit stared at him, unwilling to allow herself the hope.

Set's eyes fluttered open, and his gaze found hers.

"Am…" he mouthed.

"Set?" Nuit approached the bed on trembling legs.

"Amma?" he repeated, his voice a little stronger.

A cry of pent up pain and relief swept through the Purean queen. She rushed forward and pulled Set to her.

"My son!" She pressed him tightly against her chest. She rocked him gently, hot tears streaming down her cheeks, soaking his hair.

"Wh-what happened?" Set asked weakly. "Where am I?"

"You're safe," Nuit said. "You're safe now."

"I… I don't remember…"

"Later," Nuit said. "Don't think about anything."

"Father?" Set asked. "Where is he?"

The queen called out, "Guards!"

The door burst open.

"Summon the king! His son lives!"

The guard's shock lasted only an instant. "Yes, Majesty!" he called out and took off.

Moments later, heavy footsteps raced across the granite floor. King Geb burst in. "Our son?" His voice quivered. "Our son is—?"

"Father?" Set called out weakly.

Geb gawked at his son. He opened and closed his mouth, but no sound escaped his lips. For several heartbeats he did not move, as if afraid to break an illusion. His eyes glistened as he staggered to the bed and fell to his knees. He pressed his cheek to Set's chest and wept.

When he lifted his head, his face and beard were wet, but his eyes shone brighter than on the day his son was born.

"How…?" he asked.

"It was Harwa," Nuit said. "The truth-seer saved our son."

CHAPTER 26

HORUS LAY IN BED. He swallowed hard against another rise of burning liquid, his body numb. He had long given up on falling asleep. Every time he closed his eyes, the image of his friend's lifeless body flashed through his mind.

It's all my fault.

His guilt and helplessness enraged him, threatened to engulf him, but he clung to his newfound strength of the sentinel as if it were a tree in a windstorm. Slowly, the rage passed and anger became grief. It welled up out of his chest and choked his throat. Tears streamed down his cheeks. For once, he did not fight them. In this private moment, he allowed his emotions to run their course freely. At last, exhaustion claimed him, coming over him in waves, starting in his muscles and sinking into his bones, before pulling him into an uneasy sleep.

THE COMMOTION OUTSIDE reached him through a sleepy haze. Footsteps scurried across the corridor, and his door burst open.

"Horus, wake up!" his mother called out.

He sat up, startled. It seemed like he had fallen asleep only an eyeblink ago. "What is it?"

She rushed to the bed and grasped his hands. "Amun-Ra has blessed us all. Set is alive!"

"Wh-what? But the truth-seer... she said..." he stammered as words failed him. He struggled to shed the fog of sleep from his brain. "I thought..."

"We all did, my son. There was much confusion. His wounds were grave, and Harwa was overcome with grief, and she erred. When Set was brought to the healers, they found him alive, just barely. Together with the truth-seer they were able to save him. They brought him back from the brink of the Otherworld."

Horus's mind reeled. "Alive," he whispered, the heat rising behind his eyes. "Can I see him?"

"I sent a message to the Purean king and queen. They have graciously agreed to let us visit. We shall depart shortly."

———

A SPAN LATER, Horus, his parents, and his grandfather had gathered at the foot of Set's bed. The Purean prince's face was pale, and a thick bandage covered his neck, but his chest moved up and down in slow, regular breaths as he slept. A pair of healers attended to him diligently.

"A miracle," Isis said.

"Indeed," Geb said. He turned to Osiris and Thoth. "My words yesterday. I should not have said what I—"

Osiris clasped his hand around the Purean king's shoulder. "We shall never speak of it again, my friend. Amun has blessed our island. Your son is alive. That is all that matters."

Geb gave him a grateful nod.

Horus glanced at the queen. His smile soured when he saw her staring at his mother, an ugly frown pasted on her face. When she caught his gaze her expression shifted, and she gave him a smile. Horus returned the smile reflexively and looked away.

"We shall leave you to yourselves," Osiris said. "You have our gratitude for allowing us to visit and for sharing with you in these joyous tidings."

"Let us declare a day of joint celebration tomorrow," Geb said. "To rejoice in my son's recovery and in your son's joining with his sentinel."

Osiris nodded. "A splendid idea. It shall be welcomed by all."

They bid their goodbyes and stepped out of the room. Horus lingered and shot a final glance at his friend. As the door closed, he spotted the captain of the Purean guard enter the room through another door. The hairs at the back of Horus's neck stirred at the expression in the man's face and the bag in his hand.

He shook it off and scurried after his parents and grandfather.

They made their way to the sky carriage, each lost in their own thoughts until Horus broke the silence. "He's going to be fine, right?" he asked, trudging between his parents.

The king and queen exchanged a look, but remained silent. From behind him, his grandfather's voice rang out. "The wound was grave, and the recovery miraculous, indeed."

Osiris only nodded.

As they stepped to the terminus, a gondola arrived. The door slammed open and a Rathadi soldier rushed out.

The Purean guards stepped in his way, but he shoved them aside and rushed for Osiris.

"Halt!" the guards yelled, and drew their swords.

"Stop!" Osiris yelled at them. The Purean guards froze.

The Rathadi soldier dropped to one knee before the king. The Pureans calmed and sheathed their swords.

"Your Majesty," the Rathadi said between heavy breaths. "I bring grave news."

Osiris tensed. "What is it?"

The guard looked up, grief and anger spilling from his eyes. "A Rathadi has been slain." He lowered his voice. "A shifter, the Ursus."

"The Ursus? Slain?"

"He has been…" the guard stopped and glanced at Horus.

"My Queen Wife," Osiris said, struggling to keep his voice composed. "Please take our son and wait for me in the gondola."

"Father, please," Horus said. "I have joined with my sentinel. I am not a Rathling anymore."

The king considered. "Very well," Osiris said. He turned to the guard. "Speak."

"The Ursus was attacked last night. And he has been… decapitated."

"What?" Osiris asked. "His head, is it…?"

"It was not with his body," the guard replied.

Osiris inhaled a sharp breath.

Isis lifted a hand to her mouth. "Who would do such a thing?"

The guard shuffled nervously.

"Is there anything else?" Osiris asked.

"Yes, Majesty. We found this at the scene." He extended his arm and held up a small piece of blue cloth.

Horus gasped as he recognized the blue of the Purean royal guards. The image of the Purean captain flashed into his mind.

"Father?" he started. "What does this—?" He stopped when his mother placed a hand on his arm.

Osiris took the piece of cloth and crushed it in his fist. "That fool!" he said through clenched teeth. "That old fool!" He turned and doubled back to the palace.

"Osiris!" Isis called after him. "Wait!" She rushed after him, followed by the guards and Horus.

They turned into the corridor and spotted the Purean king exiting the chamber.

Osiris grasped him by the front of his robes and shoved him against the wall.

"What did you do, you bastard?" Osiris bellowed, his nostrils flaring.

"Osiris, no!" Isis cried.

The Purean guards drew their swords. The Rathadi drew their blades and formed a circle, blades out, around the two kings. The Purean guards stalked forward, swords raised.

"Stop!" a voice cut through the chaos. "In Amun's name, stop this instant!"

Both squads of guards froze.

"My Kings! I implore you. You must cease this madness at once!" Thoth cried out.

"Osiris, let him go!" Isis pleaded.

"Father, please," Horus begged.

Osiris glanced about him then released Geb. "Why?" he seethed.

"King Osiris, have you lost your mind?" Geb asked.

"Why did you have him killed?"

"I have no idea what you are—"

"The Ursus! Are you denying that you ordered the shifter slain?" Osiris lifted his open palm toward Geb.

The Purean king's eyes narrowed imperceptibly as he recognized the blue cloth. "If my guards acted, they did so without my knowledge," he said. "You have my word that they shall be punished."

"You mean to tell me your royal guards acted without your orders?"

"The Prince was like a son to them," Geb said. "I promise you, I shall get to the bottom of this."

"My Kings," Thoth said. "The last several days have been... eventful. I beseech you. Let us retire and cool our tempers, so that wiser heads may prevail. There is much to celebrate. Prince Set's miraculous survival, Prince Horus's transcendence. This should be a time of joy. The peace between our people has been preserved for millennia. Let it not be spoiled in your reign."

The two monarchs faced off for several moments. Nobody seemed to breathe. Finally, Osiris took a step back and gave a small bow.

"Forgive me, Majesty," he said. "I have forgotten myself."

Geb appeared to relax, but his eyes remained cold.

"I understand, my friend. I grieve with you for the loss of your kin, but I assure you, I had no knowledge of this."

The guards on both sides lowered their blades. A moment later Qar and the Rathadi sheathed their weapons, and the Pureans followed suit.

Osiris turned on his heel and strode off.

CHAPTER 27

Nuit watched the Rathadi king and his entourage depart. She moved to her husband and smoothed his cloak. He allowed her to fuss over him for a moment then gently pushed her back.

She resisted. He gave her a puzzled look.

"There is something we must discuss," she said.

"Now?"

"Yes. It is of utmost importance."

Geb raised his eyebrows.

"You, and I, and the truth-seer," Nuit said.

Geb studied her for a moment then nodded. He said to his guards, "Bring the truth-seer to my private chambers," then dismissed them.

As they strode to the royal chambers, every one of Nuit's steps had her heart thudding louder and faster, the Witch Queen's final words ringing through her head.

There are fates far worse for your son than a quick death.

They entered the room. Nuit took her husband's hand,

fighting to still the tremor in her own, and guided him to a large leather chair.

"Please sit," she said.

I must convince him.

A rap at the door announced the truth-seer's arrival. Nuit called her inside, and the old woman bowed to them before approaching.

The king's gaze moved from Nuit to Harwa. "What is the meaning of this?"

"Share with the king what you told me, Truth-seer," Nuit said to Harwa.

Harwa took a deep breath as if bracing herself for her own words. "Majesty," she began, "your son was dead. Beyond healing."

The king's eyes widened. "Then how... how did you...?" he uttered.

"The old spellcraft is powerful. I ventured into the Otherworld and reclaimed him."

"Old spellcraft?" Geb stood, but Nuit gently eased him back into the chair.

"When Harwa brought our son back from the Otherworld, a truth-vision came to her."

The truth-seer shuddered. "The most terrifying vision that ever descended upon me."

"What did you see?" Geb asked.

"Death, devastation..." Harwa said. "Our island... annihilated."

The king drew in a sharp breath. "And this vision, it will come true? Is there nothing that can be done to prevent it?"

"There was a... being... A light that shone bright and fought the destruction."

"What are you saying, Truth-seer? What was it? *Who* was it?"

"A daughter of the island. The one who shall save us."

"A Pure One?" Geb leaned forward in the chair.

Harwa hesitated.

"A Rathadi?" he asked.

The truth-seer looked to Nuit.

"Tell him," the queen urged. "Tell him what you told me."

"Both," Harwa said. "It was an offspring from a union between a Pure One and a Rathadi."

"Impossible." The king shook his head emphatically. "The Pure Ones and Rathadi cannot join to bear offspring."

Harwa bowed. "I am but a humble truth-seer. I am not one to judge what is placed before me." She paused. "Yet, there are ways of ensuring—"

"Spellcraft?" Geb interrupted. "You would use spellcraft in creating an offspring between the Pure Ones and Rathadi? And who shall be the parents of this... savior?"

Nuit held her breath as Harwa prepared to answer the king.

"On this, the vision was clearer than any that had visited upon me. It was to be an offspring between the Purean king and the Rathadi queen who would save us from certain doom."

Geb stared at Harwa, dumbstruck. He shifted his gaze to Nuit.

"An offspring between you and Queen Isis," Nuit said. She felt the bile rise up again as she recalled the Witch Queen's price for saving her son.

The king leaped out of the chair. "Insane!" he roared. "What kind of—"

Nuit placed a calming hand on his arm. "My Husband... this was as painful for me to hear as it is for you. But the fate of the island—"

"Preposterous! What kind of madness are you—"

"The survival of the island is at stake, My King," Nuit said.

"Your Majesty," the truth-seer said. "The island is doomed unless you act."

The king pinched the bridge of his nose and squeezed his eyelids tightly then shook his head. "Even if I were to agree to this... madness, Isis would never consent. And Osiris—"

"They would never know," Harwa said.

Geb stared at her, baffled.

Nuit drew close to him. "You are the only one who can save the island," she said. "A sacrifice must be made."

"They would not know?" he asked.

Harwa shook her head. "Isis and her king shall remain ignorant."

"How?" Geb asked.

"Spellcraft, Majesty... and deception."

The king considered the truth-seer's words in silent contemplation, his gaze fixed on the floor beneath him. He finally raised his head. "Tell me of your plan," he commanded.

CHAPTER 28

Isis closed the door after she and Osiris entered their chambers then glared at him, her face flushed. "Have you gone mad?" she burst out. "You could have been killed!"

Her husband's lips were taut with anger. "They murdered the Ursus," he shot back. "Do you truly believe that the Purean royal guard acted without Geb's orders?"

Isis moved closer to him with a look that started out annoyed but melted into something less certain. "Even if Geb did order the attack, what would you have us do? Start a war between the Rathadi and Pureans? I am not condoning anything that happened, but he believed that Ursus slayed his son. He was mad with grief."

"I cannot believe you are defending—"

"I am not defending anything or anybody, My Sun." She placed her hands on his arms. "But I am saying that—as painful as it is—there is not much we can do."

Osiris's fingers curled one by one until both hands were squeezed into tight fists. "His body has been desecrated.

Without his head we cannot even afford him a proper entombment."

At that Isis's shoulders fell.

"And the one responsible for the slayings remains at large," Osiris continued. "Has there been any word from the truth-seer?"

Isis shook her head.

Osiris scrubbed his hands over his scaly face, as if trying to wash away the frustration, then took a deep breath, struggling for composure. "I should not have done what I did."

Isis wrapped her arms around him. "Your actions may not have been justifiable, but they were understandable."

A long stretch of silence followed with each lost in their thoughts. Finally, Isis released Osiris and glanced at him, scrunching her brow.

"What is it?" he asked.

"Set's recovery. It is a miracle, but it doesn't feel... right."

Osiris nodded. "I may not be a healer or have your father's intellect, but the boy's injury looked grave."

"Why did he leave the ceremony to go to the palace?"

"Perhaps when he wakes up, he will be able to shed light on it."

"It must have been something important for him to miss Horus's joining ceremony."

"Perhaps Horus knows?" Osiris offered.

"Perhaps," Isis replied. "I shall ask him tomorrow. It has been a difficult day for all."

A knock on the door interrupted their exchange.

"Enter," Osiris called out.

Qar stepped into the chamber. "Forgive the interruption, Majesties. A message from King Geb."

Osiris raised his brow and waved him closer. He accepted the envelope before dismissing the weapons master, then broke the seal and read the note. When he finished, he stood in sullen silence.

"What is it?" Isis asked.

"Geb is calling for a Kings' Conclave."

"A Kings' Conclave? When?"

"Tomorrow," Osiris replied.

A ripple of unease passed through Isis. "That soon? There has not been a conclave in centuries."

Osiris considered. "With everything that has befallen us, calling for a conclave to deliberate face-to-face may be well advised."

"Are you sure you want to be locked in a room alone with Geb? So soon after what happened?"

Osiris gave a bitter laugh. "You should be thankful that we must leave our weapons behind."

"I am serious," Isis said, worry etching her voice. "I do not have a good feeling about this."

Osiris took his wife's hands into his own. "It may be most prudent to bring everything out in the open. There has been much tension between our people. Calling the conclave is a show of good faith from Geb." He brought her palms to his lips and kissed them. "I have made some witless decisions in the recent past, but I do not believe accepting the Purean king's invitation will be one of them."

Isis smiled at him, the golden light cresting the graceful lines of her face. "And you shall have my support."

"Thank you for standing by your foolhardy king," Osiris said. He lifted a mischievous eyebrow and moved his lips to hers. "You are far from the rash Rathadi girl you were when we met."

Isis pulled back and laughed. "My father may disagree with you on that."

"Be that as it may, you have always been the wiser one of the two of us."

She took stock of him as if she had eternity to stare without him noticing. A rush of warmth spread through her. "Knowledge speaks, but wisdom listens, My King," she replied, allowing him to pull her closer once again.

CHAPTER 29

HORUS STEPPED BRISKLY through the hallway of the lower level and followed the stairs that led him to the sanctuary beneath the temple. When he awoke this morning, he had found a message from his mother apprising him that she was assisting with the ceremony for the slain Ursus, and summoning him to the sanctuary.

The last two mornings had been both astonishing and daunting. It was as if he had opened another set of eyelids he did not know he had, and was learning to see and sense the world around him anew. The falcon's shadow was constant, a deep-rooted presence that smoldered within him, like an ember waiting to ignite. Yet even the newfound companionship of the sentinel could not drown out the chaos of the last two days and the memories that descended upon him when he closed his eyes at night.

He tried to put the thoughts out of his mind as he entered the substructure of the temple and crossed the bridge over the sacred lake. The ceremonial guards at the door to the sanctuary stood aside, and he entered.

His mother was surrounded by a handful of Rathadi clad in elder robes, including High Priest So'bek.

"Ra's blessings," Horus said.

The priests turned and nodded, and his mother replied, "Ra's blessings, Son." She excused herself from the group and indicated one of the wooden benches. Horus slid in, and she followed, taking a seat beside him.

"How are you faring?" she asked.

"I'm well, *Amah*, thank you. Is Father... feeling better?"

"He is doing well. King Geb called for a conclave to take place today."

"A conclave?" Horus blinked. "Are things that bad?"

"Your father made a serious allegation. If he was wrong, he owes King Geb an apology. If he was right..." She trailed off. "These are not the times for dangerous accusations, and there has been much unrest between our people—and our leaders. It is time for our kings to lead by example."

Horus considered her words. "Do the kings really go into the conclave unclad?"

Isis shot him a surprised look. "What?"

"That's what Mia said."

"I sure hope not." Isis smiled indulgently. "I'm quite certain that seeing the Purean king without attire is one sight your father can live without."

"Then it's just a rumor?"

"The Kings enter the conclave alone and unarmed, so it may feel like they are naked, but I can assure you, they are fully dressed."

"Thank Amun-Ra," Horus exhaled, relieved. "The thought of King Geb and Father locked in a room, parading around in the bare is... creepy."

"Ra's truth," Isis snickered. "If that was the case, I imagine the conclaves would be an even rarer occurrence."

Horus chortled. So'bek cast him a chastising glance, and he turned serious again. "When was the last conclave?"

"After the war with the Ba'ulati," Isis said.

"During Great-grandfather's reign?"

Isis nodded. Her gaze shifted, as if navigating some distant memories. "What do you know about that war?"

"It was the last time our island was invaded," Horus said. "But by Ra's grace, we prevailed, and the Ba'ulati were defeated."

She studied him for several moments, her face caught somewhere between a smile and a wince. "That is the official account. The part omitted from history texts is that the victory came at a terrible price for the Rathadi and nearly led to a war between us and the Pureans."

Horus's breath hitched, but he forced himself to sit still as Isis continued.

"The Ba'ulati ships breached the Brim Basin, and their forces overran the Inner Ring. Some Rathadi were able to reach safety behind the walls of the capital, but many did not." Her expression darkened. "The Ba'ulati were unable to take the capital, and the Purean forces along with the remaining Rathadi eventually defeated the Ba'ulati, but many hundreds of Rathadi died because the gates to the capital had been sealed before they could reach them."

Horus stared at Isis transfixed, struggling to process her words.

"The Rathadi were furious. Many called for open war with the Pureans. At the peak of the tensions, your great-grandfather called for a conclave with the Purean king. Only the two kings, no generals, courtiers, or sages. By tradition, both kings agreed to be locked inside the chamber and not to come out for food or water until they had resolved their differences. They were allowed to take a single bottle of wine inside, only to be consumed as a celebration of their agreement, not before."

"Were they successful?" Horus asked.

"We are still here, the Rathadi and the Pure Ones," Isis replied. "The Kings' Conclave is the lifeline of our diarchy, and one day it may be you in that room with the Purean king. It is inevitable that two people sharing one island ruled by two monarchs will encounter differences. If allowed to go unchecked, these may lead to war and tragedy. That is why the law of the conclave is absolute. When one of the kings calls for a conclave, the other must agree to it."

"What happens if he doesn't?" Horus asked.

Isis gave him a wistful smile. "I do not know. It has not happened yet, and I hope it never will."

A silence fell between them, and Horus shifted uncomfortably. Finally, his mother spoke. "Horus, I did not want to trouble you yesterday, but I have called you here because I must ask you an important question."

"Yes, *Amah*?"

"Do you know why Set left your ceremony?"

Horus's throat went dry. His mother regarded him through

her feline eyes, warm and free of judgment. He opened his mouth to tell her about what Mia found in Harwa's quarters and their plan for the night of his ceremony—then his mother's words flashed through his mind.

These are not the times for dangerous accusations.

He shook his head.

"Are you certain?" His mother cocked an eyebrow.

Horus nodded then looked away, unable to keep her gaze.

Isis sighed. "Very well," she said. "But if you remember anything, you tell me right away, promise?"

"Promise," Horus mumbled.

He looked to the altar in front of them. "Is it true what they say?" he asked, eager to change the topic. "That the Ursus will not be able to enter the Otherworld because his body is not whole?"

"The spirits of the ancestors will guide him to the best of their abilities," Isis replied.

"Is that why Father was so upset?"

"The Ursus was one of his oldest friends."

"Do you think…" Horus started. "Do you think Father and King Geb will reach terms?"

"They act rash at times, but both are wise leaders and have the island's best interest in their minds. I believe they will." She rubbed the stubble growing on his head. "I do have some good news. Queen Nuit sent a message saying that Set was awake, and she invited you to visit him."

Horus's eyes lit up. "When?"

"Anytime."

"Like, now?"

Isis smiled and nodded. "You can escort your father on his way to the conclave, then you can see Set."

Horus gave a woot, then shrank back into the bench as So'bek shot him another glare. He gave his mother a hug and rushed out of the sanctuary.

CHAPTER 30

THE SMALL STONES crunched beneath Horus's feet as he and Set meandered between the neatly manicured bushes of hyacinths and white jasmine. The royal gardens seemed richer and brighter, the scents invading his senses, lingering in his nose and throat. His wonder grew at the gift of the sentinel as it flourished within him, making him more aware of the world that surrounded him. On his way across the channel, he had spotted an ibex grazing at the foot of the highlands at a distance that would easily take two spans to traverse. When he told his father, the king had only smiled. Once they had arrived in the palace, he had escorted his father to the conclave tower, then rushed to meet Set in the gardens.

His friend tugged at the bandage that covered his neck. Horus shot him a sidelong glance. "You probably shouldn't—"

"It's itchy as a hundred prickle-ants," Set said.

Horus's lips tugged into a smile at Set's words. Two days ago, he thought he would never hear him speak again.

"What?" Set asked.

Horus shook his head. "Nothing… I'm just glad we can spend time together."

Set snorted. "I wonder how long until my parents allow me to walk around by myself again."

Horus eyed the four stern-faced soldiers that surrounded them. "You cannot blame them," he said. "Especially with the way things are now."

Set grumbled under his breath, and they continued in silence, following the curved path deeper into the gardens.

"I only hope they will work things out in the conclave," Set said.

"*Amah* thinks they will," Horus said.

"Your father really attacked mine?"

Horus sighed. "Not his finest moment. Before I knew what was happening, all the guards had their weapons out. I'm not sure what would have happened if Grandfather hadn't been there."

"Why is everybody acting so uncanny?" Set asked, frustration coloring his voice. "Nobody wants to tell me anything."

Horus considered before replying. His mother warned him not to say anything that may upset Set, but he didn't want to lie to his friend. He leaned closer, making sure they were out of earshot of the guards. "My father suspects that your father ordered the slaying of one of his oldest friends."

"What?"

"The shifter. Your father thinks he was the one who attacked you."

"Maybe my father is correct?"

Horus stared at Set, mouth agape.

Set shot him a look. "What?"

"You mean you don't remember?" Horus finally managed to spit out. "Why you went back to the palace?"

"I… I was told that I was found in the outer courtyard. They asked why I was there, and not at the ceremony. Harwa and the healers said that there would be gaps in my memory, especially the events right before the attack."

"So you don't remember—" Horus lowered his voice —"our plan?"

"Our plan?"

"You and Mia…"

"Mia?" Set's face brightened at the name. "How is she?"

"I don't know," Horus said. "I haven't seen her since the ceremony. I figured with everything that's happened, her parents are keeping her at home." He paused. "You mean she hasn't visited you?"

Set shook his head. "I haven't seen her since… I actually don't remember. She and I had some sort of plan?"

They stopped at the circular pond that made up the center-piece of the royal gardens. Horus motioned Set closer. "You and Mia left the ceremony to go to Harwa's chambers," he whispered.

"Why would we do that?"

Horus explained the claw that Mia found and their plan on the evening of the ceremony. When he finished, Set gaped at him, dumbfounded. "You sure it was me who got hit on the head? We were suspecting Harwa? The same Harwa who saved my life?"

Horus picked up a flat rock and bounced it in his hand as he pondered his friend's words. After everything that has happened, their idea did seem pretty farfetched.

"Besides, if Mia had found anything to back up her claim, she'd make sure to find a way to tell us," Set continued. "She's probably embarrassed because she didn't find anything."

Horus skipped the rock across the pond, sowing rings in the glassy surface and scattering a group of loafing ducks. "You're probably right... It does sound pretty dumb, now that I think about it."

Set chuckled at the stream of indignant quacks from the affronted fowl. "Things are going to be fine. Let's go see the horses. That'll cheer you up."

"As long as I don't have to muck the stables," Horus mumbled.

They doubled back and trudged along in silence toward the royal stables. One of the guards gave Set a quizzical look as they approached the gates.

"I'm not planning on riding," Set said. "I just want to see my horses."

The guard relaxed and opened the gate for them.

"Nothing like the smell of the stable, is there?" Set asked as they entered.

Horus wrinkled his nose, trying to take shallow breaths. "You're right... nothing like it."

Set continued unperturbed to a loose box that housed a sleek mare with a glossy chestnut coat. As he drew closer, the animal snorted nervously.

"Whoa there, girl," Set said soothingly.

As he neared, the mare stomped and flipped her head, whipping her well-groomed mane.

"What's wrong with her?" Horus asked.

"I don't know," Set said, scrunching his brow.

Horus eyed the mare. "Probably not a good idea to go in."

Set looked like he was about to argue, but nodded. The mare seemed to calm as he retreated slowly and moved to the neighboring stall. The old speckled gelding that occupied it started pawing at the ground when Set approached.

"Easy there, old boy," Set said, and slowly advanced. He lifted his hand to pat the horse, but the animal shied away and snorted, pressing against the far wall of the enclosure.

Set cast Horus a quizzical look.

Horus shrugged. "Something's got them spooked."

"I learned to ride on this nag. Now he doesn't want to have anything to do with me?"

"Maybe they're just not happy you haven't visited in a while."

Set stayed silent and studied the animals as they continued prancing around nervously.

"We should probably head back," he said dejectedly. "Mother doesn't want me out too long."

Horus nodded, and they made for the exit. The guards fell in behind them as they left the stables. They stepped along quietly for several moments when Set broke the silence.

"Ever since the attack," he said timidly. "I've been having these… nightmares."

"Nightmares?" Horus cast him a curious glance.

Set nodded and paced wordlessly for several steps, his hands clenching and unclenching. "There is darkness… all around me.

Complete and empty. I feel this… compulsion to go deeper into it. Then a pull on my body, trying to hold me back… and I can't resist it." His stoic mask cracked. He tried to continue, but couldn't put any strength into his words. A tremor rattled his hand, and he lifted it to the bandage wrapped around his throat.

"It's ok… you don't have to continue," Horus said.

Set remained silent, the fear raw in his face. His eyes watered up.

"Did you tell your parents? Or Harwa?"

Set shook his head.

"You've been through so much," Horus said. "You should not be surprised you have nightmares."

Set wiped his eyes and continued for the palace. As they approached the structure, they spotted Harwa pacing toward them. Horus tensed. The truth-seer offered them a smile, but her eyes remained cold.

"Amun's blessings, My Princes. Her Majesty conveys her gratitude for your visit today, Prince Horus, but it is time for Prince Set to meet with the healer."

"Of course," Horus said. "Please let Her Majesty know that I am grateful for allowing me to visit."

Harwa gave a small bow, the sickly smile still pasted on her face.

Horus rushed through his goodbyes with Set, wasting no time to take leave and put distance between himself and the truth-seer. He wound his way to the stairs leading to the sky carriage when he spotted a high-ranking Purean officer making a beeline for him.

Horus stopped. He recognized the man from the pristine fit

of his crisp uniform, but Mia's father's face looked harrowed, with dark rings beneath his eyes.

"Prince Horus," he said, his voice raspy. "Forgive the intrusion."

"It is not an intrusion at all, General Mehet," Horus replied. "I'm glad I ran into you. How is Mia?"

The general's face darkened further. "She has gone missing," he said.

"What?"

"She has been missing since the ceremony."

"What do you mean she has been missing?" Horus's mind reeled. "And why am I only finding this out now?"

"With everything that happened to Prince Set, I was advised to not bother him, but... as a father, I cannot continue to stay quiet. I... I was told that she and Prince Set were last seen together at your ceremony. And since the three of you are friends, I thought that maybe you—"

Horus's hands began to tremble.

"Please, Prince Horus, if you have any idea where my daughter might be, I beg of you to tell me."

Horus's heart pounded like a gavel, and heat radiated to every extremity. "I... I'm sorry, General. I... I have to go. I will let you know..." Before Mia's father had a chance to respond, he was already racing back.

"Prince Horus!" the general called after him.

Horus didn't slow and rushed along the path to the royal chambers. He skipped up the stairs, two at a time, and a few moments later he burst through the door to Set's chamber. The pair of guards in Set's room tensed for a moment, but relaxed when they recognized Horus. The healer standing beside Set jerked up, startled.

"Horus!" Set called out. "What—?"

"We need to talk. Now." Horus panted between heavy breaths. "Alone."

Set stared at him for a heartbeat then turned to the guards and the healer. "May Prince Horus and I have the room?"

The men gave Set a probing look, but bowed. "As you wish, Your Highness," the healer said.

After they left and closed the door, Horus said, "Mia is gone."

Set blinked. "What do you mean gone?"

"She's been missing since the ceremony."

"Since the ceremony? And you're telling me now?"

"Her father just told me. They did not want to bother you."

"You talked to General Mehet?"

"He looked terrible. Like he hasn't slept in days."

Set scrunched his brow, absorbing Horus's words. "Do you think it could have anything to do with what Mia and I had planned that evening?"

"I don't know," Horus said. "But we have to tell somebody. Something is wrong."

"Tell whom?" Set asked.

"*Amah* asked me earlier why you left the ceremony."

"And?"

"I told her I didn't know, but I don't think she believed me." He set his jaw. "We have to tell her the truth."

"You want to tell your mother we planned on breaking into the royal truth-seer's chambers?"

"We have no choice," Horus said. "She will understand."

"Are you sure about it?"

"The other option is to tell your mother," Horus offered.

Set reached for his cloak. "Let's go find yours."

———

A QUARTER SPAN later Horus and Set stood in the Rathadi queen's chambers. Her lips were a fine line as she digested the information they shared. She stepped to the ornate sofa in the middle of the spacious room and eased into it. After a long moment, she swallowed as if to gain her voice before she faced Horus. "So, Set and Mia planned on breaking into the truth-seer's chambers during your ceremony?"

Horus nodded.

"Because Mia said she saw a metal gauntlet shaped like the claw of an Ursus. In Harwa's chambers."

Horus nodded again.

"In a secret compartment," Set added.

Isis's mouth twitched.

"I'm sorry, *Amah*," Horus said. "I should have told you sooner… We just thought you would not believe—"

"Do not dwell on it now," Isis said, trying to keep her voice even. "You did the right thing telling me about it now."

"Do you… do you think Mia is well?" Set asked.

Isis looked at him solemnly. "I cannot say."

Set's face fell.

Isis stood and aimed for the door.

"Where are you going?" Horus asked.

"To the capital," Isis replied.

"What are you going to do? The kings are in conclave."

His mother's eyes hardened. "Perhaps a Queen's Conclave is finally in order," she said, and opened the door.

"Wait! Are you going to talk to my mother?" Set asked, panic creeping into his voice.

The Rathadi queen did not respond as she closed the door behind her.

Set stared at Horus, dejected. "She's going to talk to my mother," he said, and sank into a chair.

CHAPTER 31

Osiris rested in a chair across from the Purean king. Meager light entered the cramped conclave chamber through narrow, slit-like windows near the ceiling. He and Geb had spent the last span attempting to break the ice and discussing minor topics, akin to a pair of duelists circling each other in a ring; neither willing to provide an opening nor delve into the larger issues.

Another uncomfortable pause stretched between them. Osiris cleared his throat. "Thank you for allowing my son to visit Prince Set today," he said. "It meant a great deal to him. To all of us."

"Their friendship is important to both of them," Geb replied.

"Sometimes I wonder whether we would be well served by learning from their example," Osiris said.

The Purean king smiled pensively. His hands clenched and unclenched, betraying his expressionless face. Noticing them, he stretched them flat on the narrow table that stood between them. When he spoke, his words were careful and filled with a trace of guilt. "Osiris, I have wronged you and your people."

Osiris forced himself to remain silent, waiting for Geb to continue. The Purean king stood and pulled at his robes to straighten them. "The Rathadi shifter... I did order my men to find him."

Osiris opened his mouth, but Geb raised a forestalling hand. "Please hear me out, Old Friend."

The Rathadi king fought down a surge of temper at the words but willed himself to let Geb continue.

"Amun be blessed for the life of my son, but he was still attacked by a shifter. I had to protect my people."

Osiris blew out a frustrated breath. "It was not a shifter!"

"But the marks on Set and the others who were slain seem to confirm it. And Harwa said she saw the shifter attack Set—"

"I do not know what your truth-seer saw," Osiris snapped, anger flaring. "That shifter did not kill the two Pureans and injure your son."

"But we have evidence—"

"I have known that Ursus my entire life. He was not to blame. Thoth examined the body. He said that even though the wounds appear to have been caused by an Ursus at first glance, they are too superficial."

"What are you saying?"

"That somebody tried to make it appear as if the deaths had been caused by a Rathadi shifter."

Geb stared at him, his body rigid. "Why would anybody do that?"

"I can only venture a guess." Osiris shrugged. "Perhaps to sow discord between our people?"

Geb pressed thumb and forefinger against his eyes. "Are you certain?"

"I cannot be. But we both know that the archsage is seldom mistaken."

Geb considered Osiris's words then lowered his head. "If that holds true, I was in the wrong, and I can never undo what I have done," he said. "For that I beg forgiveness of you and your people." He closed his eyes. "I was mad with grief. Regardless of whether or not the Ursus was guilty, I should have never acted without first consulting you. But… when I found out that my son had been slain… and I thought this shifter was the one who—"

"The Ursus's body must be made whole," Osiris said. "Before his burial ceremony."

Geb looked up. "I want you to know that the head has been… kept with dignity. It shall be returned so he can be prepared for the journey into the Otherworld." He paused. "I understand my actions do not place me in a position to request anything of you, but for the sake of peace between our people, I ask you not to disclose the Ursus's true cause of death."

"You want me to lie to my people?"

"If these actions were meant to sow discord between us, as you suspect, would revealing what happened not simply serve to add fuel to the fire, and help those responsible for these heinous crimes achieve exactly what they had hoped to accomplish?"

A long breath of silence stretched to the point of breaking as Osiris considered Geb's words. Finally, the Rathadi king nodded.

Geb exhaled. "Have you any idea who may be responsible for it?"

Osiris hesitated.

"You do?"

"It is but a conjecture, brought forth by Thoth," Osiris replied. "He said my son saw something during the attack on our island."

"You think the slayings are linked to this attack?"

"The timing is too conspicuous to be coincidental," Osiris continued. "Horus described a woman who Thoth believes to be the Witch Queen on the ship that broke through the gates."

Geb stared at him, then he barked a laugh. "The Witch Queen? Tiamat?" He shook his head. "First the Ba'ulati, now the Witch Queen? Perhaps our archsage—"

"My son was attacked by a Ba'ulati wyrm that was brought to our island on that ship," Osiris said, doing his best to leach the bitterness from his words. "Thoth said that its blood had been replaced by poison. A poison created to prevent him from joining with his sentinel."

Geb's cynical grin folded into a frown.

"The Witch Queen could not have acted alone," Osiris continued. "She must have an accomplice on the island."

"And you think this... accomplice is responsible for the slayings?"

"Thoth believes that it is part of the Witch Queen's plan to mount an attack on the island."

"If there is an impending attack, we must prepare."

"I agree," Osiris said. "Give Thoth your blessing to continue his work on the weapon."

The Purean king's eyes hardened. "The weapon that can harm the Pure Ones, but leave the Rathadi unscathed?"

"It is more important than ever for us to stand united. The archsage will ensure the weapon will be harmless to both the Rathadi and Pure Ones."

Geb's jaw clenched. The muscles popped out behind his cheeks as he pressed his teeth together. For several long moments nothing happened. Finally, he nodded. "As you wish," he said. "He shall have my blessing. And any support he requires."

Osiris nodded. "Thank you."

"Then we are agreed?" Geb asked.

"The Ursus's head shall be returned before his funeral ceremony," Osiris said.

"You have my promise," Geb said. "And the cause of his death?"

"It shall remain unrevealed," Osiris replied. "Thoth will have your blessing and support to continue on the weapon."

"He shall," Geb confirmed.

"And we shall work together to find the one responsible for the slayings."

"No matter who it is, we shall find them," Geb said.

Osiris nodded. "Then on the matters most important to our peace we are agreed."

Geb gave a smile and eyed the bottle on the table. "Shall we discuss the details over wine?"

"Splendid idea." Osiris picked up the bottle.

"You are in my palace," Geb said, reaching out. "Please allow me." Osiris handed him the wine, and Geb opened it. An earthy aroma filled the small room as he poured the wine into two silver goblets. "To our sons," he said. "And to peace between our people."

"To our sons and peace," Osiris replied. The dry flavor lingered in his mouth after he finished the drink. He set the empty cup on the table.

Geb refilled their goblets. "We must not allow the island to fall," he said, "no matter the cost."

Osiris reached for his cup, not noticing the foreboding glint that passed through the Purean king's eyes as they both raised their drinks to their lips.

CHAPTER 32

ISIS PACED through the Purean palace to the queen's chambers. She wanted nothing more than to share Horus's revelation with her husband, but she knew the guards were prohibited from letting anyone disturb the conclave, even the queen. She had considered seeking out her father, but decided that this was a matter that needed to be confronted head-on. She turned the corner leading to Nuit's chambers—and almost ploughed into the truth-seer.

Harwa froze, her mouth opening and closing like a blow-fish. "Queen Isis," she finally managed. "I beg your forgiveness. I did not see you."

Isis composed her face, ignoring the churning in her gut. "Truth-seer," she replied, willing serenity into her voice. "How fares Prince Set?"

"By Amun's grace, he continues to improve," Harwa said. "A miracle, indeed."

"Word has it, it was the virtue of your skill that saved the prince, not a miracle."

"You humble me, Your Highness," Harwa said with a bow.

"One day, perhaps you will grace me with details," Isis said. "I have a keen interest in the... healing arts."

Harwa's eyes widened ever so slightly before she twisted her lips into a smile. "Of course, Your Highness. It would be my honor."

"Speaking of healing arts, have you seen your acolyte recently?"

Harwa's smile died with a downward twitch. "Mia?"

"Have you other acolytes?"

"No, I am afraid I have not seen her since the ceremony."

"Have you any insight as to her whereabouts? My son and Prince Set are quite concerned. Not to mention her parents."

"She is a headstrong girl," Harwa replied. "Perhaps a falling out with her parents?"

"Perhaps," Isis replied, keeping her gaze unblinking.

"Your Highness, I beg your forgiveness, but I fear I am keeping Her Majesty waiting."

"You have business with Queen Nuit?" Isis asked.

"Her Majesty sent for me."

"Of course," Isis said. "Just one other thing," she added, as Harwa turned. "Did you tell King Geb about the second slain Purean?"

Harwa froze. "I am afraid I had no choice, Your Highness."

"How unfortunate that His Majesty happened to ask you about it so soon after I confided in you."

"Yes, unfortunate, indeed," Harwa said when the tall door to Nuit's chambers opened, and the Purean queen appeared.

"Queen Isis, what an unexpected pleasure to see you here," Nuit said, her cold tone at odds with her gracious words.

"Queen Nuit," Isis replied coolly. Her skin prickled at the look that passed between the Purean queen and the truth-seer.

"Is there anything at all I can do for you?" the Purean queen asked with feigned sweetness.

A long pause stretched as Isis appraised the other woman. Finally, she shook her head. "No, thank you."

"As you wish," Nuit said. Harwa bowed.

Isis turned to leave then stopped and faced Harwa again. "One last question, Truth-seer."

"Yes, Your Highness?"

"Have you consulted your craft as to the whereabouts of the accomplice?"

"I fear that with everything that has befallen us, I have not yet had the opportunity."

"The accomplice?" Nuit raised an eyebrow.

"Did Harwa not apprise you of my father's suspicions? Since she advised His Majesty about the second slain Purean I had naturally assumed—"

"What suspicions?" Nuit asked.

"My father believes that the Witch Queen is responsible for the attack on the island. And that the Witch Queen has an accomplice on the island who may be guilty of the recent slayings."

Nuit's eyes narrowed. "The Witch Queen? An accomplice who slays Pureans? Queen Isis, these are incredulous claims."

"It appears we live in incredulous times," Isis said. "I do not wish to hold up your engagement any longer. Amun-Ra protect you both." The Rathadi queen turned and strode away.

CHAPTER 33

GEB PUSHED BACK his chair and rose. He stepped around the table and peered down at Osiris. The Rathadi king's head rested on the wood, his bare arms hanging slack at his sides. Geb fingered the ring with the sleeping potion that the truth-seer provided and that he had slipped into the Rathadi's goblet. After Osiris's latest revelations, Geb had almost decided not to go through with the plan the truth-seer had hatched, but she and his wife had insisted that the well-being of the island depended on it.

He paced to the back wall where his master fabricators had concealed the secret door, and he opened it. His face pinched when he found the narrow passageway empty.

Where are they?

The shuffling of rushed footsteps echoed from the corridor a moment before his wife appeared, followed by the truth-seer. He raised an eyebrow at the coldness that seemed to linger between the two women as they approached.

They stopped at the threshold, and the truth-seer glanced inside.

"He is asleep," Geb said.

Harwa nodded. She entered the room and moved to the Rathadi king.

"Truth-seer," Geb called after her. The woman stopped. "Osiris swore that the shifter was not responsible for the deaths."

Nuit whipped about at his words and turned to the truth-seer.

Geb's brow furrowed at his wife's reaction. "Do you know anything I should know?" he asked Nuit.

"I... I do not," Nuit replied. "It is just... something Isis said."

"The Rathadi queen?" he asked.

"She was here. She said she asked Harwa for help to find the one responsible for the slayings."

Geb faced Harwa. "You have assured me the visions were clear. That a shifter was to blame. What game are you playing, Truth-seer?"

Harwa swallowed. "Your Majesty, everything I have ever done was for the benefit of the Kingdom. I beseech you, you must believe that. Your son's life depends on—"

"Enough!" Geb cut in. "I have had enough of your double talk. If I am to go through with this, I will have the truth!"

His wife approached him slowly and looked him dead in the eyes. They shone with fear but also determination. "It is her price for bringing back our son," she said, her voice strangely calm.

Harwa stared at the Purean queen aghast.

Nuit met her gaze calmly. "They know about her."

"Who knows about whom? And whose price?" Geb's eyes bounced between the two women. "The truth-seer's? Why would she want—?"

Nuit shook her head.

"Then who?" Geb snapped. "Speak, woman! Whose price?"

"Tiamat's," Nuit whispered.

Geb felt the blood drain from his face.

"You…" he stammered, as words failed him. He staggered backward, pointing at his wife and the truth-seer. "You have aligned with the Witch Queen?"

"It was the only way to save our son," Nuit said.

A tremor rattled his hands. He clutched them together, but the shuddering simply migrated. "The Rathadi king… I did not want to believe…" Geb sputtered, unable to put strength into his words. Terror surged into his veins, and his face twisted into a snarl. "The Witch Queen! She is behind all of this!"

He lurched at the truth-seer and clasped his hands around her throat. He lifted the old woman off the ground and slammed her body against the wall.

"You have betrayed us all!" he bellowed. The old woman struggled in his grip, her eyes bulging as he choked the life out of her. "You are responsible for—"

"Stop!" Nuit shrieked. The despair in his wife's voice gave him pause. He turned.

Nuit held a dagger against her own throat. Geb froze.

"We need the truth-seer to save our son," Nuit said.

"She is Tiamat's puppet!"

"My life is meaningless without Set." Nuit's voice cracked. "I swear to Amun that if you kill the truth-seer, I will end my own life where I stand, and our son and his soul will forever be lost, never to enter the Otherworld." She sobbed at the weight of her own words. "Are you prepared to lose your only heir and your wife on the same day?"

Geb relaxed his grip on Harwa's throat, but did not let go. The truth-seer gulped a wheezing breath between his fingers. "Put down the knife," he said. "You do not know what you are saying."

"I may have been mad with grief, My King, but I see more clearly now than ever before," Nuit replied.

Dread pooled in Geb's stomach. He stared at his wife, then he released Harwa, and the truth-seer collapsed on the ground. He staggered back and cradled his head in his hands. "What have you done?"

"Whatever was necessary to save Set," Nuit said. "Now you must do your part."

The king sank to the floor. After several long breaths, he raised his head and locked his eyes on Harwa who lay beside him, panting. "Your life is forfeit, Truth-seer. I shall allow you to proceed with this... perversion for the sake of my son and his mother." His lips twisted into a grim line. "But after this is over, you shall be banished from the island."

The old woman's face fell, etching the lines in her skin even deeper, but she simply nodded and met his glare without blinking. "I have sacrificed all I had, Majesty. If my sacrifice will save the Kingdom, I shall gladly take the punishment."

She pushed herself up with a grunt and shuffled to the Rathadi king. "But now, I implore you, allow us to proceed."

Geb glanced at Osiris, trying in vain to ignore the feelings of dread and guilt that had settled in the pit of his stomach. "And you are certain he will be asleep long enough?"

"Long enough for you to travel to the temple and return."

Geb scrubbed his face with his hand. "Let us begin."

Harwa reached for her bag and pulled out an identical sleeveless tunic to the one that the Rathadi king wore. She began stripping his top.

"Why don't I just wear that one?" Geb pointed at the one Harwa brought.

"Because it lacks his scent," she said without stopping. When she stripped off his tunic, she slipped a dagger from her belt. She placed it over one of the candles burning on the table. She waited for the tip to glow a bright red before pulling the knife from the flame, then opened a vial and coated the blade with a dark liquid, sending up a wisp of smoke with a hiss.

"What are you doing?" Geb asked.

"Only what must be done, Your Majesty," Harwa replied.

She hunched over Osiris's back and began to trace a symbol into his scaly skin. Geb wrinkled his nose at the stench of seared flesh. When the truth-seer finished, she heated up the blade once again and doused it with the liquid then approached Geb. "With your permission, Majesty," she said.

Geb swallowed and gave a brief nod. He slipped his robe over his shoulders and turned his back to the truth-seer.

The pain shot through him when the blade touched his skin. He clenched his jaw and curled his fingers into tight fists as the truth-seer carved into his flesh.

His gaze fell to the Rathadi king's back. For an instant he thought the pain played tricks with his mind: as the truth-seer etched the symbols into him, they disappeared from the Rathadi king's back.

"How—?" he grunted, but the truth-seer continued her torturous task silently. When she finally stopped, he expelled a breath he did not realize he had been holding.

"The first part is finished," Harwa said. "We will complete the transformation in the temple."

"His wounds..." Geb hissed through the pain. "They disappeared... How is this possible?"

"A powerful illusion spell. The wounds are still there, but hidden. Just like your own form shall remain hidden beneath the illusion of the Rathadi king's appearance."

"Will he not feel them when he awakens?"

"The sleeping potion is also a powerful analgesic," Harwa said. "It will mask the pain until he heals, which shall not be long for one living with the sentinel of a scorpion."

Geb opened his mouth again, but the truth-seer held up her hand. "Time is not on our side, Your Majesty."

The truth-seer faced Nuit who stood in the corner of the room, her face blank.

"My Queen?"

Nuit drew near and helped Harwa dress Osiris in the tunic the truth-seer brought. When they finished, the queen said, "I shall be outside the conclave chamber, in case Osiris awakens prematurely."

"Very well," Harwa replied, and placed Osiris's tunic into her bag. She faced Geb. "I shall meet you at the gondola, Your Majesty."

Geb fought to dispel the throbbing in his tormented back as the two women left the chamber through the hidden door. He evened his breathing, keeping it short and shallow, and paced to the entrance.

He rapped his fist on the thick door. "The Kings' Conclave has concluded," he announced.

A moment later he heard the scraping of a key against the lock, and the door swung open. Qar gazed at him quizzically when he stepped out. "What of King Osiris?"

"The conclave was difficult for us both. Your king is in deep contemplation," Geb said. "He demands not to be disturbed."

Qar raised his brow, but nodded.

"I have business in the temple," Geb said to his guard.

"I shall call for the guard detail," the Purean replied.

"No," Geb countered. "I wish to pay my respects to the slain shifter. It would not be wise to bring soldiers."

The guard nodded. "By your command, Your Majesty."

Geb descended the conclave tower, then made his way through the palace to the sky carriage. The truth-seer waited for him on the platform. The guards snapped to attention when they spotted him.

Harwa addressed the guards as he approached, "The King and I have business in the temple—alone."

The guards' faces tightened at her words, but they opened the door. "As you wish," one of them replied.

Geb and Harwa boarded the gondola and rode to the temple in silence. When they arrived, one of the Rathadi guards opened the door for them. He raised an eyebrow when he saw only Geb and the truth-seer.

"We wish to pay our respects to the slain Ursus," Harwa said.

"Ra's blessings." The guard managed a curt nod. "Do you require an escort?"

"We do not," Harwa replied. "We shall find our own way."

They descended the stairway into the temple and entered an empty hallway. Harwa spotted a narrow alcove, and they both slipped inside.

Harwa turned to him. "Your Majesty, I must ask of you to kneel."

Geb shot her a glare, but did as she requested.

"Please close your eyes, Majesty."

When Geb complied, the truth-seer began chanting in a strange language. Bile rose in the back of his throat when he recognized the origin of the words. A creeping sensation arose in his back, where the truth-seer had carved the strange symbols into his flesh, then it enveloped his entire body like a sullied cloak. Just when he thought the nausea would overwhelm him, the truth-seer stopped.

"It is done," she said.

Geb opened his eyes, blinking, then lifted his hand. He gasped when an arm covered in the dark scales of the Rathadi king appeared before him. He reached out with his fingers and pressed against the scales. He pulled back, surprised. "It does not feel like his skin."

"The spell is not a physical transformation, Majesty. It is a potent illusion spell."

"An illusion spell?" Geb scoffed. "How am I supposed to—?"

"It will be sufficient to get you past the guards and into the royal chambers," Harwa said. "After that, you must control the Rathadi queen's mind."

"You know the Rathadi royals have been trained to resist mind control."

Harwa slipped a hand inside her robe and pulled out a leather pouch. "This will enhance your powers."

"What is it?" He reached for it.

"Fever bloom," she replied.

Geb's hand jerked back. "You cannot expect me to take—"

"I have treated it to remove most of the undesirable effects," Harwa said. "Still, you must use it sparingly. No more than one leaf every half a span. There are enough doses for three spans."

Geb clasped the pouch and pulled out one of the leaves then placed it in his mouth. When the fever bloom brushed his tongue, a jolt of electricity coursed through him. The surge of power was immediate. He inhaled sharply.

Harwa reached into her bag and pulled out Osiris's tunic and a pair of black leather trousers identical to the ones the Rathadi king wore to the conclave. "You must change into these," she said, and turned.

Geb donned the garments wordlessly as the truth-seer offered her final instructions. "I shall wait for you here. Do not delay. The unfavorable effects of the illusion spell and the fever bloom will only grow worse with time."

Geb scowled in reply before slipping out of the alcove and following the colonnaded corridor toward the Rathadi royals' living quarters. He summoned his confidence and strode assertively through the corridor for the guarded door, imitating the Rathadi king's smooth gait. The two soldiers flanking the door saluted him and opened the door. He nodded and entered the chamber.

Isis sat at a desk, her back to him, facing a tall window. She swiveled, and her face brightened into a smile, then she tensed.

Geb reached out with his mind.

I am your husband.

The Rathadi queen's face twisted, as if she were fighting some invisible battle. Geb reached out again, stronger. He ignored the throbbing in his temples that accompanied the effort.

I am Osiris. Believe.

Isis's face relaxed. "The conclave is over?" she asked.

"Yes." Geb drew nearer. He kept his focus locked on the Rathadi queen's mind. "We made significant progress." He labored to keep his voice light despite the exertion and mounting pain. "And we must celebrate."

Isis's expression fell. "Your nose," she called out. She picked up a handkerchief and rushed to him, then pressed the cloth to his nose. Geb frowned at the red specks against the white fabric when she pulled back her hand.

"Shall I fetch a healer?" she asked, concern etched in her features.

"No, it's nothing," Geb said, biting back a grunt. He lifted his palm to her cheek. The moment he brushed her skin, the connection strengthened. He pushed forward.

Calm.

A serene expression settled into Isis's features.

Geb pressed deeper against his own agony and the Rathadi queen's defenses. "It has been a long day. I am in the mood to celebrate." He lowered his arms and embraced her, pulling her in.

Isis smiled, but pushed him back gently. "Horus and Set told me something today," she said.

"It can wait until later," Geb said. The easy smile he attempted emerged as a grimace.

Isis gave him a sidelong glance.

"Does a husband, even though he may be a king, not have the right to miss his queen?" He moved his hand to her hip and pulled her in again.

Isis smacked his hand away. "I am serious. I must discuss something with you."

"I will discuss whatever you wish—after we celebrate our success." Geb summoned his remaining strength and pierced her mind with a single command.

Obey.

Isis's pupils grew, and she smiled. "As you wish," she said, her voice relaxing. "I suppose you deserve a celebration." She wrapped her arms around him.

Geb's face twisted as they embraced, the pressure threatening to burst his temples. "I must freshen up," he stammered, his limbs shaking with invisible tremors. "Will you pour us wine?"

Before Isis had a chance to reply, he staggered past her into the bath chamber, closed the door behind him and sank to the ground. His hands fumbled at the small pouch before he managed to tear it open. He pulled out two leaves of the fever bloom and forced them both into his mouth.

CHAPTER 34

OSIRIS WOKE WITH A START. He lifted his face from the wooden table and glanced around the empty conclave chamber.

Where is Geb?

Osiris stood. His head swam. He took a moment to collect himself, then spotted the empty bottle in front of him.

That wine must have been a lot stronger that I thought… I don't even remember finishing it.

He moved to the door and stepped out into the hall. Qar greeted him outside the chamber.

"Where is King Geb?" Osiris asked.

"He wished to pay his respects to the Rathadi shifter," Qar said.

"He did?" A creeping sensation prickled the back of Osiris's neck as he tried to make sense out of Qar's words, but thinking felt like running under water. "Why did you not inform me?"

"Forgive me, Majesty. King Geb said you were in deep contemplation and not to be disturbed."

"Deep contemplation? Is that what he said?" Osiris

managed a weak chuckle. "I fell asleep." He leaned closer to Qar. "I suppose the combination of wine and company of the Purean king was too much for me to handle."

Qar grinned. "Your Majesty is in a fair mood. May I assume the conclave was successful?"

"Indeed." Osiris returned the easy smile, but it wilted when his skin prickled again. "Let us return home."

Qar nodded. "As you wish, Majesty."

They made their way down the stairs and paced along the corridor when the voice of the Purean queen rang out behind them.

"King Osiris?"

The Rathadi turned. Qar pressed his fist against his heart and bowed his head.

"Queen Nuit," Osiris said. "I am surprised you are still awake."

"Sleep does not come easily to me these days," she replied. "My husband tells me the conclave was productive?"

"By Amun-Ra's grace," Osiris offered a small smile.

"And the situation with the… shifter?"

Osiris's lips tightened. "We have reached an agreement."

"Thank Amun for that," she said. "Our diarchy could not ask for two wiser leaders."

"You humble me with your words, Majesty. Amun's blessings on you. We should be getting—"

The queen's knees buckled, and she grabbed hold of the marble column beside her. Qar rushed forward and caught her before she fell.

"Your Majesty!" the weapons master called out.

"I… I…" the queen stammered.

"Fetch a healer," Osiris commanded. He moved to Nuit and offered her his arm as Qar rushed off.

"My apologies, King Osiris," Nuit said. "With everything that has befallen us in the last days... I am afraid I have not gotten my share of rest." She leaned heavily on him. "I wonder if I may impose upon you to accompany me back to my quarters?"

Osiris grumbled silently, but pasted a gracious smile on his face. "It shall be my honor," he said, as they doubled back to the royal chambers.

———

GEB LAY ON HIS SIDE, propped on an elbow, his gaze following the lines of the naked body resting serenely beside him. The Rathadi queen's eyes were closed, and her breathing was calm and steady. Her bronze skin was covered in a sheen of sweat and gleamed in the soft light that slipped into the chamber. He struggled to ignore the pounding in his head that grew worse with every heartbeat and the twisting in his gut at his deed.

Amun forgive me.

He forced the pain and guilt down. He had to get back to the truth-seer and then to the palace.

His thoughts were interrupted when something dripped on his forearm. He looked down at the small dark blot against his skin. He reached to his nose; his face tightened at the sticky wetness against his fingertips. Biting back a curse, he stood and rushed to the bath chamber, grasping for his pants along the way.

Isis moaned softly, awakened from her slumber. "Osiris,"

she called after him, drowsily.

"I shall return in a moment," Geb said. He fumbled with the pocket in his pants then found the pouch and pulled out another leaf.

The last one.

He slipped it into his mouth and chewed greedily. His headache slowly ebbed, and the familiar surge of energy rushed through him as the bitter taste of the fever bloom spread through his mouth.

He heard Isis rise. "There is a matter we must discuss," she said. "The boys told me that they hatched a plan for Set and Mia to break into the truth-seers chambers during Horus's ceremony."

"Why would they do that?" Geb asked, forcing calmness into his voice.

"They said that Mia saw a gauntlet shaped like the claw of an Ursus in a hidden compartment in Harwa's wardrobe."

A cold wash swept through Geb. He groaned.

"Osiris?" Isis asked. "What is wrong?"

Fury raged through him as the Rathadi queen approached the bath chamber. He slipped behind the door just before she stepped inside.

"Osiris?" she asked. "Where—"

Geb grasped her head and pushed into her mind with the last remnants of his strength.

Sleep.

Isis collapsed into his arms. He lifted her and carried her across the chamber into the bed then wrapped his palms around her temples and reached inside her once again, pulling her back into consciousness.

"You shall forget I was here," Geb whispered. "You had a pleasing dream about us. Now sleep."

Isis's eyes fluttered open for a moment before they closed again. She gave a contented sigh before her head sank into the pillow, and her calm breathing resumed.

Geb fumbled with his clothes, dressing as quickly as his trembling hands allowed, then exited the chamber. The guards outside snapped to attention when he emerged and fell in behind him. He struggled to maintain a steady gait through the pain clouding his mind, but drew himself tall and faced about. "I wish to be alone," he said.

"Yes, Majesty," the guards replied in unison and moved back in front of the door.

He managed a steady pace until he turned the corner, then fell against the wall, breathing hard. After several moments, he pushed off and continued, his muscles faltering as he approached the alcove where the truth-seer was waiting. Harwa gasped when she spotted him.

She rushed to him. "Your Majesty!"

He stumbled, heaving ragged breaths. "The Rathadi queen... much stronger..."

"Your Majesty, I must reverse the illusion spell immediately!"

Geb groaned, the pain in his head overwhelming him. He collapsed to the floor.

The truth-seer pulled him into the alcove. She poured a bitter liquid into his mouth and began chanting an incantation. Gradually, the agony in his head ebbed. Geb took slow, steady breaths until some strength returned to his limbs. He sluggishly pushed himself up.

"Were you… successful?" the truth-seer asked.

"It is done," Geb replied. "I wish to never speak of it again." He glowered at the truth-seer, Isis's words ringing through his mind. He fought the instinct to choke the life out of the old woman. *Was she the one?* He would learn the truth if he had to scramble her mind to do so, but this was neither the place nor the time. "I need to get back to the palace," he stammered.

"We will, but first we must pay our respects to the Ursus."

"No," Geb protested. "I—"

"This is why you came to the temple," she said. "We must keep appearances."

Geb's mind screamed for sleep, and his skin felt like it was going to peel away from his body. Harwa rummaged through her robe. She pulled out another leaf and moved it to his mouth.

Geb pushed her hand aside. He clenched his jaw and leaned on her as he rose to his feet. "Let us go," he said.

————

OSIRIS RESTED on the wooden bench in the gondola, watching the predawn sky paint the temple spires a fiery orange as he and the weapons master traveled across the channel. Before they left the palace, he had accompanied the Purean queen to her chambers and stayed with her until Qar had arrived with the healer. After a lengthy goodbye, they were finally able to leave the palace and make their way back to the temple.

The gondola docked with a familiar jolt, and they exited. He nodded a greeting to the guards and trudged to the stairs when he spotted Geb and Harwa. He raised his eyebrows at the

Purean king's appearance. His skin was ashen, and he leaned on the truth-seer as the pair ascended the last few steps.

"King Geb?" Osiris greeted him. "Are you unwell?"

"King Osiris," Geb replied. "I…"

"His Majesty was most taken when he saw the body of the Ursus," Harwa said.

The prickling against Osiris's skin returned at the sickly half-smile on the truth-seer's face, but he forced a polite nod. "I shall not hold you up, then. Amun's blessings with you, King Geb," he said.

"And with you, King Osiris," Geb mumbled.

After Geb and Harwa passed them, Qar shot Osiris a quizzical look. The Rathadi king shrugged. "It has been a long day for us all," he said, as they headed for the stairs. When they reached the bottom, Osiris turned to the royal chambers. Qar followed him.

Osiris stopped. "I can find my own way from here, Weapons Master. Get some rest."

Qar gave him a grateful look. "As you wish, Your Majesty. Until tomorrow then."

Osiris nodded a goodbye and paced to his chambers.

The guards at the door of the chamber saluted when he approached. "Back so soon, Majesty?"

"The conclave was not as long as I had feared," he replied.

The guards exchanged a confused look but remained silent as they opened the doors for him. Osiris stepped through and paced to the bed chamber. He smiled at the sight of Isis's body beneath the covers and the soft, steady sound of her breathing. He undressed and eased down beside her. Thoughts of Horus and the island filled his head before he sank into a deep sleep.

CHAPTER 35

THE SOUND of soft feet against the slate roused Osiris. He opened his eyes, trying to blink the sleep from them. The sun stood a hand's breadth above the horizon, casting a medley of shadows through the tall, slatted window. His gaze followed Isis as she moved across the chamber.

"You let me sleep too long," he said.

Isis turned and gave him a smile. "You did not rest well."

He rubbed his eyes, his head still thick, as his wife slipped into a white dress and fastened a wide, golden belt around her waist. A look of concern tarnished her face.

"What is bothering you?" he asked.

"I spoke with Father. He said that Khet has called for a gathering on the high terrace before the last rites for the Ursus."

"Khet? The Taurus?"

Isis nodded. "They are demanding an explanation of what happened."

Osiris swore under his breath. He sat up, willing the drowsiness from his head. "Khet was a close friend of the Ursus, but now is not the time to stir up tempers—or to act rashly. I should speak with them."

"Father is on his way there already."

"Good. Thoth has a way with words." He stepped out of bed. His gaze caught on a white handkerchief on the floor on his side of the bed. He wrinkled his brow at the red stains covering it and picked it up. "Where did this come from?"

Isis raised her head. When she spotted the cloth, her expression shifted into confusion, then disbelief, as if her mind was struggling to process what she saw. She reached for the handkerchief.

"I... I had a dream that you came back from conclave early," she stammered. "And your nose bled." She stared at the cloth. "And then we..." She blushed. "But... I thought it was just a dream." Isis lifted the cloth to her nose. The color bled from her face.

"What is it?" Osiris asked.

A tremor settled into Isis's limbs. Osiris watched his wife as she fought off the surge of emotions that seemed to wake inside her. Her eyes tightened when sudden comprehension dawned. She pressed a hand to her stomach as if doubling over with nausea.

"My Love!" Osiris rushed forward, but she lifted her hand, stopping him. Her lips were set in a line of dread. She glared at the cloth, as if willing it to burn in her hand.

"May I see it?" Osiris asked.

Isis shook her head. Osiris sensed a fire surging within her.

A dark suspicion rose in his chest. "Give it to me now," he said, forcing calmness into his words.

Isis extended her hand woodenly. Osiris took the cloth and

lifted it to his face, smelling the crimson stain. His throat tightened at the foreign scent. He tasted the blood with his tongue.

Purean?

Cold water, raised from a deep well, poured into his veins, sending shivers into his limbs. His cheek twitched as he lifted his gaze. "How…?"

Isis's face caved. "Amun-Ra forgive me…" she stammered. "It… it was Geb…" Her breath hitched. "I can remember… somehow he must have controlled my mind. I thought he… I thought he was you." She covered her face with her hands. "We… we…"

The realization rose inside his chest like a blaze, scorching everything in its path.

The wine… The Purean king and the truth-teller in the temple…

The conclave…

Geb's words… the promises…

All lies!

"By Ra," he said, his voice a deadly whisper. "I will kill him."

"Osiris—" Isis started.

Osiris roared. He snatched a heavy chair and hurled it against the wall, smashing it into pieces. Isis screamed with a violence that set his jaw to aching.

Before either of them could take another breath, the door burst open, and Qar rushed into the room, his hand on the hilt of his sword.

"Your Majesties! Is everything in—?" The rest of the words died on his lips when he met Osiris's gaze.

"My King…?" he stammered. "What—?" He yelled out in

surprise when Osiris barreled past him and raced out of the chamber.

"Osiris!" his wife's cry rang out behind him.

Osiris tore through the corridor, ignoring the baffled glances and yelps of the Rathadi scattering out of his way.

Horus's head poked out from his chambers.

"Father?" he asked. "I heard a scream and—"

Osiris rushed past him, not sparing him a glance.

"*Tato!*" Horus yelled after him. "*Amah!*" he hollered, as Isis and Qar shot past him, chasing after Osiris.

The Rathadi king turned the corner and sprinted up the stairs to the sky carriage.

The guard at the platform saluted. Osiris ignored him. He ripped open the door to the gondola.

"Get me across!" he yelled. "Give me the controls!"

"Majesty?" the guard asked.

"Now!" Osiris raged.

The guard's face paled. "Yes, Majesty!"

Osiris leaped inside. He seethed, pacing back at forth, as the gondola sped across the water for the Purean palace.

A warning appeared on the control panel, then an alert filled the cabin. He ignored the frantic gesturing of the Purean guards on the platform as the carriage rushed toward it. When the gondola was above the terrace, he leaped out, rolling to a stop on the platform just before the carriage crashed into the far wall of the terminus, scattering the Purean guards.

"King Osiris!" somebody exclaimed. "Are you—?"

He surged to his feet and raced for the stairs.

"King Osiris!" the guards called out after him.

He tore through the palace and charged into the corridor that housed the royal living chambers. The pair of guards flanking the door stared in surprise as he approached. They moved to block the door.

"Your Highness!" one of them said. "King Geb is not expecting—"

Osiris came to a stop. "Stand aside," he said, his voice dripping with poison.

"With all respect, Highness, you—"

His words turned to a grunt when Osiris rushed him, pinning him against the door.

The second guard pulled his sword and lunged forward. Osiris pivoted away from the blade. The guard's face knotted. He stared at his sword, buried in his companion's gut. He dropped the hilt.

His shock did not last more than an instant, but it was more time than Osiris needed. The Rathadi king pulled the sword free and smashed it broadside into the guard's temple. The man's eyes rolled back into his head, and he collapsed to the ground.

Osiris burst through the door into the royal chambers.

"Geb!" he roared, bolting up the wide stairs that led to the second floor. He spotted the Purean king.

"Geb!" he bellowed.

Geb stared in shock at Osiris and the bloody sword in his hand. "Osiris? What—?"

"You betrayed us!"

Geb opened his mouth, braced to challenge the Rathadi king's words, but he sighed and dropped his head. "I... I did not have a choice," he said. "It was for the good of the island."

"The good of the island?" Osiris seethed. He advanced on

the Purean king, sword pointed. "You will pay for what you did!"

Geb looked at him serenely.

Osiris calmed. A compulsion to drop the sword spread through him. He lowered the blade.

A rivulet of blood trickled from Geb's nostril.

Osiris roared and charged the Purean king.

"Do not try your tricks on me, Mind Queller!" He slammed the hilt of the sword into Geb's face, crushing his nose and splitting his lip. Blood erupted as the Purean king cried out and sank to the ground.

———

SET WOKE UP WITH A SCREAM.

"Father!" Panic rose in his chest, sharp and hot. His body shuddered.

He staggered from his bed and rushed out of his chamber into the corridor. His bare feet pounded against the marble as he rushed for his parents' chambers. He sped by the old truth-seer who stared at him bewildered.

"Prince Set?"

"My father!" he cried out. "My father is in danger!"

"Wait!" she called after him, but he did not slow.

Every step had his heart thudding faster, louder. He skidded to a halt at the sight of the two guards lying motionlessly in front of his parents' chambers. Dread pooled in his stomach.

"Guards!" he screamed then rushed inside and up the stairs.

He gasped at the sight. His father lay on the ground, his face and robe covered in blood. The Rathadi king loomed over him, sword raised, the dark, scaly face twisted into the snarl of a madman.

A shadow crept inside him, invading his consciousness. Set closed his eyes, letting all thoughts fall away, and reached out with his mind. He hovered on the edge of a thought, a barrier, then pushed through and let himself go, falling into something he could not explain. A sensation gripped him, a dark void humming with power. He opened his eyes.

The Rathadi king froze. He bent his right arm, moving the blade toward his throat. His face tensed, and his eyes widened, as if willing his body not to obey, but he continued, a grotesque marionette, until the sword pressed against his scaly skin, then he drew the blade across his throat.

Set screamed. The sensation collapsed, and the Rathadi king dropped the sword and pressed both hands against his throat, trying to stem the blood surging from the ghastly wound. He turned and stared at Set. His scaly lips moved wordlessly as he slowly sank to his knees, blood seeping between his fingers.

Set stood frozen. His vision blurred into crimson as tears streamed down his cheeks. He lifted his hands to wipe his eyes. He gasped at the sight of his palms covered in bright blood.

The Purean king stirred.

"Father!" Set cried out, and rushed to his side. "I thought he killed you!"

Geb's gaze fell on the Rathadi king, a pool of blood forming beneath him, then it locked on Set's face. He gasped.

"Wh-what have I done?" Set stammered.

Heavy footsteps rushed up the stairs. Before Set had a chance to react, Geb pressed past him and snatched the sword from the ground. He stood facing the stairs.

The truth-seer and a half dozen Purean guards led by Captain Nebet flooded into the chamber. They froze when they saw Geb's blood-stained form facing them with the sword in his hand.

"King Osiris tried to kill my father!" Set cried.

Harwa and the guards stared at the Rathadi king's lifeless body. Blood drained from their faces.

A moment later Queen Isis and Horus burst into the room, followed by the Rathadi weapons master.

The Rathadi queen spotted her husband's body. She collapsed at his side and pulled his blood-stained head to her chest.

Horus's body quivered as his gaze flitted between the bloody sword in the Purean king's hand and his father's bloodied form. He screamed and rushed the Purean king, but Qar held him back.

"The Rathadi king committed an act of treason against the Pure Ones!" Harwa shrilled before Geb could utter a word. "The Rathadi king attacked His Majesty in his very own chambers! He was mad. His Majesty had no choice but to defend himself."

Isis glared at Geb, and their gazes locked. Set shivered at the venom in the Rathadi queen's eyes.

"I know what you did," she spat. "You will pay for everything you—"

"Treachery!" Harwa cut in. "The Rathadi queen and prince knew what King Osiris was about to do and allowed him to attack His Majesty!"

Geb met Isis's gaze unblinking, but his expression was far away. "Arrest the queen on charges of treason," he said.

"But Father—" Set whined.

A pair of Purean guards moved for the Rathadi queen. Before they took their second step, Qar leaped forward and pulled his twin swords in a single motion. The curved blades sliced through the air, and two guards collapsed lifelessly at his feet.

"Go, My Queen!" the weapons master called out. "Warn the others!" He whirled and slashed out at the Purean guard who stood between the queen and the exit, dropping him to the ground. The five other soldiers drew their weapons and rushed Qar.

Set locked eyes with Horus for one final moment before the Rathadi queen snatched her son's hand, and they sped out of the room amid the whirling of Qar's blades.

Set marveled at the Rathadi's speed as he pounced, aiming for the nearest exposed opponent, killing him with a single stroke. Not waiting for him to hit the ground, he ducked and rolled between two strikes and came up amid three guards. The curved blades danced in sinuous rhythm, felling all three with gruesome efficiency.

The weapons master turned to the last remaining opponent, the captain of the royal guard, and lowered his blades. "I do not wish to harm you," Qar said, breathing evenly.

Captain Nebet lifted his weapon. His face was tight, but his voice confident as he spoke. "You shall not have a choice."

Qar raised his swords when more heavy footsteps reached them. An instant later a dozen Purean guards rushed upstairs and flooded into the chamber.

The weapons master spun to face them. The guards rushed him. The blades slashed and stabbed at him from every angle.

Qar's swords worked in perfect harmony with the inertia of his lunges as he sidestepped the first three strikes and parried two others, but the sixth attacker broke through his defenses, his blade slicing deep into Qar's right upper arm. The Rathadi's face twisted in pain, the sword slipping from his grasp. Still, he whirled, his left sword sliding into the gap between the breast plate and the back armor of the guard who wounded him. He faced the remaining attackers, his right arm dangling uselessly at his side, but his eyes shining fiercely.

The weapons master tensed. He froze and looked down. The tip of the captain's sword protruded from his stomach. Nebet twisted the blade and yanked it out of Qar's back, then drew his blade in a great arc, slicing at the Rathadi's neck.

Set turned away, but could not spare himself the sound of the weapons master's head hitting the floor an instant before the rest of his body collapsed to the ground.

For several moments nobody moved.

"This is an act of war," Harwa croaked, finding her voice. "My King…"

Geb dropped the sword to the ground. He faced his guards.

"Find the Rathadi," he said. "Round them up."

"They will resist, Majesty," Captain Nebet said.

"Then do what you must to defend yourselves."

Set's hot tears mixed with the blood on his cheeks as he watched the guards rush out of the chamber.

CHAPTER 36

"The Pureans have slain the Ursus!" The voice of the huge Taurus boomed over the throng of the assembled Rathadi as Thoth ascended the last steps to the high terrace. "We must not allow them to continue—"

"And what would you have us do, instead?" Thoth called out. Heads turned.

Thoth scanned their faces, looking to him expectantly. The triangular shape of the sacred monument rose up behind the crowd. *By Ra, he has managed to draw almost all of our kin here.*

"Your words are wise, Honored Archsage," the Taurus said. "And your opinion respected beyond even our king's, but what do you advise? That there shall be no repercussions for slaying one of us without a shred of evidence?"

"They were misled, Khet," Thoth said.

"And their king? Did he not order it?"

Thoth considered. "I do not know the answer to that question."

The Rathadi murmured.

"Be that as it may," Thoth said, stepping through the ranks and closing the gap to the Taurus. "King Osiris and King Geb met in conclave yesterday. They deliberated late into the night. We must have trust in our leaders. They have put aside their differences and arrived at a peaceful solution. We owe it to them to hear them out."

"And where is our king?"

"He shall be here soon," Thoth said.

A noise from the wide stairs distracted him. Thoth's brain took a moment to catch up with what he saw.

Endless lines of Purean soldiers in full battle armor and with weapons drawn surged onto the high terrace. They surrounded the Rathadi.

"This is the holiest of holies!" Thoth cried out. "How dare you come here and—"

"Hold your tongue, Archsage," Captain Nebet interrupted, stepping through the ranks of his soldiers. "By decree of King Geb, you are hereby ordered to surrender yourselves immediately to stand responsible for the act of treason."

"Treason?" Thoth called out. "By whom?"

"By King Osiris," Nebet replied. "He attempted to murder His Majesty, King Geb!"

Terror washed through Thoth as the Rathadi cried out in disbelief.

"Where is King Osiris now?" Thoth asked, dread filling his voice. "I shall not believe it until I hear his account!" The other Rathadi nodded and grunted in assent.

The captain remained silent.

"Your king lies dead at the feet of His Majesty!" one of the Purean soldiers cried out. "He paid for his—"

"Silence!" Nebet roared, but it was too late. It was as if a spark had ignited and spread through the ranks of the assembled Rathadi. Within seconds the scene erupted into chaos as the unarmed Rathadi rushed the Purean soldiers.

Thoth watched the scene before him as if in a dream. A Purean soldier advanced on him, raising his sword. Thoth backed up, tripping over someone's feet. Before the Purean could close the distance, he was lifted off the ground and brought down violently over the knee of the Taurus. The sound of his spine shattering snapped Thoth out of his stupor.

"Follow me!" Khet cried out. He wrapped his massive palm around Thoth's arm and pulled him up to his feet as easily as a father might a Rathling.

They weaved their way through the chaos when Thoth spotted a familiar figure darting between the bodies.

"Bast!" he called out.

The girl stopped and whirled, her eyes wild with fear.

"Come to me!" Thoth beckoned.

Bast weaved her way to him, and they hunkered on the ground, the Taurus shielding them with his body.

"I have a task of utmost importance for you," Thoth said. "Can I count on you?"

Her face twisted in fear, stirring the fine coating of dark fur that covered her skin, but she nodded alertly, ready to move. "Yes, Archsage."

"You must find Queen Isis and Horus," Thoth said. "Find them and tell them to gather the others and meet me at the harbor. Do you understand?"

"I do, Archsage."

Thoth grasped her shoulders. "You must find them. Amun-Ra's wind guide you."

Bast nodded again and sped off.

Thoth faced Khet. "I must reach the harbor."

The Taurus drew himself to his full size, and his eyes hardened. "Then you shall arrive there safely."

CHAPTER 37

Horus raced at full speed, struggling to keep pace with his mother. The message from Bast had been clear. Meet Grandfather at the harbor. The girl and the other Rathadi found him and his mother after they had made their escape from the palace. They had crossed the island and were now racing after the other Rathadi to the harbor.

"Do not slow down, Horus, we must not lose the others!" his mother urged.

He snapped out of his thoughts and caught a glimpse of his mother's face as they passed the lantern, her beautiful features marred by fear, the white dress stained a dark crimson.

Father's blood…

He glanced back into the darkness, to the rough voices of their pursuers.

We are the last ones. There is nobody left between us and them.

His mother turned into a dark alley and tugged him with her. The sudden jerk almost pulled him off his feet. He blinked away his tears and struggled to focus on the narrow path ahead, trying to ignore the burning in his lungs. The tears in his throat soured every breath.

"We are almost there, my son. You must be strong."

"*Amah*, I cannot go on!" he pleaded.

He tripped again and this time she almost lost her grip, but somehow managed to keep him from falling. The voices behind them grew louder, their shouts more frequent.

His mother stopped and pushed him into one of the narrow doorways. Her chest rose in shallow, rapid breaths. She peered into the darkness behind them, the shimmer in her beautiful feline eyes tainted with pain and fear.

She cupped his face with her hands. "Horus, my son, listen well." Her whisper was soft, but unwavering. The pounding of his heart and his heavy breathing made it difficult to hear her voice. "You will follow the others to the harbor. I will meet you on the ship, later."

"No, *Amah*…" Horus wanted to plead with her not to leave, but fear and exhaustion robbed him of his voice.

She pulled him into her arms. When she released him, her expression shifted. Gradually, calmness replaced the fear in her eyes. "I will always love you, my son," she said, and placed her hands on his head.

Once more she turned toward the voices. He could see the pupils grow to cover each iris. She tensed as she saw the pursuers, even though they would not be able to spot him and his mother for a long time. His own vision had begun to be worthy of the falcon, but in the darkness, none could match the sight of those living with the gift of the sacred cat.

"Why do they hate us so much? Why do they want to hurt us?" His voice trembled with fear and confusion.

"They fear what they do not understand, my son. And they hate those whom they fear." She looked at him piercingly then held him tightly against her chest once again.

"It is time, my son." She released him and gently pushed him into the dark corner of the doorway. "Stay hidden here until you do not hear them anymore, then run as fast as you can to the boats. Find Grandfather."

"*Amah…*"

She held him at arm's length. "You are Horus, son of Isis and Osiris," she said softly, then moved into the alley. She stood and waited for the pursuers to drive close enough to see her.

Horus pressed into the corner of the doorway. Breath by breath the voices grew louder. He closed his eyes.

A rough voice pierced the darkness. "There's one!"

Horus fought his terror and opened his eyes. His mother stared into the alley toward the pursuers. Somehow, he knew that the image of her standing there, tall and defiant, would forever be engraved in his memory. She glanced at him one last time. Her lips moved, whispering silently.

You shall know no fear.

She doubled back then leaped into the darkness, leading the pursuers away.

Horus turned and pressed his cheeks against the cold rock. His tears wet the rough surface as it dug into his skin while his heart hammered against his chest.

I am Horus.

Their feet pounded the cobblestones only a few arms'

lengths away, barely louder than the thumping of the blood against his temples.

Son of Isis and Osiris.

He waited for a rough hand to yank him out of his hiding place. He held his breath and squeezed his eyes shut as tightly as he could.

I shall know—

As quickly as it came, the noise disappeared. The Purean soldiers continued their hunt into the darkness. Horus stayed huddled against the rock for a long time before he dared to turn his head and look back.

Empty.

He left the dark doorway and dashed the opposite way, the wind drying his tears as they streamed down his face. He had to get to the harbor. His mother would meet him there.

She said she would.

He continued racing into the darkness, past the sloped gardens. The harbor was just ahead. Only a few more—

Strong hands grasped him, pulling him into an alley. A palm covered his mouth. He struggled against the grip.

"Be still, Horus." He settled down at the sound of his grand-father's familiar voice. The old Rathadi pointed at the harbor and put his finger to his lips. Horus nodded in understanding. He looked to the boats and gasped. Dozens of Rathadi lay at the docks motionless, strewn about like broken dolls. Purean soldiers loomed over them with their weapons drawn.

"Where is your mother?" Thoth whispered.

"She... she ran inland... to draw them away," Horus replied, unable to hold back the tears. "She said she would meet me. She said..."

Anguish filled Thoth's gray eyes as he regarded Horus, his face a shadow of agony. Slowly and deliberately, he pulled Horus to him and held him close. When he released him, the old Rathadi's face was a mask, but Horus shivered at his grandfather's eyes, two glaring mirrors of terrible pain and unrestrained hatred.

"They slaughtered everyone," he said, as he slid his hand into his robe and drew out three glass orbs.

Horus gasped as he recognized the ghostly, purple mist inside them, shifting subtly with the old Rathadi's movements. "But *Amah*—"

"We could have all lived together, in peace," his grandfather's voice quivered as he gently pushed Horus back and set off toward the Purean soldiers.

"We could have been united, One People!" His voice grew louder, startling the men near the boats. They turned and faced him then rushed forward, their weapons raised.

"We have never done you harm, yet you slaughtered my brothers... my sisters!" His voice was a shaking crescendo. "You have murdered my sons and daughters! Now you shall answer for your savagery!" He hurled the glass orbs at the running men.

The orbs flew through the air and broke on the ground in front of the Pureans as they rushed into the barely perceptible mist.

The soldiers continued for several strides before their eyes grew large and their legs refused to obey them.

"Do not look, boy. Turn away!"

Despite his grandfather's words, Horus could not tear his eyes from the nightmare before him. The image of the animal in the cage flashed through his mind as the men's skin turned the color of fire. They fell to their knees, clawing at their throats and faces, blood streaking from their eyes. Then the screams began. They grew louder and turned to the shrieks of animals. Horus covered his ears to drown out the sounds, but he could still hear them. Thoth pulled him close and held him tightly until the screams faded to a ghastly memory.

The strong beats of his grandfather's heart rang against Horus's ear, their steady rhythm a brief solace in this horror. Finally, Thoth released him and moved to the men. Horus hesitated, drawing him back.

His grandfather stopped and faced about. "Do not be afraid," he said. "This weapon can never cause you harm. It was made to protect us and bring death to our enemies. Our blood shall keep us safe." He cupped the boy's face in his palm. "Do you understand?"

Horus slowly nodded and allowed his grandfather to take his hand and lead him to the docks. He closed his eyes as they strode past the bodies of their enemies and their kin. When they stopped, and he opened his eyes again, they stood before a single-masted sloop, moored at the far end of the harbor.

His grandfather sank to one knee and rested his palms on Horus's shoulders. "Nothing shall ever be again as it was," he said, his voice heavy. "We must leave our home, and we shall never return."

Horus stared at him, unwilling to comprehend.

"They murdered your family." His voice cracked under the weight of his words. "They slaughtered them—all of them. You and I are all that remains of our people, our culture... our blood." He took Horus's head into his hands. "Our knowledge, what persists inside us, is all we have. I shall teach you all that I know, but I am old, and you must carry this burden once I am gone. You must safeguard the memory of our people."

The old Rathadi stood and lifted up his grandson, his arms surprisingly strong, and gently set him inside the sailboat. He slipped the lines off the wooden pylons, then climbed in behind Horus and pushed off into the dark water. He slipped the oars into the water.

"Stay down," he whispered, and rowed quietly to the middle of the channel.

"How will we get past the water gates?" Horus asked.

"I designed them, grandson," Thoth said. "I will get us out. Stay down."

His grandfather rowed for a long time. The sky was deeper and the stars shone brighter when Thoth finally unfurled the sail. He slumped next to Horus, allowing the wind to push them east.

Horus turned back. The single spire towered over the island, reflecting the fires that raged below. He was grateful to the darkness for concealing his tears, and the lapping of the waves against the hull for stifling his sobs, as he silently cursed the only home he had ever known.

PART 3

EXILE

THE PUREAN SOLDIERS charged through the narrow alley beneath Isis as she clung to the wall, wrapped in shadows. She waited for her pursuers' steps to recede into darkness before moving again, climbing higher until she crested the roof of the three-story building. She gazed across the channel and groaned. The sacred temple stood engulfed in flames, the faint smell of blood and smoke weaving its way through the air, threatening to make her ill. Isis pressed against the rough stone and closed her eyes, willing herself to make this nightmare disappear, to wake up in her bed next to her husband.

Osiris.

The image of her husband slumped in a pool of blood flashed across her vision.

Her king.

Her mate.

Grief surged with every expelled breath. It came at her with such ferocity, it threatened to overwhelm her.

Movement on the bridge caught her eye. Dozens of armed

Purean patrols led shackled Rathadi from the Inner Ring to the capital. A sigh of relief escaped her lips. *Not all perished.*

She squinted, straining to make out forms resembling Horus or her father when a noise below startled her. One of the patrols that scoured the city had rounded up a mother and two Rathlings and marched them through the alley toward her.

Isis swallowed the acid burning her throat and focused her pain, channeling it into something else: a pure, consummate storm of anger.

She waited for the group to draw close then leaped down, a feral growl on her lips. She crushed one of the soldiers beneath her then rolled and faced the others with a snarl. The remaining soldiers reached for their swords, then froze when they recognized her.

"Q-Queen Isis," their commander stammered.

"Release them," Isis hissed.

The soldier steeled himself. "By order of His Majesty, all Rathadi are to be brought—"

"Release them," Isis repeated.

"Our orders are clear, Highness." He drew his sword and pointed it at her. "In the name of King Geb, I order you to—"

A fit of coughs shook him and swallowed his next words. Isis's lips twitched as the other soldiers eyed their leader. The commander wiped his mouth. When he managed to speak again, his words came out in a croak. "I order you to surrender."

"Never," Isis growled.

The commander signaled the soldiers. They fanned out, encircling her, and drew their swords.

Isis's heart quaked in her chest. "Do you know what will

happen to you if you damage the king's prized prisoner?" she asked, attempting to keep her voice even.

The soldiers tensed and glanced to the commander, a hint of doubt creeping into their faces.

Isis seized the opening and lunged at the soldier closest to the mother and Rathlings. Before he could raise his weapon, her foot came down on the outside of his knee. His leg buckled with a sickening crunch, and the soldier collapsed to the ground, howling and grasping at his limb.

"Run!" Isis yelled to the woman. She ripped the sword from the soldier's grasp and faced the others.

The woman stood petrified. "My Queen…" she uttered.

"Save your family!" Isis cried out.

The woman snatched the younger child in her arm and grabbed the other's hand then took off into the alley. A soldier moved after her, but Isis stepped in his way, weapon raised. His eyes widened.

"The Queen is not to be harmed!" the commander bellowed.

The four soldiers surged at her, but their strikes were slow and hesitant as they scrambled to subdue her without causing her injury. Isis fought them with savagery and desperation, free of such constraints. Her blade whirled and danced, slashing out, finding cracks in their defense and armor. One of them barreled forward, attempting to tackle her, but she sidestepped, and before he could retreat and reclaim range, her blade slipped between the plates of his arm and shoulder. She felt the edge cut through flesh, and a scream was followed by the satisfying clang of his sword hitting the cobblestone road.

He twisted, the plates of his armor snagging her sword for only an instant, but she realized her peril immediately. Before she had a chance to dislodge her blade, the others rushed her as one. She parried an overhead slash and dodged the second—

Stars exploded in her head as the flat of a blade connected with her temple. Pain danced across her vision. She dropped to one knee.

The Pureans fell upon her. She screamed and clawed and bit as the soldiers grasped at her body from every angle, driving her to the ground. Her head snapped forward as the hilt of a sword smashed into the back of her skull, and darkness overcame her.

CHAPTER 39

NUIT WATCHED the burning temple from the terrace of her royal chambers. Her palms squeezed around the marble railing until the stone bit painfully into her skin.

By Amun, what have I done?

A hand touched her shoulder. She spun, startled, and stared into the inked face of the truth-seer.

"Harwa… what have I done?" she whimpered.

The old woman fixed her with a steady gaze. "What had to be done to save your son."

"If the Rathadi queen is not found, everything we have brought about, every sacrifice, will have been for naught."

"She will be found," Harwa said. "And she will bear the child."

"How many lives… so that one can live?"

Harwa studied her pensively before speaking. "Your Majesty, this has always been about more than just your son."

Nuit blinked. "What?"

"The vision I described to King Geb. It was not a mere tale

invented for his benefit so that he would serve our will. The vision of our island perishing did descend upon me, but it was not when I brought your son back from the Otherworld, but when the son of Isis and Osiris came into ours."

"I… I thought you had fabricated it to convince Geb to—" Nuit stammered.

"The destruction of Atlantis has been foretold when Horus was born." A grimace flickered across Harwa's face. "But there was no savior, no miracle offspring between the Pure Ones and the Rathadi who would save our island."

"What are you saying, Truth-seer?"

"The son of Isis and Osiris is the destroyer of our island. That vision befell me during his birth and has haunted me ever since. From that moment, the sole purpose of my existence has been to avert what has been foretold. I knew there was only one strong enough to prevent it."

"But her hate for the island—"

"Is exceeded by her hate for the Rathadi," Harwa broke in. "She gave me her word that our people would remain safe."

"Our people?"

"The Pure Ones," Harwa said.

An icy terror blossomed in Nuit's chest and spread to her limbs. Her voice was hoarse when she spoke. "But not the Rathadi?"

"Tiamat said it was the only way to save our island from destruction."

"And you trusted her blindly?" Nuit bristled.

Harwa opened her mouth to reply when the door burst open, and a guard dropped to his knee. "I beg your forgiveness, Majesty," he said. "The King requests your presence at once."

Nuit faced him numbly, her gaze distant, before she turned to Harwa again. "Come," she said, "we shall continue our discussion afterward."

Four guards escorted the women as they made their way to the king's audience chamber. Geb rested on a throne against the far wall of the spacious hall. The other three walls were lined with court attendants who bowed when Nuit and the truth-seer entered.

They crossed the room, and Nuit eased down on a throne to the king's right. She raised her eyebrows at the icy glare that Geb directed at Harwa as the old woman took her station beside the queen. She shot the truth-seer a questioning glance, but the old woman evaded her gaze. Before she could consider it further, the doors opened again. A murmur rippled through the assembly when six soldiers led the Rathadi queen inside. The soldiers stopped twenty feet from the thrones, weapons at the ready, and pushed Isis to her knees.

Geb stood, and a hush fell over the crowd. "Isis of the Rathadi," Geb said, "you and your husband stand accused of breaking the sacred truce that has endured between our people for millennia."

Isis raised her head. Nuit shivered at the void inside the other woman's eyes. "Every word out of your forsaken mouth is a lie," the Rathadi queen hissed.

"Silence!" the king roared. "Your husband attacked my guards, slaying one, and tried to murder me. He is a traitor."

"You dare to call him a traitor after what you have done?" Isis spat. She stood to her full height, her face regal behind her grief. "You know well what he sought. A husband's right for what you have reaped without my consent."

"These are the words of a lunatic," Geb snapped, addressing the court. "Queen Isis is no longer able to govern the—" He was interrupted by a torrent of violent coughs from the commander of the soldiers who guarded Isis. He leveled the man with a withering stare that melted when the soldier collapsed to the ground, writhing.

"Your Majesty, it is just like what befell the other soldiers at the harbor when the archsage and the Rathadi prince escaped," one of the courtiers muttered.

Nuit glanced at Isis whose lips tugged into a joyless smile. "You know about this," the Purean queen said.

"You are all doomed," Isis replied serenely.

"What do you mean?" Geb demanded.

Isis shot him a dismissive glance before turning away.

Harwa stirred. "It is an illness, Majesty," she said.

"An illness?" The anger fell away from Geb as understanding dawned. "The archsage's weapon? He turned it against us?"

"Yes, Majesty. It appears that the affliction is spread by the living and by the dead," Harwa continued.

The soldiers reeled away from their commander. The others in the chamber scurried to put distance between themselves and the writhing man as blood began to seep from his eyes.

"We must burn the dead at once!" Geb exclaimed.

"It may be too late for that," Harwa said. "The sickness may have already unfurled over the entire island."

Geb considered, dread etching the lines of his face deeper. "The boy and his grandfather cannot have traveled far." He glanced to the admiral. "Deploy the fleet immediately. Send ships in every direction. One of them will spot them and bring them back. And search the archsage's laboratory. The old Rathadi was no fool. He will not have developed it without a cure." He faced Isis. "What do you know about this disease?"

Isis regarded him, her lips pressed into a defiant line.

"As you wish," Geb said. He waved his arm, and the door opened. Captain Nebet entered the room, followed by two soldiers.

The assembled Pureans gasped when they recognized the lifeless body the pair of soldiers dragged between them. Isis's jaw dropped in a silent scream of horror at the sight of her husband. Her shoulders slumped for an instant, then she straightened again and grew still like a statue. "How dare you desecrate a king's body?"

"The treatment of his body shall be dictated by you," Geb said.

"The body of my husband is to be given a royal funeral and sent off to the Otherworld as befits a king."

"So shall it be," Geb said, "if you give me the answers I seek."

"I do not know anything about the disease," Isis said.

"You expect me to believe that your father kept his work from you?"

Isis remained wordless, her gaze locked on Osiris's body.

Geb's eyes hardened. "Very well. If you refuse to give me the answers I seek—" He signaled to Nebet who slipped his sword from his scabbard and held it against Osiris's neck —"your husband will not enter the Otherworld whole."

Nuit stared at her husband, bewildered. *No… You imbecile…* She stood to intervene, but Harwa placed a hand on her shoulder, pulling her back.

"Captain Nebet," Geb ordered the soldier. Nebet raised the sword.

Isis screamed with a violence that sent shivers beneath Nuit's skin. The form of her body seemed to shift, the muscles beneath her skin writhing.

A bolt of panic went through Nuit. "Guards!" she cried out. "She is shif—"

Captain Nebet hit the wall with a nauseating crunch. Isis ripped out of her bloodstained dress, her body molding into a massive tiger as she covered the twenty feet between her and the king in a single leap. Before anybody could react, the great cat swatted the king's face with her clawed paw, ripping through skin and bone. The Purean king's mangled head hung limply, bent at a grotesque angle, as his body slid lifelessly to the ground.

Screams filled the large hall. Two soldiers notched arrows.

Nuit leaped up and raised her hands. "Don't shoot!" she yelled.

The soldiers stared at her, perplexed.

"She is to be kept alive!" Harwa cried out.

The soldiers froze but kept their bows drawn.

"The person who looses an arrow at this cat will answer with their head." Nuit's voice rang cold as ice.

The great tigress roared, muscles rippling beneath her shining coat. The silence in the chamber was complete when she stalked to Osiris's body then circled the Rathadi king, chuffing and nudging him with her head, as if trying to wake him from sleep. Her tongue lapped at the onyx scales of his cheek before she groaned and rested on the stone beside him, gaze locked on her husband's unseeing eyes.

CHAPTER 40

THE SOLDIERS CHARGE, weapons raised. Before they can draw near, their steps falter. The men collapse to their knees, clawing at their throats and faces. Their skin turns to fire as blood seeps from their eyes.

A scream cuts through the air—

And passed through Horus's lips as he bolted upright. His right palm was clenched around the hilt of his dagger hard enough to turn his fingers numb.

A nightmare... just a nightmare.

He rubbed his eyes. The rocking beneath him was strange but soothing. A canopy of stars hung overhead, more brilliant than he had ever seen. He smiled.

Then the memories flooded him.

Tato...

Amah...

His body shuddered, the tremors surging through him in violent waves.

Across the narrow deck, his grandfather roused.

"You're safe, my boy." His voice was familiar, but his gentle eyes were empty and foreboding. He moved closer.

Horus reeled, crabbing back until his back pressed against the stern. The grief in his grandfather's face etched deeper, but he froze.

"Horus, my boy, I only wish to help," he said softly.

Despair roiled up in Horus's chest like a snake, ready to strike. When his grandfather edged closer again, he whimpered, pushing harder against the wood and drawing his legs to his chest. He hugged them, staring at the old Rathadi numbly.

Thoth sighed dejectedly. He stepped to a wooden cask and lifted the lid, then reached for a cup. Horus licked his chapped lips at the splash of the cup dipping into the barrel.

"Just a bit for now," Thoth said, holding it out to Horus. "We can use the sail to catch rainwater, but we don't know—"

Horus snatched the cup from his grandfather's hand. He gulped down the water, reveling in the moisture inside his parched throat.

"Easy, my boy," Thoth said. "Small sips,"

Horus emptied the drink and reached out for more.

"That's enough for now." Thoth took the cup. "We do not know what awaits us."

The taste of the cool liquid seemed to clear the fog in Horus's mind. A void spread inside him, darker than the seas surrounding them, threatening to consume everything, leaving him empty and senseless. He turned and stared into the vastness before him, ignoring the shudders that took hold of his body.

Thoth sighed again. "We were fortunate that there was a

boat that had been provisioned to go out to fish the seas." The sound of his grandfather's voice tugged on him, pulling him back from the void, but Horus didn't turn. "The food and water will last us for many days," his grandfather continued, "and there is gear to catch fish and even salt to preserve—"

"They're dead, aren't they?" Horus asked.

Thoth's voice choked off.

"*Tato, Amah*… the others…" He faced his grandfather.

Thoth gazed at him wordlessly, his lupine face stricken and pale in the moonlight. He nodded.

Horus's heartbeat faltered. He bit back a sob. Tears threatened to fill his eyes, but he refused to let them come.

"They lost their lives, Horus, but we must never lose our reason for living. We are alive. We have each other. We must be grateful for that. It is up to us to preserve the memories of our people, our island—"

"Ra shatter that cursed island!" Horus screamed. "They're gone! They're all gone!" He broke down, sobbing. "And we can't even bury them, or raise shrines in their honor."

"Honor them by carving their names in your heart, Horus, not in stone," Thoth replied. "Even death itself cannot kill their names and memories. They shall always live within us." A strange flicker crossed Thoth's eyes.

Horus turned away again, and a stretch of silence grew between them as the waves lapped against the hull. "Why?" Horus asked, without moving, hiding his tears in the darkness of the night. "Why did the Pureans attack us?"

"The alliance has become difficult. Even more so after the death of the Pureans had been blamed on the shifter."

"It was the truth-seer," Horus said quietly.

"What?"

"It was Harwa. She is the one who killed them."

His grandfather stared at him, dumbstruck, as Horus told him about the Ursus claw Mia discovered in Harwa's chambers, and the plan they hatched. Realization spread through Thoth's features as the scope of the betrayal sank in.

A terrible thought occurred to Horus, freezing the veins beneath his skin. "The... The Pureans... Did they attack because of what we did?"

His grandfather leaned forward and fixed him with a steady gaze. "You must never think that, my boy." His voice was gentle, but his tone brooked no dissent. "The truce between the Rathadi and Pureans has always been fragile—since the inception of our races."

"I thought we shared the island peacefully?"

Thoth gave a forlorn smile. "What have you been taught about our creation?"

"At first, we were all Pureans, living peacefully together. We all worshipped Amun as The One. When Amun created animals to keep his children company, some grew jealous of the new beasts, fearful that Amun would love the animals more," Horus recited.

Thoth nodded. "One voice rose above all, a young witch named Tiamat. Beautiful and cunning, it was she who convinced others to ban the beasts from the island, so that Amun's children could live in purity. When Amun-Ra took the form of the falcon and visited the island, Tiamat was dazzled by his power and offered herself as his bride. But Ra was wise and judged her motives to be impure. Instead, he chose her sister.

They joined and Tiamat's sister became the mother of the first Rathadi."

Horus opened his mouth, but Thoth raised a forestalling hand.

"Others followed, and the Rathadi blossomed into a powerful race. As Tiamat grew older, she and the Pure Ones became even more jealous and discontented. Eventually, the Rathadi were forced to abandon the island and move to the Ring. But despite the Rathadi's banishment, Tiamat never forgave her sister and poisoned her. Tiamat was caught by the Rathadi and brought to justice. She was sentenced to die, yet she survived."

Horus stared at him. "How?"

"It is uncertain," Thoth said. "But legend has it that she had grown immortal and became the Witch Queen—and that her power was only exceeded by her hatred for the Rathadi."

Horus shuddered. "This Witch Queen... Is that who I saw on the ship?"

Thoth nodded. "I believe so."

"Why now?"

Thoth hesitated. "I cannot be certain. But if Tiamat was involved, we had little chance, for everything she planned, everything she did, was rendered with the purpose of annihilating the Rathadi."

Horus gazed out over the water, absorbing his grandfather's words. Soon the emptiness in his gut grew again. He rose and moved to the bow and knelt. He slipped the dagger from its scabbard and pressed the tip of the onyx blade to his chest, over his heart. He hissed when he drew blood, but the void inside him grew smaller as the pain broke through the emptiness. He dragged the blade across his skin, carving a thin line. He mouthed his vow, his whisper audible only to him over the sound of the waves.

"I am Horus, son of Isis and Osiris. As Ra is my first ancestor, your names shall never be forgotten."

CHAPTER 41

DAYBREAK BROUGHT glimmers of warmth after the cool night. The sea was no longer an abyss of black. Its blues and grays glistened and blurred together into a silver mist that hung above the water. The first beam of the sun pierced through the horizon and danced over the surface, as if igniting a perfect flame.

Horus rested at the bow and stared into the golden disk, its rays burning his eyes. He did not squint, keeping his gaze glued to the sun as it rose, daring Amun-Ra himself as the vast sea reflected the countless bright sparks cast on the surface. He had never watched the sun like this. He had never noticed its beauty, or its awe.

Horus drew a deep breath of salty air and forced himself to look away. He blinked through the flashes in his eyes and faced his grandfather who reclined at the stern, one hand resting on the tiller. He moved back and eased down beside the old Rathadi. His grandfather opened a bag of cured meat. Horus wrinkled his nose at the smell.

"It is important we keep our strength," Thoth said, holding it out to him. He pointed at the barrel. "Have some water, too."

Horus nodded wordlessly. He took a bite of the smoked meat and washed it down with a long draw of the water, then took another bite. He chewed the tough meat, studying their vessel. It was almost eight feet wide along the beam and more than twice as long. A triangular sail hung suspended from its single mast, and a covered cabin midship offered just enough space for both of them to shelter from rain. A small hatch in the deck led to the cramped fish hold below.

"Those clouds are coming our way," Thoth said, breaking the silence. He studied the storm-heaped clouds that fissured the northern sky, unable to hide the concern in his face. "The winds are favorable. If we head southeast, we should be able to skirt it."

Horus nodded absentmindedly when he spotted a flash against the western horizon, reflecting the rising sun. He focused, and the outline of three tall masts and white sails took shape.

"A ship!" he called out.

His grandfather turned. "Fetch the farseeker."

Horus rushed into the cabin and returned with the glass. His grandfather's brow furrowed as he studied the ship.

"Is it Purean?" Horus asked.

Thoth did not reply. He looked up at the clouds again, studying them for several moments. He returned the farseeker to Horus then tacked, pointing the bow directly into the dark skies.

"What are you doing?" Horus asked.

"It is the *Leviathan*. We have no chance of outrunning her. Our only option is to try to lose them in the storm."

Horus swallowed, but remained silent. A few moments later, the large ship adjusted its course to intercept them. They sailed for another full span wordlessly, watching the *Leviathan* closing the distance.

Thoth pointed to the lines coiled on the deck as the seas grew stronger about them. "Secure everything in the cabin. As tightly as you can."

Horus stood to do as his grandfather instructed, and Thoth attended to the sail. He trimmed it until only a small sliver remained. He noticed Horus's quizzical look.

"We need to keep enough sail to keep moving and remain stable, but not enough for the wind to capsize the boat," he said.

Horus turned back to the ropes. Thoth gave him an approving nod after he finished. "Your amulet and dagger, too," he said.

Horus lifted his hand to the amulet and shook his head.

"The seas will be rough. The metal could injure you. Or you could lose them."

Horus opened his mouth then shut it and rushed into the cabin. He secured the amulet and dagger inside one of the chests. A moment later, he was thrown against the hull as a wave crashed into the boat. He staggered onto the deck and glanced at the sea ahead. An icy numbness spread through his body.

The clouds billowed dark and unyielding, smothering the sun and blotting out most of the sky. Thunder crackled through the air. A moment later, a small drop of rain fell against Horus's flushed cheek. Then another. Shadow swallowed the last rays of light as the wind picked up, pushing the waters into angry waves.

"Hold on to the mast, Horus!" his grandfather called to him.

The sea heaved and roiled. Dark rollers warred and clashed against each other with terrible force. The wind slammed the rain into Horus's face as he held on tightly to the ropes around the mast. The air was thick with a briny mist, the deck awash with salty waves.

Another swell crested the boat. Horus gasped for breath between the walls of water as his grandfather wrestled the tiller to keep the boat pointed into the waves. He grunted with exertion as the wind and the waves pushed the boat sideways to the surge.

A lightning strike illuminated the sky. Horus looked behind them. The pursuing ship was nowhere to be seen.

"Horus, hold on!" Thoth bellowed.

Horus whipped about. Before him was not yet another wall of water, but a sheer cliff. He whimpered and latched on to the ropes.

Every bit of air was knocked out of his lungs. Somewhere the scream of his grandfather cut through the roar. One instant he was holding to the rope then water was all around him. Time stood still as he was dragged lower and lower by invisible hands, the pressure in his ears piercing his skull. Finally, the grip loosened, and he kicked and pulled through the water as hard as he could, his lungs burning for air.

He burst through the surface, gagging and spitting. He spun around, panicked, his eyes stinging from the salt as he desperately scanned the roiling sea for the boat.

"Horus!" A mighty cry broke through the roar of the sea. He

turned to the voice. Relief washed over him when he spotted the vessel, rolling in the waves a few feet from him. "Swim, boy! Swim!" Thoth shouted, leaning over the side, stretching his arm to Horus.

Horus kicked the water as hard as he could, but despite his efforts the boat drifted farther away with every stroke. He felt his strength ebbing when his grandfather ducked into the cabin. Terror gripped him.

A moment later, Thoth reappeared, holding the end of a rope. He frantically tied the rope around his waist then dove into the sea. Seconds later his grandfather's strong grip wrapped around him.

"Hold on to me, boy! Hold for your life!" he yelled. Horus clutched to his grandfather as the old Rathadi pulled them back, hand over hand, by the rope he had secured to the boat.

After what seemed like an eternity, they reached their vessel, rolling in the waves, and Horus clenched his fingers around the side. His grandfather pushed him up, and he fell onto the deck, retching.

From one moment to the next the rolling stopped. Horus wiped his eyes and glanced up. Blue skies stretched above him.

Thoth's hands appeared over the rail, and Horus reached down and helped his grandfather into the boat. Thoth collapsed on the deck, spitting water and breathing hard.

"Is… is it over?" Horus asked, panting.

His grandfather pushed himself up with a groan. He studied the sky, and his face fell.

Horus pulled up to his knees and stared at the dark clouds all around them.

"We are in the center of the storm," Thoth said. "We are in its eye."

His grandfather regarded the sail. "The sail pushes us broadside to the waves. We will not survive another one of those breakers." He rushed into the cabin and returned with a knife. Before Horus realized what happened, his grandfather had cut the mainsail line, and the canvas spilled onto the deck. Thoth stabbed the fabric, slicing through it.

"What are you doing?" Horus cried out, alarmed.

"No time!" Thoth shouted. "I need four lengths of rope, six feet each."

Horus stared at him, bewildered.

"Now, boy!"

Horus bolted into the cabin and snatched the coiled line. He measured and cut four lengths then rushed back to the deck. Thoth had cropped the sail into a large square and folded over one of the corners. He pierced the folded section with the knife, punching a hole into the canvas.

"Quickly, thread the rope through the hole and tie it at the corner, where the canvas is doubled up," he instructed. This time Horus obeyed without hesitation, trusting that his grandfather had a plan rather than having gone mad.

He tied the rope to the first corner as Thoth finished preparing the three others. His grandfather collected the far ends of the four ropes and tied them all together, fastening them to a long line.

The wind had just begun to pick up, rocking the boat from side to side, when Horus finished. Thoth checked the knots and took the canvas from Horus. He carved out a circular hole in the middle of the square, making the contraption resemble one of the kites Horus used to fly.

Another swell rolled the boat, almost knocking him down, as his grandfather rushed to the front and tethered the free end of the line to the cleat on the bow. He tossed the contraption into the water.

The boat gave a slight tug and turned into the waves. Thoth rushed back and used two lines to fix the tiller dead ahead.

The waves were rolling over the bow by the time he returned to the cabin and sank to the deck, heaving labored breaths.

"Come to me, boy," he said. Horus obeyed, and his grandfather fastened a piece of rope around Horus's waist and his own, then secured the other end to the boat.

Horus clung to his grandfather as the boat pressed forward, pitching up, then crashing down, jarring their bones as the storm roared around them. The salty seawater mixed with Horus's own tears as he prayed to Amun-Ra that they will live to see the next morning.

CHAPTER 42

THE DOOR to the Purean queen's audience chamber opened, and Harwa entered, her expression grim. The royal confidants glanced up at the truth-seer with barely concealed distaste. The old woman did not seem to take notice as she crossed the hall to the queen's throne.

Nuit was clad in a long black dress, and a mourning veil covered her face. She glanced to her advisors and the guards. "Leave us," she said.

Several of the braver courtiers dipped their lips into the hint of a frown, but most simply bowed, expressionless, and obeyed. When the last guard closed the door behind him, Harwa spoke.

"The last ship has returned."

"From your countenance, I surmise they have not been successful in their task," Nuit replied.

"The *Leviathan* spotted them, but when the old Rathadi realized they were being pursued, he turned their boat into a storm. Our ship followed, but lost them in the weather. The ship barely endured the tempest, and the captain is convinced that a small sailboat had no chance of surviving it."

"Yet they did not find debris—or bodies." It was more a statement than a question.

Harwa swallowed. "No, My Queen."

Nuit's face tensed, as if battling for control. A moment later her stoic grimace cracked, and she set loose a piercing scream.

"More and more of our people are dying every day!" She glared at Harwa. "What of the progress you have promised? We lay our king to rest on the morrow, and I assume the crown. Am I to tell my people there is no cure?"

"Our healers have been able to slow the disease," Harwa said.

"In those whom they can reach," Nuit countered. "We do not have enough skilled in the arts to deal with the illness."

"What of Isis?" Harwa asked.

Nuit sneered. "Every day that Rathadi bitch is alive, I am reminded of what she took from me, and the bastard child she carries inside her womb."

"Yet we must not discount the possibility that her father confided in her, and that she holds knowledge that may prove useful."

Nuit nodded slowly. "Very well. Find out all she knows," she said. "By any means necessary," she added coldly.

"I shall pay her a visit," Harwa replied. "But the mother of King Geb's offspring must remain unharmed until she gives birth. Delivering the child to Tiamat is our only hope to save the island."

Nuit's lips, already thin, compressed into bloodless lines.

She turned away and gazed out of the tall window. "Whatever shall remain of this island that is still left to save," she said, more to herself than the old woman. She did not move as the truth-seer bowed and left the room.

CHAPTER 43

HARWA SCURRIED across the courtyard to the barracks. She entered without even a glance at the guard and hastened into the lower levels. Iron wall sconces hung beneath the low ceiling, casting dim shadows along the corridor. Before long, she found herself in front of a door guarded by two soldiers.

"Open it," Harwa said.

The guards complied, and Harwa entered the cell. She wrinkled her nose at the acrid stench that assailed her.

Isis hunkered on the floor, chained by her neck to the wall behind her. Her white dress hung loosely, tattered and stained. The thick iron collar was tight, just large enough to encircle her slender neck, ensuring that she would suffocate immediately if she tried shifting into the powerful form of her sentinel. An untouched plate of oatcakes and nettle stew sat before her.

The Rathadi queen glanced up. She bristled when she recognized her visitor.

Harwa swallowed before speaking, her voice thin. "It was not supposed to happen like this."

Isis lowered her head, ignoring the truth-seer.

"The welfare of our island was at stake," Harwa continued.

"The welfare of our island?" The bitterness in the Rathadi queen's voice felt like a slap. "My people lie slain in the streets. My husband is dead. My son…" Her voice faltered.

"Sacrifices were necessary," Harwa whispered.

"Sacrifices? You dare to speak of sacrifices and the welfare of our island after—"

"I did what had to be done, to safeguard our island from the destroyer."

"The destroyer?"

"Your son," Harwa said.

Isis lifted her head and stared at Harwa wordlessly, her body rigid.

"On the day of his birth, a truth-vision befell me," Harwa continued. "The most terrifying vision that ever came upon me. The annihilation of our island—brought about by your son."

A long breath of silence stretched through the cramped cell. "This is madness," Isis finally rasped.

"It was unlike any other truth-vision," Harwa continued. "I denied it, prayed I was wrong. I tried to hide from it, but to no avail. Eventually, I was forced to come to terms with it, to accept that I had been chosen by Amun himself to save us."

"You are mad," Isis said.

"I wish it were so, Your Highness. I would gladly give my life—"

"If you believed this madness… that my son was the *destroyer*… why not just kill him?"

"The destroyer would have been reborn," Harwa replied.

"There was only one powerful enough to break the cycle and prevent the destruction."

"Then my father spoke true," Isis said. "You have aligned with the Witch Queen."

"It was the only way to save the island."

Isis gave a bitter laugh. "*She* is the one who wants to destroy us!" she cried out. "Have you been so blinded by your visions that you could not see that you played right into Tiamat's hand? She used you to kill Pureans, making it seem like a shifter, to turn the Rathadi and Pureans against each other." She stared at the old woman, as if sudden realization struck her. "And… Set? That was you?"

Harwa shuddered. Her voice broke when she spoke. "Many sacrifices had to be made."

"Ra's grace," Isis whispered, and wrapped her head in her hands. "And the Purean king and queen? They knew?"

Harwa stood stock-still, her lips pressed together.

Isis studied her, pondering. "You could have stopped me from killing Geb," she said as understanding dawned. "Geb knew… the night he came to me… I told him about Set and Mia, and the children's plan… He realized what you had done. That is why you allowed him to die." Her face twisted into a sickened grimace. "You slayed the girl and savaged Set. Nuit will find out what you did to her son."

"The queen will understand," Harwa said.

"Like I will understand that you wanted to sacrifice my own flesh and blood? Prevent him from joining with his sentinel?" Isis surged forward, but the chain stopped her short before she could reach the truth-seer.

"Yet he was too strong," Harwa said. "Once he joined, a different thread of the prophecy had to take place."

"A different thread?"

"A sister. The only one who can conquer the destroyer. The one you carry inside you."

Isis glowered at the truth-seer for a long time then laughed. "Harwa, you dimwitted old woman. You were the Witch Queen's puppet all along."

"All I did was in service to the island, Your Highness. Can you not see it? Do you not understand?" She drew nearer. "I shall plead clemency with the queen if you help us defeat this affliction ravaging our people. I know you have shared in the archsage's work. Perhaps you can make sense of this illness." Harwa's eyes were beseeching. "You must help us."

Isis rose slowly and smoothed out her tattered dress. She glared at the truth-seer from behind her feline eyes. "Kingslayer," she said.

Harwa met her gaze, confused.

"That is what your guards call me," Isis continued. "But the title should be bestowed upon you."

Harwa flinched under the weight of the Rathadi queen's words.

"Because of you and your truth-vision, your king lies dead. Because of you and your truth-vision, the Rathadi king, *my husband*, lies dead." Isis took a shuddering breath. "Because of this… madness I shall never see my son again, even if he still lives. You attempted to take him from me because you believed the Witch Queen. You failed, so you violated me." Her voice trembled as it crescendoed. "I carry the son of the man responsible for my husband's death inside my womb. And you ask me if I understand?" She let out a bark of laughter that sounded half-mad. "Do not hide behind your prophecies and visions, *Truth-seer*." The word sounded like poison rolling off her tongue. "You and only you have brought this upon us all."

Isis drew herself up to her full height. "No, Harwa, there shall be no bargain between us. There can be no peace between our people. You have doomed us, Rathadi and Pureans alike. And you shall live with that knowledge for the rest of your miserable days."

Harwa stood transfixed for a long time after the echoes of Isis's words died in the cell. She trembled at the unrestrained hatred that emanated from the Rathadi queen. Finally, the truth-seer's shoulders sagged, and she spoke. "So be it, Your Highness," she whispered. "Tomorrow the people shall witness your execution for treason against the Kingdom. There shall be no entombment, no royal burial. Tomorrow, Isis, Queen of the Rathadi, shall cease to exist. But your life will continue, hidden, bereft of any pity or compassion; your sole remaining purpose as a vessel—*a slave*—to the child you carry." Harwa paused, gazing at the terror building in Isis's face. "And you will die the moment the child is born. Your daughter shall be raised by the Witch Queen, never to know who her real mother was."

She turned and banged on the cell door, ignoring the shivers of fear surging through her at the feral scream and the thrashing of the metal chain behind her.

CHAPTER 44

THE FISHING LINE TWITCHED, and the float dipped under the surface. Horus yanked on the line and was rewarded with a defiant tug from the far end.

"I got another one!" he yelled, over his shoulder. "That's three in a span."

"Strong work, my boy!" Thoth replied. "But don't count your fish until they are in the boat."

Horus pulled on the line. The fish strained against him, but he drew in the line steadily hand over hand and hauled his catch out of the water, plopping it onto the deck.

"Three in a span," he said, grinning. His grandfather gave him a smile, then he glanced at the fish, and his expression shifted.

"What is it?" Horus asked.

Thoth shook his head. "It's nothing," he said. "Like you said, three in a span."

Horus unhooked the fish and handed it to his grandfather,

then baited the hook with a small piece of meat and cast the line again.

After more than four weeks at sea, he and his grandfather had settled into the semblance of a routine. Their sail fixed, they had continued due east. They had not encountered any more bad weather, or more ships. His grandfather had taught him how to navigate by the sun during the day and by the stars at night, leaving ample time to improve his fishing skills.

"Birds!" Thoth's voice rang out.

Horus lifted his head. "What?"

"There," Thoth said, and pointed at the eastern sky.

Horus followed his grandfather's finger, using his hand to shield against the sun's glare. The sky was a deep blue with nothing but wisps of clouds. Then he spotted them. A few dark dots circling against the blue.

"Birds," Thoth repeated, his voice shaking. "When you caught the steelhead, I thought perhaps... but the birds..." He turned to him. "Horus, my boy, we are near land."

Horus flinched at his grandfather's words. Their voyage at sea had been surreal, at times making it seem like the nightmare at home had never happened. The thought of stepping on solid ground again filled him with as much trepidation as it did joy. He felt a sinking in his stomach, curling up inside him. He pushed the void aside before it had time to rob his breath.

They sailed for another two spans before Horus made out the shape in the distance. At first, he thought it was a trick of the light. A dark band rose from the water, filling the entire eastern horizon. He turned to his grandfather, awestruck.

"I see it, too, my boy," the old Rathadi said.

"It is so vast," Horus said. He shivered. Thoth seemed to

sense his apprehension. He put his arm around Horus and drew him close.

It took them another span to reach the coast. When the waves started breaking around them, they jumped from the boat. He sank in the water to his chest before his feet hit bottom. They dragged the boat ashore, until the keel ground into the sand. Thoth staggered through the shallow water onto the beach and collapsed to his knees, burying his head in his hands, quivering. Horus stared at him, alarmed, not knowing whether his grandfather was laughing or crying.

He took a step toward him in the shallows, but his legs shook, and his head spun. He staggered forward and dropped onto the sand. He rolled onto his back, staring at the blue sky.

"Grandfather… this ground… it is moving," he stammered.

Thoth glanced back, a smile ghosting the old Rathadi's face through his tears. "It is land sickness, Horus. It is normal after having been at sea for this long. It shall pass."

They rested beside each other in silence, relishing in the feel of sand against their skin and the sound of the rolling waves. Finally, Thoth glanced back to the boat. "We should unload our belongings and secure the vessel."

The sun was beginning to set over the water by the time they had finished mooring the boat and unloading their possessions, laying them out onto the sail beneath one of the trees on the beach.

Horus gathered wood and kindling, and his grandfather started a fire by rubbing two pieces of wood against each other. They fashioned a spit over the flames, and soon the smell of fire-roasted fish filled the air.

Horus's mouth watered as his grandfather took one of the

fish from the flame and handed him the stick. "Eat slowly, my boy. Your stomach has not had cooked food in a while."

He took a bite, and the taste of the hot meat filled his mouth, waking memories. He pushed them aside before they could rise to the surface and focused on his surroundings. The days at sea have left him feeling insignificant against the boundless water. He had thought that reaching land would change it, but when he gazed out at the sweeping expanse of sand and trees with no end in sight, he realized he had been wrong.

"Where are we?" Horus asked.

Thoth took a bite of his own fish then licked his fingers before glancing up. "There are ancient texts that describe a vast continent to the east of our island. The scribes called it Ortegia."

"And you think this is Ortegia?" Horus asked, the word sounding strange in his mouth.

"Perhaps," Thoth said. "Our people have not ventured that far in centuries."

"Are there people here?"

"I think that is a reasonable assumption," Thoth replied.

"Are they like us? Or the Pureans?"

Thoth looked at him. "I do not know. But it is likely that they are different from both."

"Are they friendly?"

"We shall provide them with every reason to not see us as a threat."

"So what do we do now?" Horus asked.

"We make our way inland, try to make contact. I have many

skills, Horus. Skills that people of influence will find valuable in exchange for offering us protection."

"Protection?" Horus raised his brow.

Thoth took another bite and chewed slowly. He swallowed. "We must be prepared that the Pureans will continue to look for us."

Horus's mouth went dry, the taste of the fish suddenly forgotten. "But... how could they find us? They don't know where we have gone."

"They have truth-seers. Their visions may help lead them to us."

"We have to continue hiding?" Horus's voice trembled. "They killed everybody we know, and we still have to flee for our lives?" His heart thudded in his throat as realization rose. "They sent the ship after us because of what you did to the men in the harbor, didn't they?"

Thoth's face darkened. "I took many lives to enable us to flee. I have not known Geb, or Nuit, to forget such a thing easily."

"What did you do?"

"It is... not something I wish to discuss," Thoth replied.

"Why not?" Horus asked.

"Please, my boy," Thoth said. "Let us not speak of it." His grandfather moved closer to him and put his arm around him. At first, Horus sat stiffly, anger and confusion stirring inside him, then he noticed the hurt in his grandfather's eyes, and he leaned into him. Before long, he stifled a yawn with his fist.

His grandfather pushed aside some of the items on the sail. "Here, my boy, rest now."

Horus was too tired to argue. He lay down and allowed Thoth to cover him with one of the blankets from the boat.

When he closed his eyes, the waves were still beneath him, rocking the boat gently from side to side, lulling him into an uneasy sleep.

————

HORUS AWOKE to daylight and the noise of his grandfather rummaging through their belongings.

"Ra's blessings," Thoth said when he saw him stir. "Did you rest well?"

Horus nodded, rubbing the sleep from his eyes.

His grandfather held up two tall packs, each with twin straps attached to them, fashioned from sail and rope. "We shall travel light. I have filled up one with water and the other with items we can use to barter." He pointed at the small purse at his hip. "I have a few gold coins, but we do not know their value here."

Horus scanned the rest of their belongings scattered on the ground. "What about those?" he asked, his heart suddenly heavy at leaving behind anything that reminded him of home.

Thoth noticed his expression. "We can wrap them up in the sail and bury them."

"Do you think we will ever come back to retrieve them?"

His grandfather gave him a small smile, but didn't answer.

Horus set his jaw. "I will come back for them."

His grandfather nodded wordlessly. They wrapped the rest of the items and buried them beneath a tree. Thoth slung the water bag over his shoulders and handed the smaller pack to

Horus. He covered his face with the shawl until only his gray eyes were showing. Horus looked at him quizzically.

"It is likely that none of the people we shall encounter have seen a Rathadi," Thoth said. "They may be startled enough to see two strangers. We should not provide them with another excuse to run from us—or to reach for their weapons." He glanced at the onyx dagger that hung from Horus's hip. "Perhaps it will be safer if I hold on to it for now."

Horus opened his mouth, but shut it again and handed over the dagger reluctantly. Thoth slipped it inside his robe, and they set off due east, into the new land.

Shortly after midday, Thoth gave Horus a tug and sped up. Horus followed. A few steps later, his grandfather stopped and crouched. Horus's stomach looped when he realized the old Rathadi was studying a trail of footprints in the soft ground.

"It looks like a small group of people marching next to two beasts of burden," Thoth said, unable to keep the tremor from his voice.

"Shall we follow them?" Horus asked.

Thoth scanned the tracks in both directions. "They are fresh. With the wind and sand, the tracks wouldn't last half a day. Even if we cannot catch up to whomever left these, perhaps they will lead us to a settlement."

Thoth adjusted the water bag on his shoulders and wrapped the shawl around his face tighter before setting off along the tracks. Horus fell in behind him.

The sun had begun to set when Horus spotted movement in the distance. They quickened their pace. Soon, he was able to make out several vague forms. As they approached, he distinguished what looked like three men and two large beasts, the likes of which he had never seen before. The animals were taller than horses, and twin humps grew from their backs, making them appear as if they had been laden with a great burden.

The three men stopped and turned. They were shorter than his grandfather, with sunburnt skin and brown eyes, dressed in lightweight robes that fluttered in the breeze, and shawls that covered their heads. All three eyed them suspiciously as they drew near, focusing on Thoth's form and sizing him up.

Thoth approached them with his arms wide open. "Ra's blessings upon you," he said.

The strangers tensed at his voice. The oldest-looking of the three turned to his companions, one of them thin like a reed, the other trim and broad at the shoulders, and said something in a guttural language that Horus didn't understand.

Thoth pointed at himself. "I am Thoth," he said. "Thoth," he repeated. He pointed at Horus and said his name.

A glimmer of understanding passed through the eyes of the old man who had spoken. He stepped forward. "*Kom'ter,*" he said. His mouth was filled with bad teeth, and Horus thought he could almost smell the man's rancid breath.

Thoth inclined his head. "Komter," he said, trying to emulate the man's accent.

The old man cackled. "*Kom'ter,*" he said, slower.

"Kom'ter," Thoth repeated, this time sounding closer to the man's pronunciation.

Kom'ter's yellow teeth flashed in a gnarly grin.

Thoth reached into his robe and pulled out the coin pouch. He opened it and poured three gold coins into his palm.

The men's eyes took on an eager gleam.

His grandfather pointed at the three coins then at one of the tall animals.

Kom'ter shook his head then pointed to his chest, then at Horus.

Horus grasped his amulet when he realized what the man was implying. He took a step back. Thoth held out his palm.

"I am sorry, Friend," he said, shaking his head. "That item is not for barter." He pulled back the sleeve of his robe and extended his arm, displaying a thick gold bracelet.

Kom'ter's eyes widened. His tongue flicked over his lips.

Thoth put up two fingers and pointed at the powerful beasts. "Both of those."

The weedy man poked Kom'ter in the arm and chortled. He said something, and the others joined in, laughing. Kom'ter shook his head. He pointed at one of the animals and then at the bracelet.

"One, then," Thoth said, and held up one finger.

Kom'ter seemed to consider, then nodded. He flashed another wide grin.

Thoth took off his bracelet as Kom'ter stepped to one of the animals and untied the bags the beast was carrying. He led it to Thoth.

Thoth handed him the gold bracelet, and Kom'ter turned it in his hand, examining it. He said something to his companions, then handed Thoth the reins. He bowed, and Thoth did the same.

"May Ra guide your journey," Thoth said.

Kom'ter gave a short reply then returned to the other men, and the trio continued along their way.

Thoth watched them plod through the sand until they were

only small figures in the distance, then he turned to the animal. He lifted his hand to its fleshy lips and nose, allowing it to smell him. The animal pulled at the reins at first, but his grandfather's composed demeanor seemed to calm it quickly.

"What a strange beast," Thoth said, as Horus marveled at its size. Up close it was even larger than it had first appeared, with thick muscles beneath its skin and wide, twin-toed feet.

Horus gawked at the humps on its back. "What are those?"

"I am uncertain," Thoth replied, "but I imagine the beast has adapted to living in a harsh environment where food and drink are scarce, so those could be stores of nourishment."

"Can we ride it?"

"This is a riding harness," Thoth said, examining the bridle and reins. "I believe so. It will make our travels easier."

Horus approached the animal cautiously. The beast gave him a curious glance, then offered a high-pitched bleat.

Horus jumped back.

Thoth laughed. "I think he likes you."

Horus raised his brow and took a deep breath, trying to slow his hammering heart. "If you say so."

"It is getting late," Thoth said. "We should make camp here and continue in the morning."

They tied the animal to a tree and set up camp, then ate the fruits and nuts that they had collected, but Horus's stomach rumbled.

"Tomorrow, I shall make a spear, and we will set traps," Thoth said. "And we can try our luck at hunting. I saw some small creatures that looked like hares. With luck, we shall be dining better soon."

Horus listened to his grandfather's words, struggling to

keep his eyes open. His head drooped against his chest, and soon exhaustion claimed him, and he was fast asleep.

———

"RUN, HORUS!"

At first, he thought the voice of his grandfather rang from a nightmare, from yet another reminder of their bloody escape, then Horus opened his eyes. His brain took a moment to make sense of what he saw. The two younger men they had met earlier had flanked his grandfather, their faces twisted into wicked snarls. An icy shiver ran down Horus's back at the sight of the weapons in their hands.

The thin one lanced out with a knife. His grandfather stepped aside and flung him into the dirt.

The arm wrapped around Horus's neck from behind. He screamed when he was lifted off the ground. Then he felt the cold metal press against his belly, and the scream died on his lips.

Thoth whipped about and froze. His face turned expressionless as marble, and he lifted both hands.

"Easy, Kom'ter, there is no need to—" The last word turned into a grunt as the burly man punched him savagely in the stomach, dropping him to his knees. The skinny one smashed the hilt of his dagger against the back of Thoth's head, driving him face-first into the ground.

"Grandfather!" Horus screamed.

The skinny man straddled Thoth's back and rummaged through his robe. His hand clenched around the coin pouch.

Thoth stirred weakly. "Take what you want," he groaned, "just don't hurt the boy. Leave us alone."

Kom'ter reached for Horus's amulet. Horus strained against him.

"No, boy," Thoth said. "Do not resist."

Horus doubled his efforts, but Kom'ter ripped off the amulet. Horus howled and sank his teeth into the man's arm. A fist smashed against his cheek. The pain rang through his head, setting off flashes and driving tears into his eyes.

"Ra curse you!" Thoth yelled, and tried to push to his feet, but the skinny man pressed a knife against his throat, drawing blood. The burly one strewed the contents of their bag into the sand.

Horus heard the noise a moment before the burly man raised his head and stared into the distance. His face blanched. He yelled out in his native tongue, voice panicked. The other men dropped everything and rushed into the woods.

Thoth didn't hesitate. He leaped forward and snatched Horus from the ground then rushed for the trees. They dove into the thicket and dropped to the ground.

Horus trembled and whimpered.

"Shush, my boy," Thoth said. He pressed his arm around Horus's shoulders as he peered out.

Six men, mounted on the strange, double-humped beasts, drew near. They were dressed in thin leathers, and curved blades hung at their hips. The leading rider lifted his arm at the sight of the two lone camels and the campsite, and they came to a stop. He pulled back his hood. His features were plain but hard, and his hair was bound in a tail at the nape of his neck.

Their beasts knelt down, and the riders dismounted and inspected the items on the ground, then scrutinized the tree line at both sides of the clearing. Horus followed his grandfather's gaze to the other side where Kom'ter and the other men had disappeared.

The leader barked a command, and the men returned to their animals. Two of them unstrapped a pair of strange-looking contraptions from their saddles: a long pole with an incomplete circle at the end, about the size of a man's neck. Another pulled out a net and a pair of chains.

Thoth inhaled sharply. "Slavers," he whispered.

The men spread out and began scouring along the trees. Horus moved to crawl away, but his grandfather held him firm.

"They'll hear," he whispered into Horus's ear.

They clung to the ground, barely able to breathe. Horus's heart raced as the leader drew near.

Thoth pressed his cheek against Horus's and whispered, "When I tell you, you run. No matter what you may hear, you shall keep going until you cannot run any farther. Do you understand?"

Horus choked at his grandfather's words. He desperately wanted to argue, but fear paralyzed him, stripping him of his voice.

"Prepare yourself," Thoth whispered. He tensed as the man was almost upon them.

A scream from the other side of the clearing cut through the air. The leader whirled and rushed back. A pair of the slavers had pulled the skinny man from the thicket. He wailed and fought desperately, but they quickly locked his legs and arms into chains. The other four rushed into the woods. Moments later, the sounds of a scuffle and screams reached Horus's ears, then an eerie silence followed. Before long, the four slavers returned, leading Kom'ter and the burly man before them, the circular rings at the end of the poles trapping their necks like collars. Horus gasped when he saw blood on the trapped men's chests and shoulders, realizing the collars must be studded on the inside with spikes. The slavers pushed the two captives to their knees next to the skinny man.

The six slavers shackled Kom'ter and the burly man expertly then placed collars on all three and chained them together. Dread pooled in Horus's stomach as he watched the slavers collect his and his grandfather's belongings and load them into their saddlebags. He curled his hands into tight fists, not daring to move a muscle while everything inside him shrieked. The slavers tied the other two beasts to their caravan and mounted their own animals before setting off with their captives shuffling behind them, chained to the slavers' saddles.

Horus and his grandfather remained on the ground motionlessly until the caravan had disappeared into the darkness. After another quarter span, they finally dared to move. Horus rushed out and fell to his knees, frantically searching the ground for his amulet or any of their belongings. He stifled a sob.

"Shush, my boy." Thoth's voice was little comfort. "We were fortunate. What if the slavers had come upon us while we were sleeping?"

"Wh-what kind of place is this where people enslave one another?" Horus whimpered.

Thoth had no answer for him.

"They took everything... Everything we had left to remember them by..." Horus's voice cracked. The memories rushed him. He tried to force them down, lock them away, but they burst to the surface, and great tremors washed over him.

Thoth pulled him into his arms and held him for a long time as the boy cried.

"How are we supposed to continue? Without *Amah?* Without *Tato?"*

Thoth took a long time before responding. When he spoke, his words were slow and measured. "We must learn to live without them, and learn to accept our grief, for it will never go away. It will become part of you, step by step, breath by breath. With time, you shall learn to live with the grief, and you shall prevail."

Horus wiped his eyes. "Ra's promise?"

"Ra's promise. And I shall be there with you, every day, until then."

"What are we going to do now?"

"We shall learn the ways of this strange land."

"But how? We have nothing."

Thoth shook his head. His large gray eyes shone brightly in the moonlight. "In that, you are wrong, my boy. We have far from nothing." He placed his palm on Horus's heart and then his own. "We have what is in here." He pointed a finger at his head. "And what is in here." The old Rathadi gazed at him intently. "And that is all we shall ever need."

CHAPTER 45

SET STIRRED RESTLESSLY beneath the hands of the healer.

"Please, My Prince," the man said. "Try to remain still."

"I am not ill," Set said.

"And we must ensure that it remains so. Her Majesty insists we examine you daily, in case—"

"How could I even have gotten ill? I've been kept here like a prisoner for two months!" Set bolted up. "Shouldn't you be with all the sick ones who actually need you?"

The man reached for him again. "Her Majesty—"

Set pushed aside the healer's hands. "I want to see my mother."

"Her Majesty is not in her chambers."

"Then I shall wait for her there until she returns," Set said, and stood.

"My Prince—"

Set pressed past him and left the room, entering his mother's chambers through the private door connecting their living quarters.

He entered the parlor and called out for his mother. Not hearing a reply, he crossed the room into her office then peeked into the private audience hall that led out into the corridor. The chamber was much smaller than the great throne room where the queen held formal court since she had assumed the crown, and served as a meeting space for her closest advisors. Set sighed when he found it empty, too. He doubled back to her office and eased into the chair behind the ornate desk. Absent-mindedly, he leafed through the papers resting on top of it. He scrunched his brow when he spotted a message about a sighting of Rathadi in the Brim. *They are in hiding?* He flipped past it to a report on the progress of the illness. He started reading it, but soon got lost in the numbers and the vernacular of the healing arts. He stifled a yawn with his fist, trying to keep his attention on the page, but before long, his head drooped onto the desk, and he nodded off.

He stirred when the outside door into the audience chamber opened. He hopped down from the chair and moved across the office when he heard the truth-seer's scratchy voice. He slid back behind the door.

"She refuses to eat," Harwa said, as they entered the chamber from the corridor. "And she has grown weaker."

"She must not be allowed to die before the child is born," his mother replied.

Set crinkled his brow at his mother's words. *Who are they talking about?*

"We have kept her alive and hidden for eight weeks," Harwa said.

"And you shall do so until she carries to term."

"Much can happen in four months."

"I am not interested in excuses."

"Perhaps if we moved her—"

"You know that is not possible," his mother countered. "Do you realize what would happen if our people discovered that the Rathadi queen has been kept alive while more and more of them die every single day?"

Confusion rippled through Set. *Isis is alive? And pregnant? But the execution…?*

"Yes, Your Majesty," Harwa said. "But Tiamat—"

"I do not wish to hear that name spoken in my presence," the queen hissed. "Go and see to the woman."

"Yes, Your Majesty," Harwa said meekly. The outside door opened and closed as the truth-seer left the royal chambers.

Set's mind raced. *Why would they keep her alive? And what of all the talk about a child?* He tiptoed out of the office back into the parlor. He cracked the door leading to his chambers, then slammed it shut.

"Mother?" he cried out. "Mother, are you here?"

Nuit paced through the audience hall and entered the office. She offered an indignant glare from the doorway. "Princes do not yell like commoners. Much less so when they seek the attention of their queen mother."

Set cast his eyes down. "I'm sorry. I had a bad dream and got scared."

Nuit's demeanor changed. She opened up her arms. Set drew close and nestled inside her embrace. They stood for several moments before Set broke the silence.

"When will you let me walk about the palace again?"

"When it is safe."

"And when will that be?"

"Our healers are barely able to keep the Rathadi illness at bay. I cannot risk your becoming afflicted." She clutched his hands and squeezed them, hard. "You are the only person left that I care about."

Set tried not to wince at his mother's firm grasp as he processed her words. "Why did Queen Isis kill Father?"

Nuit's face shifted for an instant before an unreadable expression spread across it. "The Rathadi are sometimes more animal than men. King Osiris has been slipping into madness. He and his woman conspired against us." She paused, looking grim. "What he was not able to accomplish, she did."

"I still can't believe that Queen Isis—"

"Betrayal is never easy to accept."

"Why did you not let me watch the execution?"

"I know you were close to her son," Nuit said, and embraced him again. "You are young and have seen enough death. I wanted to spare you even more grief."

"What happened to her body?" He allowed his mother to hold him for several more moments before he pulled back.

"She was burned without ceremony, as befits kingslayers."

Set struggled not to betray the surprise at his mother's blatant lie. "I'm glad she got the punishment she deserved," he said when he found his voice. "The Rathadi must be brought to justice for what they have unleashed upon us."

Nuit lifted her palm to his cheek. "I understand it is difficult for you to say these things. And I am proud of you."

"I may be young, but I will rule this island one day, Mother," Set said. "I must learn to become a strong leader. Like Father... like you."

Nuit kissed him on his head. "I must tend to things," she

said. "Would you like me to have the custodian bring more books?"

"Yes, thank you." Set pressed his lips into a smile as his mother turned to leave. "Mother?"

The queen stopped.

"I have spent much time studying the palace from my balcony. Could you have him bring me the plans of the palace, too?"

His mother glanced at him quizzically.

"I have been reading books for the last two months. If I am to be king one day, should I not know my palace well? And it will be more interesting than just reading—at least I can imagine I'm walking about while stuck in my chambers."

Nuit smiled. "Of course. I shall have the custodian bring them to you."

"Thank you, Mother," Set said. His smile fell from his face when the door closed behind the queen.

THE ANTELOPE LAY still in the soft soil, an arrow protruding from its neck. Thoth crouched beside it and placed his bow on the ground. He pressed a palm against the animal's head and offered a short blessing then pulled the arrow free and handed it to Horus.

"A clean hit," Horus said before wiping the blood off the shaft and sliding it into the quiver. His grandfather flipped back the hood of his goatskin robe. The old Rathadi looked leaner, his skin darker and more weathered since they had arrived in this strange land six weeks ago. At first, they had struggled to sustain themselves, but once Thoth had found a tree suitable for fashioning a bow, their fortunes changed. Horus and his grandfather had learned to live off the land, getting to know the terrain and the animals that inhabited it. As comfortable as they had grown with the wildlife, the memory of their first encounter with the Ortegians had been ingrained in their minds, and they had stayed clear of any areas that looked inhabited.

A high-pitched scream pierced the air. They exchanged startled glances before Thoth pulled Horus down and motioned for him to stay silent. They listened for several moments, but no other noises were to be heard.

"Stay here," Thoth whispered.

He crept to a hill in the direction from which the scream originated then slithered up and looked over the ridge. He turned to Horus and waved him closer, putting a finger to his lips.

Horus crawled to the ridge and peered over. A man and a woman, both dressed in gray robes, knelt beside an older woman who was writhing in pain. Next to them, a burly, bull-like animal stood impassively, laden heavy with sacks. The older woman held on to her leg and stared, terrified, at her foot, bent at an awkward angle. The younger one's face was completely covered, but her eyes were filled with dread at the older woman's injury.

"We need to help them," Thoth whispered.

Horus grasped his grandfather's arm. "Are you sure?" he asked, trying to ignore the sorrowful sound of the old woman weeping. Their last encounter flashed through his mind. "What if—?"

"We cannot judge an entire people based on the actions of a few. These three are in trouble and in need of our help."

Thoth wrapped the shawl around his face and stepped down the slope, his arms open wide. When the man spotted him, he leaped up from the ground and positioned himself protectively between the two women and the Rathadi. He slipped out a gnarled staff that hung at the animal's flank and raised it at Thoth with trembling hands.

"Easy, friend," Thoth said soothingly. "I mean you no harm."

The man's face tightened in confusion at the words, but he didn't move. Thoth stopped.

"Come out, Horus," he called over his shoulder.

Horus swallowed, but didn't budge.

"Horus, my boy," Thoth called out again, his voice firmer. "Come to me. Now."

Horus forced himself to his feet and slowly joined his grandfather. The man's face shifted in surprise, but he seemed to relax a bit.

Thoth pointed to himself then the woman on the ground. "I am a healer. Let me help her."

Horus knew none of them understood his grandfather's words, but his tone seemed to put them at ease. The man's staff dipped.

"Let me help her," Thoth repeated.

The man shot a glance over his shoulder. The young woman said something, and he lowered the staff completely.

"Thank you," Thoth said. Keeping his arms extended to his sides, he approached and took a knee next to the injured woman. The young woman stirred and watched him guardedly, but she remained silent. As Horus drew near, he noticed the young woman's eyes were a bright pink, and every bit of her skin was covered up, down to her hands that were tucked into a pair of thin gloves.

Horus stood back as Thoth placed his palm on the injured woman's forehead and whispered to her. The pain in her face seemed to ease a shade. Thoth slowly moved his other hand to her leg, but she grasped it, whimpering.

This time it was the young woman who spoke out. Horus didn't understand the words, but the old woman calmed and allowed Thoth to continue. She hissed in pain when he pressed on her knee, but lay still as he moved his hands down her leg. When Thoth touched her ankle, the woman screamed and shoved Thoth away.

The young woman spoke again, this time to Thoth, but her tone was not harsh. It almost sounded like an apology.

"I understand," Thoth said. "She is in much pain, but I can help her." He lifted a stick from the ground and motioned to the woman's lower leg. He snapped the stick, leaving it bent. "Her ankle is broken."

The three strangers nodded in understanding.

Thoth gestured to the woman's leg and then again at the crooked stick. "The bone is not lined up correctly. I need to set it first and then immobilize it." He made a show of straightening the stick. The old woman cowered and said something in the strange tongue. Thoth gently touched her shoulder.

"It will be painful, but it must be done, or your leg will not heal properly."

The woman peered into the Rathadi's eyes, then nodded. Thoth motioned the young woman to sit behind her, then waved the man close and placed one of the man's hands on the injured woman's thigh and the other just below her knee. He squeezed his palms around the stranger's hands, guiding him to hold firmly. When all were ready, Thoth grasped the woman's foot and pulled, setting the broken bone into alignment.

The woman screamed, then her head lulled back into the young one's shoulders, who stared at Thoth alarmed. Thoth placed a palm against the old woman's neck for several heartbeats, then removed her shoe and inspected her ankle before pressing his fingers against the top of her foot. After a few moments, he nodded, satisfied.

"The bones came back into alignment, and the blood is circulating well into her foot," he said, hoping the strangers would take solace from his calm tone. "Horus, fetch two straight branches, about two fingers wide." He eyed a coiled rope that hung at the animal's side as Horus bounced up. The man nodded in understanding. He retrieved the line as Horus returned with two twigs.

Thoth reached inside his robe. The man's eyes widened at the gleam of the onyx blade as Thoth cleaned the branches then cut two lengths of the rope and fixed the makeshift splint around the woman's lower leg. He stood and motioned for the man to pick her up, then beckoned the strangers to follow him. The man hesitated for only a moment, then picked up the unconscious woman and set off behind Thoth. The young woman grasped the strap draped around the animal's neck and followed, pulling the beast behind her.

Together, they crested over the small ridge and into the clearing behind it. Thoth gestured to the antelope then to all of them. The man and woman exchanged glances before the man swallowed and broke into a hesitant smile.

The young woman tied the animal to a tree, then pulled out a large pelt and spread it on the ground. The man eased the injured woman atop it then stood and faced Thoth with his hand over his heart. "*Dewa netjer,*" he said.

"You are welcome, friend," Thoth said, then motioned to Horus. "Horus," he said, distinctly, then to himself, "Thoth."

"*Ho-rus,*" the man repeated, then, "*Thoth.*" He gestured to the young woman *"Amsu,"* he said, then bowed, *"Ba'tif."* He moved beside the woman on the ground and knelt, placing a hand on her shoulder. *"Saba. Amsu e Ba'tif umma."*

Thoth repeated the names. "I believe Saba is their mother," he said to Horus, then smiled. "Fetch us some firewood, my boy. We are going to celebrate a meal with our first friends in this strange land."

———

AS EVENING FELL AROUND THEM, the smell of cooked antelope meat crept into Horus's nose, making his mouth water. Ba'tif had skinned and dressed the kill while Thoth had started the fire. Amsu had stayed by the side of her mother, who had awakened only once, drank some water, and fell right back to sleep. As the smell of cooked meat filled the air, Saba stirred again. She opened her eyes and whispered to her daughter. Amsu responded, and the woman eyed Thoth and Horus. She put her hand over her heart. *"Dewa netjer,"* she whispered.

Thoth nodded then sliced off a piece of the meat and handed it to Saba. The woman accepted the food and bit into it. The last remnant of her trepidation faded from her face as she chewed. Thoth carved up the antelope, and they ate in silence.

Ba'tif handed Thoth the water skin.

"Dewa netjer," Thoth said.

The two women and Ba'tif stared at Thoth before Ba'tif barked in laughter and clapped Thoh on the shoulder. He pointed to the antelope. *"Ku,"* he said.

"Ku," Thoth repeated. He nudged Horus. "Now you, boy."

"Ku," Horus said.

Amsu pointed to herself and her mother. "*Genna,*" she said, then pointed at Thoth and Ba'tif, "*Ta'hir.*" Thoth and Horus repeated the words for man and woman.

Thoth reached up and removed his shawl. The three gasped at the sight of his wide, bristly jowls and lupine features. Thoth motioned to Horus and himself. "Rathadi," he said.

"*Rattadi,*" Ba'tif repeated.

Amsu and Saba stared at Thoth with an equal amount of fear and fascination. Ba'tif said something to Amsu, but she shook her head. He said it again, more emphatically. Amsu looked like she was going to argue, but she sighed and slowly lowered her scarf, exposing her face and hair. Horus drew in a sharp breath. Amsu's skin was the color of ivory, and her hair was fine and white as milk. Amsu lowered her eyes, unwilling to meet Horus's or Thoth's gaze.

"You are a beautiful being," Thoth said. "You should never be ashamed of the way you have been created, for that is an affront to The One's will."

Amsu glanced up and gave him a timid smile, clearly not understanding the words, but appreciating his tone.

Horus stared at her, spellbound. "Why does she look that way?" he asked his grandfather.

"She is a pure skin," Thoth replied. "Her skin lacks the pigments that turn ours darker. People like Amsu are very rare."

"Is that why they are by themselves? Because she's different?"

"I do not know," Thoth said. "Perhaps they have been shunned by their own." His face took on a dark tone. "Or perhaps they must stay hidden because her kind is rare and valuable to slavers."

Horus set his jaw and glanced at the young woman. "Do not worry, Amsu. My grandfather and I won't allow anything to happen to you."

Amsu looked at him quizzically, but the conviction in his face made her lips curve into a timid smile.

"We should rest now," Thoth said. "Amun-Ra willing, Saba will heal well, but we should remain with them overnight."

———

THE SOUND of splitting wood roused Horus. He rubbed the sleep from his eyes and watched Ba'tif bring a long log to his grandfather and place it on the ground, next to a matching one. Amsu was busy fixing shorter cross-pieces to the long one with braided reeds. She heard Horus stir and turned to him. She had covered up her face completely, but her eyes smiled at him warmly.

"*Ba'ka nefer*," she said.

"I am unsure of the exact meaning of these words," Thoth said, "but it seems to be a greeting they exchange at the start of the day."

"*Ba'ka nefer*," Horus replied. He turned back to his grandfather. "What are you doing?"

"We are constructing a sled for Saba that can be drawn behind the auroch," his grandfather explained.

"The auroch?"

"If I remember correctly, that is what their beast is called."

"They do not have carts?" Horus asked.

"It does not appear so," Thoth replied. "Wheels do not seem very practical in the soft sand."

Horus turned to the older woman. She was resting in the same spot beneath the tree and, even though she still appeared to be in discomfort, she looked much better than the previous night. She gave him a smile that he returned.

Horus turned to Amsu. "Why are you covering yourself?" he asked, pointing at her scarf and gloves. "We are friends. You don't have to hide anymore."

She looked at him perplexed for several moments, then understanding flashed through her eyes. She pointed at the sun then at her skin. "*Akhet*," she said.

"*Akhet?*" Horus repeated, puzzled.

"Pure skins have very sensitive skin," Thoth said. "I believe she is trying to tell you that the sun causes her harm."

"I'm sorry," Horus said with a small frown.

"*Kullu tamaam,*" Amsu said.

Horus knelt beside her, then picked up a reed and started fastening it to one of the cross pieces of the sled.

"*Emmu,*" Amsu said, shaking her head. She took the reed from Horus and wrapped it around one piece, then the other, before pulling them together into a tight loop. "*Aha,*" she said.

Horus watched her secure another cross-piece to the sled then nodded. He picked up one of the branches and a reed and copied what Amsu did.

"*Aha?*" Horus asked.

"*Aha,*" Amsu replied with a wink.

After they finished constructing the sled, Thoth and Ba'tif lifted the front of it over the auroch's hindquarters, leaving the far end to drag behind the animal. They secured the frame, padding the wood with fur to prevent it from chafing the beast's hide. Amsu then used the rest of the furs to make a berth for Saba before Ba'tif gently lowered their mother into the sled.

He stood and regarded Thoth and Horus. Amsu and Saba eyed them, unsure, their faces somber.

Ba'tif spoke then beckoned to Thoth and Horus, as if inviting them to come along. Amsu and Saba nodded enthusiastically.

Horus glanced to his grandfather. "Where do you suppose they are going?"

"I do not know," Thoth replied.

"Can we stay with them, at least for a while?"

Thoth considered. "We do not know what awaits us, and we would be moving much slower."

"But they could teach us the language," Horus pleaded, "and the ways of the land. And you can check on Saba's progress."

Thoth gave him a smile. "They seem like good people, and willing to teach us. It may be good to join our meager forces for a short while." He placed a palm on Horus's shoulder and turned to Ba'tif. "*Aha*," he said.

CHAPTER 47

SET STOOD on his terrace and gazed over the island beneath him. The sun had long dipped below the western horizon, and the heat of the day had been replaced by a cool breeze. The city of Amun was lit by thousands of lights, glittering like stars that had dropped to the earth. The huge and small structures collided in a mixture of shadow and geometry, and the tangled lines of streets created twisting threads. The marvel that was the Purean capital lay still, and in the darkness and quiet it seemed almost possible to forget the last three months and the toll the illness had wreaked on the Pure Ones—or the lies and deceit that had come with it. Set turned and studied the wall before him, visualizing the route he had memorized from the palace maps. He looked to his destination, trying to ignore the quiver that crept into his limbs.

Don't be a craven, Set. Mia could do this climb in her sleep. He flinched as Horus's voice rang through his ears then gave a wistful smile. He took a deep breath and stepped onto the ledge.

"Just like climbing a ladder," he whispered, and reached for the first hold.

After overhearing the conversation between his mother and Harwa six weeks ago, he had fixated on discovering where they had kept the Rathadi queen. An entire week of sneaking and shadowing the truth-seer finally yielded the answer when he spotted the old woman heading for the conclave tower.

Remote and only used during the Kings' Conclave, the small chamber within the tower was an ideal spot to keep some-body confined and hidden from prying eyes. He had visited the cell-like room only once with his father when the king had passed down the history of the conclave to him. He recalled the cramped space and the thick door that could only be opened from the outside. It appeared his mother and Harwa did not even wish to risk any guards discovering that the Rathadi queen still lived.

He had spent the last month planning a route to reach the chamber from the outside, practicing his climbing skills, venturing farther each time. He glanced to his destination as he pressed toward it along the walls and parapets of the palace. Tonight, the prison of the Rathadi queen was within his reach.

Half a span later, Set balanced near the slit-like window. Hardly longer than a foot, and half as high, it was the only opening into the small chamber. He steeled himself and peered inside. He gasped at the sight of the woman on the floor, wearing nothing but a tattered dress that barely kept her decent, unable to conceal her bulging belly. A thick metal collar chained to the wall encircled her neck. Set's throat tightened as he fought off the surge and crash of bitter emotions that stirred inside him.

Even though this was the Rathadi who had killed his father, it was also the mother of a companion he had loved like his own brother, and had never shown him anything but kindness. He could not help but feel pity at her gaunt features and pallid skin.

"Queen Isis?" he whispered.

The woman did not move.

"Isis," he repeated. She stirred and turned, as if uncertain whether the voice was real.

"Isis," Set called out again, as loudly as he dared.

This time she raised her head and stared out into the darkness.

"Is someone there?" she asked.

Set flinched at the sound, devoid of the usual confidence and warmth that had pervaded the voice of the Rathadi queen. For weeks he had thought about what he would ask her, what he would tell her, but he froze, suddenly uncertain of what to do.

"Anybody?" Isis asked again.

"It's me, Set," he finally said.

Isis lifted her head higher. "S-Set?" she stuttered. "How?"

"I thought you were dead," Set said, his voice cool.

The queen pushed herself to her knees. "What of Horus? Is my son alive?"

"Horus and the archsage escaped. Ships were sent in pursuit, but they returned empty-handed."

Isis exhaled a long breath. "Then there is still hope," she whispered.

"How can this be?" Set asked. "Your execution? People saw you die."

"It was a sham."

"Why?"

The Rathadi queen's gaze grew distant. "I must not allow them to have her…" She looked up at him imploringly. "You must help me."

"Help you?"

Her hands slipped to her stomach unconsciously. "If it was not for the life I carry inside me, I would have done it myself, but… I am not strong enough…" Her voice cracked under the weight of her words.

Set stared at her, appalled, as realization struck. "No! I will not help you kill yourself and your unborn child!"

Isis's face twisted into a painful grimace. "They want to take her from me. They want to take my daughter. Please… you cannot allow that to happen!"

"No!" Set cried out again. "I… I can't be responsible for killing you, too!"

"Killing me, *too?*"

Set grasped the rock until it dug into the skin of his palms.

"I… I'm sorry…" he whimpered. "I'm so sorry… It's all my fault… All of it."

"Nonsense, child," Isis said. "You did nothing wrong."

"No, you don't understand!" he snapped. "The day King Osiris came to the palace… I… I thought he was going to kill my father… His sword was raised, and there was blood everywhere… and I… I…"

Isis stared at him, dismayed. "*You* killed Osiris?"

"My father told everybody that he killed King Osiris when he was attacked. He made me swear never to tell anyone what truly happened that night. Not even Mother." His tears ran freely now. "I loved you like my own parents, yet I killed your husband. I will not be responsible for killing you and your unborn child!"

Isis covered her head with trembling hands. She remained silent and motionless for a very long time. Finally, she lifted her head and spoke, her voice firming up. "A fine pair," she scoffed. "Kingslayers, you and I."

"Why do they want the child?" Set asked.

"They want to give her to the Witch Queen, Tiamat."

A cold wash swept through Set as he recalled the truth-seer uttering the name. "No..." he stammered. *Tiamat is the Witch Queen?* His heart plummeted at the implication. "My mother and Harwa..." he moaned. "Why... why would Mother and Harwa want to help the Witch Queen?"

"You have every right to hate me for what I did," Isis said, fixing him with a steady gaze, "but you must believe me. Tiamat will destroy the island and everything that is left of what we love."

"I... I don't know whom to trust anymore," he said, heat rising behind his eyelids.

Isis remained silent for several moments before she spoke. "Harwa... She is the one who attacked you."

Set flinched at her words. The ghost of a memory stirred. He squeezed his eyes shut, willing the thought to disappear. "You're lying!" he cried out. "Why would I trust you? You killed my father!"

The images flooded his mind unbidden.

Mia's lifeless body in the truth-seer's chambers, blood pooling beneath her.

The pain... terrible pain, then the truth-seer's voice, and her face leaning over him.

Set felt like every breath of air was being sucked away from him. Every muscle in his body strained with despair as he drowned under the onslaught.

Harwa didn't save me…

"The truth-seer," he breathed, a cold wash rising inside him with the memories. "She killed Mia and attacked me…"

Isis nodded wordlessly.

"My mother?" he asked, trembling. "Does she know that Harwa—?"

"No," Isis interrupted. "Your mother would never allow any harm to come to you."

Set breathed in relief. "I shall tell my mother what Harwa did! The truth-seer will be punished!"

"No. It is too late for that. The Witch Queen's hold on your mother is too great. You must not tell anybody. They must not suspect that you know. If they suspect anything—"

"We have to do something!" Set snapped.

Isis shook her head, her eyes forlorn as they sought him out. "Nobody deserves what happened to them," she said, "least of all you, and Mia… and Horus. The Witch Queen has turned us all into her pawns. Harwa was nothing but a blind puppet in Tiamat's hands." She pressed her palms against her bulging stomach. "It is too late for me, but my child, she is innocent and—"

"No! It's not too late for you. I can help you get out. There are others, on the Brim… I can—"

Isis gave him a wistful smile. "Even if you succeeded in freeing me, brave Prince, what then? We would both be caught before we could leave the island. We are hopelessly outmatched."

"Then what can I do?" he asked.

"Harwa knows when I am due to give birth. They will not let me out of their sight once time nears." Isis paused, seeming to fight a battle within herself, then her face hardened. "There may be a way to save the child, but it carries a great risk for her."

Set leaned closer and listened as Isis explained her plan.

CHAPTER 48

BA'TIF CHARGED AMSU WITH A SCREAM. The young woman's robe fluttered as she nimbly sidestepped his attack and let her brother's momentum carry him forward. She twisted, tripped him and shoved him to the ground. She smoothed out her robes and beamed at Thoth.

The sound of clapping filled the air, and Horus turned to see Saba laughing enthusiastically and clicking her tongue from her spot beneath a bushwillow. The gnarled staff she had been using as a crutch leaned against the trunk beside her. Saba's leg had healed well over the past eight weeks, and in the past two days, she had even been able to take a few steps without supporting her weight with the staff.

"You are learning well," Thoth said to Amsu in her language, drawing Horus back in. While Saba and her family had been teaching Thoth and Horus their language, which they called Khe'met, Thoth had reciprocated by schooling Ba'tif and Amsu in the art of fighting.

Amsu stepped to her brother and helped him to his feet. He shook out his furs and gave his mother and Horus a mock glare.

He said something to Saba. Horus only made out the word 'firewood,' but Ba'tif's bruised tone did not require translation. Saba laughed again, and she grasped her staff and waved to Horus.

"Come, boy. Seeing my son get beaten by his sister is too sad for a mother. I shall teach you about plants."

"And check Ba'tif's snares," Amsu said with a grin. "He is a better trapper than fighter."

"We will," Horus replied in Khe'met.

Ba'tif said something that was not part of Horus's vocabulary yet. He looked questioningly to Saba. He was picking up more and more of their language every day, but the look the old woman shot her son quelled Horus's hopes of learning the meaning of that particular word from her. He repeated it in his mind, intending to ask Ba'tif in private.

They stepped from the clearing into the woods. After a few steps, Saba pulled on his arm and pointed to a plant.

"Biteroot," she said. "Touch it."

Horus did as instructed. He yelped and yanked his hand back, then rubbed his finger as a couple of red blisters raised on his skin. He glared at Saba. "Why did you—?"

The old woman cackled. "With name like biteroot, what did you expect? Now you won't forget. Stings on skin, but very useful when made into tea. Helps with pain and brings down body fire."

"Body fire?" Horus glanced at her quizzically then understanding struck. "Ah, fever," Horus said in his own language. "When you're ill."

"Yes, yes." Saba nodded.

The old woman hobbled along with Horus trudging beside her, picking up dried wood and checking the snares as she continued her botany lesson. "Goldenseal… when stomach hurts. Rock tree… chew to make soft and put on wound. Grubberry… good to eat in spring when yellow. But when red…" She grimaced and spat on the ground.

When they returned to the camp with firewood and two rabbits, Amsu was busy preparing the fire pit while Thoth and Ba'tif seemed to be engaged in a serious discussion. Horus dropped the wood on the ground and helped Amsu arrange the stones in a circle.

He shot a glance at the men. Thoth picked up a stick and sketched what appeared to be the outline of a map on the ground. Ba'tif used his finger to add swirling lines to the west and north of the land his grandfather had drawn, then drew a small circle in the middle of it.

"We are here," he said, then marked several spots to the east and pointed to the northernmost one. "Tarris," he said. "Where we go to find *heka*."

"*Heka?*" Thoth asked. He glanced to Horus who shrugged. He had not been taught that word yet.

"An old woman. One who uses old words and plants," Saba said.

"A witch?" Horus offered in his own language.

Saba nodded enthusiastically in approval as if understanding the word.

"Why?" Thoth asked.

"She will pour color back into skin of Amsu," Ba'tif said.

Horus opened his mouth, but Thoth gave a subtle shake of his head.

Ba'tif pointed to the spot directly east of them. "Aserah," he said, his lips curling into a frown. "Many people. Not good. *Bak-anx*." He pointed to the third spot. "Estecos—"

"*Bak-anx?*" Thoth interrupted.

"People who sell others," Amsu said, her eyes flitting nervously between Horus and Thoth.

"Slavers?" Thoth asked in their own language. The hairs on Horus's neck bristled at the memory of their first encounter in this land.

"Maybe. Yes?" Ba'tif shrugged. "Not good," he repeated.

Amsu pointed at the crude map. "Where do you come from?" she asked.

Thoth's face grew somber. He indicated an area west beyond the swirling lines. "Land with water around it," he said.

"*Tahi,*" Amsu said. Horus assumed it meant island.

"Yes, island," Thoth repeated the word in Khe'met.

"Why did you leave?" Ba'tif asked.

The shadow on Thoth's face grew darker. Amsu shot Ba'tif a glare. He lifted his hands apologetically. "I am sorry. I should not have—"

"You should," Thoth said. "You are good friends and should know." He took a breath, as if steeling himself. "There was a war. Our people died. Horus and I fled."

Amsu lifted a hand to her mouth.

Ba'tif placed his palm over his heart. "I am sorry," he said.

Thoth nodded somberly. Horus drew closer to him. "Do you think *Amah* still…?"

"I do not know, my boy."

"Sometimes, when I dream, I see her," Horus said.

"As do I, my grandson," Thoth said forlornly. "The memories come alive within me."

"No, not memories," Horus said. "It's like... she's still alive, but lonely, and in pain."

Thoth's face twisted at those words. "I hope death found her quickly."

"You hope she is dead?" Horus snapped. "How can you say that?"

"That is not what I meant," Thoth said. "I meant to say that I hope she did not suffer."

"If there is still hope that she is alive, we must go back!"

"My boy—" Thoth started. He reached out for him.

Horus drew away. "She was alive, and we left her!" he cried out. "I know that. I can feel that. We left them all!"

He stood and stomped away from the fire to the edge of the clearing. He plopped down on the ground, shoulders slumped. Horus closed his eyes, letting his mind fill with the sound of his mother's voice, the subtle smell of metopion on her skin.

Like every night since setting foot on the boat that took him away from her, he recalled his mother's face, carving her every feature into his memory, longing to trap them inside of him.

Like every night, the emptiness and guilt rose within him, roiling up in his chest, threatening to rob his breath.

Forgive me, Amah.

CHAPTER 49

SET SLIPPED OUT OF BED. The slate was cool against his bare skin as he tiptoed toward the door to his mother's side of the royal living quarters. He placed his ear against the wood and listened. She retired for the night over a span ago, and by now the twilight outside his window had long faded to blackness, pierced only by the orange glow of the lamps. Satisfied with the silence behind the door, he sneaked to his wardrobe and changed from his nightclothes into the black trousers and top he had been wearing for his visits to the Rathadi queen.

Almost two months had passed since he discovered that Isis was alive and had agreed to help her. Even though Isis's child was not due for another four weeks, Harwa seemed to grow more impatient by the day, checking on the Rathadi queen more frequently. It was only a question of time before the truth-seer started to watch her constantly.

The truth-seer...

Set struggled to control the rage that overcame him every time his thoughts turned to Harwa. He wished for nothing more than to make the old witch pay for what she had done to Mia, for what she had done to all of them. Despite Isis's warning, he had almost succumbed to his grief and told his mother about Harwa's treachery, but the Rathadi queen's words rang through his head.

The Witch Queen's hold on your mother is too great.

The night after he visited Isis, he sneaked out again, his body leading him to Mia's home. Hidden in the shadows, his mind numb, he watched her grieving parents through the window, fighting his every desire to reveal himself, to tell them what truly happened to their daughter. Yet he knew he could not jeopardize the Rathadi queen's plan; otherwise Mia's death would remain meaningless. He left, his guilt gnawing at him, paralyzing him. The only thought that kept him going and allowed him to continue the daily charade was to focus on what lay ahead: helping Isis to save the child. Once his deed was accomplished, there would be time to mourn, time to set things right with Mia's parents—and the truth-seer.

Set stepped onto the balcony and took in the darkness around him. The shadows had become his comfort, the blanket that kept him sane amid the chaos that raved within him. He slung the backpack over his shoulders and tightened the straps then climbed over the railing. He descended the wall until he reached a spot between two balusters. Reaching inside a small hole, he grasped a leather pouch. He had collected all but one of the ingredients the Rathadi queen tasked him with. Unfortunately, there was only one place where he could come by the last one.

He slipped the pouch into his backpack and climbed down further until he reached the lower level of the palace. After his nightly climbs, the wall was familiar, and the movements came easy. His mouth twitched into a pensive smile. *I wish you could see me now, brother.*

Staying in the shadows, he made his way to the structure that housed the truth-seer's living space and the private herb garden on her terrace.

He jumped down and was engulfed by the scent of pungent blossoms from hundreds of plants and herbs that were arranged in a dozen meticulous rectangular beds. He recalled the description of the plant the Rathadi queen made him memorize. *Silk bay root: bright green, wispy fronds with yellow flowers and a bulbous base. Smells like anise.*

Set started on the left and examined each plant, moving across the bed. *Mia would have known exactly where to find it.* His throat cinched. He pushed the thought aside and focused on his task, methodically scrutinizing each plant. Halfway through the fourth bed he spotted a bush that matched the description. He bent down and took a whiff; a smell of licorice filled his nostrils.

He sank to his knees and tugged on one of the stems. The plant didn't budge. He wrapped both hands around it and pulled harder. The fist sized root popped out, and he staggered back, almost falling into the neighboring bed. Set allowed himself a small smile before sliding the root into the pouch and setting off for the conclave tower.

A quarter span later, he was in his familiar spot on the small ledge, just beneath the narrow opening in the wall of the conclave chamber. He peered inside.

"Isis," he whispered.

The form inside stirred. "I'm awake," the Rathadi queen

replied. She rose awkwardly, her large belly bulging from beneath the tattered rags.

"Did you find it?" she asked.

"Yes," he replied. "It was in Harwa's garden, like you said."

He pulled a rope from his backpack then fastened it around the straps and slipped the pack through the slit, guiding it down to her. She opened it and took out the pouch, strewing the ingredients on the floor. After a few moments, she nodded. "It's all here."

Set exhaled, not realizing he'd been holding his breath.

Isis reached into the backpack again and pulled out a metal bowl. She plucked the leaves of the sea sumac and placed them inside the bowl before using the bottom of a cup to grind them to a pulp. She collected the orange chicory seeds, removed the husks and stirred them in. Working methodically, she blended in all the ingredients then poured water into the bowl and swirled it around, mixing the contents.

Her hands trembled when she lifted the bowl. She paused and gazed at Set. "Thank you," she said. "No matter what happens tonight. You have my gratitude."

He met her gaze, unblinking. "As the crown prince of Atlantis, I vow to you, no harm shall come to your child as long as I live."

Isis nodded, a spark of hope breaking through the sorrow, then brought the bowl to her lips and emptied it.

"Now what?" Set asked.

"Now we wait," the Rathadi queen replied.

THE OLD TRUTH-SEER awoke at the edge of a scream, the specter of the Rathadi queen burning in her mind. Harwa sucked in air, trying to calm herself and erase the image of the tattered rags, bloodied at the womb, and the woman's glare burning into her.

A month remained before the child was due, and all of the examinations had revealed that the pregnancy was proceeding as expected for a feline Rathadi. Still, even though Harwa's truth-visions had been silenced, she could not shake the feeling of disquiet.

She made up her mind to pay Isis another visit at sunrise, then she rolled over and closed her eyes, breathing slowly, rhythmically, aiming for the place of calming seclusion. A few moments later she turned again. A lingering haze of sleep sat somewhere at the back of her mind, tantalizingly close, but just out of reach.

She sighed and pushed herself up and out of bed. A cup of dream clove tea would help ease her nerves. Her feet touched the wooden floor, feeling for her sheepskin slippers, before she stood. She threw a blanket over her body and shuffled across her sleeping chamber, aiming for the herb garden.

She inhaled deeply as she stepped onto the terrace, enveloped by the familiar scents. Slowly, the swirl in her mind settled, and the knot that had developed between her shoulder blades eased. She crossed to the patch with the dream clove when a clump of dirt on the stone path between the beds caught her eye. A ripple of unease stirred.

She moved closer to the dirt, scanning the bed.

No... it couldn't be.

She stared at the hole in the dirt among the batch of silk bay.

Bile rose in her throat, sharp and hot, and a tremor gripped her hands. The empty feeling in the pit of her stomach was as abrupt as it was intense.

She doubled back, all thoughts of sleep forgotten, and stormed out of her chambers. She rushed along the corridor, passing a pair of patrolling guards. They exchanged a quizzical glance.

"Amun's blessings, Truth-seer. Is everything—?"

Harwa didn't stop. "Come with me, now!" she panted.

The guards stood rooted to the ground, their confused looks only deepening.

Harwa stopped and glared at them. "Now!" she shrilled. "Or by Amun I will have you strung up and whipped."

The guards scrambled after her as she rushed to the conclave tower as fast as her old bones would carry her.

———

SET GLANCED at the Rathadi queen anxiously. Almost a full span had passed since she had swallowed the potion. She shifted her position again, pressing her back against the wall, her breathing becoming more labored.

"Perhaps I can find something for the pain," Set offered.

"No," Isis replied between heavy breaths. "I need my senses sharp."

"There are Rathadi hiding in the Brim. I will take her there," Set continued, filling his need to break the silence.

Isis nodded, shifting positions.

"She will give your people hope," he continued. "The daughter of the Rathadi king and queen."

"They… they must not know who she is," Isis breathed.

"But why?"

"Too dangerous…" Isis shifted again, then groaned.

Set flinched. Isis groaned anew, louder.

"Has it started?" Set asked.

Isis didn't reply. She arched her back, and her face twisted in pain. Her breathing came in rapid, shallow gasps as she forced herself to breathe in and out through her mouth.

Over the next half span, Isis's pain only magnified as the labor proceeded and the moments between the contractions grew shorter. A sheen of sweat covered her skin as she lay on the floor, panting with her eyes closed, oblivious to the world outside her. She groaned again, and a cry escaped her lips.

"What do I do?" Set yammered, unable to stave off the panic any longer. "Is there anything I—?"

"Quiet, child!" Isis grunted through clenched teeth.

Set clamped his mouth shut and stared with captivated dread as the Rathadi queen lay before him, waiting for the agony of the next contraction.

———

HARWA TURNED the corner into the corridor leading to the conclave tower.

"Truth-seer," one of the guards called out, "the conclave tower is not to be entered."

Harwa ignored him and rushed for the circular stairway.

"Truth-seer!" the guard called after her.

Harwa whipped about and opened her mouth, but her reply

was cut short by a muffled groan from above. The guards looked at her vexed.

Harwa rushed up the stairs with the guards on her heels. The groaning intensified as they ascended the last flight and rushed to the conclave chamber at the end of the corridor. A muffled scream was followed by the distinct cry of a newborn.

———

SET STARED, mesmerized, as Isis lifted the blood-stained, crying baby and held it to her breast. The baby settled down as it suckled.

"Isis…" he forced the words out of his mouth, guilty at disturbing the sacred moment.

Isis turned to him, her face wan and tired, but her expression peaceful.

"We have to go. Now."

"No…" she whispered, her eyes brimming with sorrow.

The commotion outside the door snapped them back.

"My Queen, please!" Set cried out. "It is her only chance!"

A heart-wrenching sob escaped Isis's lips. She dipped her trembling fingers in the blood that had puddled on the stone, and pressed them against the child's blanket, then swaddled the newborn and placed her gently inside the backpack.

Set pulled on the rope, hoisting up the bundle, when the door flew open, and Harwa rushed inside, followed by a pair of guards.

Isis's expression changed. Her eyes filled with a threatening darkness. She seemed to summon up all of her remaining strength and staggered to her feet.

The truth-seer surveyed the scene before her. She stared at the Rathadi queen's blood-soaked rags. Then she spotted the backpack.

"Seize it!" she screamed.

One of the guards rushed for the bundle. Isis surged into him with a feral growl, driving his head into the wall. She lunged again, but the chain around her neck snapped taut, yanking her back and throwing her to the floor. The second guard chased after the pack. Isis whipped up the chain, catching his feet and toppling him to the ground. She dove on top of him and flung the shackle around his neck.

Set hauled up the rope frantically as the truth-seer scurried for the pack. She reached for it, stretching her gaunt arms high in the air, but the cloth slipped through her grasp. She howled as the bundle disappeared through the narrow gap.

"Truth-seer." The voice behind her was barely a whisper.

Harwa faced about. The Rathadi queen loomed tall, both guards lifeless at her feet, her hand clutched tightly around the hilt of a sword. Blood pooled beneath Isis's trembling legs, and her breathing came in ragged gasps. She swallowed, face twisting with pain, but her eyes shone with relief and triumph.

She plunged the sword into the truth-seer's chest.

Red blossomed around the blade and spread through the truth-seer's robe, soaking the coarse fabric. Harwa's mouth opened in a silent scream as she pressed her hands against the wound.

"You shall never have her," Isis spat, then her legs buckled, and she and the truth-seer slumped to the floor.

Set stared at the Rathadi queen, bloodied and gasping on the cold stone, then at the bundle with the newborn girl in his hands. A surge of panic coursed through him, starting in his gut and resonating throughout his body. He forced it back. He had a promise to keep. He opened the backpack and shifted the bundle, freeing the child's head.

Isis faced them. The corners of her mouth tilted into a smile as she locked her gaze on her daughter. Her eyes began to grow distant, the glint fading from them with every halting breath. Set remained motionless, holding the Rathadi queen's daughter until a tranquil expression spread through Isis's face, and her chest heaved for the last time.

Tears soaked Set's cheek as he pressed it to the child's head. "This is your mother. Isis, the great queen of the Rathadi," he whispered, his voice cracking. "She knew no fear."

The baby gurgled softly. Set secured her inside the backpack when he spotted a single word that stood against the white of the blanket, inscribed in the Rathadi queen's blood. A name. Set mouthed it, swearing his loyalty to the girl entrusted into his care, before slinging the bundle over his shoulders and disappearing into the darkness.

CHAPTER 50

A CHILL PASSED through Horus as if something cold reached through his breastbone and seized his heart. He groaned and staggered.

"Horus!" Saba called out. She rushed forward and grasped his arm, concern darkening her features. "Are you unwell?"

"I… I'm alright…" he managed. The feeling ebbed, but his heart still quaked. He tightened his grip on the firewood in his arms. "Better now."

Saba studied him, unconvinced. "We should get back to the camp," she said.

Horus nodded, too rattled to argue, and followed her back. The old woman's leg had healed completely since she had broken it three months ago, and she set a brisk pace. The gnarled walking stick had been demoted to little more than a prop, its main use consisting of being shaken at Ba'tif or, increasingly more often, at Horus. He and his grandfather had grown close to Saba and her children, and the old woman had begun treating him as one of her own—which included the occasional kindhearted chiding.

As they drew closer to their campsite, the skin on Horus's neck prickled. At first, he could not discern what caused the feeling, then he realized.

It's too quiet.

The sound of the friendly banter between Thoth and Ba'tif that had blended into routine during their daily camp rests was absent. He turned to Saba and placed a finger to his lips then carefully lowered the firewood to the ground and sneaked for the camp.

The sight before him robbed his breath. Four strangers dressed in thick hide and armed with blades had surrounded his grandfather and the siblings. One of them, a bald man with hard eyes, had clamped his arm roughly around Amsu and pressed a dagger to her skin. Ba'tif called out to a huge man armed with a sword who appeared to be the leader of the gang.

Saba crept up beside Horus. Her face paled.

Horus's mind raced. He glanced up at the tall rock beneath which they had set up their shelter. He pointed to himself, then the rock, and motioned Saba to stay. She grasped his arm, but he shook it off.

Before he had a chance to debate the wisdom of his resolution, he had crawled around the rock and had climbed halfway up. He crested it and slid on his belly to the edge. The bald man clutching Amsu stood directly beneath him while Ba'tif appealed to their leader. He raised his voice in a desperate plea. Without warning, the huge man smashed the hilt of his sword into Ba'tif's face, dropping him to the ground. Amsu wailed and pressed for her brother, but the bald man held firm.

Horus's hand curled around a large stone. He leaned out farther and caught his grandfather's gaze. The old Rathadi's eyes widened ever so slightly behind his shawl, then he gave a subtle shake of his head. Horus moved closer to the edge. His grandfather shook his head again, more emphatically.

Horus clenched his jaw then pushed off the edge, plummeting onto the bald man. The stone cracked against the man's head as they both collapsed to the ground. Amsu screamed and leaped away.

Horus struck the ground hard, his teeth rattling from the impact, and he flipped to his back just in time to see the third man lunge at him, dagger raised. He rolled aside and skittered back, barely escaping the blade. The man slashed out once more, and this time the blade drew blood. Horus cried out, grasping at his injured arm. The man lifted the blade again.

His grandfather barreled into his assailant, driving both men to the ground. They rolled across the sand, struggling for the dagger. The burly leader charged forward. He grasped his grandfather by his robe and yanked him off his companion, throwing the old Rathadi across the clearing like a ragdoll. His grandfather crashed into the dirt, and his head smashed into an old tree stump with a thud. His eyes rolled back, and he lay on the ground, unmoving. Horus screamed as the leader rushed at Thoth, sword in hand. The huge man froze when he spotted the Rathadi's lupine face, free of the scarf, unmasked in the struggle.

The leader reeled back. "*Shaytan!*" he bellowed, his voice hoarse with terror.

A hood dropped over Horus's head, and a pair of hands clamped around his arms. He heard Ba'tif's voice then the sounds of a scuffle. A high-pitched scream from Saba's throat pierced the air, then cut off abruptly before silence descended on them, interrupted only by pained, heavy breathing.

"Grandfather!" Horus screamed, his own pain forgotten. "Amsu!" He cried and kicked in a panic, but the grip around his arms held firm. Strong hands shoved him into the sand, then heavy irons clamped around his wrists and ankles.

———

"THOTH..." a voice croaked in the dark.

The old Rathadi groaned and stirred. He lifted his hand to the back of his head, wincing at the touch and the stickiness against his fingertips.

"Thoth..." The sound of his name morphed into a wet, wheezing cough.

He forced his eyelids open, straining to focus.

Ba'tif lay on the ground, blood seeping from a wide gash across his stomach. Thoth pushed himself to his feet with a grunt, ignoring the pounding in his temples, and staggered to Ba'tif. He sank to his knees beside the young man and pressed his hand against the ghastly wound.

Ba'tif pushed Thoth's hand away. "Mother..." he choked out, tilting his head to a body at the edge of the clearing. Thoth scurried to Saba and pressed his fingers against the side of her neck, knowing the answer before his fingers felt the absence of a pulse. He turned back to Ba'tif and shook his head.

The man's expression wilted completely. "They took them," he groaned. He swallowed, face knotting with pain. "They took Amsu... and Horus."

"Who?" Thoth asked. "Who were they?"

Ba'tif took a gasping breath.

"Who took them, Ba'tif?"

"Slavers," he replied weakly.

Thoth felt a wave of terror wash over him, his worst fears confirmed.

"Where are they taking them?"

Ba'tif's eyes rolled back.

Thoth grasped the dying man's face between his palms and locked his gaze on him. "If you cannot give me an idea of where they took them, my grandson and your sister will be lost forever."

Ba'tif's face caved under the words, but he grasped Thoth's arms and squeezed them with his remaining strength. "The slave market," he rasped. "The slave market in Aserah." Ba'tif shuddered, and his palms slipped off Thoth's arms. He stared into an empty space between them, then his face closed in a grimace, and his head slumped to his chest.

CHAPTER 51

"HORUS?" Amsu's whisper pulled him back from the darkness that surrounded him.

"Amsu?" he stammered. The heavy metal against his wrists and ankles bit into his skin, and the coarse hood that covered his head smelled of sweat and made him labor for every breath. He crouched, squeezed between two others, lurching with the motion of the crude skiff as they were pulled across the sand. "What's happening?"

"I... I don't know," Amsu's voice cracked. "There was a fight... Ba'tif... I saw him being struck..."

Horus's heart plummeted. "And Grandfather? Saba?"

Amsu stifled a sob.

"What of Grandfather?" Horus pressed. "Is he...?" Horus's words choked in his mouth, uncertain of whether he wanted to hear the answer.

"They were scared of him when they saw his face. They left him."

Horus sighed. "Then there's hope."

"There is no hope," a man's voice behind him rang out.

Horus turned to the voice. "Who are you? What do you mean?"

"My name doesn't matter. And yours won't either, soon enough."

"Where are we going?"

"Where they take all the slaves," the man said. "To Aserah."

Slaves? Dread pooled in his stomach. "I am not a slave," he snapped. "My name is Horus. I am the son of Isis and Osi—"

"Quiet!" He flinched at the loud thud against the wood near him.

"But there's been a mistake," Horus started. "I am—"

He yelped as a thick palm smacked the back of his head.

"Enough! Or you'll taste the whip! And nobody wants damaged goods."

"Keep your mouth shut," the man scolded him quietly. "You'll get us all into trouble."

———

THE JOLTING STOPPED. A moment later the hood was pulled from Horus's head. He blinked in the brightness of the golden sun that rose over the barren land. They stood at the edge of a town. Dozens of small, hut-like buildings protruded from the endless desert. All around them, dunes rose and fell like a rolling sea, punctuated by silhouettes of wooden skiffs, gliding like ghost ships over the sandy waves.

He found Amsu's eyes. They were red and swollen. Beside her, another man and two women blinked against the glare as their hoods were removed. Their expressions mirrored Horus's confusion and the raw fear that had curled up inside him.

The huge man leaped into the cart and unlocked their leg shackles from the thick metal ring in the floor of the skiff.

"Get out," he growled.

Horus scurried out as quickly as his shackled feet allowed and huddled beside Amsu at the side of the cart. Instead of wheels, the cart rested on two broad skids that glided across the sand, pulled by four muscular aurochs.

The huge man and the three others shoved them into a single line as a newcomer drew near. He was short and dressed in colorful garb. His hair was thin and receding like his chin, but he had the eyes of a fox. He and the huge man exchanged a curt greeting before he approached Horus.

The man appraised him wordlessly, like a horse master might appraise a new steed. His eyes were flat, devoid of any emotion. He grasped his upper arm and squeezed it.

"Do you understand me?" he asked in Khe'met.

Horus nodded shyly, and the man flashed twin rows of gold-capped teeth.

"Very good. Open your mouth," he said.

Horus glanced at him confused.

The smile fell from his face like a cracked mask. "I will not ask again."

Horus opened his mouth, and the man examined his teeth.

"Good," he said before moving to Amsu. He lifted her shawl and gasped then turned to the huge man. He said something in a language that Horus did not understand. A grin spread across the large man's face.

The colorful man cupped Amsu's chin and examined her

face. Amsu winced, but she held his gaze. The man said something over his shoulder, earning lewd cackles.

After examining all four captives, he addressed the huge man who drew back, as if taking great offense at the other's words. He gestured to Amsu and Horus, his tone challenging. The men traded what appeared to be insults before Horus realized that they were engaged in a haggling ritual. Finally, the colorful man pulled out a string purse and threw it at the huge man with an exaggerated sigh.

The huge man barked a command, and Horus and the other male captive were shoved forward. A shiver of panic shot through him when he realized that Amsu was led in a different direction.

"Keep moving!" one of the slavers grunted.

"Amsu!" Horus shouted. He cried out at the sting of the lash across his back and was shoved forward again, harder. He fought back his tears at his pain and the despair in Amsu's face as he and the other man were herded into town after the colorful man.

The narrow street opened into a large square that was enclosed on all sides by long, flat buildings. A raised platform stood at its center. The colorful man guided them to one of the buildings and opened the door.

The smell of sweat and waste assaulted Horus's nose as he and the other man were shoved inside. Horus tripped over the shackles and fell.

He lifted his head—and gasped at the sight. Dozens of men and boys of all ages were strewn on the floor of this cell that should have been at least twice as large to accommodate all of them comfortably. The colors of their clothes were as diverse as the tone of their skin and hair, but their shackles gleamed the same rusty tinge, and they all shared the same look of fear and uncertainty that Horus felt in the pit of his stomach.

He flinched at a touch.

"Easy, Young'un," a man's voice sounded near him. A pair of hands wedged into his armpits and helped him sit up. He turned. An older man with sunburnt skin and gentle eyes gave him a kindly smile, but he, too, could not hide the dread from his face.

"Wh-where am I?" Horus stammered.

"In Aserah," the man replied.

"What is going to happen to us?"

"Auction tomorrow morning."

"Auction?"

"Sell you," the man said. "To the highest bidder."

"F-for what?"

"That depend on who buy you," the man said. "If you be lucky, you get to some big house and work kitchens or tend camels. If not, you be working fields." He lowered his voice. "Or, if you be truly luckless, you be sold to one of them wild nomad tribes, caught up in their endless, bloody wars."

Horus listened to the man's words, but he struggled to process what he was hearing; his mind and body willing this terrible nightmare to end. He ignored the man's words until he felt a nudge against his ribs.

"I say, where you come from, boy?" the man asked. "You speak strange. What of your family?"

Horus gazed at him forlornly, biting back the tears welling up. "There is nobody left," he whispered.

HORUS WOKE to the sound of a key scraping against a lock. He squinted against the glare of the light as the door swung open, revealing the silhouette of the colorful man. He bore a different garb, but it was equally flamboyant. He banged a long, thick staff against the door to rouse the few that still slept.

"Come out. One at a time." He pointed at the man crouching closest to the door who wore a gray shirt that was ripped at his back. A long gash marred his face. "You, first," the colorful man said.

The man rose slowly and approached the door. The colorful man reached for his shackles and tethered him to a long chain.

"Do not make any trouble," the old man whispered, and grasped Horus's arm. "Be strong, Young'un."

Horus counted silently as the colorful man and his entourage chained forty-three captives into a long procession and led them into the square. He gasped at the transformation of the space since he last saw it. Hundreds of people crowded the area. A twinge of pain shot through him as he was reminded of the festivities of the Day of Unity, until he spotted street vendors who peddled shackles and whips as easily as they did their foods and drinks. He cringed.

What kind of people are those who value others so little?

They were led beside the raised wooden platform where other groups of shackled men and women stood waiting, their expressions empty. Around them, tough-looking men armed with swords and cudgels glowered as if daring them to step out of line. Horus craned his neck in every direction, keeping his eyes peeled for Amsu, but he came up empty.

As they waited in the glaring sun, the crowd before them grew even larger. Some of the latest arrivals included men and women who were dressed in the most dazzling garments, and who were ushered to the front of the assembly. When the square looked like it could not handle another person, the colorful man stepped atop the platform and began speaking in a strange tongue.

The next spans passed Horus by like a dream. One by one, the captured men and women were escorted onto the platform and displayed, before being claimed by the highest bidder. When his time came, he ascended the stairs numbly. The words of the colorful man reached his ears, but his mind was empty. He barely registered the voices of the people in the crowd as they raised their hands, placing bids on him. Before he knew what had transpired, it was over, and he was ushered off the platform.

———

THOTH SQUEEZED his palm around the hilt of the onyx dagger as he watched one of the attendants lead Horus down the wooden stairs. As the next bidding began, the man who bought Horus fought his way to the front of the crowd. He talked briefly with the attendant then slipped out a purse and exchanged coins for the boy. Bile rose in the back of the old Rathadi's throat when Horus was led away behind his new owner. He pulled the shawl tighter around his face and followed the man and Horus into one of the side alleys.

Once he draws far enough from the crowd...

His hopes were dashed when the man joined a group of

three others at the edge of town. They gathered around four aurochs that were laden heavy with sacks. The man approached each of the large animals and inspected them. After several moments, he nodded to the other three, seemingly satisfied. The others barely spared Horus a glance before the small caravan set out into the desert.

CHAPTER 52

THE SUN BEAT down on Horus, its malevolent eye unblinking, as he trudged behind the four men and their beasts. With each step he seemed to sink deeper into the searing sand, and breathing was like inhaling steam from a hot spring. The desert breeze blew sand into his eyes, mixing it with the sweat that rolled off his forehead, caking his eyelids.

His leg buckled, and he tripped, falling face-first into the sand.

The man closest to him shouted something, and their caravan stopped. He drew closer and glared at Horus.

Horus forced himself onto his back. "Water," he whimpered, spitting sand, his throat and lips parched. "Please…"

The man stepped to one of the beasts, and a moment later he bent down and lifted a water skin over Horus's lips. He poured a mouthful, and Horus swallowed it greedily. The man waited a moment then poured another sip.

Horus reached for the water skin, but the man knocked

down his hand, then slapped him across his face and grabbed a fistful of hair.

"Long road. Water for all," he said, pointing to the others. "You drink what I give."

Horus clenched his jaw and nodded.

The man glanced at the shackles around Horus's ankles where the metal had rubbed his skin raw. He stepped to the auroch again and returned with a fist-sized block of wood. He used it to hammer out the pin that held the shackles together, then he repeated it for the cuffs around Horus's wrists. Horus gazed up in gratitude, but before he had a chance to say anything, the man fitted a metal collar around his neck, then fixed one end of a long chain to the collar and the other end to one of the beasts.

"Walk easier without shackles. Will need less water," he said, then set out again.

They continued to trek through the desert, keeping a steady pace, but the man made sure to stop before exhaustion over-whelmed Horus again. During one of their longer rests, he brought dried meat and a handful of sweet nuts to Horus, who devoured the food eagerly.

He spoke a guttural language with the others. It was differ-ent, harsher than the language Horus had picked up from Ba'tif and his family. Horus's mood darkened even further when he thought of the trio and the kindness they had shown him and his grandfather.

Just before sundown, he spotted smoke rising in the distance. Before long, he made out a shadow against the sand, then individual skiffs. As they drew closer, he counted over thirty large sand skiffs that appeared to have tall tents affixed to their beds. They were arranged in a great ring, forming a wall and protecting the inside of the circle.

A shout rang out from up ahead, and the man leading their caravan yelled back. They rounded the enclosure until they arrived at an opening that was just wide enough for an auroch to pass through. After they entered, a smaller skiff was pushed in front of the opening, securing the encampment.

The interior bustled with activity. A fire smoldered in the center of the camp, and a collection of pots and meats hung suspended from a high bar, looked after by a handful of women and girls. Others sat on hides beside their skiffs, sewing or mending clothes. They passed a group of older boys busy with making arrows and sharpening weapons, supervised by an older man. At the edge of the settlement, dozens of camels and aurochs were cordoned off and tended to by two boys with collars around their necks. As they wound their way through the camp, Horus was met with curious glances, especially from the countless children that scampered about, but most of the adults heeded their group no attention.

Horus was brought before the largest skiff, and the man who bought him called out a name. A moment later, a woman's head poked out. The man shoved Horus toward her.

The woman ambled forward and appraised him. She was dressed in a loose yellow robe that stood in stark contrast to her raven black hair. Her face could have been pretty, but her lips had a scowl to them, and her wide, almond-shaped eyes were hard when they met his. She said something in the guttural language. Horus stared at her and shook his head.

"Your name," she asked in Khe'met.

"Horus," he answered.

"How many summers have you seen?"

"Seven," Horus said.

The woman blinked. She drew near and cupped his cheeks in her palm. Her grip was hard, and Horus winced. He forced himself not to whimper. Instead, he held her gaze, unblinking.

"Do not lie, boy," the woman said, her tone threatening. "You look too old for seven summers. You look like you've seen twelve."

"I speak true," Horus said.

The woman studied him, still unconvinced. "Your eyes and features. They are strange. Where are you from?"

"From… from the west," Horus replied. "I… we were traveling with our family when… when we were taken."

For a brief moment, Horus thought he saw a shadow of pity in the woman's eyes, but it passed as quickly as it had appeared.

"I am Zera. I am your mistress, and you belong to me now, Horus," she said, her tone cold. She nodded to the man, and he untied Horus's chain from the auroch and handed it to her.

"Do as you are told, and you will be given food and water, and you will be treated well," she continued, her voice almost kind. Before Horus had a chance to react, she pulled on the chain, and he staggered and fell to his knees. She snatched his collar and brought his chin up to face her again. "Disobey me, and you will live to regret the day you were born."

Horus flinched at her words.

"Do you understand?" she asked.

"Y-yes," Horus managed.

"Yes, what?"

"Yes, Mistress," Horus whispered.

———————

THE SUN HUNG low in the sky and cast beams of light through the circle of desert skiffs, stretching long, shadowy arms across the open sand. Thoth shaded his eyes against the glare as he watched the men and Horus enter the nomad encampment, and the makeshift gate slid close behind them. The old Rathadi cursed himself for not attempting to ambush the four men earlier. He had hoped they would make camp, perhaps even try to sleep out the hottest part of the day, but their small caravan kept pushing until they had reached the settlement. He counted at least thirty-five tented skiffs. He assumed it meant at least that number of able-bodied fighters.

Thoth wrapped the tunic about his shoulders and tightened the shawl as the desert cooled around him. He shivered, partly from the chill in the air and partly from the rage he tried to quell. He would bide his time, but he needed to be ready when the moment presented itself. The old Rathadi took a sip from his water skin and hunkered down in the sand, his gaze fixed on the camp.

CHAPTER 53

"No, boy!"

Horus flinched at Zera's voice. He tensed, readying himself for the blow, but it did not come. He exhaled.

"Hold it this way," she said, and repositioned the sharp stone in his hand. She placed it against the oryx hide that hung stretched between two poles and edged it down with practiced strokes.

"Press against it, but not hard enough to damage the hide," she warned.

"Yes, Mistress," Horus said meekly, and tried his best to scrape the coarse hair from the animal skin.

After his introduction to Zera last evening, he was given food and water and a camel pelt to protect him against the chill, and had spent the night chained to Zera's skiff. Even though he was exhausted from the grueling march, sleep did not come to him until the morning hours. Instead, he had lain awake, watching the dozen other figures that slept on the sand, collars chained to their owners' skiffs, and tracking the two men on patrol who circled the perimeter of the camp. At first, after Zera had dismissed him for the night, his fingers found their way to the lock of the collar, searching for some way to open it, but he quickly abandoned the idea of trying to break free. Even if he somehow managed to escape and could avoid being captured, trying to cross the desert by himself without provisions seemed like certain suicide.

He was roused at sunrise by Zera and spent most of the day in a haze, cleaning and feeding the aurochs and camels and tending to his mistress's needs. He learned that Zera was the wife of H'met, the chief of the Tehesu tribe, and the mother to his young son. Each of the tented skiffs housed a Tehesu family that was headed by the oldest male. He had counted thirty-eight men old enough to bear the crude swords that hung on their hips, and forty women. Even during the day, the Tehesu continued their patrols that scanned the desert, prepared for an attack from one of the other tribes. It seemed—

"Stop dreaming!" Zera snapped. This time the blow came. His cheek stung from the slap, and he felt the blood rush into it.

"I-I'm sorry," he stammered, heat rising behind his eyelids. He willed the tears back.

"The next time you notch the hide, you will go to sleep hungry," Zera scolded.

"Yes, Mistress," he whispered.

He continued his task, heedful not to let his mind wander again. When he finished, Zera drew near. He fidgeted nervously, kneading his cramped fingers as she inspected his work. She gave him an approving nod then pointed to a skiff across the camp.

"Take it to Ullah for tanning," she said. "When you return, see to the aurochs and camels. Then you can eat and rest."

"Yes, Mistress. Thank you," he said.

The skies were gray by the time he staggered to his spot beside the skiff, and Zera secured his chain to the thick metal ring at the side of the wagon. He stretched out his pelt and ate his meal of cooked meat and date-stuffed bread, washing it down with sips of warm water. His eyes drooped as he chewed the last few bites, and sleep claimed him as soon as his head hit the camel pelt.

The next three days were spent following the same routine, learning more tasks from Zera and others in the camp. The Tehesu were harsh teachers, but equally as fair, and far from cruel. His meals came from the same pots as theirs, and he was never denied water. As long as he paid attention and worked hard, Zera seemed mostly satisfied, at times even losing her habitual scowl when addressing him. Most of the other Tehesu ignored him as he passed them during his daily chores. Some of them, especially the flocks of children that scurried about the camp, even offered him a curious smile, but a quick slap from Zera after he stopped to greet a young boy had made it clear he was not to speak to anybody unless she approved.

After that, Horus kept his head low when going about his tasks, his days too busy to think about anything but ensuring he did not upset his mistress. It was not until he lay down to rest, and the large fire in the middle of the camp had died down, that images of his family came to him, choking him as if he had swallowed sand. In this darkness, the tears he worked so hard to hide during the day came unbidden, streaking his cheeks before soaking into the rough hide beneath him.

On his fourth night in the camp, he lay sleepless once again, exhausted, but unable to find relief from the itching of the sand that seemed to have found its way into every crevice in his body. He imagined himself in a hot bath when the hairs on his neck stirred.

He sat up and glanced about.

Where are the sentries?

He strained his eyes into the darkness then stifled a gasp when he spotted two forms between the skiffs, lying motionlessly in the sand. A dozen shadows flitted between the wagons. The glint of a blade flashed in the dim moonlight.

A bolt of panic shot through him.

He leaped to his feet. "Zera! H'met!" he shrieked. "Danger!"

An instant later, H'met rushed out, thick muscles rippling beneath his bare skin as he drew his curved sword. He stared at Horus who pointed to the figures. H'met took in the scene in a heartbeat and bellowed a command, then chaos descended upon the camp.

Horus stood, petrified, as dozens of forms flooded the gaps between the skiffs, weapons raised. Before he could take another trembling breath, the tent flaps flew aside, and the Tehesu warriors leaped from their wagons, their eyes as sharp as the blades in their hands. Battle cries and the staccato clack of metal against metal rang out into the night.

A scream shrilled from Zera's skiff. Horus raced inside just as a man burst in through a wide gash in the tent wall. He towered over Zera who clutched her son in her arms, her face bloodless.

Horus surged forward, but the chain snapped him back. He

grasped a clay pot from the floor and hurled it at the intruder, striking him square in the back of his head. The man whirled, his scarred cheeks twisted into a snarl.

Zera dashed past him, squeezing the child against her body. She pressed off to dive from the wagon, but the man reached out and caught her arm. She lost her hold, and the wailing child flew out of her grasp. Horus watched, horrified, as Zera's son tumbled through the air before his head slammed into one of the wooden skids. The wailing ceased abruptly, and the child's limp body rolled to a stop in the sand.

Zera's terror-filled scream pierced the air as she scampered after her son. The raider lunged after her.

Horus dove at the man's legs, tumbling them both to the sand.

The man vaulted to his feet with a growl and pulled his sword. Horus crabbed back, but the man stepped on the chain, snapping it taut and yanking him to a halt. He stalked forward and raised the blade. Horus cowered, whimpering.

A glint of metal streaked through the air, burying into the raider's chest. The man opened his mouth in a silent scream then crumpled to his knees. Horus stared at the onyx hilt protruding from beneath his attacker's sternum.

He whirled—and found his grandfather's gleaming eyes.

A tremor blossomed in his chest, robbing his breath. He froze, unwilling to move, afraid to disrupt the vision before him.

The old Rathadi rushed to the dead man and pulled out the dagger, then raced to Horus. He slipped the blade into one of the links in the chain that leashed Horus to the skiff and twisted.

The link snapped. He grasped Horus's arm as the fighting raged all around them.

"Quickly, my boy!" he shouted.

Horus bounced up and followed his grandfather when he spotted Zera, bent over the body of her motionless child. She looked up at Horus, her eyes hollow.

He tugged at his grandfather's arm. "We have to help them!"

Thoth stopped and followed his gaze. His expression darkened, but he pulled Horus back. "We must leave, now. This is our only chance."

"No!" Horus cried, and held firm.

For a heartbeat, the old Rathadi looked like he would dissent, then he took stock of Zera and her son again. He sighed, the tension draining from his shoulders, before he nodded.

CHAPTER 54

THOTH KNELT IN THE SAND, grimacing with pain behind the shawl that concealed his features. Two Tehesu warriors gripped his arms, twisting them behind his back as H'met towered before him, his bare skin stained a dark crimson. The ground around them was strewn with dead Tehesu warriors and their enemies.

The raid had come to an end as quickly as it had begun. After the attackers lost their element of surprise, they were overwhelmed by the Tehesu. Only moments after Horus and Thoth had turned back to help Zera, H'met had spotted them, and they had been captured.

H'met stalked for Thoth, his wide face twisted with battle rage. Sinewy muscles bulged beneath his skin as he lifted his curved sword.

"No!" Horus cried out. "He is on our side! He killed Zera's attacker! He wants to help your son!"

H'met ignored him and placed his sword against Thoth's throat.

"He is a healer! He can save your son!" Horus screamed. He faced Zera, pleading. Her face was empty, eyes half in this world, half elsewhere as she cradled her son's limp body. "Zera, tell him!"

Zera flinched at the sound of her name. She cried out in the language of the Tehesu. H'met froze.

"Can you really help my boy?" Zera asked in Khe'met, her voice barely a cracked whisper.

"I must lay eyes on the child to answer that," Thoth hissed through the pain.

Zera said something to H'met, and he barked an order. The Tehesu released Thoth. The Rathadi groaned as he rose and tightened the shawl around his face. Zera carried the motionless boy to him.

Thoth examined the lump on her son's head, then lifted the boy's eyelids. His expression darkened. "This boy is gravely injured and will likely be dead by sundown, but there is a small chance that I may be able to save him."

The woman cried out at Thoth's words and reeled back.

"There is only one way to save your child," Thoth continued. "The pressure inside his skull is increasing, killing his brain." He paused. "I have to make a hole in his head to relieve the pressure."

Zera stared at him in horror. H'met's blank gaze flitted from Thoth to his wife. She translated the Rathadi's words. H'met bellowed and raised his sword again.

"If you kill me, your son is dead!" Thoth cried out, but he didn't flinch.

Zera slipped between H'met and Thoth and lifted her arms protectively. H'met bristled, glaring at his wife, but he backed off. He pointed his sword at Thoth and spoke, his voice harsh, before lowering the weapon.

"He said that if his son dies, you shall share his fate," Zera translated.

H'met barked another order then turned on his heel and strode off. Horus stared at his grandfather numbly. His thoughts raced. So many questions splintered his mind, he couldn't keep them straight.

Thoth rushed to Horus and pulled him close.

"Grandfather," Horus sobbed, pressing his body against the old Rathadi. "I'm so sorry…"

"Shush, my boy," Thoth whispered. "All is right." The old Rathadi broke the embrace reluctantly. "We have work to do. Fetch water and boil it in a clean pot."

Zera stepped forward. "What can I do?" she asked. Fear sullied her face, but a spark of hope flickered through the sea of anguish.

"I will need clean cloth, as much as you can get," Thoth replied. He looked to the large sand skiff. "And space in your wagon."

Zera translated his words, and two women who were not busy tending to the wounded Tehesu rushed off. Moments later they returned with handfuls of linen. Horus emptied a waterskin into a pot and hung it over the fire. To his surprise, his grandfather took the cloth and the onyx dagger and pitched them into the pot.

"What are you doing?" Horus asked.

"There are things we cannot see, Horus, that are even deadlier than the things we can," he said. An odd shadow dimmed the old Rathadi's eyes at his own words.

After the water boiled, Thoth took the pot off the flames and carried it to the skiff where Zera waited with her son. He rolled up his sleeves and fished out one of the cloths. He winced at the heat, but methodically cleansed his forearms and hands, one finger at a time. When he finished, he pulled out another piece of linen and placed it on the floor of the skiff.

"Lay the boy down, with his head on the cloth," he instructed Zera, then poured water over the boy's skull. The boy gave a soft moan, but didn't move.

Thoth removed the onyx dagger from the pot and carefully shaved one side of the boy's head. After he finished, he placed the point of the knife over the flame of a candle.

"I need you to hold his body very still," he told Zera and Horus.

Zera blanched but nodded. She held her son's shoulders while Horus grasped his legs.

Thoth took a deep breath. He clasped the boy's head with one hand and touched the tip of the blade against the shaved section, then began rotating it, drilling into his skull.

The child whimpered again.

"You are killing him!" Zera cried out.

Thoth stopped and raised his head. He fixed her with a hard gaze. "Right now, I am the only one who can save his life," he said. "If you are unable to help, leave and fetch me somebody who can."

Zera matched his gaze for several breaths, then swallowed and nodded.

Thoth bent over the boy again and continued drilling until a gush of blood surged from the skull. He tilted the head to allow the blood to drain out then waited for several moments before placing another cloth against the wound. He wrapped the child's head and exhaled deeply. "It is done," he said.

"What now?" Horus asked.

"Now we pray for Amun-Ra's favor, and we wait," the old Rathadi replied.

CHAPTER 55

HORUS HUNKERED beside the sleeping boy. He and his grandfather had spent the rest of the night and the following day with Zera at her son's side. As they waited, Horus watched the old Rathadi go through the same ritual every span, pressing his fingers against the boy's forehead and neck, lifting his eyelids, and smelling the wound in the boy's skull.

At midday, one of the Tehesu had brought them food and water, and Horus had nodded off after the meal, unable to keep his eyes open any longer. When he woke, his grandfather was still alert, keeping a watchful vigil over the injured boy.

Thoth stood again and approached the narrow berth. When he lifted the boy's eyelids, a small sigh of relief escaped him.

"What is it?" Horus asked.

His grandfather waved him closer. "Look, Horus," he said, lifting the child's eyelids again. "Both pupils now point in the same direction, and they shrink when light falls on them."

"That is good?"

"It means the pressure in his head is decreasing," Thoth replied.

"So he will be alright?" A timid smile flickered across Horus's face.

"It is too early to say," Thoth said. "There are many things that could still go awry. I could have been too late, and his brain may already have been damaged. And even if I intervened in time, he may develop a bad fever." He watched Horus's smile falter and added quickly. "But it is a step in the right direction." He patted him on the head. "Try to get some sleep, my boy."

———

When Horus woke again, Thoth rested beside him, his eyes drooping in slumber. Horus turned to the berth, and his breath hitched. The boy was resting in Zera's arms, playing contently with his mother's hair.

Horus rose and approached the pair quietly. Zera glanced up. Her face was wan and tired, but relief shone in her eyes.

"How is he?" Horus whispered.

"In good health," Zera replied.

"Amun-Ra has blessed you both," Horus said.

"Amun-Ra?"

"The Sun," Horus said.

Zera gave him a quizzical look, but nodded. "Yes, Amun-Ra has blessed us by sending your grandfather." She looked to the old Rathadi. "While you slept, he also tended to our wounded."

"And H'met?" Horus asked. "Is he still…?"

"My husband shares in my gratitude to your grandfather— and to you, for staying his hand."

Horus exhaled. He moved closer. The small boy reached out to his face curiously, and Horus smiled.

"What is your son's name?" he asked.

Zera shifted her child, so Horus could see him better. "Horemheb."

Horus repeated the name in his head. "A strong name," he said.

The tent flap opened, and H'met entered. Thoth roused and got to his feet, adjusting the shawl around his face.

"*Ab-ba*," the boy babbled and stretched out his small arms for his father.

H'met's expression softened as he stepped to Horemheb and cradled him. His eyes glistened when he faced Thoth and spoke at length. When he finished he turned to Zera.

"My husband says that he is in your debt twice over, Thoth the Healer," Zera translated. "His son lives, and the men to which you tended are recovering quicker than he has ever seen, even the ones with grave injuries. The Tehesu are in your debt." She paused. "I am in your debt," she added.

Thoth nodded at her words.

H'met continued, and Zera translated again. "Because you have saved the life of his firstborn and the lives of his warriors, my husband will grant you two favors. If it is within his power, no demand shall be deemed too large."

"Release my grandson from his bonds," Thoth said instantly.

Zera translated. H'met replied with two words.

"It is done," Zera said. Horus's heart lurched at her words, struggling to absorb what just transpired. His gaze bounced between Zera and her husband.

"And the second?" Zera asked.

"Allow us to leave in peace," Thoth said.

Zera translated. This time H'met's response was longer.

"You and your grandson are free to leave anytime," Zera said, after he finished. "But the land is hostile, as you have discovered. My husband invites you to stay with our clan."

Thoth glanced at her guardedly.

"As our honored guests," she continued. "You are wise, and your healing skills are beyond any we have seen. Your presence would be most welcomed and valued."

Thoth glanced from Zera to H'met, then to Horus.

Horus met his gaze. "These are not evil people, Grandfather," he finally said in their own language. "Despite—"

"You wish to stay with them after they enslaved you?" Thoth cut in.

"You have gained the trust and gratitude of their leader," Horus countered. "Is that not what we had hoped for?"

"They kept you chained up like an animal!" Anger hardened his grandfather's voice.

"That is their way. Perhaps when we spend time with them, we can teach them that it is wrong to enslave others."

A flicker of surprise passed through Thoth's eyes. He studied Horus, as if seeing him for the first time. When he spoke, a strange quiver tinged his voice.

"I may have saved the lives of the chief's son and his warriors, but my achievements shall pale next to the plans Ra has envisioned for you in this strange land, Horus."

Horus blinked, puzzled at his grandfather's words.

Thoth faced H'met and Zera who gazed at him expectantly.

A long breath of silence stretched through the tent before Thoth spoke again in Khe'met. "Please tell your husband that we would be honored to accept his offer," the old Rathadi said. "We have much to learn of your land." He paused and added in his own language. "And much to teach you."

THE BRIM BASIN LAY BLACK, its surface smooth, as the narrow boat glided across the expanse. The moon broke through the murky clouds that hid the stars, blending the sky with the water. A gentle breeze stirred the boy's hair; it had a chill to it that wasn't there when he set out from the other shore a span ago.

Set pulled the oars into the boat then laid another blanket over the bundle that he had carefully stowed in the bow of the boat. A soft cry rang out from beneath the covers as he dipped the blades into the water again, pulling them closer to the distant shore.

A span later, the bottom scraped against sand. He jumped from the boat and dragged it ashore before gently lifting the bundle and wading through the water. He settled onto the beach and waited, holding the sleeping baby in his arms.

Three hooded forms approached him noiselessly. The trio stopped before him and lowered their cowls.

Set stood and addressed the girl in the middle. "I am thankful my message reached you."

The dark fur on the young Rathadi's face bristled, and she pulled a dagger. "Tell us why we should not kill you where you stand," Bast hissed. "After everything your kind has done to us."

Set lifted the bundle. The girl gasped at the sight of the newborn.

"Is it...?"

"It is Rathadi," Set replied.

"Wh-where did you find her?" Bast stammered.

"She was born to a female prisoner," Set replied.

"What happened to the mother?"

Set swallowed. "She... died," he said, straining not to choke on his words.

Bast sheathed her dagger and reached for the girl, but Set pulled the bundle back protectively. "Give me your vow that you will protect her with your life," he said.

The girl raised her eyebrows and fixed Set with a glare.

Set matched it, as firm and unyielding. "Give me your vow," he repeated.

Bast drew herself to her full height. "As Ra is my first ancestor, I vow that I will protect this child with my life," she said.

Set exhaled and allowed Bast to take the baby into her arms. The child woke and gave a soft whimper. Bast's expression thawed.

"What is her name?" she whispered.

Set gazed into the child's golden eyes. They reflected the moon, glowing in the dark like cold fire.

"Nephthys," he said. "Her name is Nephthys."

END OF BOOK ONE

ACKNOWLEDGMENTS

When I started working on Heir of Ra, the thought of completing an entire trilogy seemed quite ambitious; the idea of penning a prequel to the trilogy seemed little more than a starry-eyed dream. The fact that you're holding this finished work in your hand is testimony to the love and support of countless people who have been part of this journey, and without whom this book would not have been possible.

Soon after beginning work on the prequel, the world and story took on lives of their own, and I found myself drawn back to my teenage years and the wonder I felt when reading Tolkien, Frank Herbert, Ursula Le Guin, Terry Brooks, Robert Jordan, and many others. To those pioneers of fantasy and science fiction, thank you for building immersive worlds and crafting fantastic tales that shaped my imagination and inspired me to become a writer.

To my family: Vera, Sarah, and Misha. Thank you for putting up with me. It is immensely fun to see the ideas we throw around the kitchen table transform into worlds and come alive as characters on these pages. Being able to share those creations with our readers is gratifying beyond words.

Vera, thank you for your unwavering optimism and for supporting me every step of the way since we set out on this journey. Thank you for standing by me at my highs and lows, for being an honest sounding board for the storyline and art, and for hunting down the gremlins in the early drafts. Thank you for being my best friend and co-conspirator in life. I am eternally grateful.

Sarah, thank you for taking time from your school work and college applications—and from writing your own book—to critique your old man's work. Your comments are as astute as they are wise. (Yes, I did call you wise in a moment of weakness…) Now go out and conquer the world!

To my amazing beta readers, who took weeks from their busy lives to provide me with insightful feedback, edits, and criticism: Your efforts helped shaped the manuscript into the finished work, making it a far better product for those who pick it up after you. From the bottom of my heart, and on behalf of all the readers, my sincere thanks to Calais Fitzmaurice, Scott George, Patti Grayson, Amber Hodges, Kim Johnson, Nicole Lopez, Marion Marchetto, Jessica Morris, Kathy Parsons, Tim Riley, Mike Snodgrass, and Tanisha Wallace-Roberts. Every author should be so lucky to have such perceptive and ardent friends.

Igor Voloshin, for gracing the book with another gorgeous cover. Thank you for translating a concept of Atlantis into a stunning visual.

My stellar editor, Pam Jones, for her sharp eyes and sage advice.

Finally, to my readers: Thank you for your messages. Thank you for the fan art. Thank you for your loyalty. It's humbling, and sometimes still a bit unreal, to see how passionately the series has been embraced. You make all the hard work worthwhile.

If you enjoyed reading Dawn of Ra as much as I enjoyed creating the backstory of the Rathadi and the Pureans, please consider taking a moment to leave a review on Amazon or another book site you frequent. It is difficult to overstate how incredibly valuable every single review and recommendation is. There are almost three thousand books published every day in the USA alone, and it is a fight every day to get our work noticed, so we can continue creating and sharing our worlds with you.

Please visit our social media pages and drop me a message. I'd love to hear from you!

If you'd like to be notified when my next book comes out, please visit our website, where you can sign up to receive an email about new releases and exclusive content.

Thank you for allowing me to share my world with you.

Pursue your dreams and know no fear!

   - M. Sasinowski

WWW.HEIROFRA.COM

facebook.com/heirofra

instagram.com/heirofra_book

twitter.com/heirofra

M. Sasinowski is the author of the bestselling Blood of Ra series. He lives in Williamsburg, VA, with his wife, Vera, daughter, Sarah, and stepson, Misha.

When he's not busy annoying his ex-wife's cat, or perfecting the vacuum cleaner dance, he can be found typing furiously at his keyboard that is sometimes connected to a computer.

Printed in Great Britain
by Amazon